One

CARVER'S HOLLER, ARKANSAS
1893

"Hoo-ooo-ie, she's het up!"

Margaret Rose shook a spatula at the men in her kitchen. "If you plan to eat supper, you'll not be egging him on."

All three bearded jaws dropped.

"I mean it." Never once had she made that threat. In her five years of cooking and caring for a baker's dozen ragtag of old men, Maggie managed to tolerate plenty. Love made it easy to dote on them and overlook blunders. Most often, her "uncles" showered her with affection, appreciation, and endless amusement. Today, however, was different. Their discussion frayed the edges of her patience so badly, a tattered sock would have looked brand-new by comparison. She didn't often rue being the only woman in Carver's

Holler, but this counted as such a time. "After being hounded for six days, I deserve some rest."

"You'd get more rest as a married woman," Uncle Bocephus encouraged. "As a wife, you'd feed and doctor only one man. Not thirteen."

"Nonsense!" She nibbled on a broken cookie. "I'd have fourteen men."

"All the better reason." Paw-Paw rose from the table. Breath hissed though his teeth and his features tightened. "Thirteen's unlucky."

Alarm shot through her. "Paw-Paw, you're hurting! What's a-wrong?"

"Wood leg's giving my daddy fits," Jethro tattled. "Wore a hole in the stump sock, and now he's going to rub a raw spot on what's left. He doesn't want to tell you so."

"Mercy's sake, Paw-Paw. Take off your leg and pass over the sock. I'll have it darned in a trice."

Paw-Paw plopped down and yanked up his pant leg. "Take it from an old man, Maggie. Life is full of surprises." He gestured in a wide arc to the view out her window. Meager beams of sunlight snuck through the heavy gray clouds, the sky promising a rare snowstorm. Maggie had seen all of three snowstorms in her whole life, and the wicked chill sweeping through the holler promised a mean fourth. "Even the critters know a change is on the wind, lass. They're planning ahead for what's to come. You should, too."

She laughed. "I am! I'm planning on having thirteen hungry men at my supper table. Sure and for certain, *they* won't change one bit. They'll all come early because of the weather. The Flinn twins will give us a storm update and Mr. Collier's suspenders are going to be twisted," she predicted.

Uncle Bo let out a sigh powerful enough to flip over a sack of potatoes. "Don't you see, girl? Deep as this holler—that's my love for you. Only things that matter a whit to me are tramping in God's footsteps and doing what He wants—especially regarding you." His Scots-Irish accent grew thicker as emotion built. "My callin' is to walk you down the aisle and see you waltz off with a good man. The Lord's got the right one for you, and I'll not bind you here to me. We clung to each other in our sorrow after my Maude went to the bosom of the Almighty—"

"And in His infinite mercy, the Almighty gave us one another to lean on." She gazed adoringly at Uncle Bo, her only living relative.

"Lass, grief mellowed into sweet memories, yet we've leaned ourselves right into a rut."

"Rut! I know you're not talking about emotions, because you just said our grief has mellowed. You taught me resilience and even moved me into my own house so I'd stand on my own." Slapping away Jethro's hand as he tried to sneak his fourth cookie, Maggie frowned. "Surely you aren't calling my pretty house a rut, not when I'm happy as a magpie in her nest. You'd crush my feelings!"

"Feelings cloud the senses, and I've come to mine at long last." Uncle Bo pointed at her. "The time's a-comin' for you to meet the future God has planned for you."

"You ain't gettin' any younger, Maggie." Paw-Paw arched a scruffy brow and didn't even have the grace to look guilty.

"I'm shocked! Back when your wives were with us, bless their souls, you would never mention a lady's age!" As she turned to add almost seven dozen oatmeal cookies to the goodies in her pie safe, laughter tinted her voice. "Time must be sneaking up on you just as fast as it's creeping up on me."

Wagging his head side to side, Jethro folded his arms on the tabletop and sagged forward. "Old age took us captive the moment we picked up our rifles and fought for the Confederacy."

"Since we forfeited our larking years," Uncle Bo shared a glance with the others, "we reckon time owes you a few extra."

He considered it a mark of honor to shield her from the soul-deep burden he carried from the War Between the States, so Maggie pretended not to hear the sadness dragging at his voice. "First you said I'm getting old, but now you're telling me I'm still young and owed more youth." She made a show of tapping her chin with her forefinger as though deep in thought. "That must make me an old maid, Uncle Bo. I'm sure keeping me underfoot makes for a heavy burden, but this will shore you up." She handed a mug of steaming chicory to him.

Maggie brewed chicory special for him. Everyone else in Carver's Holler, Arkansas, drank coffee, but she'd do just about anything to make her uncle happy—other than getting married. She held firm to the belief that marriage ought to be grounded in faith and promises of love. The only grounds she could claim swirled in the bottom of a chicory pot.

"You don't listen any better than those bullheaded Belgians out in the barn," Jethro grumbled about the draft horses. "Ornery things only do one thing: eat!"

Neither Adam nor Eve would do a thing for anyone but her, so Maggie couldn't disagree with that part of the comment. "I do listen. You've told me I'm tottering on the edge of decrepitude, so let's not waste our limited days nattering about something that isn't going to change." Pleased with how she'd put an end to the conversation, she turned away to get the silverware.

"It is gonna change." Uncle Bo stepped up beside her. "That's what I'm a-tellin' you. Plain and simple, I've got it pressing on my heart to ask God to send a man for you."

The drawer came out completely when she yanked it, flipping silverware into the air as though the cutlery wanted to slice through her hopes of changing the topic. "How many times have you told me just because I pray for something, it doesn't mean God's going to follow my wishes?" She handed him the empty drawer and knelt to pick up the mess. "You taught me to pray for His will, not for my wants—but now you've turned it around."

"Nothing's turned around a-tall. Told you it's been pressing heavy on my heart. Sure as can be, God's easing me into letting go of you."

"Nonsense!" She sorted through silverware and conversation, picking which pieces best served her. "I'm where I belong, with the people I love, right in the center of God's will for me."

Her uncle gave her his don't-try-my-patience look. "Can't expect the Creator, who has an imagination big enough to build this whole wide world, is going to stop putting things together or pulling them asunder. Our lives change at His bidding."

This was a new direction in his argument. But Uncle Bo couldn't pray a groom out of thin air.

"I'll respectfully disagree in part. Regardless of what life brings, God lets us grow and stretch—but that just means we improve. Some things last forever. Like love. And my roses. Mama and Aunt Maude made sure to pass those legacies down to me."

Jethro broke in. "You're making the argument for him, because they're both gone. So's your daddy."

She lifted her chin. "Daddy will live on as long as I thirst for knowledge and enjoy reading. But I'm still blessed with lots of loving 'uncles'—and the rest of them will be here soon. Jerlund will show up first—probably in the next minute or two."

Within a heartbeat, a slightly garbled voice called out, "Maggie?" Upon hearing his distinctive shuffle, Maggie filled a cup halfway with milk. Jerlund had the body of a strapping man, but the mind of a seven-year-old child.

When Maggie flashed a victorious smile at Uncle Bo, he gave her an exasperated look. Still, his voice sounded kind. "C'mon in, Jerlund."

Helping him shrug out of his coat, Maggie told Jerlund, "You may snitch one cookie. I won't have you spoiling your supper."

A couple men bumped shoulders and wedged into the kitchen just behind Jerlund. "Cookies?!"

Maggie giggled softly. "See? Things don't change. Every last one of our neighbors is going to be here by quarter past the hour." She shoved corn bread into the oven. "And no one should be surprised. I bake cookies every Monday."

"Thass why I wan more'n one," Jerlund pouted. "You got gobs of 'em. And they're liddle cookies."

"One or none at all, Jerlund. You need to save room for the stew."

The door stayed wide open. Men kept coming in, their hats and coats bearing a telltale shimmer. "Colder 'n blue blazes out there!"

Maggie dashed to the window. "Oh! It's snowing! I thought we'd get sleet, but it's pure snow."

As if they hadn't just come inside, three men crowded by her at the window. One said, "So much snow, Elding is stringing a clothesline for us to follow home."

"It's the only time that stinker uses a clothesline!" Uncle Bo shot back.

"He's not the only one capable of raising a stink," Maggie gave her uncle a meaningful look.

"What's that?" Another man stopped shedding his coat and gave her a perplexed look.

"Margaret Titania's in a dither because I've reminded her God's got a man for her."

Real trouble loomed whenever Uncle Bo used her middle name.

She hadn't lived among men for all these years without knowing this situation called for a deft mix of humor and gumption. "But you'll all notice I'm not sashaying to the altar."

"Weddin' calls for a groom," someone concurred.

"Exactly!" Maggie resisted the urge to cheer. Finally someone was going to put an end to all this nonsense.

Paw-Paw chortled. "Once Bo sinks hisself into a notion, a rabid wolverine couldn't shake him off. Magpie, you need a man to hunt and provide for you, to love you and give you a passel of young'uns."

A chorus of "Aye," "So be it," and "Yep" rumbled the walls of her kitchen, yet Maggie refused to give in. "If that's God's plan, He'll work it out. He created man. If—"

"Exactly!" Uncle Bo smacked the tabletop. "He's a-gonna bring your man here, and it's fitting for me to remind you."

"Several times a day for a week." Maggie couldn't bear it anymore. "After six days of work, even God rested!"

"Told ya; she's het up!" Jethro leaned back and elbowed his dad. "Ain't seen anyone this hotheaded since Maude took an axe to Bo's bagpipes."

"Aunt Maude? Bagpipes?" Deep chortles and chuckles filled the room, but Maggie gaped at her uncle. Color crept up his neck and turned his ears barn red.

"Wasn't no secret." When Maggie continued to lock gazes with him, he muttered, "Just never occurred to me to mention it is all."

"Then you can tell me what drove a serene woman like Aunt Maude to such action while I darn this sock."

"He can do that later. Stick to the important subject." The grizzled man beside the stove inched out of her way. "Last week I told y'all that my Genevieve"—a chorus of "God rest her soul" ran as an undertone while he continued—"has sisters planning to come live in the holler. Us men will have womenfolk to help us out, but you got a future to mind."

"Stop kickin' and start listening," Uncle Bo growled. "You're of an age to mull over matrimonial considerations."

At twenty, I'm also of an age to make my own decisions. Biting back that retort, Maggie let out a slow breath and wrestled with the whole situation. She didn't want to sound disrespectful. *I'll always be their little girl. The only time they treat me like an adult is when I barter or heal. . . . Aha!*

She'd exercise her skills as the region's barterer and concoct a diplomatic bargain. "You can talk to the Lord all you want about it. If He has designs on me marrying up, He can send that groom on by. God or groom—them I'll listen to. That's the best deal you'll get."

Everyone agreed—all except Uncle Bo. "Nope. Not me. I got the rest of this sixth day to wedge in important points as they occur to me."

Maggie tried to look outraged, but she felt the smile tugging at her lips. Keeping face among his friends mattered. Uncle Bo couldn't just give in, and she reckoned as long as the nagging would end, she could endure a wee bit longer. "Bartering is my profession, but you're making a counteroffer? I suppose I'll have to settle for twelve silent men and you exercising discretion for the rest of today."

"I didn't say a thing about discretion."

Maggie brushed a kiss on Uncle Bo's cheek. "But you're a man of honor, and I trust you. The rest of today—then you'll forever hold your peace." Quickly, before he could add on anything, Maggie sealed the agreement. "You've got a deal."

"Forever?!"

Lifting the lid on the pot and filling the kitchen with fragrant steam, Maggie mused, "Isn't it a perfect match—how I like cooking and you're always hungry?"

Anger coiled inside Todd Valmer as the train chugged away, leaving him and Ma behind in an obscure valley in the Arkansas Ozarks. In the middle of a growing snowstorm, too. Between violent gusts of wind, he spotted smoke curling out of a distant cabin.

"Here, Ma. Soon you'll be warm." Ma held fast to him, her right arm hooked around his neck and the rest swathed in a blanket. Todd left their valise to sink in the slushy mess and took long strides toward the smoke. With no road to follow, he forged his own path.

Drawing closer, he noted well-traveled trails from various directions converged like stems to branches, as if the house ahead were the trunk that kept everyone rooted here. But Todd's steps slowed. Surely this couldn't be the right place. He squinted and scanned all around, finding two other, smaller, cabins. Neither boasted a picket fence, though—and according to the porter on the train, a doctor lived at the only house with a picket fence.

All confidence in this doctor's capabilities evaporated as Todd stared at the ludicrous array before him.

Someone had hooked or tied washtubs, horseshoes, cookie tins, and whisk brooms to the pickets. More than a few sets of praiseworthy antlers, some plates, and multiple pelts joined them. If that display wasn't mind-boggling enough, an array of brightly painted whirligigs fluttered madly in the wind all around the eaves in merry mockery of the heavyhearted people who'd walk below them.

Up closer still, a sturdy lean-to shielded contents from the weather—lengths of chain, rope, and a plethora of farming implements. What use would a doctor have for such equipment? None. But what if he'd taken it as payment and by doing so ruined a man's ability to provide for his family?

I've got three bucks to my name. Either he helps Ma or he doesn't, but at least she'll be warm. Resolve hardening his jaw, Todd started up the stone steps to the porch.

A woman's voice reached him. "Jerlund, get back here and give Paw-Paw his leg, or I'll not feed you a lick!"

"We're right on target, Ma. This has to be the healer's place if someone inside has a wooden limb." To his relief, Ma stayed quiet. The icy wind cut across the landscape, whipping at her blanket and hem.

Once he reached the top porch step, a gust of wind sent a stupid whirligig careening toward him. He evaded the wheeling wings and wooden body painted like a magpie, of all things. The realization twisted his lips in a wry smile as he recalled the odd bounty adorning the fence. A sign he'd thought was the doctor's came into focus. It read MAGPIE'S BARTER, BUY, OR SELL. If ever someone hung a sign that truthfully proclaimed their business, this was it. Magpies collected whatever caught their fancy and cluttered their nests with the madcap mixture.

The sign explained the mess, and perhaps the doctor shared the building. Moaning wind obscured his knock, so Todd opened the door, concerned for his mother's welfare. He carried Ma in, convinced the door to shut with the sole of his boot, and looked up.

And up. And around. He couldn't help himself.

No one in their right mind would ever imagine anything as ludicrous as the sight before him. Like a magpie's nest, shiny, sparkling, odd and appealing things filled this habitation. But the ridiculous birds lived only a short while. Whoever had been nesting here must've been adding on to the collection for ages.

Todd's mouth went dry. *Ma's done for.*

He stood rooted to the floor, stunned by the dizzying array surrounding him. A flash of movement drew his attention. Yanking off her apron, a young woman with coal black hair came into view. She called to someone in the other room, "A caller just let himself in."

Several men flooded after her. One growled, "Gotta be a Yankee. Southerners got better manners than sneaking in."

" 'Course it's a blue belly." Another snorted. "No Southerner's dumb enough to go strollin' out in this weather."

Never taking her focus off Todd, the woman tossed her apron onto a spindled chair. "Do you need something, mister?"

"The doctor. For my mother." Ma didn't move or make a sound.

An old man stepped in front of the young woman. "Stand back, lass. We got no reason to trust this Yankee. Don't even know yet what he's toting there."

"Women's boots are sticking out." Ignoring the order, she approached, pulled back just the corner of the blanket, and gently touched Ma's face. "Poor soul, she's chilled to her marrow!"

Honesty wrenched an admission from Todd. "More, too, is wrong."

Startling bright blue eyes studied him. He met her gaze and silently pled for help.

Two

Snowflakes plastered the stranger's hair, so Maggie couldn't be certain of its color. But blue eyes radiated worry, and the set of his square jaw hinted at a determined nature. A sturdy jacket stretched across wide shoulders that weren't snow-covered—odd, until he hefted the heavy burden he bore. Ahh. That movement knocked away the last remaining flakes. The coat ended at the hips— a workingman's jacket. Denim work pants wet clear up past the knees tattled he'd waded through snow for a fair distance. The stranger must be miserable as well as cold, but he'd asked only for help for his mother. Aye, and he'd been mindful to stomp the worst from his boots before coming inside.

He showed integrity, telling her something more ailed his mama. Several times in the past someone sought her healing skills and left out the important fact that they or their loved one suffered a contagious ailment. Faster than corn popping in her kettle, thoughts burst in her mind and ricocheted around.

"He put his mama's needs ahead of all else, and he's been dead-level honest with me, so I'm gonna help him."

Air whooshed from his lungs. "God bless you!"

His deep voice held more grit and less lilt—yet beneath the grit she detected a cadence unlike the Scots-Irish rhythm that flowed in all the holler's men's voices. The difference intrigued her. She'd like to hear him speak more. His accent—could it be German? Or mayhap Dutch?

"Don't take 'em in," Jethro warned. "Betcha what she has is catchy."

"Since it's my home, I'll decide what's to be done. My guests are chilled." Maggie slipped past the stranger and opened the door to her spare room. "Bring your mama on in here."

A swift nod acknowledged her invitation, but the stranger had yet to show a hint of a smile.

Poor man's worrying himself sick. Hope his mama's in better shape than he thinks. "We didn't swap names yet. I'm Maggie Rose. Yonder's my uncle, Bocephus Carver."

"Valmer. Todd Valmer."

"Mr. Valmer, you and yours are welcome to my home."

"Thank you, ma'am." His hold on the blanketed form tightened, but his voice softened. "Ma, there's a gal here who's going to help me tuck you into a nice warm bed."

His mother stayed still and silent until he reached the bedside, then made a garbled sound.

"Knew being in here would perk her up. Everywhere she looks, your mama's seeing specials and sparkles." Maggie unlaced her patient's boots. Mrs. Valmer kept her right arm about her son's neck, clinging tight and going slack-jawed. "You're not dreaming, ma'am. You're surrounded with wondrous, beautiful things."

Mr. Valmer cleared his throat. "First thing, Ma, I'll move that chandelier."

Maggie's hand shot up to touch a prism dangling from the chandelier she'd hung over the bed. "You're welcome to, but the endeavor is needless. It's safely chained to a strong beam."

"Nonetheless, I will move it."

Tugging off both boots and stockings roused the woman, but Maggie ignored her splutters of protest. Given the merest scrap of sympathy, folks ofttimes imagined themselves to be in dire straits. Only this woman was in sad shape. A quick scan of her set Maggie's mind awhirl—especially when she pulled the rest of the blanket open and Mrs. Valmer's left arm drooped from her shoulder and dangled like a pendulum. "Go on. Lay her down."

Todd felt like a rooster caught midcrank of a killing neck twist. He'd put Ma on the bed and turned loose, only Ma took exception to them parting. She curled her right arm around his neck even tighter and hung on for dear life. Todd reckoned he might survive if he ever got a chance to draw a breath again. "Whoa, now, Ma. You're fine."

Cramming one knee into the mattress and easing her elbow over his head proved difficult but doable. "Easy. Easy g—" He caught himself, realizing he was talking to her as he would to an unbroken mare. Not that he meant any disrespect. Simply put, she looked as wild as a ready-to-buck-and-bolt mustang. Right hand shooting up, she grabbed for him.

Thwack! He brained himself on something when he sprang out of her reach. A series of tinkling sounds reminded him what hovered above the bed. "Ma, settle down."

From the other side, Miss Rose leaned over Ma. "Ma'am, your boy's got two big, strong arms, but if you're in them, he can't help you much—and neither can I."

Still wild-eyed, Ma trembled.

"Just as surely as God sends angels to protect us, I'm thinking He sent your son for such a time as this, where Mr. Valmer can stand watch and you can rest easy."

Panicky features going soft with uncertainty, Ma turned toward him. "I'm right here, Ma. You rest."

Miss Rose plucked out Ma's hairpins with a deft hand. "Pale, but it could be from the cold or fright as much as from illness. We'll have to check on that in a while again. Took a bump to the head?"

"Ma swooned."

Blotting a damp cloth against Ma's goose egg, Miss Rose nodded. The lamps someone brought in illuminated her face, and his estimation of her age dropped by a solid five years. His already-shaky confidence in her plummeted.

"Swoon, then fall; or fall, then swoon?" she asked.

"Where is the doctor?"

Black eyebrows pulled together in consternation, Miss Rose countered, "I'm needing you here to answer important questions."

"Ask Ma."

"I doubt she knows whether she fainted first or last." Fingers tracing Ma's features like a blind woman trying to memorize a new face, Miss Rose didn't bother to draw a breath. "What was she doing immediately before she fell?"

"Just sitting there, riding the train. Then she keeled over."

Voice as calm as a summer day, the gal continued on. "Anything happen to get her dander up or cause an uproar?"

"*Nein.*" Uncertainty struck. Had the upheaval in her life triggered this? "She is moving to my farm."

24

Miss Rose flashed him a grin that lit her whole face. "Judging from the way your mama clings to you, I'd wager the arrangement's fair pleasing to her." Her assessment relieved him of that concern. "Is your mama given to any weakness? Any drooping of the eyelids, one side of her smile being lower, her voice being reedy, or her grip feeble?"

"Nein."

"Her laces . . ."

Todd reared back. Such things were not spoken of. He shook his head once.

Fingertips bumping down Ma's ribs, Miss Rose insisted, "Aye, they're tight."

Gritting his teeth, Todd considered the topic both unnecessary and unnerving. Men wore suspenders to keep their britches in place, but women wore corsets to keep themselves in place. Never particularly good with words, he'd embarrass this black-haired beauty and make a fool of himself by discussing such an indecent garment. "This is not a breathing problem. I need to fetch the doctor."

An enormous shadow appeared at the foot of the bed. *The doctor! Glory hallelujah. He's—* Todd dropped Ma's hand, turned around, and frustration swamped him.

The huge man standing there had the guileless eyes and smile of a child. "Maggie, we're waitin' supper. I wan 'nother cookie."

"One and only one." She held up her forefinger. "Jerlund, I've a lady visitor in this room. You must ask permission before coming in here from now on."

"Does she wanna have milk and a cookie, too?"

"Mayhap later." Miss Rose waited until the boy left, then addressed Todd as if they'd not been interrupted whatsoever. "Do her kin have heart problems or sinking spells or apoplexy amongst them?"

"Heart."

The odd woman's startlingly blue eyes narrowed. "And the other problems?"

"Nein. Otherwise, I would have said." As soon as he added the harsh words, Todd regretted them. The gal was doing her best, but that still wasn't near enough. Ma looked mighty bad. "Where's the doctor?"

"Nearest one is miles and miles away."

Terror shot through him. "On the train, they said there was a doctor here!"

Miss Rose kept right on checking Ma. "They told you wrong. I—"

"How far to the doctor?" he interrupted.

"Next train stop, there's a boneheaded man who declares himself to be a doctor. His brain and heart are as empty as his ridiculous top hat. Seven miles beyond that, there's another stop. Doc Wyant's there. He's capable of diagnosing and treating folks so long as he hasn't been sampling his corn likker. A few hits of Oh Be Joyful, and he's safe as a rabid wolf." Empathy radiated from her. "Wish things were different."

Staring at Ma's pasty coloring, he rasped, "What can be done?"

"Pray. That's the most important. I'm the healer for folks hereabouts, and I'll do my best for your mama." Stroking Ma's shoulder with compassion, Miss Rose slowly used overlapping movements and petted her way down Ma's arm.

But compassion didn't make anyone a healer. Knowledge and experience did. Her questions hinted at a scrap of knowledge, but her youth and isolation robbed her of any claim to experience. Somewhere, someone had to be able to do better by Ma. He reached to bundle up Ma, but Miss Rose was doing what Doc did back home—pressing the wrist to check on Ma's heartbeat. How did an Arkansas mountain girl know that trick?

"Your ma feels a tad unsettled. Won't you please sit by her and hold her hand?"

Phrased as a question, her order allowed him to save face. But Todd refused to yield control. "For now." He leaned over and cupped his hand around his mother's.

"Awww." A smile lifted the corners of Miss Rose's mouth. "Sure is sweet how your mama's fingers curl 'round your big old hand." Her skirts whispered as she moved. "Mrs. Valmer? Mrs. Valmer?"

"Mrs. Crewel. Her name—it is Mrs. Crewel."

The ivory comb in her inky hair glinted as the woman nodded. "Please, Mrs. Crewel, raise this foot." She tapped Ma's right foot.

Ma's toes curled, and she drew her foot beneath her hem.

A quirk of a brow, and the woman tapped Ma's left foot. "This leg now, too."

Leg? Did Ma shiver like that because she was scandalized by such brassy language? Afraid? Cold? Whatever the reason, she didn't comply. Todd squeezed her hand. Perhaps if he spoke in German. . . . *"Bitte, Ma, verschiebst du deine linken Fuß."*

Nothing.

"Very well. Mr. Valmer, turn her toward you. I'll see to releasing her fastenings."

Straightening up and folding his arms across his chest, he stared at the young woman. Not one thing about this whole situation was right. "Get another lady to help you. I'll fetch the doctor."

"Another woman's not to be found for a good ten miles."

If she exaggerated about that, she could have embellished the physician's shortcomings. Desperate, Todd rasped, "I'll help with her, then go."

He put his hands where Miss Rose directed, pulled Ma toward

him, and slammed his eyes shut. With the layers of clothes, it took an eternity for Miss Rose to undo everything. The sound of laces being pulled through grommets ended with both women inhaling deeply.

Blankets all drawn up snug to her chin, Ma finally looked better. Not that she looked good. But not as bad. Miss Rose pulled him from the bedchamber.

All the old men who'd followed her into the room when he arrived immediately crowded around. "Is it something catchy?" one man demanded.

"No." Miss Rose moseyed across the parlor. "You men need to pray."

"She always says that," another old man grumbled to the group. Others asked what had happened.

"Ma fell facedown in the aisle."

"So did mine." The speaker elbowed the man beside him. "But I went on ahead and said my wedding vows!"

Chortles filled the room, but Todd clipped, "Where's Miss Rose?"

"Likely fetching something. Keeping track of that lass is like balancing a book on an acorn. Can't be done." The speaker waggled his brows. "So is your ma a widow? Always did like a woman with meat on her bones."

For a second, Todd's jaw dropped, and then he went straight back to gritting his teeth. Stepping to block the door, he fiercely stared the man down.

Miss Rose exited a room diagonal to Ma's. "Y'all give Mr. Valmer a chance to catch his breath." Shaking her finger, she scolded, "And don't you think for a minute I'll put up with any roosters strutting in my parlor." Arms full, she went back in to be alone with Ma.

Suddenly the door to Miss Rose's parlor banged open. The same large man who'd barged in on Ma now tromped inside. "Tracking. Thass wha' I done. Lookie what I found!" He held aloft their valise.

Stepping toward him, Todd extended his hand. "Thanks." When the man shuffled back, Todd halted. "I'd like to shake your hand."

The leather bag hit the plank floor with a resounding bang. "Paw-Paw, Daddy! Watch. The man wans to shake my han!"

A stubborn water pump got cranked with about the same force his arm did, but Todd couldn't think of a time when he'd seen a handshake matter more. Jerlund must have repeated his name four times.

Jerlund reminded him of Uncle Buddy. Ma's baby brother was probably about Jerlund's age when he'd come to live with them. Todd was eleven. Buddy claimed twice his years and thrice his strength. Though Todd might have boasted he had twice the smarts, it never seemed right to do anything but stick alongside his family. Plenty of folks felt differently. They hid away their slow-minded kin, so seeing how Miss Rose treated Jerlund lent significant reassurance of her compassion—even if she wasn't medically trained. "Thanks again, Jerlund. We'll need those things."

"Son, I done tole you to fetch his horse and take it to the barn." Expression every bit as mean as his voice, a man grabbed Jerlund's elbow and yanked him toward the door.

"But, Daddy—"

Todd jumped in, "I don't have a horse with me. I need to borrow one so I can fetch the doctor."

Jerlund's father snickered. "And I thought my son was a dolt!"

Mr. Carver rested his hand on Jerlund's shoulder. "Just because we think different ways don't make any of us a dolt."

"How in thunder did he get here without a horse?"

"The train." Mr. Carver raised his voice. "Flinn twins! About the storm . . ."

"Hitting faster than we thought," someone shouted from the adjoining room.

"Bet we get a good two feet by morning—" A similar voice began.

The first continued. "And a solid foot or more each day." Their report sounded the death knell for him riding out for help. Until the storm stopped, they'd be stuck here with that young woman's caring touch the only help on hand.

Miss Rose opened Ma's door and stepped back out. "I'm hoping these men haven't bent your ear reciting cockeyed stories. Aside from carving, telling grand tales is what they do best."

He looked down into her eyes. "I'm from Texas, miss. Tall tales are to be respected."

A pretty blush washed her cheeks as a soft smile lifted her lips . . . like they'd shared a secret or something. "Respecting traditions and seeking out new tales can only improve one's lot. Mr. Valmer, I'm fixin' to spend a while with your mama." Miss Rose made a shooing motion. "Go join the others. There's food aplenty. Worry ofttimes leaves a fearsome appetite in its wake."

Suddenly the aromas of a good meal registered. So did the stampede of men heading toward him. Survival and hunger—both instincts kicked in. He headed in the direction she'd gestured.

What a kitchen! He could have fit his entire cabin in it. A trestle table lined each side, and the center held a big worktable, a circle of chairs, and a pile of wood shavings. The largest stove Todd ever saw commanded the corner of the inside wall, providing heat for the whole building. Expensive white enamel smoothed across the doors of that oven, and fancy nickel doodads added embellishment. Savory steam rose from a gigantic pot on it.

Suddenly everything made sense. "So this is a restaurant."

Bo Carver let out a shout of laughter, and the men did likewise. "Valmer, you got yourself a fine sense of humor."

In a matter of minutes, they all had corn bread and bowls of stew in front of them. An old gent offered a blessing and slipped in a word concerning Ma. Afterward, he sat down next to Todd. "Eat hearty and enjoy it. A finer healer you'll not find for a far, far ride."

Please, God, don't let that be one of the tall tales. From what Todd had witnessed, reactions in this crowd came fast and clear. So far he'd seen these men be protective of the gal, fall readily into mirth, and display their curiosity. Not once had any of them uttered a lie. No chuckles, snickers, or throat clearing followed the declaration that Miss Rose knew her way around sick folks—just the sounds of men diving into good food.

A full baker's dozen crowded around the tables, and they all seemed remarkably hale, considering their ages. Perhaps Miss Rose did have some skill. Todd spooned in a bite. The incredible taste of venison stew filled his mouth. If Miss Rose cured her patients half as well as she cooked, Ma ought to be square dancing by breakfast.

He had no choice but to depend on Miss Rose to care for Ma. Trusting no one else might be more capable—that was a horse of a different color. He needed to weigh his words, consider his actions, and make a decision. But while he did, he was going to satisfy his hunger with this tasty stew. The aroma brought back memories of when Pa and he would go hunting. Ma always made Victory Venison Stew when they returned. Only this was seasoned a little differently—better, actually. Not that he'd ever tell Ma.

"Mmm-hmm. That little gal's a dab hand at patchin' up ailin' folks. And if she can't heal somebody, at least our Maggie sure will serve 'em up a dandy last supper!"

Todd choked on his bite. He swallowed and rasped, "Good food."

"Yap. Our Maggie says it don't take more time to stir a pot with three gallons in it than it does to stir one with three quarts. She cooks everything—and makes it tasty."

The oldest one—Paw-Paw, they called him—slurped from his spoon. "Ain't a thing I wouldn't do for that gal. She's one of a kind."

Others nodded or echoed his sentiments. Mr. Carver carefully set aside food for his niece before the men relished seconds. Todd wasn't shy about accepting. His ability to cook included beans, rice, grits, and searing side meat or fresh kill. Oh—he boiled eggs, too. But the yolks never failed to turn a sickening green. These men had no notion what a treasure they had.

Well, maybe they did. As they put on their jackets and left for the night, two of them set things on the worktable. No wonder her home resembled a magpie's nest—perhaps Miss Rose wouldn't accept money for cooking and caring for this bunch of men, so they paid her with gifts. If she didn't display the stuff, the old men's feelings would be crushed. It all made sense in a backward sort of way.

Ma would only be here a few days. He'd talk to her about ignoring the mess.

A couple of days. Todd grimaced. Added on to the time he'd already been gone, it was an eternity. Barely a handful of times had his father left their farm in Virginia for three days—and never once any longer. Yet to fetch Ma in Virginia and carry her back to Texas took a walloping five days—and that was allowing for five scant hours in Virginia. Stretching the already-unheard-of time to a full week not only increased his debt to his neighbor, John Toomel, who was caring for his stock; it endangered the farm.

"Hope you're good at washing." Mr. Carver jarred him from his worries. "I always dry."

Todd eyed the pile of dirty dishes. "For that supper, I would wash all of the dishes twice."

"You've a silver tongue, Mr. Valmer."

At the sound of Miss Rose's voice, Todd whipped around. Somber stillness replaced her sparkle and sass. "Uncle Bo, I'll see to the dishes in a bit. Mr. Valmer, we need to talk about your mama."

Maggie crossed the kitchen. "Would you prefer we speak in private, Mr. Valmer?"

He paused a second. "Is it something a woman would wish to keep private?"

She fought to keep her shoulders from slumping beneath the weight of the bad news. Best he hear it straight out; shilly-shallying just stretched folks' nerves. "What's befallen your mama can occur to either woman or man. It's not something that will remain a secret."

With a gentleman's fine manners, he pulled out a chair and motioned for her to occupy it. And he scooted it back in just right, too. Then he sat down and leaned his elbows on the table, abandoning those manners. "So, then, tell me."

"Your mama had an attack of apoplexy. Just how severe it is, only time will tell. Some folks, they're almost good as new in a few days. Others never do recover at all. Most fall in the middle, and with hard work they learn how to do some things for themselves again."

Maggie paused for a moment to let that sink in, taking a sip of the tea her uncle slipped to her. Bitter, but certainly less bitter than what she'd be saying next. "As soon as we opened the blanket and her arm dropped and hung there, I suspected she'd suffered a stroke.

I've books and a journal to which I refer. They all concur after such an episode, the patient is expected to be exhausted and confused."

His light brown brows crinkled. "Confused?"

"Unable to recall where she is, or even who you are—though it's safe to assume she recognizes you from how she responds to your nearness. She's not uttered a word for me. Has she said anything to you?" *Please say yes. Please recall her having spoken even a few sentences. . . .*

Wiping his rough hand down very worried features, Mr. Valmer paused. "Sounds. She's made sounds. As for words . . ." He shook his head slowly. "What would this mean?"

Experience taught Maggie to save some good news to give after the bad, so she folded her hands on the tabletop and continued to meet his gaze. "Very often, when someone suffers like this, when they lose their ability to speak, they keep functioning abilities of the right side. She might well struggle to communicate, but your mama will be able to do lots for herself."

The muscles in his jaw twitched as he clenched it tighter and tighter with every word she spoke. That tattled on a stubborn temperament—and Mr. Valmer was going to need plenty of dogged persistence in the next several months to hound his mama into relearning how to do things for herself. "Ma's left-handed."

"I see." Immediately realizing she needed to change the comforting things she planned to say, Maggie nodded to give herself a moment. "We'll see how much use she regains in her limbs. As I said, there's a possibility she'll regain some of her abilities again. But as she's left-handed, that means she'll most likely have preserved her ability to speak. Praise Jesus, she'll be able to talk and make herself understood, to sing and to pray. Of all the losses a body could suffer, I'd imagine that not being able to speak would be the most frustrating of all. We still have another hand that can take over if the other's injured, but we've only one voice box."

Mr. Valmer remained silent.

Folks needed a chance to weigh the information given them. Maggie doubted the stranger would need long, though. He'd been swift and sure in deciding how to treat Jerlund. One glance, and it was plain that Jerlund was one of those special individuals who'd remain a child all his days, but Mr. Valmer treated him like the man he wanted to be. The selfsame attitude—to look past a problem and see the person—that would be the best medicine his ma could get.

A single deep inhalation expanded Mr. Valmer's already vast chest, and he let it out slowly as he stood. "Miss Rose, I know you did your best by Ma, but a physician might know something more. I must give Ma that chance. Mr. Carver, I need to borrow a horse."

"Son, that's a fool's errand."

"It's a son's duty."

Uncle Bo set down the dishrag and came closer. "Your going out, getting lost, and freezing both yourself and a horse won't do your ma a lick of good."

"I'll follow the railroad tracks."

"At night? In the worst weather we've had in years? In territory you don't know? It's fifteen miles to Big Dip. Doc Wyant's probably away at his still, but if he's in town, you don't want him. Tomorrow is Tuesday." Uncle Bo shook his head.

Bafflement painted Mr. Valmer's features, so Maggie explained, "He's usually sober Mondays because of the train going through."

"Cold weather and hot coffee—they will sober him." Determination filled his voice.

Maggie walked around the table and touched Uncle Bo's shoulder. " 'There's small choice in rotten apples.' Mr. Valmer needs a medical opinion from a healer he approves. We may as well let him take our biggest and strongest horse so he stands his best chance."

Her uncle gave her a frustrated look.

"I couldn't live with myself if we didn't seat him on Adam." Chin rising a notch, she willed Bo to go along with her ploy. He dipped his head and nodded. Thank heavens he'd said nothing. One word, and Mr. Valmer would have known something was afoot. "But, Mr. Valmer, you have to make us an honor-binding promise that you'll turn around and come right back if you run into trouble or if Adam balks even once. He's one of the smartest horses God ever made, and he'll keep you alive if you let him have his head."

"Agreed! You have my word of honor. You will see to my mother until I come back?"

"Of course I will. Now out to the barn with you men. I'm going to take my bowl of stew and go sit with your ma." *And if Adam behaves like I expect him to, you'll be sitting by my side, fuming, in about fifteen minutes.*

～⁂～

She was quite a woman, Miss Rose. Even with worry nagging at him, as Todd bent his head into the wind and walked alongside Mr. Carver to the barn, he couldn't help thinking the young gal was what Ma called a touch of serendipity—something unexpected that brought gladness or thanksgiving. In the midst of this whole tragedy, God couldn't have arranged a better example. *Ja,* Miss Rose was the only bright spot in this mess.

And what a mess it was. He'd had to impose on John Toomel while he fetched Ma. Since the two bachelor farmers owned adjoining properties, they bore one another's burdens most heavily. Now John worked both places, waiting for the promise of Ma's good cooking—a promise Todd and Ma might not be able to uphold.

Lord, you know Ma's needs and what will cure her. If a miracle's what it'll take, then I'm begging you for one. Minding the sick isn't my gift. If Ma's in a bad way, I can't take her back to the farm. I'm barely hanging on . . .

A sudden thought caused him to turn to Mr. Carver and shout through the wind, "What other day does the train go through?"

The old man shook his head. "First and third Mondays are westward bound. 'Twas off schedule for them to stop today. It'll be by next week."

Todd strode ahead and started to open the barn door. He might well lose his crops and maybe even land over this, but he wasn't going to lose Ma. He'd haul the doctor back here so she'd have every chance of recovering.

By the time Todd drew the door shut, Mr. Carver had lit a lamp. The sudden glow sent a pair of mules shuffling off to the right. A kid and nanny goat lay in fresh-smelling hay across from a row of three stalls. On the near end, a gelding stirred, but in the center's side-by-side stalls stood a matched pair of sorrel draft horses. Todd didn't blink for fear the miracle might disappear. Belgians! There stood steeds that could plow through snow as easily as farmland fields.

Mr. Carver walked to the stallion. "You won't find a stronger mount than Adam. Has endless stamina, but he's stubborn as sin. He'll save your life if you let his judgment prevail."

"Belgians—they are smart." Todd extended his hand so the horse could catch his scent. Even in the meager light of one lantern he could see Adam clearly rated as one of the best of his breed. Honor warred with need. "Your niece—she is a good woman, but people sometimes do not appreciate what a certain horse means to his owner. If you would rather I use the gelding . . ."

"You gave your word to abide by the horse's inclinations, so it's only right that I lend the smartest mount I own."

Looking into the man's unwavering gaze, Todd knew he'd freely given not only his consent, but his blessing. "Thank you." As Todd turned to grab a saddle blanket, Adam nuzzled the huge mare in the adjoining stall.

"Stop being a lover boy," Mr. Carver muttered as he produced a halter. Adam was ready to ride in mere minutes.

Rapidly winding his scarf around his lower face and neck, Todd nodded. "He's good-tempered."

"*Hmmpf.* When she awakens, your ma's going to be a handful. Ain't a creature on earth more high-strung than a woman worrying over her child." Mr. Carver pulled a stubby pencil from his pocket and pointed at an unpainted board. "Before you hie off, leave us with the names and whereabouts of your kin. Don't mistake my meaning—your ma would be treated like family here. Other than my wife, no other woman ever walked the face of the earth who cared more, worked harder, or had a bigger heart than my niece. But your ma deserves to be with her own if the worst happens."

Arletta couldn't be reached. Even if she could, his sister let him know Ma permanently wore out her welcome. Ignoring the pencil, Todd strode toward the stallion. "The worst cannot happen. I'm all my mother has. I will return."

As Mr. Carver went to the door, Todd swung up into the saddle. About two thousand pounds of powerful horseflesh rippled beneath him, testifying to God's providence. *Lord, I put my trust in you. Lead me to safety so Ma can have the best of care. Amen.* Todd kneed the horse and made a clicking sound with his tongue.

The stallion stood stock-still.

Some horses were trained with a jiggle of the reins. The Belgian's only reaction to that cue plopped onto the straw behind them.

"Barn-sour, saddle-backed mares move better," Todd muttered.

Adam set out, took one step, and then shook his head. A firm hand on the reins, a tightened clamp against the beast's sides with his knees, and Todd gained his cooperation. Adam took a few more steps and corrected course.

This stallion needed praise and encouragement, but he'd do well. Many a horse needed a coaxing—not often this long, but Todd felt as well as saw the change. The tension that came with carrying an unfamiliar rider eased out of Adam's muscles. A solid pat on his slightly arched neck acknowledged the trust. Man and beast had an understanding.

Todd felt some of his own tension ease as he urged Adam ahead. Carver opened the barn door, and snow gusted in. Adam huffed to clear away a few flakes he'd inhaled and kept walking . . . in a large arc back into his stall.

⟡

"The snow may let up in the morning. I'll try again then." Mr. Valmer set a pair of crates inside the kitchen. Without another word, he walked back outside.

"Margaret Titania," Uncle Bo's voice held an unnecessary warning tone. This was the second time today he'd used her middle name. "No more sneaky tricks. That's a smart man." He shook his finger at her. "He reckoned Adam's a clever horse, but if you pull another stunt, you'll rightfully incite Valmer's wrath. No man appreciates a woman making a fool of him."

"I didn't make a fool of him. I owed it to his mother to keep him from killing himself. Her heart would break if she lost him—and I'd have failed them both."

Uncle Bo pursed his lips, stared at her, and finally nodded. "Reckoned you'd say something like that. These crates are for your treasures. Start a-packin'. Whilst you have both a cot and a patient in there, stuff's liable to get broke. 'Specially with her strapping son hovering."

"He's got rare wide shoulders and huge hands."

Uncle Bo shot her a telling look.

"I noticed because he needs a change of clothes, just as his mama did." A little niggle of doubt crept into her mind. Was that the only reason? His stature and strength were among the very first things she noticed about him. His deep blue eyes . . . Well, she'd had to pay attention to those in the first few moments, too, to take his measure. And his wet denims had clung to long muscular legs. *I noticed his hair's sandy-colored, too—and there's nothing untoward about simple observations.*

"Seein' as your scheme trapped him here, best you pack away all that you can. The nicest things from the parlor, too."

Dread swamped her. While the men ate supper, she overheard them weasel out the fact that Mr. Valmer was a bachelor. The notion of Uncle Bo playing matchmaker was enough to make her take to a sickbed herself. "I've no reason at all to pack anything from the parlor."

"If you treasure them, you will. Big, brawny men cause a lot of unintentional damage in small places. One expansive gesture, and he'd sweep everything straight off a shelf. Little Magpie, we both know you could fill a dozen crates and barely take away a glimmer from the cave."

Aladdin's Cave. Daddy said she'd gladly live in Aladdin's Cave, but Mama was from here in the holler and expressed herself in a more natural way. She'd said Maggie gathered up pretty things like magpie, and the nickname took. Uncle Bo knew her all too well—he'd said the very thing that would gain her cooperation. But she'd prove him wrong. From her trading trips, she'd learned to fit a lot in a small space. He predicted a dozen; she'd surprise him. "I'll stack the crates in my bedchamber." Needing to go sit with Mrs. Crewel again, Maggie washed her hands.

"Suppose storing them there's a possibility. I'll talk it over with Valmer."

"That man's got no call deciding on anything for me or my house. Certainly nothing about my—"

"Sure he does." Uncle Bo closed his hand around hers. "Maggie, my magpie, I gave him leave to sleep in your bed."

Three

You what?!"

"Now, Magpie—"

"Don't you *now* me!"

Looking wounded, Uncle Bo reared back. "You'll need to sleep on a cot by Mrs. Crewel, and Mr. Valmer's got to sleep somewhere."

"We both know he should sleep at your house!"

"Granted, 'tis true, but Jethro and his daddy are having a set-to, so Paw-Paw sent Jerlund to spend the night at my place. He's already upset, and Mr. Valmer's not going to sleep a wink, worrying and not bein' able to check on his ma."

Thoughts tumbled through her mind. This was just what she and Uncle Bo had been hoping for—that Jerlund would come to Uncle Bo in a troubled time. Sensitive to others' moods and any change,

Jerlund wouldn't settle in at Uncle Bo's with Mr. Valmer there. If the first stay didn't work well, he'd never go back again.

But it wasn't right, having a man spend the night in her house. A big, strong, handsome man. Well, maybe it wasn't so bad. His mama was in the house. That changed things. *But appearances count. And this still gives a bad witness.* "The barn. He can sleep in the barn."

"You'd withdraw the hospitality I extended?"

"How could you possibly allow a bachelor to stay here for a full three days until the storm passes?"

"Magpie, my lass, I trust you full well." He hooked his thumbs into his suspenders. "Aye, and I've taken that man's measure. He's one you could ride the river with."

Inhaling so sharply she set herself into coughing, Maggie made a sound of disbelief between coughs.

"I'm giving you just what you asked for, lass. This very day, you said God could 'send that groom on by. God or groom—them I'll listen to.' You made that deal, and I'm holding you to it."

"Hold your horses!" Grabbing him by the arms, she resisted the urge to shake some sense into her uncle. "Just because Mr. Valmer's a man doesn't automatically turn him into my groom."

"He's the most promising prospect around." Uncle Bo brushed a kiss on her cheek. "You're the one who let the man stay when everyone wanted to pitch him out."

"He carried an ill woman."

Smiling as if he'd won the final point in a debate, Uncle Bo stepped back. "Can't get a better recommendation than that. Men wind up treating their wives just like they treat their mother and sisters. Feelin' concerned 'bout his loved one, he wants to stay close. You can't fault a man for doing something praiseworthy."

Making a living by bartering taught her plenty. Cocking a brow, Maggie said, "Whenever someone talks fast and fancy as you are,

I know better than to trade. They're trying to pass off a skunk as a swan."

"I'm not trading a-tall, lassie. I'm fixin' to go on home. Calm Jerlund. Talk to the Lord. I reckon this buck can talk for himself." The kitchen door opened. Bo lowered his voice. "But you can't listen to the man if he ain't under your roof."

꿍

The next morning Todd looked expectantly at Miss Rose as she exited the room she and Ma shared. "Your mama's looking much the same this morning as she did last night."

Disappointment hit him. "No improvement?"

Voice soft and steady, she said, "Making it through an entire day and night bodes well for survival. Her stability is encouraging."

"Then I will be satisfied." Walking toward Miss Rose, he noticed several objects were missing from the parlor, and a pair of crates sat beside the spindle chair. Another wave of disappointment hit. He would have rather she start ridding Ma's room of some of the stuff. For Ma's sake he'd offer to help pack after breakfast. Miss Rose already did far more than he should have hoped for.

Todd went to see Ma. She slept soundly. Looking up from her, he jolted. Instead of bursting at the seams, the room looked comparatively normal. "Where is everything?"

"My specials and sparkles? They're in those crates in the corner."

Frowning at the four crates, he chided, "They're too heavy for you. You ought to have waited. I would have carried the others out for you."

Miss Rose arched a brow. "I did wait. That's all I needed."

Todd's jaw dropped. She'd rounded up all those bits and pieces, corralled them into . . . "Four crates?"

"Well, there are two in the parlor." Miss Rose gestured to a shelf. "I kept out those angels so when Mrs. Crewel first awakens, she'll be looking at a reminder of the Lord's protection and mercy. She'll have a few foggy days, resting up and gathering strength for the rough road ahead. Where are you bound for?"

"Gooding, Texas. I farm there. We're a sight over halfway home." Ma had always been strong, healthy. That would help her bounce back quickly. "Ma enjoys riding the train, watching out the window."

"Seeing the countryside change . . ." Miss Rose's smile returned. "It all goes by so quickly. Like taking a picture book and flipping through the pages real fast."

Her description amused him. "Have you traveled much?"

"Each season I take the men's carvings off to trade or sell." Miss Rose straightened a lacy nightcap she'd put on Ma. "There."

Ma would be horrified by that thing on her head and would gladly trade anything to get rid of the nightcap. Then again, Todd reasoned, it stood to reason if her apoplectic fit happened someplace in her head, keeping her brain warm would help it recover.

Miss Rose's blue eyes held his. "Once she awakens, we'll get her on soft, runny foods. Eggs, custards, and thickened broth will help from the inside while you help her from the outside."

He shot her a stricken look. "Doing what?"

"Stretching her muscles and having her push against you—it'll build muscles. Trips out onto your veranda will be a nice treat."

"Three days could be enough time for this all to pass—you said so yourself. That's what I'm praying for." That's what he'd been beating down heaven's gate about. Ma couldn't go home like this. He couldn't take care of her—or afford a nurse for her. As soon as the weather improved, he'd ride for the doctor.

"To the kitchen with me, now. I only cook supper for the men, but Uncle Bo and I encourage Jerlund to be our guest anytime he'd like. Dangling breakfast is a bribe, but I'm unashamed to do it."

46

"Food is a good plan." Todd followed her across the few steps of the parlor and into the kitchen. His voice dropped. "It troubled me, seeing how his father treated him. Whatever I can do to help—just tell me."

"If I think of anything, I'll let you know." Direct and straightforward—that was Miss Rose. She didn't dither or put up pretenses—just laid out the truth without a bunch of fuss.

The kitchen door burst open. "Maggie! I'm starvin' real bad."

Throwing his arm around Jerlund's shoulder, Todd jostled him good-naturedly. "Strapping men earn their meals. What about you and me doing a few projects around here after breakfast?"

⁕

"Best you men come in and fill up. You've been working so hard, steam's puffing off the barn roof just like a locomotive." Maggie stood over by the barn door and scanned the place. Stacks upon stacks of shingles filled the empty horse stall. Uncle Bo's house and the barn both needed roof work, but the notion of him being up there gave her nightmares. Could Mr. Valmer . . . ?

"I been cuttin' joys, Maggie. Me. With a saw." Jerlund finished cutting through the mark on a piece of wood. "Todd Valmer showed me how."

"Jerlund's a natural at cutting joists." Mr. Valmer climbed down from the ladder and scribbled numbers on a scrap of paper. "He's got a powerful arm."

Though not academically bright, Jerlund had an uncanny ability to perceive the true feelings others tried to hide. Simply stating the fact in a bare-bones, man-to-man way, Mr. Valmer sparked a look of pride on her friend's face she'd never before witnessed. Of all the beautiful treasures she owned and bartered, none came close to Jerlund's squared shoulders and lifted chin.

Mr. Valmer shut the barn door, then caught up with her. His elbow jutted out, and his brows rose in a silent offer. Jerlund rushed to her other side and stuck out his left elbow, too. "Miss Rose is on your right, Jerlund. Offer her your other elbow. When you walk beside a lady and the ground is slippery, it's good manners to allow her to borrow your strength."

Looping her hand into Jerlund's arm was sweet. Sliding her hand around and onto Mr. Valmer's forearm was something entirely different. Even through his coat, the power of youth and vigor radiated to her. All the men in the holler were well past their prime. It was surprising to discover the tensile strength and bulk of a hardworking man at the zenith of his health. Up close like this, he smelled . . . good. If she were to take out her precious oils and try to match his scent, she'd start with musk and add sandalwood . . . then a touch of something complex. . . .

"Is anything wrong?"

"The wind robbed me of my breath for a moment." Maggie took a step, and they all headed toward her house. "It's extremely unusual for us to have such harsh weather."

"Here. Use my scarf." Mr. Valmer had it off and around her in a flash.

She'd already noticed how its blue matched his eyes. Now a deep breath gave her an overwhelming urge to gag. She wanted the wind back. That scarf hadn't been laundered in . . . Had it ever been washed?

Looking pleased with himself, Mr. Valmer smiled. "The blue. It matches your eyes."

It's going to match the color of my face if I don't get into the house and rip it off before I take my next breath!

Whisking off the scarf once they reached the kitchen, Maggie shoved it into Mr. Valmer's hands and croaked, "Lunch is ready!"

Not that it mattered to her; she'd completely lost her appetite. "I'll go see to Mrs. Crewel whilst you men eat."

Maybe because she was built like Mama and Aunt Maude, Mrs. Crewel drew forth a special warmth in Maggie's heart. Funny, how all three of them had dimples in their elbows and at their knuckles. Arms and hands like those gave engulfing hugs and the softest of caresses. The women Maggie loved had gone to the Lord, and she wanted to do everything humanly possible to help Mr. Valmer continue to enjoy his mother.

As a result of lying on her weak side, she'd drooled. Maggie reached over, replaced the soft cloth beneath her cheek, and used the edge of the damp one to tidy up the corner of her patient's mouth.

Mr. Valmer walked into the room and took a deep, noisy breath. "When she sits up, will this problem end?"

"It may still be an issue, but not as much. It's one of the reasons why helping her learn to swallow again is important."

"So." He said the single word with the same finality a few of Paw-Paw's generation used to say, "So be it." With that one word, he showed he'd begun to accept things were different.

They soon left Mrs. Crewel's room, and Mr. Valmer stopped. "I'm obliged for all you've done for Ma. You need only ask for the exchange you feel is fair." The tips of his ears went red. "Tilling soil fills the heart but not the pocket."

He's embarrassed, and for no reason at all. I can take care of that right quick. She shrugged. "Southern hospitality. You, on the other hand, have been working your fingers to the bone."

He held up big, square, callused hands. "It would be impossible for me to dwindle to skin-and-bones eating at your table." He cracked his knuckles. "Sitting idle, I get antsy."

They'd both downplayed what they brought to the

exchange—striking a deal without a big to-do. She flashed a smile. "I'd best get some laundry done while your mama is sleeping. I want to have plenty of time in the kitchen for supper so the only skin-and-bones thing around here is the ugly-as-sin warthog's head at the Flinn twins' house."

"How did they get such a thing?"

"They traded a whole fresh deer. Which accounts for why *I* do the bartering around here. Trading comes naturally to me as breathing." Breathing brought to mind his scarf, which reminded her, "I'd best hie on over to Uncle Bo's to do the wash."

"Work's calling me, too." He turned to go, then pivoted back around. "Miss Rose? I wish to leave my scarf with you in case you need to go out in the storm today."

"I can't think of anything that would bring me more comfort." She silently tacked on, *than washing it.*

While Mr. Valmer went back out to work, Maggie slipped over to Uncle Bo's. Weather being so bad, she used his cabin as a laundry. Even if she hadn't planned on washing today, laundering bedding was necessary. Mr. Valmer had offered to sit up with his ma last night, but Maggie wouldn't hear of it. Had he understood her when she said his ma needed care that a son oughtn't render? Bright-minded as he was, the truth should have registered; but in her experience, family members could be blind to obvious facts until she specifically pointed them out. Like the drooling. Upset as that minor inconvenience made him, she'd have to nudge facts in one at a time.

How could he smell so wonderful, yet his scarf reek? Out of sheer self-preservation, she dunked it first.

Uncle Bo came in. "Looked in on Mrs. Crewel. Sleeping sound and snug as a babe."

"Well, then, I'm calling you at your word. I want to hear the story about Aunt Maude and the bagpipes."

"Knew you'd nab me." He straddled a chair. "It all goes back to the Arrangement."

The Arrangement. She loved hearing Carver Holler's own happily-ever-after fairy tale of arranged marriages. " 'Twas well past time for the youngsters to marry up," Maggie began.

"Aye. And so the lassies were invited to list a few bucks they respected. The lads put in for three possibilities they'd gladly take to wife. Then the fathers prayed and got to work. Nine matches came out of it, and every last one was a marriage made in heaven. I'm the luckiest man in the world, because I got Maude."

"Seven were from heaven," Maggie said for the first time. She wobbled her brows. "Daddy admitted he'd already claimed Mama. You can tell me the truth, too. It's every bit as romantic as having the elders match you."

Combing his fingers through his beard, Uncle Bo let out a rueful chuckle. "I was bullheaded enough to think the elders took leave of their senses when they concocted the Arrangement, but Paw-Paw pointed out the Bible is full of marriage agreements that worked out right fine. Lo and behold, God's Word instructs a man to love his wife. It's his duty. Turned out cherishing Maude was the easiest thing I ever did."

"But the bagpipes?"

A plethora of memories flickered across her uncle's face as he stood and reached for an old book. "A handful of years later your granddaddy done went and spilled the beans. He told Maude about me not writing her name on my paper, and Maude ran home shrieking like a banshee. Before I could explain, she grabbed my axe and made kindling of my bagpipes."

Insatiably curious, Maggie took the slip of paper he handed to her.

I'll take any woman as long as she's godly.
I'll learn to love her.
Bible tells me to, and I will—heart and soul.
Bocephus Carver

"I was livid that day. Not because of what Maude did, but at myself because she wasn't convinced of my devotion. I never replaced those bagpipes to prove something to her: They were just bags of wind—but she was my very breath and heartbeat."

"Oh, Uncle Bo! You more than proved yourself. You adored each other."

His eyes shimmered, and his voice trembled. "You said you'd listen. Harken to the voice of God and of that Valmer man. If marriage comes up, I approve. You'd be going to the same kind of arranged marriage your aunt and I had, and a finer, richer marriage there never was."

"Has he said anything?"

"Not a word. Not yet." Embracing her, he urged, "But I'm sure he will."

As she finished rinsing the sheets, her uncle left her to her thoughts. Did she want Mr. Valmer to say anything? Or to stay silent? It was so confusing. Year on end, she'd been content. And as soon as he left, life would go back to normal. Or would it? *This is silly. Uncle Bo's wild notion and nagging have addled my wits. I'm not going to fret.* Well, that wasn't quite true. She said she'd listen to God or groom. *I have no reason to think Mr. Valmer is my groom. And God hasn't said anything. . . .*

Not yet.

⌐◈¬

Tonight was the night he and Ma should have arrived in Texas.

Instead, Ma's furniture would be unloaded at the Gooding train station with them nowhere in sight. Folks would reckon he'd been delayed.

Delayed? Todd shoved the saw with such force, the teeth cut through four inches of the board. The train wouldn't come through again until next Monday. He was stranded for a whole week while his farm withered. With telegraph strung across the entire nation for thirty years, it was reasonable to assume every place had one. But nothing about this situation was reasonable: Carver's Holler didn't have a telegraph. For him to remain silent for an entire week . . . folks back home would know something bad happened. Maybe even deadly.

His neighbors would probably parcel out his beloved horses—the ones he hoped to someday use for his breeding stock. He'd get the horses back, but the chickens and hogs were a different story. With so many mouths to feed, some neighbors might slaughter a hog even though it wasn't fat enough for butchering. They could fry up his chickens, too. He had to provide for Ma now, and they'd need eggs, chicken, pork, and lard. . . .

The next train won't get us home until eleven fifteen Thursday night. I'll be gone a full eleven days. He couldn't help imagining the disaster awaiting him—scorched wheat, withering alfalfa, and missing tools. By now he should have planted sorghum, but that field remained an unplowed patch of dirt. Whoever said "time is money" must have been a farmer. Lack of time on the farm equated with a huge loss of money. A hired hand's help would probably turn the tide, but Todd couldn't promise to pay someone when every last cent went toward the mortgage. The stack of boards grew higher as he sawed out his frustration.

Finally, he went back inside to check on Ma. A mouthwatering aroma hit him as he entered. "Mmmm!"

"Last night's stew and tonight's roasts are from a buck the Flinn twins downed."

"I could tan your hide." The moment the words came out of his mouth, he groaned. "Not yours. The deer's."

Her merry peals filled her kitchen, making the huge room bright and warm. "I'm eternally grateful the Flinns kept that buckskin. Tanning reeks to high heaven." Sweet-smelling steam bellowed out of the oven as she opened the door.

"I'd rather get a whiff and taste of that any day. What is it?"

"Pie. Tuesday's the night I hold Sweets 'N Swagger, where everybody gets a taste of dessert and the men admire one another's work."

Tuesday. His gut clenched. Any reference to time reminded him of the disaster awaiting him upon his return. But that was his concern—not hers. He refused to drag her down.

"Carver's Holler is known for the beautiful work her men do. It's a shame for something to be sold or traded before we can all appreciate it."

"Do you carve, too?"

"Only roast." She wrinkled her nose. "My whittling lessons ended when I dropped my knife. It stuck straight into Paw-Paw's wooden leg."

Her admission charmed him. "I'm positive the other men will agree with me that your cooking is the masterpiece of the night."

"Not necessarily. I bartered for shells a couple years back, and the men took up the challenge of teaching themselves how to carve on something that fragile and unforgiving. The first pieces were atrocious. Once they adapted the skills of carving wood to carving shell, some of the men turned out to be gifted craftsmen, but all of them do wonders with wood."

He watched with wonder of his own as, with hands moving

at blurring speed, Miss Rose chopped enough carrots to fill the biggest mixing bowl. With his help, she dumped the carrots into a roasting pan.

About five minutes later, Todd stood on the side of Ma's bed. She'd been facing the far wall earlier. Now she faced the door. Miss Rose tucked a nest of pillows around Ma to make her stay put. *The woman just has to build nests—whether with mixing bowls, her "treasures," or pillows. But Ma looks okay, and that's what matters most.*

Todd moved to assist her. "I'll do that."

"I'm done." Miss Rose sidestepped something.

He went to pick it up, but she tried to stop him. Towels. But she hadn't had anywhere near enough time to bathe Ma. So why . . . ? His eyes narrowed. Those weren't sheets. It was a stack of flour sacks inside a towel. Rooted to the floor, Todd looked from her to his mother, to the diaper-like thing on the floor, and back as the truth dawned on him.

"Such lovely hair your mama has." Miss Rose's lilting observation warred with her stern look. "The silver and brown look like sugar swirled with nutmeg."

He nodded curtly to acknowledge the unspoken message. Miss Rose was kind to give him something to talk about. "My sister, she inherited Ma's brown hair and eyes."

"You have a sister?" Did relief tinge her voice?

"Arletta. She and her husband left last Friday for France." Even if he reached his sister, it wouldn't matter. After marrying a rich man, Arletta lost her values. When their stepfather died, Ma went to live with Arletta. Infrequent notes from Arletta accused Ma of being nosy—even making a pest of herself. At that time he'd been breaking sod and living in the barn. When he wrote that he'd take Ma as soon as possible, Arletta didn't respond. Then, out of the blue, months later, a curt note arrived. They were going to Europe, didn't know when they'd return, and it was his turn to take on the "burden" of keeping Ma. Ma knew nothing about it, and he'd make sure she never did.

It was supposed to be so easy. Now it's impossible.

Miss Rose bent and scooped up the laundry. Lithe. Lively. She moved with such purpose. On this trip, Todd enjoyed ample opportunities to watch women. Oh, the pleasure of listening to a voice that wasn't in a low register! Hearing the rustle of petticoats and catching a whiff of perfume could make him stop dead in his tracks. Some of the littlest things were most potent of all: the flutter of a narrow ribbon, the way sun skipped all over the peaks and valleys in a woman's hair, or the glint of her jewelry. Even at a distance, he appreciated how women gestured as they spoke.

Back home the longing for a wife had him praying earnestly for a helpmeet. Privileged city women who dropped lace hankies, swooned, and didn't know the working end of an animal—they'd make sublimely ridiculous farmers' wives. Not that it mattered— they'd have tilted up their noses and sailed past him. Miss Rose moved more gracefully than all of them, and he'd bet she raised her nose only so she could appreciate the stars.

"Have you ever swooned?" The question surprised him; he didn't realize at first he'd spoken aloud.

Her eyes twinkled. "I have more sense and better things to do with my time." She dumped the towels into a wicker basket. "Earlier, you mentioned your farm. What are your crops?"

Walking back to the kitchen in her wake, he noticed the tiny little straggles of hair that teased away from the rest. They were a bit damp. And starting to curl. Was taking care of Ma putting too much strain on her? She turned around. "Hmm. I see. Cats. You have a cat farm, and one of them got your tongue."

Spirited little filly. "I've been in Gooding two years. Both years showed yield on the wheat. The second year more, since I cleared more land." Her smile invited him to tell her more. "Most of the soil's rich. I have a Dempster windmill. The water is sweet, but we're suffering drought. Lack of rain for a third year is brutal on the wheat."

"Bet that's hard on your garden, too."

"Didn't do much gardening," he confessed. "Makes me half wild—you opening that pantry door." A rainbow of jars filled the pantry—fruits, vegetables, jams, jellies, crocks . . .

"I've gracious plenty. I'll send home a crate with you." When she put the lid down on one pot and lifted the lid on another, the aromas mingled. Her kitchen was a feast for the senses. "Everybody's got their likes and loathes, so don't tell me you'll take anything. You may as well take your favorites."

"Corn. Beans and tomatoes, please." Scanning the kitchen, he spied a small oilcan. The back door needed attention, and Todd needed to stay busy.

"As for your mama, we'll feed her warm grits gruel. Mashed 'tatoes and gravy. Thick applesauce. Then I'll steam and mash up vegetables."

His mouth went dry. Todd could handle the worst mess in the barn; he'd dealt with the bloodiest wounds on horses. But everything Miss Rose listed was fit for a baby with two teeth. His stomach churned at the memory of church picnics where mothers fed mushy food to their babies. *Even if I had the time, I couldn't spoon that vile stuff into Ma.* Immediately on the tail of that thought came, *Miss Rose would be good at it. Real smooth and patient.*

"It shows good sense, you thinking about these things."

Todd let out a mirthless laugh. She'd think he lost all his good sense if she knew what was twirling like a desperado's lasso in his head. Marrying Miss Rose would be an answer to every prayer—for a godly wife, a hard worker, a good cook, and now, someone who could tend to Ma. He started formulating a plan.

"Fair warning: grab yourself gravy straight away tonight, because my uncles hog it."

Splurp! Oil shot from the can as he wheeled around. "Uncles? All of them—"

"Are like kin to me." Affection coated her words and glowed in her eyes. "Uncle Bo's the only real blood relative I have left, but don't breathe a hint of that around the others. You'd break their hearts. Jesus and my uncles and Jerlund—they're my world."

She'd just summed up a life he'd heard about only once before. "My sister loved a book about a maiden who made her home with many little men. Dwarfs."

"Snow White." A winsome smile tilted her full lips. "By the Brothers Grimm. It's Jerlund's favorite."

After putting away oil, he cleaned up the mess. "When you said there's not another woman here, you weren't joking, were you?"

A plethora of emotions flickered across her face. "I wish I had been. Cholera stole Aunt Maude, the granny woman who taught me her healing ways, and three other women. I lost them and the last five children all in one wave. Most of the men were off installing the altar, pulpit, and pews in a new church, so they escaped it. I tell myself to be grateful, because had they been here, I would have lost some of them, too."

"It's been hard on you."

"Aye. But I have learned to open my heart wide so I hold no regrets of what was—only of what might have been. And then, I'm second-guessing God. So I enjoy those God gives me." Turning, she began to mash the potatoes.

Todd took the funny implement from her hand. "I'm no cook,

but this I can do." She added milk, butter, and a bit of salt, and he massacred the boiled potatoes. "So this is how they are made."

"Mashed potatoes drowning in gravy would make a rib-sticking meal for your ma."

Ma. For a few moments, he'd let the predicament slide from being his primary focus. With Miss Rose on hand, he could set aside his worries . . . and with all these men depending on her, there wasn't a hope he'd pry her away. Or could he? "Ma's in a bad way."

"Forsooth, she is—now. Time will reveal her true condition. If God granted requests based on the number of prayers dedicated to an issue, sure as snow's a-fallin, your ma will be skipping all the way back to the train station."

Another prayer got added to the count at suppertime. Tender roast, carrots, mashed potatoes—every bite tasted ten times better than the one before it. Afterward, the men set out what they'd been working on so the others could "take a gander."

Miss Rose lifted a small box from the midst of the work and carried it to her pie safe. "We have some cameos this time."

"They're her favorites. She wears one every day," Jerlund said in a loud whisper. "I like the birds best."

"Everything is special in its own way if you pay attention." Miss Rose lifted a cameo and held it before the kerosene lamp. "This only takes a glance, and the graceful profile proclaims it as a thing of beauty."

Todd studied the woman instead. The lamplight cast a glow about her. Graceful and beautiful—those words fit her far better than a thin piece of shell. Ordinary conversation filled the room— weather, animals, memories of happy times. Todd would much rather talk with Miss Rose.

Time to see if his plan stood a chance. Elbowing in, Todd planted himself by her side. They'd stood close while mashing the potatoes, but this was closer still. Her response to his touch would reflect either instinctive withdrawal or acceptance. "By the time that cameo gets to me, I'm not going to know who made it." His fingers slid beneath her hand, and he pulled it just a little to the right so he could see, too. For an instant, her hand shook. Did she feel the same jolt he did upon contact? He wasn't disappointed in the least when her hand relaxed trustingly in his, but her voice trembled as she answered Jethro's question about her parents.

Todd wondered aloud, "Do you take after your mother or father?"

"Both. Mama liked to bake and grow roses; Daddy loved books and folktales." She passed the cameo to the nearest old gent. "How about you, Mr. Valmer?"

She'd ignored appearance. Interesting. And telling, too. "My love of the land comes from my father; to my great regret, I have none of my mother's cooking ability."

"An affliction common to men." She kept a straight face. "Daddy couldn't fix anything in the kitchen unless he used a hammer for the job."

She refilled his coffee mug, then her own more delicate cup. But that cup crashed to the floor when a hair-raising wail sounded in the other room.

Four

I t must've been vinegar pie. It always gives me nightmares. Opening her eyes again, Helga Crewel felt sure the wild vision would be gone.

It wasn't.

Even after the biggest slice of vinegar pie, she couldn't possibly dream up anything this . . . junky. Gaudy, frivolous things that cost too much hard-earned money cluttered the room. Shelves along one wall held wood carvings. Angels—one or two would be tasteful, but nobody needed a whole host of them. A tattered rag doll slumped beside an exquisitely hand-painted china doll. Glass, ivory, and jet buttons and beads filled glass tubes . . . a few spools of ribbon and cording. Was this a dressmaker's?

Maybe so. Her Todd was such a good son. She'd grown terribly weary on the train, and he'd no doubt considerately arranged for them to stay at a stopover and rest. *I must have been utterly exhausted. I don't recall changing into my nightgown.* Her arm and leg had gone to sleep. In a second her limbs would begin to tingle with a vengeance. Wanting to stave off that eventuality, Helga buckled to the shameful temptation to roll over and laze a moment before she left the mattress.

Flipping onto her back proved difficult. Pillows abounded—even a few behind her back, of all places. Silly to have to work at such a thing, but she made it. A chandelier dangled above her head. *No. Oh no. Father, don't let this be real.* She reached up to test if it truly existed, but her arm refused to budge.

Bang! The door hit the wall. Todd dashed in with a black-haired girl chasing behind. "Ma. Ma!" He cupped her face in his hands and got so close, he was all she could see. "Ma!"

It wasn't until her lungs burned and she needed to draw another breath that Helga realized she'd been screaming.

"Shhh. Ma. Shhh. Shhh."

"You're doin' a fine thing," a twangy voice said. "Panic makes . . ." Whatever the stranger said got lost in Helga's terrible fright.

Todd repeated the slow shushing sound, and Helga couldn't help breathing along with him. She pulled herself together, only to burst into tears. "I can't make my arm work."

"I know, Ma." He eased back and glanced off to the side.

"Don't make her go through this again. Present fears are less than horrible imaginings." The girl who came in with Todd stepped into view. "If it be your druthers, I'll speak with her."

Todd cleared his throat. "Ma, something went bad." He halted and searched for words.

Each moment that passed without him saying something, Helga's fears grew. A hand clasped hers and squeezed. "Mrs. Crewel, ma'am, I'm Margaret Rose." Pretty thing had steady eyes. She mopped away the tears. "Ma'am, I need to know straight away: Are you suffering pain?"

"N-no."

Todd let out a gust of a sigh. "God be praised at least for that."

"Indeed!" The girl—Helga couldn't recall her name—nodded a few times. "You had yourself a problem on the train. For now, both your left arm and leg aren't working."

Panic's fingers started tightening around Helga's windpipe again. "Leg?" She tried to move both of them. The right one bent immediately: the left didn't budge. *Dear God, please—*

"I didn't want you to find out all on your lonesome," the girl's comment interrupted Helga's supplication. "I'm sorry we weren't by your side when you awoke. There's a more than passing fair chance a portion of the use might return."

While the girl spoke, Helga kept trying to make her arm and leg work. Even just her hand and foot. A simple wiggle or twitch . . . Yet nothing whatsoever happened. "A chance. But how much?"

"We can't predict such a thing." Todd gave her shoulder an awkward pat.

"I'll teach your son how to help keep your limbs supple, and he tells me you're a strong woman. That bodes well. You can learn to do things right-handed and keep taking care of yourself—at least partway."

Combing her hair. Braiding it. Pinning it up. Getting dressed . . . Simple, everyday personal tasks required both hands. Walking . . . Walking! Balancing herself on a wagon seat. Getting up on tiptoe to gather eggs hens laid in odd places. Myriad chores and tasks whirled around in her mind. All required her to be of sound constitution.

" 'Tis a powerful sorrow these words brought with them." Miss Rose—that's what Todd called her—wiped away more tears for her. Voice low and caring, she continued. "The train comes through next week, and in that time, I'll help all I can. Even more, though, a legion of prayers has been a-marching up to God's holy throne room, imploring His Eternal Majesty to grant you recovery."

Next week? That wouldn't be nearly enough time to recuperate.

"I'm stepping out to give the both of you time together."

What would become of the plan for her to help out on her son's farm? All she'd be now was a burden. Todd hadn't said a word, but that was his nature. It made her feel far worse.

"Son, what are we to do?"

Todd finally sat on the edge of the bed. Pressing both of her hands between his, she felt his strength seeping into her. "We'll trust in God, Ma. He has never failed."

⚜

"A lovely morning to you." Maggie pulled opened the curtains and allowed the natural light into the room. "After three days of a fearsome storm—Paw-Paw said he's not seen one that bad in all his years—well, the sunshine on the snow sets everything a-sparkle. Take a look-see."

Mrs. Crewel drearily turned her head away. "Go pester someone else."

Maggie took no offense at her patient's rudeness. Quite often, folks had a few testy days after taking ill. "I already fed the men. Even that storm hasn't kept them from accomplishing enough to warrant a pair of new toolboxes, and they're still going strong. Today they're reroofing sections of the barn. Mr. Valmer already reinforced Mr. Elding's porch. You must be proud of that boy you reared." Maggie slid a hand beneath the woman's shoulders and pulled out the pillow.

"He sees a need and tends it." Mrs. Crewel grabbed the pillow with her right hand. The two women stared at one another, sizing up the foe in the sudden tug-of-war.

"Ma'am, you stayed abed yesterday and had time to accustom yourself to the news. But the longer you laze, the less you'll recover. I have breakfast here for you, too." Having made her point, Maggie took full possession of the pillow.

Mrs. Crewel lay stubborn as a board nailed every two inches to a foundation. "I choked on water and broth. It's no use trying anything more."

"Once we kept fingers pressed to that side of your throat, you didn't choke." Maggie stuck the pillow against the headboard and tapped an arm of the chandelier. "Reach on up here with your good hand. Bend your good knee and push against the bed whilst I scoot you upward. We'll work together, and you'll be pulling your own weight."

"I know I'm fat; you didn't have to tell me. But it's all the more reason why I won't eat."

"I spoke of responsibility, not weight. When you get to Texas, your son needs to rig up something similar. That way, as you start to regain use of your limbs, you can work the muscles for strength, as well." Ignoring her patient's grumbling, Maggie sat her against the headboard. "And now for a treat!"

Mrs. Crewel spied the invalid cup. "I'm not using that! I used one just like it to feed my babies."

The device looked much like a teapot with the handle reglued to be at a forty-five-degree angle from the spout. Instead of a lid, half of the top remained open. "Nonsense. I'll brace your throat muscles. You hold the cup and keep control of the flow."

A truculent expression warned Maggie the woman had dug in her heels. "Once you've eaten, we'll wash you up and sit you in my wheelchair. Just think how much that will please your son." Those words earned her instant cooperation.

After his mother successfully ate some breakfast, Mr. Valmer helped set her in the wooden wheelchair. A deep, pleased chuckle rumbled out of him as he stepped back. "Look at you!" Almost immediately, she sagged to her left. "Ma!"

In less than a blink Maggie propped her with a pillow in a strategic spot. Next, she took a wide strip of cloth and draped it across her patient's shoulder and tied it to a thick grosgrain ribbon by her hip. Now Mrs. Crewel wouldn't slump and slide straight out of the chair. "You look regal as a queen a-wearing her ceremonial sash."

"I can't believe you have a wheelchair." Mr. Valmer stared at the back of the wooden, cane-seated premier model.

"The mark of a professional barterer is that they anticipate needs. If I waited until someone got hurt, they'd have to wait two weeks to get one."

Mrs. Crewel stared out the window and gasped. "The storm blew over someone's house! How heartbreaking. They've lost everything they owned. Just look at that pathetic mess out there."

Mr. Valmer went ruddy. "Uh, Ma?"

Maggie raised a hand and shook her head. No need trying to correct the poor, misguided woman. Her heart was in the right place. Combing the woman's hair, she reassured, "In time, everything out there will wind up right where it belongs."

⌒⌘⌒

Each day for five days, Todd grabbed every opportunity to pass time with Miss Rose, exchange stories, and pitch in with anything Ma needed. Convinced Miss Rose was the one for him, he strove to give her cause to trust and rely on him.

He needed her, if any hope remained of keeping his farm. He

could picture his winter wheat withering, weeds abounding, and wolves eating his chickens—or worse, preying on his hogs or horses. He'd almost lost his colts to the wolves weeks ago. Though the vet had discounted his fees significantly, it drained what little Todd had stashed away. He needed bumper crops this year to keep his head above water.

At any moment he could state how much time had elapsed since he'd worked his own land and how much more time remained before he'd return. Two more nights, two more days, and he'd finally be on the train for thirty-one hours. Somehow, he had to convince spry old Bo Carver to give his blessing, appeal to Miss Rose with a proposal she'd accept, and marry her—all before the train came.

One step at a time. Tonight, the consent. Tomorrow, the proposal. Then Monday, we'll marry and depart. Todd knew he'd petitioned the Lord for a string of miracles. Heal Ma. Keep the farm going and the animals well. And now this desperate timeline . . .

Todd had noted that occasionally, Mr. Carver helped him wrangle a little time with Miss Rose. He'd think of something urgent to tell his niece, then send Todd as his messenger. No matter where Miss Rose sat at the table, one of the men beside her would move—allowing Todd to take his place. Those things ought to have boded well.

They didn't. For every instance when Mr. Carver assisted his courting efforts, there was another when he just as surely blocked it. Today Miss Rose's uncle volunteered him to repair a neighbor's roof. That reeked of keeping him away from his niece. It worked, too.

Absence didn't just make the heart grow fonder; it made Todd more stubborn. Miss Rose's stunning appearance caught his attention, and her kind ways and spirited nature charmed him. Most of all, her Christlike heart captivated him. He'd waited for the right woman. Now that he found her, Todd wasn't going to let go.

Barely quelling a snort, he cast a rueful glance at Mr. Carver as they headed toward the barn. Those trips to carry messages were probably his way of providing Todd with an excuse to check on Ma. And the old fellows—they'd done all the musical chairs because they teased Miss Rose. Blinded by their love, the old men probably didn't even consider she might ever leave them. The minute he brought up the subject to Mr. Carver, the two of them would undoubtedly tangle. But Todd was determined to win this war.

"Can't thank you enough for all the help you've given," Mr. Carver said as Todd opened the barn door.

"I'm happy to be of help." Todd followed him inside. "Though, tonight, it was a sacrifice to stay and finish that last section while the other men went ahead and ate supper."

"Nothing's better'n one of my Magpie's meals." Mr. Carver set his toolbox down in the barn and looked up with glee at the roof they'd repaired a few days ago.

"One thing sounds better to me."

Bocephus Carver looked at him, agog. "Something sounds better than Maggie's food?"

Todd nodded curtly. "The girl herself." Seeing the old man suck in a deep breath, Todd paused for a second. Yep. He'd just dealt a big shock. But now was the time to make his points before Mr. Carver shouted out his refusal. "Miss Rose cooks well, but she is more. Kind. Healthy. Pretty. And she is good with Ma. I want your niece to become my wife."

The old man cupped one hand over his eyes for just one moment, then dropped back his head and exhaled loudly. Pain radiated from every line on his wrinkled face as he finally stared Todd in the eye. Slowly he extended his right hand. "Son, you don't know how I've prayed for God to send the right man for my sweet Magpie."

Todd didn't accept the old man's hand. Omitting a truth was

every bit as bad as lying. Honor forced him to lay out the facts. "I'll protect her. Provide for her."

The lantern spat and sparked in the sudden silence. Withdrawing his hand, Miss Rose's uncle glowered. "But you don't love her."

Five

The old man cut to the heart of the issue—or the lack of heart, repeating the stark fact. "You don't love her."

Unflinchingly, Todd stood his ground and met the man's stormy eyes. "Miss Rose is a remarkable Christian woman. I admire her and like what I've seen so far, but that's as much as I can admit."

"That ain't much, son."

Raising his chin a notch, Todd clipped, "Any man who declared his undying love after a few days—he's the one you ought to be wary of."

Shaking his head side to side, her uncle groused. He turned and walked off a few paces, wheeled around, and narrowed his eyes. Then waggled his finger as he came stomping back. "That child grew up reading happily-ever-after fairy tales. She saw her daddy and me doting over our wives with overflowing hearts. You expect her to settle for less? You haven't even courted the lass."

"I'm honorable. I won't pretend what I don't feel, but a woman of her caliber is certain to fill a home will love. As for courting—that can happen on either side of the wedding ring."

"You're wrong. A wise man knows courting never ends. A little effort on his part cultivates a garden in her heart. Him not bothering—what should have taken seed, sprouted, and flourished just blows away." His eyes narrowed. The corners of his mouth went tight, as did his voice. "Supposing I put Maggie's hand in yours . . . just supposing . . . would you give her the courtship she deserves?"

"I could do that." Was the old man softening?

Mr. Carver leaned a little closer. "You sure you don't love her maybe a little?"

A slow smile slid across Todd's face. "If your niece turns out to be half as sweet as her jams, falling in love with her will be easy."

Bocephus clamped his hand around Todd's arm and plowed over toward a pair of hay bales. Once they both plopped down, Maggie's uncle said, "What if I give my blessing for a courtship? Your ma could stay here with Maggie, and you could write letters for a spell."

"They both go with me now." Todd wasn't taking any chances. Some other man might steal his bride. Besides, when he was alone with Ma for even a second, she begged him to get her out of here.

Carver scowled. "You sound mighty sure of yourself."

"You can come visit us anytime. Ma's got only me. Leaving her when she's helpless and struggling—even with my bride-to-be . . . I can't. Especially with my bride. I'll not ask Miss Rose to bear such a responsibility alone. A man takes care of his own."

Rubbing his chin thoughtfully, Mr. Carver studied him for a long moment. "Then . . . you might could be betrothed. The women live in your house whilst you stay in the barn."

"You're more likely to find a barking cat than an eligible woman where I come from. I'd be ten kinds of fool to dangle a prize like her around a hoard of randy cowboys. I won't endanger her like that."

"Hmmm." A slow grin crossed Mr. Carver's face. "My Maggie Titania's a princess, and any man would be blessed to be her husband. I ain't about to send her off to someplace full of woman-hungry bucks with slick ways and smooth words." His smile faded. " 'Tis my duty to see she's with a good, solid Christian man who'll follow God's Word. The Bible instructs a man to love his wife as Christ loves the church—to cherish her so much he'd be willing to give himself up for her."

He's laid it on the line. And because I stuck with the truth, he's going to turn me away.

"I got the biggest decision of my life to make, and it's only right you answer me."

Todd nodded. "Fair enough." *I've still got a chance.*

"A man whose heart is right with God and grounds his life in the Holy Scriptures—he can't help but love his woman. Might take some time, and there are bound to be some bumps in the road, but that's the truth. The questions are, do you love God that much? Are you a man to study the Bible each day and follow it in word and deed? Do you trust Him enough?"

"You're making it downright easy. The answer to all of those—"

Mr. Carver lifted his hand. "Don't you answer me yet. You see, there are some other things that might make a difference."

Nothing would make a difference. Nothing . . . except if she couldn't have children. He wanted several. But they'd adopt if it came to that. Any child under their roof would wriggle right into his heart in no time at all.

"There's things you ought to know. First off, I'm not talking outta my hat. My own marriage wasn't a love match. I took Maude to wife and said my vows, leaning on the promises of God. She, too, loved the Lord with her heart, mind, soul, and strength. I know it's not the way of things in these modern times, but there are still times when the hand of God reaches down to arrange situations. We have to recognize them."

"I've been praying for a wife. Ma took sick, so I prayed for the best of care, and the train kicked us out right here. Miss Rose is the answer to my prayers, and—"

"Son, you're eager to get her hand. I'm making sure the details won't become burdensome."

His jaw clenched. "Ma's not a burden. I wouldn't want a wife who viewed her as such. Miss Rose—"

"Dotes on your ma. You're plowing off course. I'm talking about legacies. My niece has one she counts most precious."

"Thus I would wish her to keep it."

"Mountain women are tough, but they're also tenderhearted. They know their minds, too. There's a wildness that love tempers but won't tame."

"Intelligent women have spirit. I'd want it no other way. What else could I tell you to put your heart at ease?"

Mr. Carver glanced away. "Your actions speak louder than anything comin' out of your mouth. I saw you beseeching the Lord for your ma's sake. A man who can love so much he'd risk his own life—he'd be a good husband."

He's softening. I actually have a chance!

"I've been on my knees, praying about the right man for my niece for years. Only in the last two weeks, the matter weighed heavy on my heart, and that's how God let me know things were due to change." The old man's voice quavered with emotion. "In the six days before you set foot in Maggie's parlor, I told her each day that God was going to be bringing a husband her way. I prayed. You came."

Todd looked him in the eye. The old man met his gaze, unashamed of the tears wending down his careworn face. "Sir, you asked if I would lay down my life. Now at this very minute, you are setting the example. For your niece's future, you are making a great sacrifice, letting her go.

"There is a word: serendipity. It is when something unexpectedly good happens in the midst of the trials of life. For me to meet my wife now—it is because God has worked in a bad situation. Let Margaret become my bride. I will heed God's commands, and I will come to love her as you loved your wife and as Christ cherishes the church. Until that love blooms, your niece and I have serendipity—this providence from God—that brought us together. It is a fine start."

For a moment, they shared a profound silence. A bittersweet smile tugged at the old man's lips. "Son, you're gonna have to talk her into it. I've done my best to get her ready. Problem is, Maggie's as headstrong as you are proud."

"Ah, but just as the man is to love his wife, the woman is to respect her husband and submit to him. I'll be good to her."

"You have my blessing." The funny old man chuckled softly and extended his hand. "Just remember; there's a world of difference between submitting and submission."

༺✦༻

A blast of cold air blew out Maggie's lantern just as she reached the barn. For all the work Mr. Valmer accomplished, he ought to be triplets.

"Mr. Valmer, a strong young man like you could undoubtedly spell Atlas and hold up the world for a while, but my uncle's recently taken to telling me he's so old, I almost believe he and

George Washington played marbles together. Come inside, eat a hot meal, and rest."

Chuckling, Mr. Valmer reached her side. He offered his arm, and she readily took it. For a moment, she looked up into his handsome face, and her heart pitter-pattered. *Oh my. Granny would have laughed and said the sap was running a mite early.*

"What's for supper?"

"Sap. I mean, soup." She didn't even tell him what type. The less she said, the safer she'd be.

A few minutes later, they were inhaling the soup.

"Maggie? Maggie?!" Panic edged Jerlund's voice.

Maggie dashed toward the back door to help her friend. But Mr. Valmer had shot to his feet, too. Gripping her securely, yet gently, he murmured, "I'll help. No man wants a woman to see him frightened. Go check Ma."

Everything within her railed. "He's . . . Jerlund's . . ."

"Yet a man." Mr. Valmer turned her shoulders and ducked his head to whisper in her ear. The warmth of his breath tickled and made her shiver. "I've trusted you. Trust me."

He had trusted her. Now the tables were turned. Jerlund wasn't on death's door, either. *I do trust him.* Maggie nodded.

"*Sehr gut.* Very good." Mr. Valmer squeezed her shoulders and turned loose. The loss of contact left her feeling . . . alone. Adrift. In the past few days, she'd had more contact with a man of her own age than the entire rest of her life, and it left her breathless. Before she blurted out something to embarrass herself forever, she fled to the sickroom.

Mrs. Crewel was stirring. Gently, Maggie stroked a few wisps of hair behind the woman's ear. Mrs. Crewel's right eye opened. With her left eye drooping, it didn't open much unless she was wide awake. "Let me sit you up and give you some nice, thick soup."

After a few sips, Mrs. Crewel signaled she'd had plenty. "That ruckus—it's the child-minded man, isn't it? Go help him, girl. Strife in a home is hard on anyone, but that boy must be in anguish."

Maggie kissed her fingertips, pressed them to Mrs. Crewel's temple, and whispered, "I now know where your son got his kind heart." She went out and started stacking dishes. "Hi, Jerlund."

"Hi, Maggie. I'm gonna sleep in your bed—the one at Uncle Bo's." Nodding, Jerlund added, "Bo Carver said I can. It smells like your perfume."

Uncle Bo puffed up his chest. "My Maggie Rose makes it herself. Has nothing a-tall to do with her daddy's family name, neither. My Maude, she taught her how to coax things from the rose. 'Twas the legacy she passed on."

Turning his head toward her, Mr. Valmer inhaled deeply. Gazing into her eyes, he rumbled, "A sweet one indeed."

❧

The next morning, Maggie looked at the bottles of her perfume while brushing her hair. He liked her perfume. Should she dab on a little as was her custom, or omit using it because he might consider it flirtatious? He'd leave tomorrow, and he'd forget her perfume . . . and forget her.

"Miss Rose." Mr. Valmer's deep, morning-husky voice whispered across the distance.

I'll miss the sound of his voice. Glancing up in the mirror, she spied him over in the doorway. The intensity of his unwavering gaze made tingles go up and down her spine.

His eyes met hers in the mirror, and one side of his mouth kicked upward as he beckoned her. *I'll miss his crooked grin, too—though it doesn't mean anything. That's what I have to keep in mind.*

Setting down the brush, Maggie chose a comb. She held it

between her teeth and twisted her hair into a long rope as she walked to the door. Once the whole length gave just the right tension, she coiled her hair and grabbed the comb. Daddy formed the comb with only three teeth—but they were all an inch apart and five inches long. Wiggling it back and forth from scalp to bun, she whispered, "Your mother had a difficult night. I'd like her to gain another hour of sleep yet."

"Fine . . . good." Mr. Valmer stared at her as she crossed the room, but as she reached him, he tore his gaze away and muttered, "Sleep. The raveled care . . ."

" 'Sleep knits up the raveled sleeve of care.' " Even though he'd jumbled Shakespeare, it was touching. He slipped in a quote from the Bible here or there and occasionally even a line from Shakespeare! Since Daddy died, she hadn't spoken to anyone with the same ability.

As Maggie squeezed past him and out of the room, they brushed against one another. She felt breathless and tingly. Funny, she never really noticed her heart picking up pace around any other fellow, but it kept happening around Mr. Valmer. *He's the only man near my age I've seen more than once. Well, other than a few of the fellows who come a-trading—and business is strictly business.*

Maggie wished to give Uncle Bo a piece of her mind. If he hadn't been yammering about her "marryin' up," she wouldn't be making such a goose of herself. These momentary reactions were nonsense, plain and simple. Besides, even if she were absolutely full-on smitten, nothing would come of it. This farmer must get back to his fields in Texas, and she was still needed in the holler.

Pulling the door shut, Mr. Valmer cleared his throat again. "The door—it was ajar. I did not mean to intrude."

"The way you check on your mother warms my heart." One

last wiggle and stab, and the comb secured her hair. Maggie entered the kitchen.

"It wasn't my intention to eavesdrop." His eyes sparked with humor. "As much as she's cried, I worried you might be in danger of drowning. I came to rescue you."

Maggie found his admission disarmingly clever. "Especially at the start, it's normal for a body to be sorrowful. As time passes, if your mama keeps a-crying a pond of tears and wallows in it, you'll need to set her straight. Christ Jesus did the ultimate work when His precious arms and legs couldn't move anymore."

He nodded curtly. "So will I tell her. The thought—it is sehr gut."

Maggie reached for her mixing bowls. "Now, what can I do for you?"

"I need to ask you something."

The door banged open. "Maggie! I'm starvin' again!"

Grudgingly, Todd set aside their discussion until later.

"Let's see to breakfast." As Miss Rose spoke, deep rumbles of male conversation converged on the porch.

For pete's sake, every last one of the holler's inhabitants had showed up for the meal. As far as Todd could see, St. Peter was the only one not sitting at the table. Left up in heaven minding the pearly gates, he was probably having a good laugh at Todd's predicament. Todd wanted a nice, quiet breakfast and hoped to escort Miss Rose on a walk after church, where he could propose.

Earlier, he'd lost his breath when he'd spied her with her hair spilling down in inky splendor. She'd refrained from scorching his ears for gawking at her in such a compromising state. Instead, she spun her tresses round and round, disciplined them into that bun, and nabbed it in place with the comb. His fingers itched to pull it back out and test the texture of her hair.

Why did the "uncles" have to show up for breakfast?

All the noise and laughter woke up Ma. Miss Rose bundled Ma into a robe, braided her hair and secured it in the same across-the-head-and-back arrangement Ma favored. Ma screeched as Todd picked her up. "Where do you think you're taking me? There are men out there!"

"You'll be eating breakfast with us and sharing in the worship. It's Sunday, and everyone under my roof attends church." Miss Rose bustled ahead. "Mr. Valmer, please position your mother next to yourself." After setting the invalid cup of soupy oatmeal in front of Ma, Miss Rose took a seat across from her.

Mr. Collier said a prayer, then Miss Rose poured milk into her oatmeal, heaped in some sugar, and stirred it. Setting aside the spoon, she picked up the bowl and drank her oatmeal! It didn't take but a minute before the men at the table followed suit. Ma blustered. Todd added more milk to his own oatmeal.

"Nein. *Fresst du nicht!*"

Todd shot Ma a scowl for ordering him not to eat like an animal. His fingers curled around the china bowl, and the warmth radiating to them matched his feeling toward the young woman across the table who'd abandoned her own manners in order to make Ma feel less self-conscious. He spoke to her in German. *"Don't worry about how I eat, and I won't worry about how you eat."* The oatmeal went down easily. He nudged Ma's invalid bowl closer. *"Das Wichtigste ist, dass wir essen."*

"Yep," Mr. Carver declared. "That's a smart son you got there, Mrs. Crewel. The important thing is that we all eat."

"Sprechen sie Deutsch?" The side of Ma's face that didn't droop turned into a mask of embarrassment.

"Only me and Maggie. Lot of her books are in German. Once in a blue moon, she even barters in German. Brings to mind the time my Magpie traded that wagon wheel. . . ."

Soon Ma sipped oatmeal while Mr. Carver related how that wheel skipped about like a stone on the surface of a lake from one trade to the next—all with his niece's brokering—until nine trades later, that wagon wheel came back to her possession along with an apron and so many quarts of berries.

"No wonder you've got so much stuff!" Ma scanned the kitchen.

"I'm aiming to bring in more." One of the men planted his elbows on the table and leaned forward. "That gnarled old tree finally gave up last night. I already marked what sections I want for carving. The rest can go for our Magpie's stove. It'll take at least six of our horses or your Belgians to drag the tree, Bo. The pair of them could probably tap it once and send it skidding here."

Ma huffed. "Today is Sunday."

"Yep. But if we don't move it today, tomorrow's train could derail and kill folks."

Mr. Carver cleared his throat. "Magpie'll have to do it." Chortles filled the room. He looked Todd in the eye. "My niece spoilt them horses. They won't listen to a single command I give. Just the other day I told Paw-Paw that pair is Maggie's dowry because they'll do me no good staying behind."

"Uncle Bo!" Miss Rose turned a fetching shade of pink.

"I had all my kitchen goods, thirteen fine quilts, and a *milch* cow when I married Todd's father."

"But no bride brings a dowry of such great worth as matched Belgians!" Todd didn't want Miss Rose to witness his delight. She'd assume he'd proposed to get the horses. "The man who wins Miss Rose's hand has received treasure enough."

Jerlund gestured around the room. " 'Cuz of all her treasures she'll take."

"Beauty's in the eye of the beholder." Ma pushed her now-empty cup away. "But I'm seeing plenty of trash and very few treasures."

"Ma . . ." Todd said in a low undertone.

At the same time, Jerlund scrambled to his feet. "That wasn't nice. I don' like her bein' mean to our Maggie. We love our Maggie. Uncle Bo, Paw-Paw, Daddy—you tell her."

"Shhh, Jerlund." Miss Rose stood and patted Jerlund. "It's like when I bake cookies. You like all of them. Mr. Collier favors the oatmeal ones, but if they have raisins, he doesn't eat them. Different people have different tastes."

Jerlund frowned. "But Mr. Collier never tole you your cookies are trash."

"Nothing you cook could be mistaken for trash, Miss Rose." The minute she'd stood, Todd shot to his feet. "The good Lord above knows my gratitude's robust when I gave thanks for your meals. Even more, though, I'm indebted to you for the tender care you've given Ma."

He meant every word, but he feared it was too little, too late. Miss Rose wouldn't ever leave these men who hung on her every word and competed to earn her smiles—not to be the wife of a stranger, bribed with a pair of horses into proposing so she would care for his ailing, sour-tongued mother.

Only Todd Valmer wasn't a quitter. He'd concoct a way. But fast. Because they'd have to get hitched tomorrow morning. First, he'd get Miss Rose alone. "I insist on hauling that tree here after church. Lives hang in the balance. Please, Miss Rose, won't you come along to show me where it is?"

Ice on the ground crackled as the men unhitched the tree she and Mr. Valmer dragged over. As long as they rode side by side, Adam tolerated carrying Mr. Valmer. Back in the barn, they groomed the horses—but Adam wouldn't allow Mr. Valmer to touch him. Eve endured his ministrations with a rather twitchy response. "I want to apologize for Ma. The way she talked at your breakfast table—"

Maggie held up a hand. "She's not herself right now. Besides, God has forgiven me for worse. How could I hold a few words against your mother?"

The way his body changed—from ready-to-snap tension to strong and able astonished Maggie. Just a few words of honest Christian charity, and the poor man looked as if she'd relieved him of a two-ton burden. "You are most kind, Miss Rose."

Thinking of all the help he'd given to her uncles and the extra time and attention he lavished on Jerlund, she responded. "I thank you for the compliment, but most of all for jumping in and being so hardworking."

Mr. Valmer cleared his throat. "That is something I wanted to discuss with you before breakfast. I don't believe our exchange has been fair."

He wanted to renegotiate? "In the spirit of being a straight dealer, I should warn you: You might wind up with a wagon wheel or an apron. Just how brave are you?"

"I have no wife to wear the apron. I would exchange it or the wheel for the berries you undoubtedly preserved."

He isn't thinking of having a wife anytime soon. Maggie didn't want to think about why that disappointed her so much. *The barter. I need to stick to business.*

"My uncle had no business repairing roofs. You've been a hardworking man, putting your hand and back to the heaviest chores. As a result, I gained peace of mind that's worth every last teakettle in

Russia. Just as I pitched in with your kin, you pitched in and helped mine. I reckoned we'd already decided to call it an even swap. But I insist on sending you away with a crate of food."

"That's not enough."

Since he didn't consider it fair, he ought to counteroffer. Only he stood there, staring at her. He'd done much harder physical labor in horrible weather. She'd been up several times a night with a grumpy, sick woman. But men loved sweets, so he undoubtedly wanted more jam. It was no hardship. "We'll make it two crates, and I'll be sure you have plenty of corn and peaches."

He shook his head, and his brow furrowed.

"What is it you want, then?"

His gaze swept over her. A slow, handsome smile kicked up one side of his lips. "You . . ."

Six

"You . . . you have a sled!" He pointed to the sled hanging in the shadows behind her. "I have never ridden one. For the trade to be fair, I will have one crate of food and you will teach me to ride the sled."

"The sled!" Turning to look at it, Maggie let out a shaky laugh. "This kind of snow is such a rarity, I forgot it existed. Mama, Daddy, and I would all ride it together."

Mr. Valmer lowered the sled. "Now it will hold us as you teach me."

Being that close to this huge man? Barely brushing by him in the house set her into a tizzy. Each time he sat beside her at the table, she couldn't believe the difference between his Viking physique and the age-tempered, smaller stature of the holler's men. *The glory of young men is in their strength: and the beauty of old men is the grey head.*" Proverbs 20:29 expressed the feeling perfectly. Until she sat alongside Mr. Valmer, Maggie hadn't known the sheer sense of physical shelter and protection a young man exuded. Would she feel that way toward any other man?

No. No, it was definitely him. The notion of sitting with him on that sled? She shook her head.

"Come," he rumbled, the word half temptation, half order.

"No." Dusting the sled with a burlap sack, she avoided looking at him. With every second the sled shrank more. "I'm sure you have the necessary coordination to sled by yourself."

"You would rob a man the joy of your laughter when he first learned to play thus?"

If she hadn't been flustered earlier, his attentive gaze set her to stuttering. "I-I-I'll watch."

"But if you aren't with me, how will you teach me? Dragging the tree, you used tricks with the horses. Sledding must have tricks, too. I'd rather learn from example than exasperation." He tugged the burlap from her and tossed it over a stall gate. "So are we agreed? Riding together is reasonable."

I agreed to nothing of the kind. How is a woman supposed to deal with such an imposing man? Mee-Maw Jehosheba's sage words flashed through her mind and straight out of her mouth. "Whenever a man calls a situation 'reasonable,' any sane woman ought to run screaming into the dark."

Merriment sparkled in his blue, blue eyes. "You would not want me to call you unreasonable. That was clever, but 'A witty saying proves nothing.' "

"Voltaire." Maggie blinked at him. He'd quoted Voltaire. Daddy would be so pleased. *But Daddy wouldn't get asked to share a sled with Mr. Valmer.* "Mee-Maw Jehosheba's wisdom is what I cited.

Mee-Maw Jehosheba lived to be ninety-one, and I'd take her advice over Voltaire's."

Mr. Valmer pretended to look serious, but the corners of his eyes wrinkled. "I can't say if she was wiser. Her advice is more current . . . But just slightly."

"By a whole century." Maggie couldn't quite contain her smile. Mr. Valmer's humor was disarming. She'd almost think him wise—except for the fact that he still believed she should sled with him.

He hunkered down and tilted his head. "I don't see more than the runners—is there no way to steer?"

"Daddy said leaning together was more fun, and if it didn't work, falling and laughing was part of sledding. According to him, it was cheating to use a fancy sled. It robbed us of the thrill when we made a perfect run."

Mr. Valmer nodded thoughtfully. "Your father sounds like a wise man."

"He was. Mama and I adored him." *Would you become the kind of husband that Daddy was to Mama?* She closed her eyes against such useless thinking. "Shall I take you to the incline I first learned on?"

Rising, he looked down at her. Stared at her, actually. *His lips are right at the level of my forehead. What would it be like if he brushed them across . . .* Heat filled her face.

"Your blush gives you away. Likely, it is no more than a bump in the road. Take me to the last place you went sledding."

"I wouldn't want you to hurt yourself." *Please don't ask what I do want.*

Adjusting the collar of her coat, he said, "I won't get hurt; I have seen pictures. The person in front is smaller. Thus will you teach me."

How could such a simple gesture feel so intimate? Warm, callused hands brushed against her neck as Mr. Valmer pulled up the collar and straightened it. "I won't let you chill." He rumbled the words in a soft, deep voice that made her want to sit on the sled with him. Right now.

"We'll need rope."

"I'll keep hold of you."

That's exactly what I'm afraid of. "It's easier to hang a rope down the hill. After the ride, you tie the sled to it, use the rope so you don't slip on the ice when you climb back up, and then draw up the sled."

"Brilliant! Let us go."

Winsome memories threaded through her mind as they made their way to the top of a sloping road. Mr. Valmer positioned the sled perpendicular to the drop and held her hand as she sat down. Immediately memories dimmed and doubts abounded. Days ago, bracing her hand as they looked at cameos, he'd made her tingle. When he climbed onto the sled, it felt as if a gentle bear enveloped her. His arms wrapped snugly and his entire bulk overshadowed her. Maggie couldn't decide whether to hop up and run or to lean back into his engulfing warmth.

What have I gotten myself into? He made it sound so simple!

"See what being reasonable gets you?" Delight resonated in his voice. "Before we go, show me how much to lean to steer this."

Move? Surrounded by him? Heaving with all her might, she almost tipped them over. Todd's firmly planted feet prevented disaster.

"Whoa!" He straightened the sled. Leaning close, his breaths washing over her cheek, he chided, "You thought my strength would work against you. Never. Now we will work together, ja? To have fun?"

"Agreed," she rasped. Just then the cold, crisp air carried the sound of a fiddle.

He plunked one leg up onto the sled. "Now, so, with my other leg, if I push backward . . . and I use the opposite arm thus, we face downhill." Several folks had their own special little twist on how to get going on a sled, but Mr. Valmer's technique would leave every last one of them gaping. "So what song is—"

Gravity and the slick ice took over—but his right foot still wasn't up. "Whoa! Ho! Ho! Ho! Ho!" His boisterous laughter echoed around them. Trying to get his right foot up, he swung too hard and made the whole sled veer. Maggie accommodated for it, making them zigzag. She leaned forward to grab the hem of his pants, and he leaned forward, too, practically mashing her. "Ho! Ho!" he belted out, sending her into breathless laughter. Mr. Valmer kept hold and straightened them up together, but he pulled too far.

Maggie let out a shriek as he tumbled off the back of the sled . . . and took her along. They logrolled in the shallow snow and ice, none of it providing decent padding. When the dizzying rotation stopped, Maggie realized Mr. Valmer hadn't let go of her. Somewhere in the tumult, he'd gotten her turned around and curled one arm around her waist, the other about her shoulders to cup her head against his chest. His protective-instinct reflexes shielded her as they kept skidding, and he'd made sure he was downhill so he took the brunt of the impact.

Ice tinkled and rained down from the barren shrub branches. Maggie lay there for a moment, cold and stunned. She could hear his heart thundering—or was it hers? "Mr. Valmer? Are you hurt?"

"Nein. How are you?" Concern etched his features and roughened his voice as he stroked her cheek with his gloved hand.

She pulled away from his gentle touch. Tiny shards of ice continued to shower around them. She cocked a brow. "See what being reasonable got me?" *Cuddled up with a warm, caring man. I should have followed my instincts and run.* Pressing her hands on his chest, she pushed away and huffed. " 'Rose That the Wind Blew Down.' "

"It was not the wind. It was my doing. I—"

"The jig the fiddler played. It's called 'Rose That the Wind Blew Down.' My uncles delight in teasing me and are likely fighting about which tune to use. I don't mind it, but when we get home, I'll make a big to-do." While speaking, Maggie fought to get her skirts all back down and in order.

Thankfully, Mr. Valmer turned his head to the side to allow her privacy. Even so, the rustle of cotton and the heavier flop of flannel petticoats would let him know just what a sight she'd become.

"Music is particularly important to mountain people. Someone from the Arkansas 3rd fiddled a square dance as they marched into battle at Antietam. The Flinn twins declare it kept them alive because they were so proud, they had to go shake that man's hand." Skirts in order, she let out a sound of relief. "There."

"You aren't hurt?" She assured him with a shake of her head, and a blinding smile lit his face. "So will you sled again with me?"

I wanted to escape this, but now I wouldn't trade it for the world. "I'm too selfish to let you have all the fun."

The next run showed very little improvement, but Maggie didn't care. Neither did Mr. Valmer. He kept hold of her hand afterward. "So what was that song?"

" 'Maggie Lauder.' "

His lips twitched. "Louder?"

"Goodness, no. As much as you've set me to laughing, no one would urge more noise from me. *Lauder* is an old Irish word for strong."

"They've used your given name and your family name. Is there a song for your middle name?"

"I don't believe so. 'Maggie's Apron' gets played when the men are hungry and want me in the kitchen!"

Sweeping his arm about her waist, Mr. Valmer assisted her uphill. "Let's hurry and have several more rides before we hear that one." His arm about her felt warm. Strong.

Looking down at her, he gruffly ordered, "Your arm—twine it about my middle. Given the icy ground we climb, it is rea—prudent." When she complied, he gave her a tiny squeeze of approval.

Prudent and practical never felt like this.

"Third time's the charm." His lips barely grazed her temple, and Todd set them in motion before he caved in to the temptation to kiss her. *A perfect run. This third run will be perfect, and then I will propose.*

Wind blew past them as they gained speed. His eyes burned and cheeks stung from the cold, but holding Miss Rose—that warmed him clear down to his toes. Detecting the slightest lean on her part, he'd tilt his shoulders, then immediately straighten out when she did. When the sled finally scraped along the ice at the bottom of the hill, he let out a long, satisfied sigh. "Ahh. To do it right brings great satisfaction!" He stripped off his gloves, rose, and helped her to her feet.

She grabbed his arm. "Let's go for another run!"

Before he'd lose the opportunity, Todd went down on one knee. "Miss Rose, I'd gladly go on another run. But first, you have the ability to make this the proudest day of my life. Will you marry me?"

Eyes and mouth wide open, she stared at him.

"I owe you complete honesty, Miss Rose. My farm in Texas is only two years old, and so much work remains to be done. But the land is rich. I've prayed long and hard for a wife, so though I readily confess I need someone to care for my mother, it is not only because of her that I now propose."

"I . . . see." The words came out faintly. A somber expression replaced her usual free-and-breezy smile. Fiddled music swept over them on the chilly wind. " 'Magpie's Nest,' " she identified.

She's stalling. With her hand held firmly in his, she couldn't run away.

"Paw-Paw's favorite." Love saturated her voice. Sudden panic transformed her features. "I can't leave my family! No!"

Staying awake most of the night, he'd anticipated Miss Rose's objections and developed several points to convince her. "Leaving your uncles will cause homesickness. But the love between you will not end just because you leave. Letters and visits will keep ties strong."

"That's not enough. My love for them runs too deep. I can't—"

"You can't believe your uncles want you to sacrifice having a husband and sweet little babies to love. You are the last generation from Carver's Holler. Passing on your people's tales and lore is the ultimate way of showing your respect. You'll tell your father's stories. Uncle Bo will visit and teach our sons to whittle. Our children will learn the songs from today."

Tears filled her eyes. "You barely know me. I know even less about you."

"In the early morning hours and late at night, I've seen your constancy and kindness. The men speak to me of your virtues and talents."

She cleared her throat. "They're biased."

"The truth stands, nonetheless. You work hard. And with a willing heart. It makes for a happy home. You respect your elders. Finer food I've never eaten. Most important: you hold your faith most dear."

"So I'd be an acceptable helpmeet."

"Far beyond acceptable! My future sons and daughters could have no better mother." There. They'd agreed, and he'd paid her the ultimate compliment. Todd rose and sought a kiss.

Reclaiming her hand, Miss Rose compressed her lips. Clearly she didn't agree. Hugging herself, she whispered, "Have you prayed about this?"

"For years. And also specifically about us since I met you. To marry is the right thing."

Her lashes dropped, hiding her expressive eyes from him. "How can it be right? It'll start with a lie if you vow to love me."

"Oh, Miss Margaret." He dared to use her given name as he slid his hands across her shoulders, turned them to cup her neck, and used his thumbs to lift her face to his. "There are many things to say here. Some very frank. You must excuse me, for there is no other way to speak."

Chewing on her lower lip, she thought about it, then nodded.

"There are different kinds of love. Between us, there is already Christian love. Since that is understood, I will talk about romantic love. You are most fair—so beautiful to look upon. Happiness glows on you, and your hair is a crown of glory I would relish taking down at night." He indulged in lifting his right hand a little higher and finally discovering the softness of her hair. Up this close, faint freckles showed beneath the scarlet of her cheeks. He'd love to brush them with his fingers, then his lips. . . . He cleared his throat. "Physically, I am drawn to you—but to call such attraction love is to . . ." *Lord, please give me the right words.* "To say such stirrings are love is like us calling one apple an apple pie. It cannot be a pie until many other important elements are included."

Blushing from his earthy honesty, she dipped her head. "What other elements?"

Todd cupped her cheek and tilted her face back to his. "Faith. It is vital. Hard work. Nothing worthwhile comes easy. Honesty and forgiveness—they are the soil of trust and cleansing rain. If you think on it, those things are what it takes for love to blossom in a sound marriage—for God to be the head, for the husband and wife to work hard and honor one another, and for them to appreciate the special gift of unity marriage brings. From all this, love and a family grow. On these things do you agree with me?"

"They seem . . ."

Don't say reasonable. It would be the same as saying no.

"Sensible."

"What is not sensible is that I want to kiss you silly. So now I ask you two questions. Miss Rose, will you marry me tomorrow, and—"

"Tomorrow!"

"My farm—I must get back to it." Todd didn't pause to take a breath. "Will you marry me tomorrow and permit me the joy of a first kiss now?"

"Now?" Tension sang through her, but Miss Rose didn't blurt out a refusal.

"Come here." Drawing her into a loose embrace, he sighed. She failed to hug back, turned her face to the side, and rapid breaths warned a firm denial was still a heartbeat away. "Shhh. Quiet your heart. Under normal circumstances, such questions deserve consideration."

"Then why ask me for an answer now?" A plaintive quality ached in her voice.

Resting his cheek against her soft, fragrant hair, he murmured, "In this situation, there is no luxury of time. I'm not proud to push so fast. Neither am I ashamed."

"You ought to be," she muttered. "You didn't take my no for an answer and are debating like a Yankee senator."

At least she'd gone from tears to being disgruntled. He could handle anything but tears . . . or a refusal. "On my tenth birthday, my father directed me to pray for the woman who was to become my wife. Each day for a whole decade I've lifted that girl in prayer." Gently tipping her chin so their faces were inches apart, he said, "You are the one. Of this I am sure."

She pulled away. "Anyone could claim that. A woman would be a fool to act on a man's say-so."

"You have time today to think and pray. Deep in your heart and soul, you will see God's will."

"What I need," she sighed, "is a burning bush like God provided for Moses."

"Moses hesitated at first. Still he set out on the journey."

She arched a brow. "He was concerned because he couldn't speak well. I, on the other hand, more than make up for that lack."

"Then you can come with great confidence." Todd stepped to the side and kept his arm about her waist. "You promised me another ride. I'm claiming it." Of all songs, the fiddler started to play "Johnny Todd." Todd sang along,

> "If you'll wed with me tomorrow
> I will kind and constant be.
> I will buy you sheets and blankets
> I'll buy you a wedding ring.
> You shall have a silver cradle
> For to rock the baby in."

Pushing free, she went whiter than the snow. "Mr. Valmer, Uncle Bo takes notions at times. If he's put you up to this, you didn't have to go through with it. For true, you didn't. I've a happy life here. Their bothersome nagging to make a strange mountain girl your wife is scarcely reason to ask."

"You have it wrong." Pulling her into the lee of his body, he stared into her wide eyes. "This is all my idea."

Mr. Valmer's proposal set off a cavalcade of emotions. He wanted her? It wasn't at Uncle Bo's urging? For true? They'd scarcely met, yet she felt . . . tingly. Confused. Undeniably impressed by his strong presence and protective ways. His thoughtfulness. And, she admitted, his deep voice and warm looks disturbed her in a thrilling way. Yet fear gripped Maggie. How could she ever leave Uncle Bo? And Carver's Holler? Jerlund and Paw-Paw? Her uncles?

She shouldn't pass more time with Mr. Valmer, allow him so close if she wasn't seriously considering his suit. Before, it was innocent fun—now it wasn't. But Maggie had promised another sled run. She endured the tumult of emotions long enough to sled twice more, then claimed she needed to go see to lunch.

Ever since proposing, he'd called her Miss Margaret. No one ever called her that—unless they paired it with Titania, and then she knew she was in trouble. Hearing the sound of her full name on this handsome buck's lips confused her even more. Formal, yet oddly personal. She still addressed him as Mr. Valmer, though. If Uncle Bo heard him address her informally, he was liable to plunk himself square in the middle of everything.

When they returned home, Uncle Bo was waiting to meet them about twenty yards from the barn. "Margaret Titania, I need to have a word with you." Slowly, she nodded. They needed to talk. Alone. Uncle Bo looked at her with an intensity he reserved for the few times she'd gotten herself into a sore and sorry mess. She shivered, but not from the cold. A chill swept through her soul, warning her of the utter desolation she'd feel if she left Uncle Bo.

"I will put the sled away." Mr. Valmer strode off.

Her uncle took her hands in his. "Margaret Titania, I've important things to say."

"So do I. Uncle Bo, I love you. You've been with me—"

"For a long spell. Todd Valmer's a good man. Could you come to respect him?"

The question caught her off guard. "I already do. Look what he's done for his mama and how he's helped out everyone I love."

"I'm wanting to see you settled with a godly man, one who'll fill your heart with love and house with laughter. If it means I travel a ways to dandle your children on my knee, so be it."

Most of what he said was a repeat of his marry-you-off speech. But the part about him having to travel was new. It never occurred to Maggie that she'd leave the holler, but Uncle Bo suspected it. How could she do without his wisdom and insight?

A bittersweet smile lifted the corners of his mouth. "Growin' you up as I have, I can read your heart like your daddy could read a book. Don't let your worries for me and the others hold you back. Elding's got women coming in who can cluck and fuss over us."

"That's not the same."

"Aye, but to everything there is a season. Glowing inside you is a spark I recognize well. Your mama and aunt both wore the same radiance, and it gained more luster every year. Love's budding in your heart, and happily-ever-after dreams are beckoning you."

She couldn't deny her feelings. Were they that strong, though? Love? Could her heart have turned to a man she barely knew?

"I'm shovin' you outta the nest, Magpie. Even if it means that man don't ask until he puts his foot on the train, you fly away with him."

Rattled by his order, she gulped. "He asked."

A rusty chortle bubbled out of Uncle Bo. "The boy didn't let grass grow 'neath his boots."

"You suspected?"

Her uncle nigh unto bust his buttons. "More than that. He asked for your hand last night."

"And you didn't warn me?"

"Stop fighting the inevitable and take care of essentials—like your legacy."

Maggie folded her arms across her chest. Mr. Valmer didn't even know about that. Goodness only knew he'd tossed every other skill and tradition into his argument. But her legacy was rooted in the holler. "My legacy dictates I stay. A duty to the generations before me rests on my shoulders. I owe them—"

"A daughter to whom you pass the legacy. All the history and generations gone by are for naught if you die without passing those roses on. They crossed the ocean and took root in this holler six generations back." Uncle Bo wagged a finger at her. "With the weather gone so cold, the bushes are dormant. Couldn't be a better time to take 'em to a new home. By the time you get settled in and have a plot ready, they'll be eager to grow and bloom."

"Uncle Bo . . ."

"Maggie-mine, you're a woman full grown. Stop clinging to your past and open your heart."

⌒⬥⌒

Leaning against a barren tree, Miss Rose stared toward the house. Todd made no attempt to muffle his steps. Edgy as she was, he owed her fair warning that she wasn't alone anymore. "Tell me you see a burning bush and have made up your mind."

She turned to glower at him. "Uncle Bo made up *his* mind.

For me. I haven't decided anything, but he's in there, packing my things!"

"Your uncle is a ball of fire." Todd waited a heartbeat while she nodded. His lips twitched. "God used a pillar of fire to direct Moses and the Hebrews. When the time came, they left quickly. Look where it got them."

She turned away, buried her face in her hands, and her shoulders shuddered.

He moaned. "Miss Margaret, there is no call to weep." He moved so his chest grazed her back and wrapped his arms around her. She couldn't muffle the sound any longer.

Turning, she looked up into his eyes. Choked laughter shook her voice. "Have you forgotten all the wars the Hebrews fought throughout the exodus?"

Relieved she wasn't crying, he gave her waist a tiny squeeze. "No doubt we will disagree on occasion, but the only weapon would be the sword of truth."

"Next you're going to tell me the pillar of fire will bake that silly apple pie of love and the sword will cut it."

"Nein. I misspoke. I will have to get a sword—to fight off men when they discover how well you cook." He softened his voice. "But the apple pie—that will be something only you and I share. Come, Miss Margaret. Be my bride."

She studied him. Indecision played across her features. At long last she set her jaw and lifted it, and his heart missed a few beats. "I'm a magpie through and through. *If* I agreed, would you allow me my treasures and legacy?"

Six silly boxes and one more thing mattered that much to her? Undoubtedly she'd fill a crate with her clothing and a few more with kitchen necessities and bedding. All brides brought such essentials to their marriage. She'd expect that, and they needed those things. Ten.

Maybe twelve crates, considering her magpie-like nature. "Absolutely. I wouldn't mind at all."

Yet she scrutinized his face. He hoped and prayed she'd see what she sought in his steady gaze. A slow exhalation shivered out of her. Hesitantly Miss Rose extended her hand, as if to shake on a business deal. "Then I'll marry you."

"Come here, my little magpie!" He brushed aside her hand, swept her up, and spun around. She let out a shriek of laughter and insisted on being put down. He leaned close and rubbed noses with her. "Margaret?"

"What?"

"Waiting to kiss you was worth it." His head dipped.

"Was?!" She jerked away. "Oh no. You promised me all day today. You got my decision about marriage, but you asked about the kiss separately. You won't have my kiss until tomorrow."

He groaned. Loudly.

It wasn't until almost the end of lunch that she spoke to him again. "Mr. Valmer?"

"Hmmm?" A spoonful of jam hovered an inch from his lips. He felt guilty as a hound with a maw of feathers—about the jelly, not about coaxing her to wed him.

"I'd like to make a proposal." She rushed on, "If, perchance, you went home and your mother stayed here awhile, then you and I could wed comfortably."

Ma shouted, "Absolutely not!"

Seven

"Absolutely not!" Mrs. Crewel repeated. "I'll not stay here one minute longer than necessary. Furthermore, girl, you have no couth or manners. A lady waits for the gentleman to propose. She doesn't pounce upon him and decide they'll wed."

While Maggie gaped at her, Uncle Bo started chortling.

"Todd, you must get us away from here at once. They're—"

"Going to be family by this time tomorrow, Ma." He reached across the table and took hold of Maggie's hand. "My Margaret didn't propose marriage; she proposed delaying it. I won't stand for such a notion."

My Margaret. Why did every thought in her mind flutter straight out her ears once he took her hand and spoke in that deep, sure voice? She'd assumed Uncle Bo's hopeful thinking made him see a glimmer of love in her eyes . . . but dear mercy! He was right. She could sit and listen to Todd Valmer forever. Look at him, too. But that was attraction, not love.

Mrs. Crewel wailed, "Nein! You are not marrying a backwoods hillbilly. We will get a nurse to take care of me."

"Hold your horses." Uncle Bo's knuckles rapped the table.

But Todd cut in. "I've longed and prayed for a wife, and well you know it, Ma. A man can't build a defense against what he yearns for. Sure, I need help with you, but had I met Miss Margaret under other circumstances, I still would have pursued her. A finer bride I'll never find."

Very well, this was more than attraction. Her heart was involved . . . and it did a little jig. Then she looked at his mother and every bit of warmth melted in the ice of her glare.

Todd squeezed Maggie's hand to gain her attention. "This surprised Ma—that's all."

"Appalled is more accurate," Mrs. Crewel snapped. "Before you proposed, you should have spoken to me. I would have talked sense into you."

"I chose my bride with prayer and care. I'd not be swayed." Todd gave his ma a stern look.

The other men mumbled under their breaths or stayed silent. Paw-Paw rose. "Mrs. Crewel, I'm leastways old as your parents, probably older. So I'm gonna stand on my age and speak a truth that you'd best hear. My Maggie's cosseted me aplenty through my infirmities, and I've done my best to show my thanks. Knowing how much care she'll lavish on you, what with you lying about needin' her help and you not lifting a finger about the farm—" He shook his grizzled head. "A kind heart ain't gonna cost you nothing. Best you sow love instead of strife." He sat down amidst hearty "Amens."

"Mrs. Crewel is fatigued. Let's help her retire." Maggie turned loose of Todd's hand and rose.

Todd lifted his mother into bed. "Once you're finished, come out to the parlor. We'll start off right by having devotions together."

"That would be nice."

He wrapped his arm about Maggie, pulling her close to his side. "Ma, I don't ever again want to hear you speak to or about my bride the way you just did."

Mrs. Crewel's lips quivered. "I-I'm sorry. I w-was s-s-surprised, is all. Margaret, stay with me now. You and Todd can start having devotions tomorrow."

Several niggling doubts beset Maggie. But Paw-Paw's words of wisdom never failed to open eyes, and the Holy Spirit would convict Mrs. Crewel if she kept on this mean path. The calm support in Todd's eyes reassured her. "That's a right nice offer, ma'am, but I was taught to start on the path I intend to follow. My man wants us to have holy time, and I agreed. Harkening to my Master and my man—that's what's right. When you wake up, we'll talk about the wedding. Mayhap you can think on a hymn for the ceremony."

"Very good! Margaret, each day I read a chapter of Proverbs. Surely our marriage is ordained by the Lord, because today is the thirty-first: the qualities of a godly wife. I'll get my Bible and meet you in the parlor." Todd left the room.

Immediately his mother's expression changed. She didn't say anything; she didn't have to. Clearly, she believed the marriage would be anything but good.

⌖

"Ain't you the purdiest sight?" Uncle Bo's breath caught. "Proud I am to have you on my arm."

"Thank you, Uncle Bo." Maggie turned to the mirror. She'd not slept much last night. Had she known Uncle Bo was ironing the wedding gown she'd taken in trade years ago, she wouldn't have slept a wink. Funny little crinkles puckered a few spots on the skirt, but all the love Uncle Bo showed more than made up for it. God be praised, the fragile-as-a-fairy's-wing bobbin lace sleeves and bodice escaped her uncle's ministrations. The swath of the Rose clan tartan Daddy draped over Mama's shoulder when they were wed now graced Maggie's.

"Your aunt talked with you about the special union betwixt a husband and wife. Don't go blushing on me. Inside marriage, those feelings are pure. God wouldn't order us to be fruitful and multiply if He didn't intend us to share that intimacy. It fosters a special closeness." Uncle Bo gave her a crushing hug and added, "You'll see 'tisn't a duty, but a joy."

He'd ordered her not to be embarrassed, and then he said that? As soon as he turned loose, Maggie reached for Mama's veil. Even ten times thicker, it wouldn't hide her virulent blush. She took a few deep breaths. Todd had waited until today for a kiss. Perhaps he'd grant her time before they'd become . . . close. Comforted by that thought, she pinned the veil in place with her most cherished possession: the small oval hatpin of a girl sitting beneath a tree. With painstaking skill, Daddy had depicted the very tree she often read beneath. On the day he died, he'd given it to her, kissing it and sticking it through her old straw hat as though it were a fancy silk bonnet. Mama's veil and Daddy's kiss on her hatpin—they were with her on her wedding day.

"You're giving me away, but I'll always be yours."

Uncle Bo's eyes glistened. "I wouldn't give you away if I wasn't sure of the man. More, though, I wouldn't let you go if you didn't love him. You do, don't you?"

"Yes." The admission suddenly steadied her shaking hands and voice.

Uncle Bo walked her out, and Jerlund jumped in front of Todd. "Maggie, I'm th' bes' man!"

Todd stepped to the side. Maggie said to both of them, "You make me proud."

Jerlund whispered loudly, "Todd Valmer don' got no plaid."

The enormity of that comment shot through her. Showing her honor and support in the Scots-Irish way, all of her uncles wore their plaids; her husband had no tartan, no clan, no inkling of all the traditions and lore steeped into her bones. By marrying this man, she'd step into a completely different way of life. But he'd told her their children would hear her stories, learn to carve, and learn her music.

"Constant and True"—Uncle Bo spoke her father's clan motto— " 'tis the stock you come from. This man will be both constant and true."

"Maggie, you gotta plaid on th' chair. If you don' want Todd Valmer stuck in pants, he could wear it."

She looked into Todd's steady gaze. "I'll take him just the way he is."

Uncle Bo escorted her to the parson he'd sent for, and everyone formed a horseshoe about them. Maggie said her vows, looking at Todd's chin. She pledged her love honestly, but if he saw the tenderness she already felt for him in her eyes, it would make her too vulnerable.

When they knelt for Holy Communion, his knee landed on the edge of her gown, and as they rose, he stepped on her dress. His mother laughed outright, and he didn't seem in the least bit embarrassed or apologetic. Maggie noticed an odd little trail of grain across the floor, a small pile where he'd stood, then some on her dress. He glanced down as she twitched her gown to dislodge the grain, and a smile creased his face. So he was being a bit mischievous?

Joyous events like weddings seemed like a perfect time for a little lightheartedness. He'd best know he'd gotten himself a lively woman who'd get in the last word. She knew exactly what she was going to do, too. . . .

"I now pronounce you man and wife. What God hath joined together, let no man put asunder. Todd, you may greet your bride."

Todd curled his hands around her waist, lifted her a little, and dipped his head. Before his lips met hers, he murmured, "Salt and grain for the pie." She let out a nervous giggle. This was the first kiss of her life, and they had an audience. At the touch of his lips, her laughter died out. . . .

Once the kiss was over, his hands squeezed tighter still. "Now you are mine!"

"Are you so sure of that?"

His eyes widened. "You're standing on my toes?!"

Witnessing her son marry so far beneath himself tore at Helga. It was her fault; he needed help and she'd let him down. Now she was a burden—just as she had been with Arletta. Only instead of sending her away, he'd bent over backward and married this no-account hillbilly to be her nurse and his housekeeper. Magpie said it all—both her endless chatter and vast collection of junk.

She'd failed in her first duty as a bride to carry salt and bread in a small purse to represent plenty. Todd made sure to have grain in his pocket to represent wealth and good fortune. If her failure stemmed from ignorance, that proved what an unsuitable wife she'd be. But Magpie knew the custom of stepping on the groom's toes. Todd knelt on her hem and stepped on it for good measure to symbolize how he'd keep her in control; but her action countered that with the traditional sign a defiant bride used to declare her husband wouldn't keep her in line!

Now that strong-willed girl plucked ugly dresses from a crate, measured them, and chose three. Until Helga could lace up her corset extra snug so she'd fit in her own gowns, she'd be stuck wearing frumpy hand-me-downs like a charity case. "Put in the mauve and take out that blue stripe. It looks like cheap mattress ticking."

"Actually, it's green, and specks of color are threaded betwixt them. The skirt's generous, whereas the mauve is—"

"So I'm fat." Arletta told her so dozens of times.

"I'd say you're sturdy-built and a fine testament to the quality of your mama's cooking. She taught you her recipes and you stayed true to them. A woman who honors her family's traditions and lore—that's a lady to be admired, not belittled."

Helga blinked in surprise. "Todd's father . . . he thought so, too."

A soft smile lit the girl's face. "My own mama and aunt were bountiful and just as beautiful on the outside as they were on the inside. Had I not given away their gowns, I'd be buttoning them on you. My heart's full up of memories spent at the stove and in the rose garden with Mama and Aunt Maude. Someday, God willing, you and I'll be teaching a passel of our own daughters and granddaughters."

Her words warmed Helga—until she mentioned the next generation. A cold shiver went up her spine. Goodness only knew what odd things Maggie would pass down to her children. *Before she has daughters that age, I'll rub off her rough edges and polish her up.*

Magpie was nice; Helga wouldn't mind having her for a neighbor. The problem was, she wasn't anywhere near Todd's match. They were as unequally yoked as a purebred quarter horse and a flea-bitten puppy. But it was too late to say so. During the ride to the train depot, she fought the urge to weep.

Livestock, coal, and shipping cars formed a long line on the tracks. Two men yammered on about the railroad strike and how lucky Todd was that passenger cars were attached at all. The only lucky thing was, they were getting out of this benighted place.

Maggie came over with tears on her cheeks after kissing her uncle, and Jerlund burst into sobs. Using her good hand, Helga tugged on Jerlund's arm. "Paw-Paw needs you to keep him company and take care of him. Todd needs Maggie to keep him company, and I need her to take care of me. Give me a kiss, and we'll send you your very own letter in the mail."

Convinced he wouldn't get a letter if they didn't leave, Jerlund cooperated.

Maggie whispered, "Thanks, Ma."

The wheelchair wouldn't fit through the train's narrow door, so Todd carried her aboard to discover only the least-desirable seats remained: those in the very front of the car, where the metal curvature blocked the view; and those in the very back, where the car had a necessary.

"Let me flip the seat. I did it for my family." A stranger fiddled with something, and soon the seat tipped backward to face the one directly behind it.

"Isn't that a cozy arrangement? Thank you for your help," Magpie chattered. "You're so kind."

Worry speared through Helga as Todd lowered her onto the wooden bench. *I cannot sit up alone—I'll fall to the side.* But Todd understood; he'd sit next to her. Immediately she started slumping sideways.

"I need rope to tie Ma in," Todd said in a low tone.

Horror shot through her. Her own son would bind her up like a common criminal and make her a spectacle?

Someone boomed, "Easiest fix is to hook the nice old lady to the seat with suspenders. I just got new ones, so you can have the old. They're in my carpetbag."

"Thank you, but we already have a better solution." Magpie whispered, "Don't fret. I know just what to do!" She hurried to the door and sent someone running. "Jethro's gone to fetch you his favorite chair. For him to let you take it away is a mark of his honor and respect."

A favorite chair. Helga hoped it had a well-cushioned seat. The train's wooden benches ceased to be tolerable after a few hours. A nice tall back would help support her head. Maybe Jethro's chair had arms, too. "The train's going to depart," Helga worried.

"In a few minutes." Someone shouted her name, so Magpie went back to the door.

Helga breathed a sigh of relief. "Lift me up, Son. I want to be in my chair. Anything's better than this miserable bench." As he did, she scrunched her eyes to shut out the pitying looks people gave her.

Thumping and rustling sounded. "I've padded the sides with a quilt. Settle Ma in."

Helga letting out a long *aaaahhhh* of bliss. Cocooned in softness, she eased into unbelievable comfort. That little gal did know what she was talking about this time. Helga owed Magpie her thanks. "Child . . ." She opened her eyes as she began but halted as every scrap of benevolence evaporated. "You put me in a whiskey barrel!"

"It hasn't held a drop of white lightnin' in ages. Jethro took away nigh unto half the staves and glued a seat inside to fashion himself a gambling chair. The staves here on either side . . . ? He hinged them. We can open them in daytime, and at night, shut, they'll hold a pillow close."

A gambling chair made from a whiskey barrel. What has the world come to? "I will not sit in this. It held whiskey." Then Helga Valmer Crewel spoke words she had never considered uttering: "I'll wear the men's suspenders."

"No need now. This'll work far better, and your comfort matters."

"Margaret," Todd took her arm and seated her. "The train is departing."

He'll teach his bride proper behavior. A dirt-poor farmer already had far too much to do without shouldering the burden of a bad bride. More than anything, Helga wanted better for her children. She'd married Mr. Crewel because he'd agreed to provide a good education for both of them. Arletta went away and soared. Indeed, she'd done so spectacularly, she'd caught the attention of a very eligible bachelor and married into a family of class and distinction.

The minute Helga moved in with her daughter, however, she realized she didn't belong. A self-sufficient farmwife with a German accent and homemade clothing stuck out like wooden bucket amidst hand-painted china teapots. Two years of Arletta's suggestions, complaints, hints, and lessons certainly changed her into a woman with a modicum of polish. No matter how hard she tried, though, Helga still said or did something wrong. After nearly every outing, Arletta highlighted her mistakes so she wouldn't repeat them.

If Arletta saw me now! The things she would say!

Two years passed, but no grandbaby; then Arletta and her husband planned a trip overseas, and Helga jumped at the chance to live with Todd. And though a lady was not to travel alone, Arletta didn't instruct any of the staff to accompany her to Texas. Instead, Todd came—at great sacrifice both financially and for the state of his farm. And know-it-all Arletta set off on her voyage without leaving so much as a cent for this grueling trip halfway across the continent. Helga slumped slightly, and the side of the barrel kept her from tipping. Bitterness filled her.

Land rich and money poor, Todd clearly had money concerns. Helga winced along with him as he stuck his hand in his pocket. Suddenly a puzzled expression chased across his features. Turning to Maggie, he slowly said her name. "There is something in my pocket."

"For as long as it lasts, that's where it belongs. Yoked together, we are. Aye, and all that's mine is yours."

The porter came by. "Accompanying a patient, Miss Rose?"

"She's Mrs. Valmer now." Todd acted proud as a stallion with a whole bevy of mares.

Magpie plunged into a conversation that sounded like a tightly wound music box. She introduced the porter to them, told him she'd be living on a farm in Texas, and discussed a rash the man had. A rash! Maggie produced a small jar of unguent from a nearby bag. "Just you take this, then."

"Thankee, Miss Ro—um, Valmer?"

"That'd be Mrs. Valmer," Todd said, reaching into his pocket. "As there wasn't a ticket office in Carver's Holler, I need to—"

Waving his hand dismissively, the young man scoffed. "The horses and such are all reckoned for, and I'll use the money I'd have paid for the medicine for the lady's ticket."

"That's not necessary—"

"It's so nice of you to give us that as a wedding gift," Maggie interrupted. "It's like you're sending me straight to my husband's arms, but we want to pay for one more seat."

Why did she have to point out this horrid barrel takes up two seats?

Chuckling, the porter shook his head. "Every last man in four counties is going to hail me as a hero for getting rid of Jethro Bugbee's good-luck gambling chair."

"Their wives will thank you more." Maggie flashed him a grin.

Wearing a dubious look, Todd shook hands with the porter and sat down. He shot Maggie a sizzling glare. "Valmers do not accept charity."

"Neither do folks in these parts. Our tickets, transporting my treasures and your Belgians—it pert near evens the books on a right hefty debt. Rest easy, Husband. You don't owe anyone a cent or a favor."

A few hours later, the porter approached again. "Mr. Valmer, your wife's good at calming and healing folks. We sure do need her—"

Hopping up before Todd heard the full request, Maggie ordered, "Show me the way."

"Do you need me?" Todd asked without first considering how that would leave Helga alone.

Maggie grazed his sleeve. "Thankee for the offer. Should I need help, I'll send for you."

When at last she returned, Todd voiced everyone's curiosity. "What happened?"

"Nothing much, really." Magpie shrugged. "When I treat someone, I won't be speaking with you about it."

Helga's mouth hung wide open. "A wife keeps nothing from her husband!"

"Ma'am, you would as lief leash a bird or try to teach a pig to sing as to get me to betray a patient's confidence."

Todd leaned forward and murmured, "The day you took ill, she showed you this respect and dignity. It is wrong to deny someone privacy."

Helga stared at Maggie. "Things should still be done quietly and discretion—"

"Exactly!" Todd's wife cut in. "Discretion. I knew you'd understand."

Crooking her good brow, Helga gave Magpie her most chilling look. "It's impolite to interrupt someone. Impulsive actions and blunt words can be a woman's downfall. You must curb your impetuous nature." There. She'd said it just as tastefully as Arletta would.

"Ma'am, I'm not one to dither. Sitting on my hands when something needs doing goes against my grain, and I'm up-front with others, just as I appreciate their candor. My nature is set. It isn't going to change. Uncle Bo's a wise man, and he said, 'Love means we gotta see each other through God's eyes, not with a mind of molding them to our own wants.' I reckon Uncle Bo wouldn't have put my hand in Todd's if he weren't dead-level certain Todd would strive to see me as I am instead of with a goal of transforming me into something I'm not."

"Spirit is important in a woman." Todd and she exchanged besotted glances.

In disgust, Helga gave up. She slumped into the whiskey barrel chair with the absolute knowledge that even if she'd guzzled every last drop it once held, it wouldn't begin to numb the pain of dealing with Todd's wayward bride.

༺❀༻

Todd woke to the scent of roses. Maggie snuggled against his side, and he squeezed her shoulder. Caressing the darling wisps of hair that curled at her nape, he couldn't decide whether he was the luckiest man alive to be married to her, or the most wretched for having spent their wedding trip sitting on a hard bench, in a drafty train, with his mother sitting across from them. Lifting her head from his chest, Maggie gave him a sleepy, puzzled look. Cheeks sleep-flushed and lips slightly puckered, she tempted him to abandon propriety and kiss her. *Okay, so I'm blessed and wretched all at the same time.*

Suddenly, her eyes grew huge. Snapping into perfect posture, she tried to scoot away. "You . . . I . . . umm. G'morning. Did you sleep at all? What time is it, anyway?"

She didn't get far. His hand kept hold of her shoulder, anchoring her to his side. "I slept some, and waking up to you made this a very good morning." Tearing his gaze from her lips, he cast a quick glance to the side and spied Ma's valise. "At the first stop after breakfast, I will send a telegram ahead. Between your crates and Ma, we need help to get home tonight."

Whispering softly, they got to know one another a little better and let Ma sleep . . . until Maggie let out a little squeal. "For true? I'll finally have women for neighbors?"

He'd taken her away from all she knew and loved—but this was something she wanted and he could provide. Todd smiled. "You will have lots of woman friends."

In her excitement she'd awakened Ma. Ma groused about being awakened, so Maggie quickly began unloading a basket she had stowed beneath the seat. "I packed us a picnic breakfast: hard-boiled eggs and prune bread."

Prune bread. He hated prune bread.

Ma snickered. "I'm sure Todd will be certain to do it justice. Won't you, Son?"

He plastered on a smile and choked down a piece.

"Since you like my prune bread so much, eat my slice whilst I peel Ma's egg."

"I could not."

"Sure you can," Ma and Maggie said in unison.

Just then two porters carrying linen-covered trays entered the car and stopped by them. "Mrs. Valmer, Mrs. Ludquist sends her

114

respects and asks if you might consider sending her a bottle of your fine lotion."

Margaret pulled out a bottle of lotion and added a cake of soap. "Please thank her for us."

The porters whipped the linen off the trays. While Todd moaned in pleasure, laughter tinkled out of Maggie. "Dear Gussy, what a fancy spread!"

After setting the tray in front of Maggie, the porter accepted the soap and lotion. He managed to look blasé as he said, "I was directed to tell you the meal is compliments of Ludquist, Littlefield, and Mouse."

Instantly, Todd understood. Someone needed calming yesterday. A rich woman named Mrs. Ludquist got spooked by a little field mouse. And Maggie, who talked a blue streak and loved to tell stories, stayed entirely silent about it. Truly, he'd married a woman of discretion and compassion.

Except for the gleam in her eyes, she schooled all emotion from her expression and concentrated on the tray. "Ma, holler out what appeals to you."

Ma gritted, "You've created *a scene,* and everyone is watching. I won't be a part of it."

"Since you won't accept anything from the trays, eat this." Todd pushed the unwanted slice of thick, sticky prune bread into Ma's hand. It wouldn't be right to thank the Lord that he didn't have to choke down prune bread. But Ma needed to eat something, and she'd turned down Maggie's previous offers. Todd turned his focus on his bride. "I have crops in the field, God in my heart, and you in my arms. Already I awoke feeling blessed . . . and now we have this fine meal, too. Why don't you pray this time?"

Later, when Maggie slipped off to personally thank Mrs.

Ludquist, Todd boasted, "I got quite a bride. My Margaret has a kind heart and willing hands."

Impossibly weary, Ma sighed. "So do many maids and servants. Still, it does not mean they are suited to marrying the man of the house."

Todd snorted. "You sound like Old Frau Schwartz. 'No girl is good enough for my son.' Those old men back in Arkansas are saying I am not good enough for Margaret."

"But I . . . I am right. In the days ahead, you'll come to see she doesn't know how to be the wife you need. She lived with carvers, not farmers."

"My Margaret gardened, put up food, and cooked for a dozen men. She is more than capable. If there are small details she misses, you'll be there to instruct her."

Margaret returned with a wide smile. "I just swapped cookie recipes. Would you care to know what kind?"

"What kind?"

"Prune?" Ma guessed in a glum tone.

Eyes sparkling, Maggie lilted, "Wishes Come True. I'm going to make Wishes Come True."

Todd couldn't take his eyes off of his beautiful bride. "Yes, you will."

⟊

Gas lamps glowed a late-night welcome to Gooding. Ma let out a moan as Todd carried her off the train.

Dropping their satchels on a bench, Maggie cooed, "We made it, Ma. We're here." Concern puckered her brow as she tucked quilts around Ma. "We've got to get her home and to bed."

Todd grunted agreement.

Maggie pulled her shawl close against the midnight chill. "I'll ask the porter to bring the wheelchair straight away, and I'll fetch the horses."

Sure enough, Ma's chair arrived. Getting her comfortable was impossible; Maggie always did that. Truth be told, he didn't think there was anything his wife couldn't do.

I have everything I could ever wish for. Todd watched Maggie step down onto the ramp with huge, shaggy Belgians following her like obedient pups. He'd gotten himself quite a bride, all right. The sight pleased him immensely—until Eve moved forward and he spotted the hames about her neck. For a breath, he wanted to give his bride credit for dressing the beasts with the heavy pieces so they'd be ready to hitch to a wagon, but Margaret halted the horses a step before they'd be on the ground and scampered back up into the car between them. That could mean only one thing: His bride sneaked some kind of conveyance along!

The gas lamps illuminated the magnitude of her deception. A whole wagon. She'd brought a whole blessed wagon full of more of her clutter! He bet an unreeled fishing line couldn't be shoved between the stuff Margaret crammed in. Not Margaret. Not Maggie. Magpie—the hoarder of junk. Todd's throat ached with the restraint it took to keep from bellowing her name.

"Good evening, Mr. Valmer." Linette Richardson stepped closer. "Daddy's fixing to back our buckboard up here for you to use. Why don't I stay with this lady until someone comes for her?"

His telegram had said Ma was ill. As usual, Linette had her heart in the right place and ruined it by putting her foot in her mouth. "This is my mother, Mrs. Crewel. Ma, this is Miss Linette Richardson. Thanks for staying with Ma." A curt nod, and he strode away toward his wife. Relief flooded him. As a married man, he wouldn't have to suffer through Linette's husband-hunting schemes anymore.

Linette's father let out a low, appreciative whistle. "Look at those, will you? Belgians!"

"You're an old married man, Richardson." Toomel chuckled. "The real beauty holds the reins!" The neighbor who'd been minding his land slapped Todd on the back. "I'll see you later. I'll be grabbing the chance to meet—"

"My bride."

"Your bride!" John Toomel roared.

Half running from the other direction, Piet Van der Vort stopped in his tracks. Though he owned the livery and appreciated fine horses, the Belgians weren't what grabbed his attention. Jealousy colored his booming voice. "Valmer, you'd better not be talking about that pretty young gal who just drove—"

"I am." Vexed as he was with Magpie, Todd admitted she'd made quite an entrance. He lifted her down, kept her clamped to his side, and made some brief introductions.

Piet scuffed the ground with his boot. "You fooled us. We never expected you were bringing home a bride. The telegram said your mother needed a wagon."

" 'Mother ill. Need wagons tonight,' " Magpie recited softly. When it came to telegrams, shorter was cheaper. She might chatter a lot, but she'd been economical when helping him compose the message.

"Huh? That's not what we got." Toomel pulled a crumpled sheet of paper from his pocket and smoothed it out as best he could. " 'Mother'll need wagons tonight.' We reckoned she was shipping a bunch more stuff. Big Tim hauled everything that came a week ago out to your place."

Chuckling, Piet slapped him on the back. "The mistake on the telegram is understandable."

Maggie inched away from Todd and stepped toward Adam. The

stallion had started acting up, and Todd reached out to yank her back. To his alarm, she skirted out of his reach.

"Thou flea-bitten hunk of wayward will, be still." She served a solid smack to the stallion's shoulder, and he whipped his head to her.

Every man there dove to spare her the horse's tantrum.

Adam nuzzled the side of her face, and she petted his forelock. "We're in Texas now. You're to show these men how well-behaved you are. No more fretting. You'll get Eve all worked up." Adam nuzzled her again, and she giggled.

One arm banding her waist, Todd pushed the enormous horse's head away. "Woman—"

"Please don't be upset with your new horses. Given time, they'll adjust. Adam didn't mean to offend you with his little show."

"Show?" Piet wiped the sweat pouring from his brow. "Ma'am, that stallion could trample you in a couple of seconds."

"A heartbeat," Todd corrected in a raw tone.

"Adam's harmless as a speckled pup to me." She smiled. "I'll grant you, he could pose danger to others, but he trusts me. The trust was hard-won, and true love casts out fear." The crazy woman nodded as if the Bible verse applied to this situation. "I'll lead them over to the side whilst you unload things." She pursed her lips, made a kissing sound, and the pair of behemoths trundled after her.

"Todd, you can have her. She'd have me gray and babbling by the end of a day." Piet shook his head. "Never saw a stallion put up with that, but one of these days . . ."

Shoving his hands in his pockets, John mercifully changed the topic. "There's more to unload? The woman and the horses are already a staggering booty."

Groaning, Todd got into the boxcar. John stood below and let out a low whistle. "What a cache!"

"Don't be so sure." Passing things down a line and into the buck-boards, Todd grated, "Some of this will be useful, but my bride is sentimental. I promised she could bring her treasures—but I thought she meant a dozen crates."

John belted out a laugh. "Women confuse the daylights out of me. Let me know when you figure out how to understand what she means when she says something."

"Only men in the Bible lived that long."

⁓⁂⁓

Betwixt the stingy sliver of a moon and the heavy clouds, Maggie couldn't see much of their farm. Mr. Richardson and John Toomel veered left and continued on toward the barn. Pulling the buck-board to a halt alongside the one the liveryman drove, Maggie barely glanced at the house.

Todd sat beside her, holding Ma across his lap. Poor Ma sagged against him, too exhausted to open her eyes as she whimpered, "Did that man at the station say my bed's waiting?"

Maggie set the brake and dropped the reins. Fussing with Ma's blanket, she confirmed, "Aye. Before anything else at all, I'll tuck you in."

The liveryman reached up to take Ma.

Todd handed her to him, hopped down, and immediately took her back. He strode off toward the cabin, leaving Maggie standing on the edge of the buckboard, waiting for him to help her down.

The liveryman gawked at her, shook his head, and stepped up. "Ma'am."

A good wife covered for her husband's missteps—even when they trampled her feelings. "Thank you. My man's sore worried o'er his ma." Embarrassed, Maggie kept talking as she grabbed the valise and satchel they'd need for the night. "You're most kind to help us, sir, and I'm chagrinned I don't recall your name."

"Piet Van der Vort. Go. After you see to the old woman, you can decide what you need for tonight."

She rushed toward the house and called over her shoulder, "Don't move that buckboard. Adam won't approve."

A hint of light sneaking around the door led her to her new home. *I ought to take comfort in how Todd left the door ajar to let the light guide me here.* She pushed it farther open with the satchel. Still, she couldn't help herself. Eyes focused downward, Maggie stepped over the threshold. *Suppose it doesn't make a whit's difference if a groom carries his bride o'er the threshold the second time instead of the first.*

A soft circle of light from a lamp on a pretty bureau drew her attention to a matching bedstead. Maggie kicked the door shut and hastened over to Ma's side. "Here we are now—home at last."

"It's f-f-freezing in h-h-here." Ma's teeth chattered.

"I am starting a fire." Todd's confident words, alone, warmed Maggie. There was something fundamentally reassuring about how he immediately saw to their basic comforts.

Removing Ma's shoes, Maggie soothed, "I'll pile on plenty o' cozy quilts. Come morning, when we've plenty of warm water, I'll wash the aches out of you."

Ma groaned as Maggie eased the covers from beneath her. "Poor Ma, miserable after sitting all that time." Tugging the quilts back up, Maggie promised, "My willow and menthol salve will heat up those joints and ease some of the hurt. I'll go fetch it."

As she straightened up, she noticed with pleasure how well the cabin wall had been chinked. After seeing this lovely corner prepared for Todd's mother, Maggie could scarcely wait to see the rest of her new home.

"Come show me what else you need brought in."

Maggie turned toward Todd's voice and halted about halfway. Between the lamp on the bureau and the lantern he now held, she got her wish. Her heart leapt from her chest, rolled across the uneven dirt floor . . . and Todd stepped directly on it as he opened the door.

Eight

⚜

A starter place. He'd told her it was small. When Maggie had asked what furniture he'd like to take, he'd been quick to suggest they take her nice bed. But with him going on so about the barn with all the stalls and his beloved horses, the land, and the God-fearing neighbors, Maggie hadn't pressed for details about the house. Now that lack hit her square on and left her breathless.

Fitting in essentials would be quite a trick. Three shelves hung on the wall over by the toy-sized potbellied stove. Nails served as hooks beneath them for a skillet, a battered pot, an enormous coffeepot, and a washtub. On the other side of the room stood a drop-leaf table, a washstand that matched Ma's dresser and bed, and a cot with a couple of crates beneath it. If someone sneezed, the soundly built place probably would have lifted and dropped back onto the foundation logs.

She'd initially thought the cabin extended back a ways more—that he'd set up a place for his mama near the stove so as to keep her extra warm whilst he took the back room. Only there was no back room.

This was it.

"Magpie." Other than when she accepted his proposal, he'd never used her nickname. Then it had been endearing. Now he might as well have called her Margaret Titania.

"Just taking a moment to prioritize what we need." She scurried past him into the night, her mind cartwheeling like a kite in a sudden windstorm. He'd brought her home to be his bride, and many a woman lived in a single-room cabin. But how could she ever become his wife with her mother-in-law's bed right beside them?!

Aye, and Maggie's bed was the very first thing Todd and Mr. Van der Vort toted in. While they did, she grabbed her medical box and set it on the buckboard seat. Pillows, quilts, and clothes—those all had to go inside at once. Without inspecting the shadowy shapes on the shelf, she didn't know what grocery supplies her husband had on hand.

The men came back out, and she smacked a bag of rice. "Bare essentials here. Bedding, clothing, and viands."

Todd helped her down. She filled her arms with bedding. He and Piet each laid a large sack of flour or rice across a crate and carried the load to the cabin. Second time across the threshold—but Todd was busy. So was she. And their arms were just as heavily laden on the third trip. By then, it took something akin to a folk dance to get about the crowded cabin.

"Rub that medicine into Ma. I'll move the buckboard."

Maggie paused and took a deep breath. "Uncle Bo didn't jest when he said they'll obey only me. Adam's skittish, but for good cause. I bartered him and Eve away from a wicked-mean man who ruled them through fear and pain. Quick you were, to remind me a beast of his size is dangerous."

"I do not want you handling him anymore."

"Soon as it's safe, I'll pass his handling to you. Uncle Bo told me you saddled and sat upon Adam. He neither bucked nor brushed you off. That's far more than any man in the holler ever managed."

"So you seated me on a horse knowing full well he'd carry me nowhere."

A guilty smile twisted her mouth. "It's called horse sense for a reason. Neither of the other horses would have gone, either." Maggie started for the wagon, and Todd matched her stride. "Seeing you with Adam proved what a talented horseman you are. There's nary a doubt in my mind that you'll soon be driving those Belgians."

"But not tonight. I'm displeased, Wife."

She reached Eve and gave her a loving pat. "Are you looking two gift horses in the mouth because you'll have to win their loyalty?"

"I am glad to assume responsibility for them." His eyes bored into her. "But I hold *you* responsible for withholding a truth. This was the same as telling a falsehood. That causes my displeasure."

Maggie couldn't exactly argue. He was right. At least they didn't have an audience for this squabble since Todd's friends were dropping off things in the barn.

It took little time to unload everything. As everyone rode off, Maggie took a final look around. Foods and household goods sat in one stall; tools, furniture, and miscellaneous things filled another. Before she'd reached the barn, the men had already unloaded everything that went toward her precious legacy. Roses, vegetable garden, household, food, tools and trade goods . . . With this being a very lean starter farm, everything she brought was needed. Surely realizing that their place was on a better footing had soothed Todd's irritation with her. He'd accepted the tools with alacrity.

Walking side by side, they passed the other stalls. Maggie sensed he wanted to thank her but couldn't find the words. He waited to one side to shut the barn door and let out a low growl. "You brought too much."

"You don't need to thank me, Husband. Everything I have belongs to you."

"And you brought it all. This is not good, not right."

"Nonsense. You're tired. After a delicious breakfast, you'll see how perfect things will be with me by your side." Recalling his admonishment about withholding truth, she added, "Besides, this isn't everything. I only brought the essentials. If we need anything more, I'll have Uncle Bo send it."

Obviously overcome with gratitude, Todd didn't speak another word but shut the barn door. Maggie stepped close and placed her hand on his forearm. He bent his arm and escorted her home. When her groom paused at the threshold, Maggie's pulse started to race.

He set down the lantern and opened the door. Any second now, he'd sweep her off her feet, kiss her, and carry her over that threshold. She prepared her mind to take in each word and gesture so some day when he was grumpy, she could recall them and still feel cherished.

"Sleep on my cot tonight. I'll sleep in the barn."

⌒☙⌒

Predawn's stillness woke him. Todd rolled over and shoved off the quilt. Stupid thing kept him awake most of the night. Made of several shades of green, it would appeal to any farmer—or so he told himself as he kicked it to the foot of the pile of hay he'd used for an erstwhile mattress. But the cotton pattern deceived him, because the other side turned out to be a deep, soft velvet. And it smelled of roses. He couldn't blame Magpie for torturing him. He'd grabbed the quilt for himself.

But she'd made it. And certainly, she'd slept under it.

Oh, to have had her beneath it with him! They were husband and wife, so the desire was not wrong—but Ma couldn't be left alone, and the cot barely supported him. He and his bride couldn't share it. No matter what, he'd get their bed put together today.

He grabbed a pair of buckets and hiked to the windmill. It wasn't until he stepped out of the barn and onto dew-covered ground that Todd remembered his boots. He stalked back to the barn. That woman had his mind so turned around, he should be ashamed of his lack of self-control.

Slamming his right foot into a well-worn boot, he snorted. "Who am I kidding? I left her alone last night. That's either self-control or stupidity."

Carrying a full bucket of water, he eased into the house. Rickety creaking drew his attention toward the cot. The leaves of the table were propped up, and stacks of garments formed tidy piles. Just beyond that, slender arms extended heavenward in a long stretch. "Mornin', Savior. 'Twas a rough night, so I'm asking you to help me keep a sweet spirit today."

The cot's creaking must have covered the door's sound. Eavesdropping on her prayer wasn't right. Intriguing, to be sure, but he couldn't spy on his wife. Todd mule-kicked the door, and it sounded as if it slammed shut.

"Oh! I . . . um . . . could you please give me a few moments?"

Her hesitation could only mean one thing. He grimaced. "I don't have a chamber pot."

"We do now, but I was so tired last night, I forgot to bring it over for Ma. That'll be at the top of my list. Well, almost at the top. I need to get dressed, Mr. Valmer." She clutched his old wool blanket to her fortified flannel nightgown.

"Ja, you do." He folded his arms across his chest and grinned. In a few lighthearted moments on the train, she'd called him Todd. Shyness now sent her careening back to formality—at the most informal time they'd ever shared. Amused, Todd stood and unabashedly stared at her. His bride was cute, all morning-mussed and embarrassed.

"You're being a rascal, aren't you?" Swiping a stack from the table, she still refused to turn and meet his gaze. His Magpie tried to act unaffected, but the way her hands shook as she tried to hide her petticoats from him before sneaking them beneath the quilt gave away her frazzled state of mind.

He raised both brows.

"Yes, you. Don't you dare have the nerve to feign innocence." She muttered, "Clearly, I'm not going to get an honest answer here. A rascal wouldn't admit to it."

Wiggles, squirms, and a few undulations that left his hands itching to yank off the blanket ensued. *I ought to be catching up on chores.* Yet he didn't so much as shift in place. Chores would always be there nagging at him, but he promised Bo Carver he'd court Maggie. Right now that vow and the one to make this girl his wife both provided ample cause to stay put. All promises should be such fun to keep!

"If your mama was awake, she'd be scandalized by your horrid manners." Maggie snatched another stack of garments.

"We're . . . a . . . well-matched pair. You . . . I don't think . . ." He shook himself. He could scarcely talk while watching absolutely nothing. His maddening, modest bride drew the blanket entirely over her head. Something started to slip out off the cot, and she barely caught it in time, muttering unintelligible things.

He opened his mouth and couldn't recall what he'd just said.

How had she done this to him? Stuck a mud-brown wool blanket over her head and set him to blithering.

"Well matched," she huffed, head exiting the blanket. "If we were well matched, you'd notice I'm a lady and you'd be gentleman enough to give me some privacy."

Ah, yes. That's what he'd said. The spark in her eyes drew him, and he decided to egg her on. "But you say I'm a rascal. This means you are—"

"Severely inconvenienced at the moment." Making an exasperated sound, she lay back and then clamped the blanket between her teeth. By raising her chin and tenting up her knees, she kept the cover away from herself so he could scarcely detect the slightest wave of activity as she put on all of those frothy things.

He sucked in a deep breath. "I'm not the only one with a wayward streak. You put her in a whiskey barrel for the trip home. To Ma, that will always be the worst of all possible transgressions."

Rustling of cloth sounded, punctuated only by Ma's occasional light snore.

"Oh!"

"Is something wrong? Need some help?"

"I can . . . get . . . it. . . . There!" Giving him a frown, she made a show of chomping into the blanket to hold it away from herself again as her other hand snuck out to swipe her blouse. While she went through more gyrations on the cot to fasten something more, Todd studied the clothing on the table. Everything on there was far too big for his bride—everything except for the brown-and-rust checked skirt. Casually sliding it over his arm, he smiled at her.

She gaped, and the blanket fell out of her mouth, revealing a misbuttoned blouse. "So help me, Todd Valmer!" Keeping hold of the blanket, she swung her legs over the side of the cot, used the cover as a skirt of sorts, and rose. Or tried to. A second effort didn't work, either. Lying back down and covering up, she let out a jaw-cracking yawn. "Travel exhausted me more than I realized. Mayhap a tad more sleep will strengthen me."

Tapping the gate leg back into its storage position beneath the center of the table, Todd lowered a leaf. A simple half-arc drag moved the now smaller table out of his way. One large step forward, and he reached his sweet bride's side, where he hunkered down and fingered her nighttime plait. Every husband ought to be a rascal—to let his woman know he found her desirable. Or so he'd imagined. But he'd miscalculated.

Skittish. That was the problem. His bride needed to get used to him. Cupping the back of her head in his hand, he smoothed the wisps of hair at her nape.

She froze.

He cleared his throat. "Breakfast—"

"Will be ready in about two hours. When I can break free from this sudden affliction—" she yawned once again—"then I'll cook. I'll fix you a sound meal."

"Best I not kiss you, if you're feeling sickly." He rose, dropped her skirt on the table, and walked out the door. *Was it my imagination, or did she look relieved when I said I'd not kiss her?*

The dirt beneath his boots made a gritty sound as he strode away. If Maggie truly was sick, he'd fetch the doctor; but if she was misleading him as he believed, she deserved to be caught. He gave it a few moments before borrowing Adam's trick of circling back unexpectedly.

He couldn't believe his eyes.

Nine

ᘛ❦ᘚ

Maggie wheeled halfway about and almost killed herself. While tying her corset, she'd gotten the laces wrapped around a side slat of the cot. Now she stood looking like a human letter *T.* And Todd had come back to witness it. "Don't come— Ouch!" She softened her voice to an imperative whisper. "In here." *How am I going to hide this?*

"Woman . . ." Todd's lips twitched, but he kept from laughing. "What have you done?"

Resting her elbows on the side of the cot and clamping her hands near each end of the frame, Maggie held it at waist-level behind her. She couldn't hide it, so how should she explain it? If he had even a wee drop of mercy, he'd saunter off.

He didn't move an inch. He didn't even blink.

"What have I done?" She let out a small laugh. "Other than

getting dressed and putting on my boots, I've done nothing much yet."

"Wife." He took a step closer, stalking across the tiny cabin like an Arabian tiger. "What are you doing with the cot?"

"As I arose, I felt a sudden urge to rearrange the furniture."

His voice dropped to a dangerous purr. "Is that all?"

She inched backward. "I ran into a little trouble but know how to work it out. I'm almost done!"

"Tight as that cot's pulling your laces, you're almost dead."

A minute later, he'd freed her from the cot and retied her stays. Burrowed against his chest, she didn't want to part from him. Maggie knew for certain she couldn't look him in the eye. Probably not for a week or two.

"You are still breathless."

She stopped his fingers from loosening her ties. "Embarrassed," she corrected. "If you ease those any more, it'll fall off and I'll perish of mortification."

He kept his arms about her and squeezed. "You are my wife." The pronouncement sounded as if it carried an entire list of reasons to counteract her emotions. Todd didn't give a single one. Instead, he nuzzled her hair. "Rearranging the furniture is a priority, and we will do so later today. To have our bed."

Our bed. That was supposed to calm her? Maggie pushed away. "We have other things to accomplish. Important things. I told you, once I broke free from my affliction I'd make you breakfast."

With an audacious wink, he corrected, "You didn't break free from your affliction. I rescued you."

"So does that mean you'll cook breakfast?"

"Not even the doctor could rescue us from such a result." His eyes twinkled. "Hmm. Breakfast before all else. I am happy with you just as you are, but do you not want your skirt?"

Heat filled her face. "You bawdy rascal!" She grabbed the garment and got mad at herself for having looked him in the eye after she'd just promised herself not to for at least a week. Sparkling blue those eyes were, and crinkled at the corners. If that didn't prove how right she was about him being a rascal, the unrepentant grin he continued to wear testified how he'd proudly misbehave just to keep her off balance.

Why, oh why couldn't this cabin at least have a screen for her to hide behind? Her hands shook as she donned her skirt and apron. There. Now she could face the day.

"I'll show you the windmill and where the outhouse is."

"Thank you." No indoor pump? She didn't bring an extra pump, but wondered if someone in the area had one she could trade for.

"The buckets you brought—they will be useful."

She nodded. Out they went, each carrying buckets. It would be days before she'd get this place whipped into shape. For now, though, Maggie determined to start in with a good attitude. If she strained to be extra observant, she'd pay her husband five compliments by the day's end. She hurried to keep up with his long stride. "That's a clever setup you have with the water trough fed from that pipe so the beasts don't get close to the household supply."

Nodding, he started filling a bucket.

"You're a tall man. I'll need a crate to stand on to reach the diversion."

"As soon as I have an empty one. Lumber is very expensive here. I use the wood from crates."

It took mere moments to fill all four buckets. "Water looks nice and clear." Regardless of the cold, Maggie cupped her hand, dipped it in, and took a sip from her palm. "Mmm. Just a tad sweet, too."

While she dried her hand on the hem of her apron, she turned and felt her jaw drop. "What is that hairy wall?"

Todd laughed. "It is grass, not hair. When I broke ground, I constructed the sod wall. It gave shade and acted like a windbreak until I could build the barn."

He lifted all four buckets and jutted his chin off to the side. "Outhouse is behind the house, near the cottonwood."

The closer she drew, the more grateful she felt. Her husband had overlapped crate slats to construct a clapboard-styled outhouse! Here was one thing on the place she didn't need to fix up. Except . . . It couldn't be. She reached out, testing with her fingers so the vile vision would dissipate, but it didn't. In the space where a door should have been, a frayed and tattered section of wool blanket hung limply from the top beam.

After slipping behind that dusty blanket, Maggie mentally reviewed what she'd packed. Everything from andirons to window sashes, but not a single door. Not even a piece of wood that would serve as one. An empty nail hung on the wall. No. Surely there had to be an old catalog or magazine or something! He'd stranded her in a doorless necessary without the necessities! *Oh my word! He mentioned the cottonwood. He actually expected me to use those leathery, toothed leaves to* . . . Paper in her apron rustled. She slid her hand in and pulled out the recipe she'd gotten on the train. Her sigh ruffled the blanket-door. Todd had no one to blame but himself that he wouldn't have his Wishes Come True.

Not wanting to awaken her mother-in-law if she still slept, Maggie peeked in the curtainless window. One look at the cabin set her mind awhirl with plans, but those plans came to a screeching halt the second she spied the stove. With room for only one pot at a time, cooking would be an either/or proposition: either she served hot food and cold coffee or cold food and hot coffee. No two ways around it: she needed to set a cook fire outside, too.

Since Ma still slept, Maggie dashed to the barn. Eggs, ham, and biscuits with a steaming cup of coffee—that ought to be a grand start for her man's first day home. A search turned up only two measly eggs. Neither was any too fresh.

The trip didn't take any time at all. But when Maggie opened the cabin door, Ma shrieked, "You left me! How could you be so cruel?"

While Maggie changed Ma's linen, Ma kept a steady stream of rebukes, complaints, and criticisms flowing. No amount of soothing calmed her. Knowing embarrassment fueled the attack, Maggie forgave her but quickly escaped to start a fire outside.

With coffee perking over one side of the washpot and water heating on the other, she went back inside to make the biscuits. Cooking for three felt odd. Stingy, even. A glance at the tiny stove made her wince. *My heart ought to overflow with gratitude that I'm only cooking for a few,* she reminded herself. The folding metal box which was to be set atop the stove to turn it into an oven couldn't be found. Making do, she flipped a kettle upside down over the biscuits.

Nudging the table flush against the wall, she gained a little breathing room. "With one leaf up, Todd has his rightful place at the head of the table and we'll sit side by side." She patted Ma's hand as she squeezed past her wheelchair. "Using a spoon or fork is the next step. Practicing when it's just the two of us here will make it easy."

"Easy? Nothing about this is easy." Tears filled Ma's eyes.

Though tempted to dab away the tears, Maggie tucked a handkerchief into Ma's right hand. "Aye, that's true. Learning new ways is hard work, and you're a private sort of lady. My intent was to say we're kin, so your heart can be at ease as you improve because it's just me."

While Ma gathered her poise, Maggie almost lost hers. Todd's hideous dishes ruined her appetite. Gold rimmed the plates' edges and ringed them again where the center began to slope upward. That inner ring measured at least half an inch—probably an attempt to corral all the fruit in the middle. Between the edge and inner gold ring, pansies fought marigolds for dominance. A gorgeous set of her great-grandma's china—appropriately bearing graceful swags of roses—rested in a barrel out in the barn. Assured she'd only eat off these monstrosities for a single meal took the sting out of looking at the eye-crossing trio of place settings.

The door barely opened, and Ma said, "Breakfast isn't ready yet."

"Oh." Todd sounded befuddled as well as disappointed.

Accustomed to hungry, impatient men, Maggie patted his arm. "If you'd be so kind as to fetch the coffee brewing outside, I'll have your ham all fried up and ready." Relocating the biscuit pan with the overturned kettle to the table, she freed up the stove. *Thank you, Jesus, for ham. It fries up so fast.* Laughter bubbled out of her.

Thump. A solid knock sounded as warning, and the door opened. Todd entered, sniffed, and grinned. "What makes you laugh?"

"I thanked Jesus for ham. Ham! Jesus is Jewish. Jews don't eat pork. It never occurred to me how I've ardently asked Him to bless food He wouldn't touch."

"You have nothing better to think about?" Ma groused.

Todd sat down. "In the New Testament, some believers ate of the meat offered to idols. Others did not. Paul exhorted us to act according to our hearts but not to make a brother stumble. I gladly eat ham. God looks upon the heart and knows I am thankful."

Maggie served her husband first—two thick slabs of ham and the pair of pitifully small eggs. While the ham for her and Ma sizzled, Maggie quickly poured coffee into all three cups. Why hadn't Todd seen to that task? Uncle Bo always did when her hands were full. Just those fleeting memories brought pangs of homesickness. *Naturally I'll miss my uncles, but I have to work on pleasing the man who matters most to me now.*

"Push me to the table, Son." Maggie served up the food for Ma and herself.

Todd drew back Maggie's chair, and she stepped in front of it only to miss the nudge of the seat against her legs as he scooted it back in. Baffled, she turned around. Her chair was gone! Todd had moved it sideways, to the spot farther from him.

"Breakfast is getting cold." Ma wore her cat-that-ate-a-spider smirk.

Patting the other spot, Maggie forced a smile. "This place has the most room for your wheelchair. You'll catch some nice heat from the stove here, too."

"I'll get as much heat at *my* place."

Her place? A wife belonged at her husband's side! Ma knew it, but she was trying to usurp her place as mistress of the home. Ready to confront the situation, Maggie's chin went up—and then she saw the look in Todd's eyes. She didn't know him well enough to read the emotions there. Pain? Regret? Anger? A wife owed it to her husband to try to keep harmony in the home just as much as manage it. Did it matter if this is how things worked out right now? They could be different at dinner. Giving a little shrug, Maggie slipped to the side.

Todd asked a blessing, then ate with lightning speed. Ma complained that the biscuits were too dry on the bottom but dunking them in the coffee made them passable. Maggie chopped the ham into tiny bits for her.

"You made it into a baby's food."

"No, if it was for a baby, I'd put it through a grinder."

"Hmm." Todd agreed. At least Maggie assumed he'd agreed. His mouth full, he nodded once and reached for his coffee.

"Here. Have another biscuit. Oh! I forgot the jam!"

He perked up. "Yeah!"

Scooting her chair back a little, Maggie hit an obstacle. At a slight angle, Ma's wheelchair managed to block her exit. *Another reason why I should be sitting there.* A glance made it clear she couldn't wiggle her chair free, nor could she lift her skirts and step over both her chair and the smaller rear wheel jutting from the back of Ma's chair. Sinking back into her seat, Maggie started cutting her own ham. "Todd, I brought in two jars of jam—blackberry and plum. They're in the poke at the foot of Ma's bed."

"The wife serves her husband!"

While his mother gave her opinion, Todd took the few steps to get the jam and returned. He grabbed another pair of biscuits, sat down, and attacked them.

Maggie started chewing her first bite of breakfast. Did Todd agree with his mother? But he couldn't—or he'd have stayed in place. Hadn't he seen how he'd trapped her? Or was he too busy eating? *His mother as much as called me lazy. And he's allowing her to.* Confusion and pain pulled at her.

"The only good thing about this meal," Ma declared theatrically, "is that it's on my beautiful china."

Sitting through breakfast took every last shred of Helga's reserves. While in the Ozarks, she had been a guest. For her to do nothing was understandable—expected, even. On the train, no one did anything. But this morning she couldn't make excuses any longer. She was useless. The truth galled her.

From the moment moving to Texas came up, she'd looked forward to all that entailed. Instead of being a burden who needed to be shuffled around and told what to do, she'd be the lady of the house. Once again, she'd set the daily menu and make trips to the grocer, earning her own egg and butter money. Now that she knew more about fashion, she'd choose feed sacks with a more discriminating eye instead of just for what matched, so even her everyday dresses would be admired. As Arletta taught her, it wasn't sufficient for a woman to simply blend in and be part of her community. She needed to stand out and be an example. Didn't the woman of Proverbs 31 do just that? Ja, she did.

Upon awakening today, Helga had lain in bed and looked about the cabin. All of her hopes, plans, and dreams had crumbled. She wouldn't be deciding between oatmeal or biscuits and gravy for breakfast. Gone was the vision of curtains on the window, the same violet shade of pansies . . . With her tacky ways, Todd's bride would likely nail up a pair of mismatched sacks.

At least for now. But those kinds of things could be corrected. The list of lessons and admonishments she needed to give this girl grew. Magpie treated Todd like a servant instead of the man of the house! Helga knew her son couldn't possibly have fallen in love. Oh, he was nice to a fault, but deep beneath that reserve he was just like his father. When he fell in love, there'd be no mistaking the fire in his heart.

"What God hath joined together, let no man put asunder." The line flashed through her mind. Only Helga knew deep in her heart God hadn't intended this union. He paired like with like—and this was the most unlikely couple on the face of the earth. Since she couldn't jerk them apart, Helga hoped she could coach Magpie into being a good farmwife. The task was staggering. Examples often helped; she'd keep a keen eye out for neighbors to use to illustrate points.

"We must have good neighbors. They set up all my furniture so nicely. Todd's best piece was his cot, so we brought mine, you see." Affecting a half smile, Helga looked at Maggie and rubbed her right hand back and forth just below her beloved plate on the very table she'd begun housekeeping with as a bride. "This has always been my place at my table."

"I can understand why." Magpie flashed a grin. "A wife should always sit beside her husband."

Bold as brass, that girl! She won't stop at anything to get what she wants—even if it means taking away what's familiar to me when I have nothing other than my memories. It wouldn't hurt her one bit to yield to me.

"Todd and I will be putting our bed up today. As we arrange the furniture, we'll try to do something about the table."

"Yes." Todd looked about. "The Bible?"

"On Ma's pillow. She was reading earlier."

That was a lie—not Maggie's, but hers. Ever since she'd had her apoplectic fit, Helga hadn't been able to read. The letters all looked like hieroglyphics. Their shapes made no sense whatsoever. After losing her first husband, all through her second unhappy marriage and the years with Arletta, Helga had found great solace in the Scriptures. She'd read them avidly. Only she'd never been good at memorization. Now that lack haunted her. It was bad enough she couldn't walk or tend herself; she refused to let anyone discover that she'd reverted to being no better than an illiterate child. So when Maggie offered the Bible, she always accepted it. Sometimes she'd even turn the page.

Guilt prompted her to snap, "Don't tell him where the Bible is. Get it!"

"I'll be happy to fetch the Bible, Todd." Maggie simpered. "Ma's chair is at an angle, and I'm stuck here. As soon as you straighten her out—"

"Straighten me out! I am not a wayward child in need of discipline."

Todd stepped behind her but said nothing. A slightly jerky maneuver, then he pushed her back in. "So." He motioned to his wife to stay seated and got the Bible himself.

Yet another reminder that I'm in the way.

The hillbilly took hold of her hand. "Ma, I didn't mean to hurt your feelings. The chair was cockeyed is all, and my man set it to right."

My man. Not "Todd" or "your son." Like the bird she'd taken her name from, Magpie chattered on, "We'll find ways to make things work. I'm going to do every last thing I can to help you get back to where you used to be."

As shakes started to overtake her, Helga couldn't say whether it was from anger or fear. It wasn't enough that she was being pushed away from her own spot at her own table; she was being told she wasn't welcome in her son's home!

"Speaking of which, I'll be needing a nice, thick dowel, Todd. About an inch in diameter and so long." Magpie held her hands about a foot and a half apart.

His brows knit. "Wood is expensive."

"I already have rope, so that part's taken care of. I saw the nails in the barn, too. So with a dowel, I can hang a bar over the bed for Ma."

"Nein!" Helga grabbed her son's arm. "This bar she plans—it is a punishment. She left me alone this morning until I couldn't wait any longer and I—" Unable to actually say aloud what she'd done, she sobbed and shook her head. "I could not help it. That hurt my pride—but it was in private. This bar would shame me. Anyone who pays a visit will see it." Swiping madly at her tears, Helga tried in vain to stop crying. "She knows it was her fault, and she hides the truth from you—but you watch. Soon sheets will be laundered."

"The laundry is already boiling. I'd best go check on it." Magpie scooted back her chair. The door shut behind her with a scrape of the latch.

Eyes trained on the edge of his mug, her son used his thumb to move it clockwise by the handle. "Back in the Ozarks, Margaret kept this a secret even from me—that you messed the bed. On the train, my wife woke during the night and early in the morning in order to spare any embarrassment." Neither his face nor voice reflected any emotion. "I do not need a chamber pot, nor does she. But she brought one from her old home for you. This morning she went to the barn to get it."

Rising, Todd rested his hand on the Bible. "At dinner, I will read." Then he, too, departed. Having been widowed twice, Helga knew she could lean on the Lord and her children. Now she couldn't read her Bible, Arletta abandoned her, and Todd . . . He hadn't even come to her defense. He'd just soundly put her in her place by standing up for his bride.

Gott, how could you do this to me and leave me all alone?

❧

When Todd came in for dinner, Maggie purposefully sat in her rightful place at the table. Acting as if everything was right in the world, he pushed Ma to the other spot and took his own seat. For all her talk earlier, Ma now kept silent. Ignoring her snit, Maggie conversed with Todd.

"John left my gelding, Axe, here last night. All my horses are named after tools." Todd scooped in another gigantic bite. "Tomorrow I will reclaim my hogs from John. The Richardsons have the hens. Creighton kept my other horses at Never Forsaken in my absence. I told him I would fetch them this afternoon."

As dinner ended, Todd gave Maggie a solemn look. "You pray before you eat. We also pray after the meal. It is not enough to be thankful for the food. After partaking, one should dedicate the strength it gives to God's service."

The custom appealed to Maggie. "The sentiment must be pleasing to the Almighty. Do we do it after every meal, or is it just after dinner and supper since we didn't this morning?"

"You left the table." Ma scowled at her. "No one can force you to dedicate your service to the Lord, so my son didn't call you back inside."

Todd ignored his mother's comment and instead gave a short, heartfelt prayer. Once done, he stated, "The train ride exhausted Ma. I will put her to bed for a nap, and then I will do today's reading from Proverbs."

Substantial as she was, Ma wasn't easy to move around. Maggie appreciated how Todd saw to such matters. She rubbed Ma's back while he read the third chapter of Proverbs.

At the very end of the chapter a verse jumped out at Maggie. " 'Surely he scorneth the scorners: but he giveth grace unto the lowly.' " She'd seen the way her husband's mother changed. Maggie understood all too clearly: As a temporary caregiver, she'd been acceptable, but she wasn't up to snuff for wife material. Her scorn came across, but Maggie knew God was calling her to meet it with grace.

Todd went back out to work. Maggie slowly coaxed Ma's left hand open, rubbed lotion into each little nook and cranny, then grabbed a small jar and slid it into Ma's palm. "Hands ofttimes curl up tight when someone suffers apoplexy. This'll keep everything opened into a wide arc and help your fingers stay limber."

"You're doing it to make me look ridiculous." Ma pushed away the jar.

"I waited until we were alone." Maggie replaced the jar and held it in place.

Arguing wouldn't help, so Maggie set to washing the dishes. Ma kept up a commentary that was just as ugly as her plates. Nothing suited her. Maggie's dress, the way she'd left the back part of her hair down, and the song Maggie hummed all came under attack. "You're not taking my bed away and sticking me on that rickety cot."

Maggie stacked the last dried cup on the shelf. "That's a needless concern."

"You took my place at the table. You're just as likely to want my bed. Don't think I didn't see you put something in my dresser."

"I put away some of your clothes."

"Those hideous castoffs aren't mine. They're hillbilly rags."

Biting her tongue, Maggie stepped out the front door and leaned against it, only to jerk away. Sure enough, she'd gotten a splinter from the rough door. Pulling out the half-inch nuisance, she glanced back at the cabin. *"By the pricking of my thumbs, something wicked this way comes."* The line from *Macbeth* shot through her mind. *I'm not going to think like that. I'm not. I came out here to get a fresh breath of air.* In the distance, Todd rode off. *"Thy mother's name is ominous to children"* from *Richard III* resonated in her brain. She shook her head. Of all the times for lines from Shakespearean plays to echo through her memory, this had to be the worst. A smile tugged at her lips. The lines were pertinent.

Impertinent, too. Disrespectful. I'm like that proverb my husband just read—being scornful instead of lowly and humble.

"Holy Spirit, you're going to have to heap grace onto me. It befuddles me how an acid-tongued woman like her reared such a kindhearted son. My man's trying to honor his ma, and that's something to be admired. He deserves a home filled with laughter and love, not sadness or strife. He'll be out of the cabin and I'll be here with Ma all day. I knew that up front when he proposed, but his mama hadn't shown this mean side of her nature. If you'll help me turn the other cheek to her, I'd be much obliged."

Feeling she'd set her heart to rights, Maggie faced the afternoon. While Ma was awake she kept thinking up something she needed; when ready to fall asleep, any movement in the cabin bothered her. Maggie did the best she could. Straight off, she seized every old catalog and outdated almanac and took them to the outhouse, solving the lack of essentials. Cottonwood leaves would not suffice!

Good thing she'd brought rope for clothesline. A short row of nails on the eaves had been Todd's "clothesline." Because wood cost so dearly, she devised a dandy V-shaped clothesline from the cottonwood to the corner of the cabin. A breeze soon made Ma's sheets wave and whuffle dry.

It never occurred to Maggie how many of her recipes included milk, butter, or eggs. Without any of those three things, it made planning meals difficult.

Todd had said the Richardsons would soon return the chickens, but a milk cow was expensive. A goat would do just as well—and it was cheaper to feed, too. *Tonight, I'll make do. Tomorrow, though, I'm going to barter for the necessities.*

༺ঔৈ༻

Tall in the saddle, Todd led a string of fine horses home about an hour later. Maggie made sure Ma was okay, then lifted her skirts and ran to the barn. "Aren't you a sight! Riding off on a handsome gelding, I thought you a prince among men, but I was wrong. You're a king, and you came back with treasures of your own, didn't you? A whole caravan of them. Their lines are grand. Strong. Sleek legs and shiny coats. After you told me about the wolves attacking your colts, I worried about them. But they both trot true—not an off step or a wobble!"

Todd grunted as he dismounted and immediately hitched the fractious stallion to a post.

Since he had told her at dinner that he planned to keep the colts stabled, Maggie took them into the barn, and their mama trotted right behind them. Nuts and Bolts gladly accepted the oats. Wrench nosed them away and lipped some for herself.

Across the way, Todd charmed Eve with a stream of compliments. Dusting off her hands, Maggie watched Todd concentrate on the mare. "Eve likes the sound o' your tongue. Scared as she was when first I traded for her, I thought a different language might make her feel safe. She's partial to Deutsch."

"*Schon, schon.*" He reached out and rubbed Eve's neck. She leaned into the contact. Something mystical happened between a man and a horse when they decided to accept one another.

Watching Todd and her mare cross the river of trust, Maggie stayed silent until he stepped away. "Sure and for certain, Eve's taken to you. You've got a firm hand and a kind voice. Adam's preference goes contrary to your bent." At Todd's quizzical look, she explained, "His original owner cursed at him. Unless he's insulted first, Adam won't obey. If you use a fresh string of words so he's listening to a new song, he's more likely to mind." She flashed him a grin. "Seems to me, stallions get the quirks."

Todd let out a snort.

"It'll be a long while ere I trust your stallion or he trusts me."

"Stay away from the stallions. Women have no business around such dangerous beasts. I don't want you trampled."

Her husband meant Hammer, of course. She'd proven how

tame Adam was with her. "I reckon I'll fetch a few things whilst I'm out here."

Todd grunted.

Those all-purpose grunts, "So," and "Good food," were the staples of his vocabulary. The man could speak tenderly and beautifully, but he also had this annoying side that dominated his communication. How could it be, he barely spoke at all, yet his mother spoke far too much? Maggie wished she could change both, but she'd settle for the first. Short of a miracle, Maggie knew Ma wouldn't change.

It would have been an insult to inspect the horses when he collected them from Never Forsaken, but Todd needed to look them over. He unlatched the gate, and Wrench came right to him.

Humming like a berserk bee, Maggie crossed the barn. Banners of sunlight filtering in the wide-open doors glossed her black hair, and the way she walked sent his mind spinning. Wrench nudged him and nearly knocked him over. *Two legs or four, females have me off balance.*

He'd barely begun to check Wrench when Adam plowed through his stall's gate in a bid to get to her. Intent on not getting killed, Todd didn't know Maggie responded until she'd made it halfway across the barn. "Maggie! Get out of here!"

"Whooo-oo-ie! Thou bilge-bellied miscreant, hie back. Hie back!"

Adam turned to her, stomped and snorted—a sure sign they were in for a fight. Todd's blood ran cold. Focused entirely on the stallion and keeping himself between it and his wife, Todd ordered her, *"Geh zum haus."*

"I taught him *stall*, not *house*." The lunatic woman raised her voice again, "Hie back! Geh zum *stahl*! Go to your stall."

Like an eager-to-please hound, Adam looked about. He spotted the broken gate and walked across it, splitting the boards into kindling.

"Can't rightly say why, but neither horse will barge past rope nor leather barriers. If they take a mind to wander, wood won't contain them." She started to take a coil of rope off her shoulder. "I brought—"

"I ordered you to safety, Wife. In defying me, you put yourself in harm's way. This will not happen again."

"It won't." She promptly added, "Now you know you need not protect me from Adam. But rest assured I'm wary of your stallion. He's got fire in his eye."

"As do I, when I'm defied." From her quick inhalation, Todd knew he'd made his point. He took the rope and secured both Belgians. Eve put up a show to get his attention. "Settle down and settle in." He'd aimed his words at his bride every bit as much as he had to the mare. Todd held out his hand, and Eve nuzzled his palm.

"She's smitten with you. You've got the touch. To my thinking, 'tisn't just a talent, 'tis a rare gift from God. Had you not told me you're a farmer, I'd have guessed you to be a horseman."

Is this just flattery because she feels guilty? His eyes narrowed. "What makes you say that?"

"Carrying twins ofttimes taxes a mare, yet Wrench is fit and feisty. And twins are usually smaller than a single-born colt; yet Nuts and Bolts are sizable. Aye, and they had to be strong to pull through those grievous injuries—but more, they had to have been calmed and pampered."

She'd put thought behind her comments, and her opinion pleased him. Still, Todd felt compelled to set forth a bitter truth. "But Hammer is a dangerous knothead. Unpredictable. If it weren't for his history of siring prime offspring, he would be completely worthless."

"Not every horse is what Uncle Bo calls a 'good usin' ' horse."

Leaning against a post, Todd decided to confess his ambitious dream. "I have an affinity with horses. Hanging on to mine this past year—it has been expensive and difficult; but I have hopes of someday running horses on the side." He watched her carefully for her reaction.

Her posture remained relaxed. "You got enough land to do it, and the barn still has room for you to stable a few more."

"Time, water, and money—the lack of them limits me."

"Droughts end, and you've got quality starter stock. I think it's farsighted of you to plan ahead." Chewing on her lower lip, Maggie shifted her attention to her feet. "Do you want to keep the line dedicated to plow horses, or would you consider crossbreeding with the Belgians?"

She'd listened to his vision and endorsed it, knowing full well they were barely meeting their bills. Just as important, Margaret brought up a topic he needed to address but that men didn't discuss with women. Stud fees from Adam would bring in a bit of money—some he'd already figured on because those men would have bargained on Hammer servicing their mares—but Adam's fee would be higher. "Crossbreeding would give more strength to the plow horses, yet temper the size of the Belgian. Once I tame Adam, people will undoubtedly ask for him to stand stud."

Tightly clasping her hands at her waist, Maggie stared down and whispered, "You needn't wait. Put a ready mare in a paddock. I'll lead Adam in and leave."

"So."

Immediately, she turned away. "I . . . um . . . I thought to take birdseed back to spread outside the window. Coaxing beauty nearby should cheer Ma."

Todd followed her over to the stall where she knelt by a beautifully carved chest.

Pink filled Maggie's cheeks, and she still didn't meet his eyes. "Uncle Bo took care of those . . . um . . . business deals. You will, too, won't you?"

"Of course." Just days ago, he'd thought about how a farmhand's labor would make a difference—but now Maggie planned to work beside him. Her help and the small revenue he'd get from the stallions both hedged against failure. For the first time since he'd heard the price on crops had dropped, Todd felt a tiny glimmer of hope. The tension drained from his shoulders. As his hands eased downward, they hit boxes.

Todd shuffled to the side, searching for space. He loathed being closed in. For punishment, his stepfather had whipped him with the razor strop, then locked him in a crowded little shed. Being in tight spaces brought back bad memories.

"Here we are!" Oblivious to his dark thoughts, Magpie lifted the trunk's lid and took out a quilt. Reverently, she traced her fingers over the flowers and leaves. "Mama and I made this quilt together for my dowry chest. Sick she was, sore sick on the inside. But each day I'd sit right aside her and we'd stitch away on my Rose of Sharon. ' 'Tisn't right for a bride to make her bed without the newlywed quilt on it,' Mama would say. A vase full of memories comes along with each flower, and I know my mama prayed hard I'd find the happiness she did in marriage."

Todd saw the uncertainty in her eyes. Tamping down his growing apprehension, he asserted, "You will."

"Daddy and Uncle Bo made my dowry chest together, and Aunt Maude helped me fill it." Magpie reached down and caressed the plaid cloth she'd worn as a bride, then fleetingly touched the thin-as-air hair covering she'd worn, as well. "I brought Mama's veil along so someday our daughter can wear it, too."

He'd hit his limit. Standing amidst her boxes, barrels, and crates made him feel closed in. He wanted to start pitching things out of the barn or stride away. By tackling the issue now, he'd solve it. Pointedly looking about, he growled, "Far more than a veil you brought."

She shut the lid on her trunk. "Aye, and so you said last night. Betwixt then and now, I had no opportunity to rid us of anything. I'm tending your ma and especially came to get this since you said we'd put together the bed later." She'd choked on those last words and her face went scarlet.

Drawing in a shaky breath, Magpie lifted the lid on her dowry chest again. Beneath the veil lay a stack of embroidered linens.

The notion of having fresh, crisp sheets on a bed in his own home instead of a cot sounded like a slice of heaven. Being with his bride under that newlywed quilt . . .

Maggie lay the quilt back inside and shut the lid.

Ten

Todd glowered at her. "You got close to an antsy stallion and risked your life for birdseed and that quilt? Yet now you leave the quilt out here."

Blue fire. Her eyes shone with the same blue that simmered at the very bottom of the hottest flames. "I wouldn't put myself in jeopardy—heart or being—for anything in the world but you. It wasn't safe, you alone with—"

"Talk wastes time." Todd strode past her and out the barn. Whether he liked it or not—and he didn't—she was right. He'd been in danger, and she'd turned the situation around.

But a woman didn't point out such things to a man. Now that he thought of it, she'd asserted her opinions freely in the holler. Ma was right about her not knowing how to be a farmer's wife. *They* followed their husband's orders and edicts. Challenging a husband showed a lack of respect. German culture held to the biblical model of the man being the head of the home. For that matter, all of the women on the other farms—German, Dutch, English—all of the women deferred to the man.

His wife would, too. This wasn't Carver Holler, and she'd best mend her ways here and now. Just as surely as she'd closed the lid on that trunk, she'd have to close the lid on her past and adhere to the right way.

For a short while, he'd let himself believe life would get less complicated. Easier. He snorted. Impossible. An ailing, cranky ma; a fresh-mouthed, opinionated bride, and a heavily mortgaged farm teetering on the edge of disaster amounted to anything but easy. Given a little time to heal, Ma ought to sweeten up, so that didn't weigh too heavily on his mind. *I'll pull the reins as I need to, to keep my wife in step with me.* Teaching her, though—that would take time—time he didn't have. Sassy back talk wasted her breath and drew them both away from their tasks and chores. Todd came to the unsettling awareness that she'd meant it when she stepped on his toes at the wedding. But he'd keep her in line.

"You vexatious, dog-hearted clodpole!" Maggie watched her groom stride away. Grabbing the bag of birdseed, she stomped out of the barn's side door. Along the way, she spied one of the outdated catalogs she'd put in the outhouse and snatched it up. Clearly, her husband knew nothing at all about a woman's needs. Any of them.

His mother is going to have to explain this one to him. I'll set this beside her bed, and he can try taking it away from her. After casting a handful of birdseed by the cabin's window, Maggie went inside, took the catalog from her apron pocket, and set it on the foot of

Ma's bed. "That's from 1891, so I figure at two years old it's fair for using as an essential."

"Arletta had wonderful paper specifically made for the necessary—this last year, it was even rolled instead of little sheets. If my son had gotten a good education, he could live in the city and afford those kinds of things."

"Todd seems very well educated to me."

"Of course he does." Ma cast her a look and paused slightly. "For a farmer."

That wasn't nice—not to me or to Todd. Straightening and bending her mother-in-law's left arm, Maggie decided she could work on Ma's attitude as she worked on her body. "Your husband—Todd's daddy—must have been a strong example of finding contentment working the soil. The Bible talks of Boaz being a husbandman, and God was so pleased with him, he sent Ruth his way. Christ Jesus came from their line. Let's work your shoulder now. Up and down, side to side, and in circles."

"Boaz sought his family's permission ere he took Ruth to wife, so there is no comparison. I'm Todd's ma, and I know him better than he knows himself. Stop twisting my arm off and pay attention." Ma reached over with her good hand and squeezed Maggie's wrist. "Don't delude yourself. He'll do right by you, but he doesn't love you."

"Ma'am, you're calling your son a liar."

Ma spluttered and huffed. "I am not!"

Maggie started working on Ma's fingers. Each one needed to be bent and straightened half a dozen times, and her wrist needed to be rotated. "Sure and to be certain, you did. In our wedding vows, Todd pledged to love me. Now I grant you, we've only been acquainted a short time, so the feelings we carry for each other are just taking root and sprouting. But they're there. With time and tending, we'll reap a rich marriage and a crop of children." She stared the woman in the eyes. "I won't hear anyone suggest that my man's a liar or that he doesn't care for me. That's sinful gossip and lies."

"Oh, he cares for you—but he'll never fall in love unless you adjust and . . . transform."

"You spoke your piece." Maggie refused to listen anymore. Each sentence Ma uttered stung—and partly because Todd's treatment of her suddenly reflected anger and disappointment. Ma's attitude that she wasn't suitable already hurt, but for Todd to feel the same way made her sick inside. Not sick, she amended herself, determined. Things were going to have to change, but she wasn't. At least not much.

The way to a man's heart . . . "I decided on apple crisp for dessert tonight. I can get it made and let it set out of the way whilst supper's bubbling on the stove."

"Sweet things don't keep a man going, girl."

The sound of a wagon pulling up spared Maggie from having to answer. "We have a caller!" Without bothering to remove her apron or smooth her hair, she dashed outside to escape Ma.

Maggie recognized the man's unmistakable build and horses from the night they arrived. "Mr. Van der Vort! Welcome!" When he turned around after helping a strikingly handsome woman alight, Maggie halted. "You're not . . . I'm sorry. I'm Margaret Valmer. Maggie." *I didn't stumble and say Rose instead of Valmer this time!*

"I am Karl Van der Vort. My brother, Piet, helped you the other night. This is my wife, Dr. Taylor Bestman-Van der Vort." He handed his wife a leather satchel.

Maggie turned to the man's wife. "Ma'am, my husband told me about you, and my heart leaps to make your acquaintance. Won't you both come in?"

"Actually, this is a sick-and-dying call." The laughter in the doctor's eyes and tone kept her words from being overly alarming. "Piet said Todd's mother is quite ill. And even if she weren't sick, Karl's dying to go see those Belgians."

Holding an immense wicker hamper, Karl grunted, "Just meeting Todd's missus would have made me visit."

Maggie couldn't smother her smile. "That's right friendly of you. Todd's on the other side of the barn. Adam—the stallion—is a mite touchy."

"The male of the species usually is. Drop off the food and go admire the horses." Leaning forward, the doctor murmured conspiratorially, "Mercy, my sister-in-law, is a commendable cook. Every half mile or so, I've had to rescue your supper from Karl."

"You should stay for supper. We'd be honored to have you."

"Perhaps some other time. This is really just a quick stop, because I need to visit one more patient before supper." The doctor patted her outraged-looking husband's chest. "I must abide by my instincts, and something tells me I'd best be home this evening. Maternity cases are notorious for ignoring the calendar."

Karl Van der Vort set the hamper just inside the door and disappeared. Introducing the doctor to Ma, Maggie assisted her with her wool cloak. Scrubbing her hands at the washstand, the doctor changed in a way Maggie understood quite well. She'd set aside the neighborly-ness and became briskly professional. "Good afternoon, Mrs. Crewel."

"That pretend healer there already had her chance and didn't make a lick of a difference. Get me a man. With a degree."

"I assure you I am a real physician with a medical degree." The doctor walked over to Ma. "The only one for miles around. After I've examined you and posed several questions, you may decide it's far less embarrassing to have a lady for a doctor."

Maggie transferred Ma from her wheelchair to the bed. Ma put no cooperative effort into the move. Her answers to the doc were surly, but Doc kept right on. When she finished, the doctor folded her arms across her chest. "Mrs. Crewel, you suffered a vascular incident in your brain commonly called an apoplectic fit."

"A fit." Ma spat the word as if it were dirty. "Like I'm demon-possessed. Next thing you'll tell me it was a 'stroke of God's hand.' "

"Ma!" Maggie started to reach for her hand, but the doctor waved her off.

"It's unfortunate that in the unenlightened past, when we didn't have medical knowledge, people attributed things they didn't understand to the spiritual realm. *Stroke* is a medical diagnosis and no longer carries such implications. Only the very foolish or ignorant would stand in judgment of another's walk with the Lord. You'll work yourself into worse health if you suppose anyone using *fit* or *stroke* is disparaging you."

"Easy for you to say. They aren't judging you."

The doctor lifted a brow. "Like most others, you made a snap judgment because I'm a professional woman. Just as I had to earn the community's respect, you will have to earn back your abilities. It is urgent that you exercise daily. Any delay, and the rehabilitation will be fruitless."

Maggie's admiration for the doctor grew even more.

"You're starting off in prime condition." Doctor's brisk, positive approach robbed Ma of the pity she both wanted yet hated. "You were blessed to keep a sharp mind, and your right limbs are strong. Ten days after a stroke, your joints are supple and your hands haven't begun to claw up. For most patients, they'd be curling and stiffening. A fair number would have bedsores, too, from lying in one position for prolonged periods of time."

"Stiffen? The way Magpie picks on me, yanking and twisting on my limbs like I'm a rag doll, it's a marvel I'm still in one piece."

"The marvel, Mrs. Crewel, will be how much you'll be able to do if you cooperate. There's no reason you can't stitch, button, shell peas, or do dozens of other tasks." The doctor produced a suturing needle and took two stitches on the edge of Ma's sheet, then she switched the needle to the other hand and stitched another pair. All four were identical. "Learning to be ambidextrous is a challenge, but you're a strong-willed woman. If you completely regain your left hand, you'll be twice as useful; if you don't, you'll become independent again. I'm sure you'd rather tend to yourself than need your daughter-in-law, wouldn't you?"

"Yes." Ragged with emotion, the word promised cooperation.

"Excellent!" Doc's features pulled. "I need to go, yet I ought to see those Belgians, too. Men admire horses the way women admire babies, but the men in my life and your husband are particularly knowledgeable and discriminating. You see, my husband and his brother run the smithy and livery, and my twin brother is the veterinarian. I'm bound to hear all about Todd's new horses."

"Oh, mercy." Maggie gave her an empathetic look. "Men are all full of vinegar and beans. They're liable to feed you a crock of nonsense just for the fun of it."

"Precisely." The doctor gave her a wry smile.

"You don't have to dirty your pretty boots out in the barn. I got a much better way of handling this. It's a foolproof cure against men's shenanigans." Maggie pulled a box from beneath Ma's bed. Jars rattled merrily. "Take one apiece—the cure's specific, you see. What'll work on your husband might not take hold of his brother or yours."

The doctor inhaled sharply. "I won't turn you down. Only I'm not promising the men will get any of it."

Maggie laughed. "Of course they will. But I have plenty. Do you trade goods for services?"

Jars of jelly conveniently tucked inside the doctor's bag, Maggie and the doctor exited the cabin. Having left the barn, Todd and Karl came over to join them.

"Doctor?" Todd's voice held a thousand questions. Maggie slipped her hand in his. Being engulfed in his larger hand warmed her clear through.

"The stroke was significant, but she's mentally sharp. Time will tell how much she'll regain—time, and repetitious exercise. Your wife's kept her limber." She finally smiled. "Maggie's given her extraordinary care."

Todd flashed Maggie a grateful look and squeezed her hand.

"I've challenged Mrs. Crewel to learn to use her right hand. Urging her to do things for herself and helping with small chores will aid recovery and improve her mood—though she's likely to resent it at the beginning. Suspend a trapeze-like arrangement over the bed. Your mother could then assist with moving herself and strengthen her arm."

While their first visitors drove off, Maggie waved good-bye. "We've been blessed with supper by someone named Mercy. I'll go—"

Instantly Todd tugged her toward the house. Maggie laughed as he washed up and she set out the food. "I was going to warm up things."

"Should have done that when the doctor was here," Ma accused.

"It will all taste fine." Todd scooped Ma from the bed and put her in the wheelchair. For an instant, Maggie's heart stuttered. Did he plan to seat Ma next to himself again? "Margaret." To her joy, he seated her beside his place.

A loud gasp filled the house. "Son, I am not hungry anymore. Put me back to bed."

A big fuss over who sat where at the table? Todd gave his mother an exasperated look. Maggie started serving food onto his plate. Still warm from being in cast iron and surrounded by cloths, the casserole steamed. Irritated and hungry, he started shoving the wheelchair toward the vacant spot.

"I said, I'm not hungry!"

"Hungry or not, everyone joins at the table in my home."

"But it is my turn. To sit beside you. I yielded it at dinner."

"The other place is for you. You have more space, and your chair fits in more easily." He positioned her chair without another word.

Todd sighed heavily as he sat. Ma was being childish, yet Maggie filled a teacup with corn and a high-edged saucer with casserole. *Generous of heart, my wife. With her loving care, Ma can't help improving.* Todd bowed his head and asked a blessing.

Maggie turned to Ma and draped the dishcloth over her bodice. "I thought we'd try something new." She threaded Ma's left forefinger through the teacup handle and curled her hand about it, resting it on the tabletop.

"I can't lift it." Ma sounded on the verge of tears.

"I didn't intend for you to." Maggie tucked the saucer against the cup and put a spoon in Ma's right hand. "Your left hand will steady the dishes, and you can feed yourself. How is it, Todd?"

Todd took a quick gulp. "Sehr gut!"

Turning back to her plate, Maggie served herself. "If it's as toothsome as it smells, I'll have to get the recipe."

Pleased as could be, Todd shoveled in the meal. His bride treated his mama nice even when Ma was in a rare mood—though it seemed less and less rare these days. Ma's low opinion of his bride vexed him. A wife deserved her husband's honor—and he'd see to it Maggie got her due. He owed Ma his respect, too—but Ma knew where he stood. Maggie figured it out, too, when he ignored Ma's snit and seated Maggie in her rightful place at the table.

Dealing with two emotional women after living alone tested a man. Ma had been a handful since she took sick, and as he'd told Bo Carver, she was the worst patient in the world. But his wife—he'd been wrong about her. Todd expected her to be more biddable. Back in the holler, she'd been calm, easygoing, and predictable. Today she'd shamelessly disobeyed him and could have been trampled, then gotten angry because he'd mentioned her outlandish collection of junk. Not that he was especially good at picking up what women thought, but her slamming the wedding quilt back inside the trunk wasn't a subtle hint as to how riled up she felt.

His bride scooped another big helping onto his plate. "Ma, you'd better start eating, else your son will inhale every last speck."

Ma dropped the spoon. "You expect far too much. The next thing I know, you'll say the doctor wants me to have that vile bar over my bed."

Maggie choked on her coffee.

"The doctor ordered such a bar," Todd confirmed. "Tomorrow, it will be so. You will work hard and strengthen yourself with it. Make me proud."

The droop on one side of Ma's face already made her appear melancholy, but something about the angle of her mouth transmitted more emotion. "You will be ashamed when you find out what happened. Like a tramp peddler, your wife traded instead of using credit."

"Ma, many of the folks here barter with Doc. My wife was clever to do so."

"I promise you, you will not approve. She arranged for two visits—"

"Then I'm very pleased."

"—with jelly," Ma tacked on.

Todd half roared, "You gave away my jelly?"

"No." His wife didn't have the decency to show a scrap of regret. Calm as could be, she reached for her glass. "Your jam and jelly are safe. I used my trading supply."

Drumming his fingers on the table, Todd thought for a moment. "Everything of yours is mine. Thus all of the jam and jelly are mine."

"Aye. You could say that." Maggie nodded. "But Valmers don't take charity. Paying in advance makes sure we don't have to go begging or borrowing someday. That assurance is sweeter than any jelly." She took a sip. " 'Neither a borrower nor a lender be,' " she quoted from *Hamlet*. "I'll owe no man."

Sobered by her words, he grated, "Maybe not a man, but the bank."

"We owe money?" She sounded scandalized.

"Of course I do. The Oklahoma '89 Land Rush was before I came west. Land in Texas is not free. I bought enough land to support several sons, and I needed funds for the barn, to drill for water, to buy starter seed, and all the essentials."

"Todd, I'd like a word with you." She turned and stepped outside, expecting him to follow, which he did despite the look in his ma's eyes.

Maggie didn't stop until she was standing by the windmill. "Your family sent you here with nothing?"

Todd looked into his bride's shocked eyes. "I grew up in Virginia. Dad passed away when I was eleven. Ma's second husband and I farmed the Valmer land. It was my birthright. I took on extra

CATHY MARIE HAKE

work for a neighboring widow, and I earned a matched pair of
horses. Those horses were my pride, and that land was my joy. The
week before I turned eighteen, my stepfather had an accident while
cleaning his gun. Then the banker informed me Mr. Crewel used
my land as collateral on a loan."

"He couldn't!" Maggie grabbed his arm. "He didn't—the
snake!"

"While I was a minor, he had the legal power. I was desperate,
and I pledged to sell the horses or put them up for collateral. But
Mr. Crewel already had. We lost everything—all but the furniture
and dishes the banker let Ma take with her to Arletta's."

"My ancestors settled Carver's Holler," she said in a soft, strained
voice. "Land passed from generation to generation—as yours should
have. Finding out about our debt—it surprised me, is all. We'll work
hard and pay it right off."

A new tenderness took root in his heart. Such innocent resolve
on her face! That only made it worse. She deserved to know the
galling truth. He should have told her before they married. Anger
at the situation and at himself for saddling her with such a burden
filled his voice. "It'll take years before this farm is free and clear."

"Seeing as we're going to grow old together, I reckon we'll have
plenty of years together to succeed."

"Years, Maggie. If a farm is in arrears, the bank can foreclose—
and it has. Two farms last year, and already one this year." He waited
for that ugly piece of information to sink in. "The Panic last year
only made the situation worse—costs are greater, and grain prices
are low. Very low."

She clutched his hand. "We'll do our best, and we'll do it
together."

Todd studied his wife. In a span of minutes the woman who said
she'd owe no man went from thinking things were a little tight to

learning she'd married a heavily mortgaged man and they were barely hanging on. She didn't look shocked or scared or even angry.

"I'm right proud of you, Husband. You've built all of this— gone from penniless to paradise. Aye, with God's help, you'll pull us through." Determination made her chin tilt up a little and courage lit her eyes. She made him believe they could do it.

Yes, he'd gotten himself quite a bride.

Later that night, after washing the dishes, Maggie again stepped outside to find Todd waiting for her.

Drawing her to himself, he made the distance between them disappear entirely. Even in the light of the skimpy moon, his eyes glittered as he studied her. At complete odds with that intense look, the corner of his mouth kicked up in his boyishly endearing, lopsided grin. "Mercy's apple cobbler tasted fine, but I had a little taste of your apple pie, and there's no comparison."

A nervous laugh shivered out of her. Todd silenced it with a hard, swift kiss, then he tucked her beside himself and grumbled, "After all the layers you put on this morning, I don't see how you can be cold."

"Todd!"

"There is no need for you to be bashful." Keeping her close, he reached over with his other hand and tenderly ran just the tip of his forefinger along her hairline. "You are my wife, and I am your husband. We belong to one another."

He was right. Uncle Bo even reminded her of that reality before he gave her away. Maggie let out a shaky breath. "I'm not used to thinking that way. It'll take me a while."

"Walk with me." They ambled toward the house. After a pause, he mused, "You always put Ma's chair to the right side of the bed."

"That way, she'll be able to use her strong side to help herself in and out."

Compressing his lips, he stared off at the fields.

She followed his gaze. "The winter wheat looks good. You put in a dandy crop. This section here would be convenient for a vegetable garden. Penned in as they've been, Adam and Eve be rarin' to turn the soil. I brought seeds from home—but if you have some on hand that're favorites, I'll be sure to nurture them along." *I'm babbling. I can't help it.*

After a day of near-frantic work, the walk should have given her a sense of peace—but it didn't. Once they got inside, Todd plucked her plaid from its peg. Stretching out the abundant length, he waited for her to back into it. She did, yet he didn't merely drape it over her shoulders. Her husband used it to wrap her into an engulfing embrace. Though unmistakably present, his strength altered—his arms transmitted the same tenderness his eyes and words carried just moments ago. One kind of shivers stopped and another began when he murmured into her ear, "I'll put together the bed. Get the quilt."

The light jumped as the lantern jostled atop the carefully loaded wheelbarrow. "Lord, yonder's my home. That's the family I'm supposed to fit in with. Right now, it's pinching like a new boot. Maybe we all need to be broken in before things will be comfortable. I'd have a gladsome heart if that's how you worked matters out, and a mighty thankful one if you'd see fit to make it happen fast."

She looked down at the quilts she piled in with her supplies. Her Rose of Sharon newlywed quilt was the last thing she wanted to put on her bed. *Our* bed, she corrected herself with a gulp. She didn't feel like a bride.

But Todd was her man, and the Holy Bible said she was to honor and respect him. He'd told her to go get the quilt. Temptation tore at her to leave it behind and bring others, pretending to misunderstand. Only they'd both know the truth. That was no way to start out as man and wife. So along with sheets she'd embroidered with roses, she brought three quilts, two fat feather pillows, and a pretty nightgown that was far too lightweight for this time of year.

Light shone through the window. Sewing curtains would pretty up the place. Surely some fabric in her trade goods would look nice with her Rose of Sharon and the Virginia Rose she'd hung in the center of the cabin for privacy. Knowing full well Ma was watching every little thing like a hawk, Maggie made a point of counting logs to show she'd been scrupulously fair in giving Ma a full half of the sleeping area. With a bed against each wall, there was just enough room for the dresser between them. The washstand and stove filled the third corner, and the table occupied the fourth. In a move to please Ma, Maggie even hung her quilt so the pretty appliqué faced Ma's bed.

Cold as the night was, Maggie tried to determine whether she ought to put her other quilts beneath the Rose of Sharon. She'd freeze half to death wearing her summer-weight nightgown.

Good thing Ma slept like a hibernating bear. Maggie thought she might work up the nerve to take her bath once Ma fell asleep. Only then could Todd come back into the house. If she blew out the lamp. And kept her eyes closed. Oh, dear goodness . . . Try as she might, she couldn't make herself take another step.

Her pretty quilt as a backdrop, she could see her handsome groom in the window. More to the point, he saw her. He waved.

Todd must know I have feelings for him, but they run far deeper than he's guessed. What if he finds out? She let out a rueful laugh and waved back. A husband discovering his wife was fond of him wasn't a bad thing. No, it truly wasn't at all. Ma said Todd didn't love her—or if he did, the how and how much were to be considered. Well, the time had come to explore the possibilities. And with the lamps extinguished, her groom would have to know she was blushing clear down to the tips of her toes.

In the last twenty-four hours she'd developed tempered-steel composure, she reminded herself. Sure and for certain, after all that the day brought, she'd cope with whatever came up and not be upset.

Then she opened the door.

Eleven

❧❧❧

"Almost done." Standing *on* their bed because the proximity of the beds left him no floor space, Todd beat a nail into the wall with a solitary slam of the hammer.

Almost dead. What was Todd thinking? All he needed to do was build their bed opposite Ma's, keeping the dresser in between. It would provide ample room for Ma's wheelchair, give them some privacy, and split the space in half. But he didn't do that. Todd scooted the dresser where the bed was supposed to be. Ma's bed filled the middle third of the wall, and their bed . . . he'd crammed it where Ma's had been. The quilt that divided the room in half now draped down the center of Ma's bed.

Todd finished moving the divider, but the whole thing was ludicrous. The sides of the beds lay all of three inches apart, and they had perhaps a foot of space between their bed and the wall.

They didn't have room to make their bed. Certainly, they wouldn't have the room or privacy to—

"It took you half of forever. I still want my bath."

"Ma." Todd's voice stopped her. As he reanchored the rope, the quilt swung off Ma's bed and hung free.

The full extent of the division sent Maggie reeling.

"Margaret?"

"I brought things in the wheelbarrow." Clutching the wire handle of the lantern, she rasped, "If you'll excuse me . . ." A before-bedtime trip to the necessary—it was reasonable. No one else would give it a second thought. But she was having plenty of second—and even third—thoughts. *What have I gotten myself into, marrying this man and coming clear out to Texas?* A few minutes later, Maggie heard Todd calling her. She buried her face in her hands. Even in the outhouse, she couldn't have privacy.

"Margaret, I want to talk to you."

"Go away."

"A wife does not speak thus to her husband."

"That might well be the case." She gave up and exited from behind the ridiculous flapping blanket-door of the outhouse. Chin high, she glowered at Todd. "But you and I are not husband and wife yet. With that arrangement, I promise you, we won't be, either!"

His brows slammed together. "We are married. You are my wife."

"Nay." She shook her head. "I'm your bride."

Even in the slight moonlight, she could see his eyes spark as they had just a while ago. "Ja. I have readied a bath for you, and Sharon's Rose will be across our bed." Slipping his arm around her waist, he pulled her close and murmured, "And two shall become one."

Maggie rested her forehead in the center of his chest. It kept some distance between them. "And a man shall leave his mother—"

He lifted her face to his. "You knew Ma would be with us."

"Not in our bed!" Maggie caught herself before she added, "Not even in our bedchamber." She'd made assumptions, and that was her fault.

"Ma begged for a change, but tomorrow, I will measure. Things must be moved."

Relief poured through her. Any change would be a vast improvement.

Rubbing his rough thumb down her cheek, he rumbled, "*Besser, ja?*"

"Aye, that would be better." The heat of her embarrassment nearly roasted her, yet she couldn't remain silent. "But tonight—" Her throat closed up.

He continued to caress her cheek. "After a time, when Ma has fallen asleep—"

As she shook her head, her hair cascaded down.

"You ask much of me." His voice sounded strained.

She felt his fingers threading through her hair, and the intimacy of the act made if difficult to speak. "I've done my best to do everything you've asked of me. Aye, and I've agreed—until now. So for me to ask we wait until you set our home to rights . . ."

"I'm not sleeping in the barn."

Negotiations could be difficult, but this was nigh unto impossible. Maggie knew they'd both have to yield to some degree. She whispered, "I'll settle Ma, then I'll go sleep in the barn."

"No, you will not." He yanked her back into his arms. "We have a bed. We are sleeping in it."

"Only if I nail barbed wire between the headboard and footboard."

He let out an impatient sound. "Okay. For tonight. Tonight, I will stay on my half."

"If that was meant to reassure me, it didn't. I saw your idea of half in the house already." She poked her finger in his ribs. "And don't tell me you're bigger. I'm meaner."

"Ja, Wife, you are." Scowling, he pushed away her fingers.

"Agreed!" There. That had to be the toughest bargain she'd ever made, and she closed it before he had a chance to add on any additional terms or have second thoughts.

⌒✿⌒

Helga sat in her wheelchair and looked out the window the next afternoon. When Todd looked up, she made it a point to wave. Ja—that went along with her telling him how she needed to be able to sit by the window in her chair.

When Magpie hung the dividing curtain yesterday, Helga felt closed in. By getting her son to promise her the window side, then insisting she'd be too cold at night with her bed directly against the glass, she got her own little reception area. A caller could pay her a visit and sit with her by the window. Coming and going at will, Todd and Maggie didn't need much room. Stuck inside like this, Helga deserved more space.

Magpie didn't see it that way, though. While oatmeal cooked this morning, she'd put photographs of her family on the dresser! Wasn't it enough that Helga's dresser had five drawers and she'd only kept two for herself? The space should be hers, alone, so she insisted Magpie put her things atop the washstand. After all, it was on her side of the house.

Tight-lipped, Magpie then went about the cabin, hanging pictures. Without asking, she hung two samplers and a mirror in Helga's space. Samplers—a reminder that she couldn't read or stitch anymore. That doctor showed off yesterday, but whipping out a few simple stitches with both hands didn't compare with the tiny, precise stitches required in needlework. And the mirror? With Helga's face now drooping, having her image reflected back mocked her. That was so cruel, she'd burst into tears. Magpie took down the mirror and hung it up elsewhere—but that didn't lift the sadness weighing on Helga's heart.

This wasn't the woman for her son. Uncouth and uneducated, Magpie certainly wasn't the mother for his children. The hillbilly wasn't simply thoughtless—she was mean. She ordered her husband around, telling him to fetch jam or the Bible. Had she baked anything in the dish from last night's supper and arranged for it to be returned to that nice woman? Etiquette dictated a dish never be returned empty. Heathenish girl probably didn't know that.

If only I could write! It is hard for me to remember so many things at once. It never was before. But these are all things I should fix, or she will disgrace the family. Speaking aloud to the empty cabin, she declared, "It is my fault for getting sick. So it is my responsibility to fix the problems I cause."

Helga stared at her left hand. Useless thing. *Come, now. Move. Open just a little. Or my fingers. If I can wiggle them . . .* Nothing happened. Why not? Why couldn't God heal her? Hadn't she been serving Him? With that left hand there, had she not crocheted and quilted blankets for orphans? Following the doctor's suggestion, Maggie unearthed a canvas and yarn so Helga could do some crewel stitching. But Helga knew she'd never manage.

What good was she without her hands? She couldn't roll out pie dough or make noodles. She couldn't braid hair. Crocheting, knitting, tatting, sewing—those were all lost to her, as well. Such simple, everyday activities and things. How many dozens of hankies had she tatted a lacy edge around? How many hundreds of pies had she baked? How she'd loved to brush Arletta's long hair and braid it! And to read. She'd read stories to her children. Now she would have to be like a child and have others read to her.

I no longer have anything to offer. And even worse, Maggie wasted time needed for vital work tending her. Helga had to ring a bell and halt everything if she needed anything at all.

The door opened. "Hello, Ma. It occurred to me that—"

Helga cut Maggie off. "It should occur to you that your whirligigs would bother me."

"Whirligigs?"

"Was it not enough that you dragged your trash in here and started nailing it to the walls? Did you have to hang it from the outside so you'd embarrass your husband?" As the girl lathered up at the washstand, Helga couldn't help herself. "The silly wooden birds are just as crude as this thing you want me to stitch."

Drying her hands, the hillbilly stared at her. "Whirligigs—what a fun word to say. Back home we called them woodicocks, and I thought one directly out the window might cheer you up. But I've reconsidered. You see, folks I love carved those pieces, and I take exception to you calling my treasures trash."

"Then by all means, take it down and get rid of all this garbage you tacked up today. At least the things on my side."

"Ma'am, the outside ain't your side. Since you're so set on me taking down my kin's masterpieces from the inside, I'll just have to honor my folks from the outside. I already moved the mirror and apologized for bruising your tender heart. 'Twas my lack of thoughtfulness that caused the problem, and I owned up to it. As for the stitch work—since you don't appreciate it, I'll move it. But that woodicock is staying outside. I can't help feeling you're sitting there, stewing and brewing up things to grumble about."

Embarrassed at the truth, Helga snapped, "You speak to an elder this way?"

"You speak to the woman of the house in the same manner. If you didn't care for the taste of your own medicine, mayhap you oughtn't be dispensing it."

"Those old fools let you have your head. They—"

"Those fine gentlemen gave you the clothes on your back." Magpie folded her arms across her chest. "Caring for them was my joy, yet fearing they'd encumber me from having a happy future, they nudged me out of the nest."

She used encumbered *on purpose.* Stung, Helga snapped, "We will be happy to send you right back."

Maggie drummed the fingers on her right hand against her left arm—a definite sign of impatience and ire. A long minute passed. "I reckon by 'we' you mean you and the woodicock." She pulled her skirts close and weaseled past. Taking down the first sampler with the pansies and daisies, a funny sound caught in the girl's throat. She took the one with a trio of roses worked with a shamrock, too.

Trying to determine what those samplers said had nearly driven Helga crazy. Without them taunting her, her space felt . . . safer. But then she saw how that backward girl cradled those pieces. The way Magpie's cheeks went pale and her nose got red tattled that she'd start crying any minute. Arletta hadn't hung a single thing Helga stitched for her—a painful rejection because Helga often took the county fair's blue ribbon for her needlework. But this girl cherished the things others made for her. She had a sentimental heart and appreciated what others did for her. *And I do appreciate what she does. But I can't let myself go soft over this.* In the end, she was doing the girl a favor. Things weren't just rough on the Texas plains; they were raw. They'd be hard-pressed to eke out a living. She needed to learn to be satisfied with what she had instead of imposing on others.

Maggie tacked up the samplers on either side of the washstand, then turned to go.

"He did not marry you out of love." Helga raised her voice. "He did it to get those horses. Years ago he had a pair of Belgians that got taken away, and he'd do anything to get another set. Anything— even marry you."

A brittle smile creased the girl's face. "I'll add a matched pair of Belgians to the list. Todd also married me to get a gardener and a cook so he'd have thrifty, wholesome food grown, served, and preserved. Aye, and he covets my jellies and jams, so by wedding me he'll enjoy those aplenty, whilst he'll not have to trouble himself with laundry or ironing or cleaning. But you're discounting your worth, ma'am, for sure as I stand here, your son married me most of all because of love. Because he loves his mama and needed someone to tend her. I'm supposing I can go right back out there now and hold my head high, knowing just how useful I am to your son—even if you say he had to be bribed to take me."

Left alone, Helga wept. Shame scalded her. She'd blurted out vicious things—some true and others not—but she didn't feel any better for it. She didn't even know why she did it. No wonder her hand wouldn't move. No work of the hand would be worthy when done with an impure heart.

"It *is* a stroke of God's hand that has made me half dead." She turned and caught a glimpse of herself in the washstand mirror. That momentary sight was all it took to assess the reality of what had become of her. "A useless leg and arm, one side of my face sagging, and a mouth that grows uglier each time I open it. How can I ask God to heal me when it is He who has done this to me?"

"Lord, you're going to have to do something quick, because we both know your Word says I'm to be slow to anger, but that woman in there has me hair-triggered. Do you know what I almost said to her? Of course you know. But I'm a-gonna quote Shakespeare right now anyway because he and you feel like my only friends. If I don't shed some of this wrath, it's bound to spill out on that crotchety old woman and hurt her feelings." Maggie inhaled and struck the pose she'd seen her father use when he depicted Othello. " 'You, mistress, that have the office opposite to Saint Peter. And keep the gate of hell!' "

A chilly breeze blew and birds twittered. Nothing had changed. Maggie let out a deep breath and shook her head. "Jesus, that didn't help one iota. I acted just as self-indulgent as she is. Well, not quite. At least I didn't do it to her face, intending to make her miserable for the rest of her days. But 'twas poorly done of me.

"You and me and Uncle Bo—we made it through dreadful rough times together, but now it's just you and me. I'm supposed to lean on my man, but I can't. Not just yet. Specially when he still favors his ma over me. I can't say anything. And if I'm wrong—I'm sure I'm not—but if perchance I were, and he didn't favor his ma, I'm merely a convenience. I never knew a heart could be so empty and cold. Back home, each day left me brimming o'er with happiness. Weeks and months flew by. Now each hour plods by in weighty boots . . . and I have a leaden heart to match."

She trudged on, wondering what she had done. Loving Todd and wanting to be loved in return had brought her to this lonely place. *That dreadful awful debt casts a pall over Todd, and it will for years and years to come. He's using up all his feelings, worrying about money and Ma. Will the leftover scraps of his attention be enough to make him fall in love with me?*

Todd met her at the edge of the field to accept some water. He drank four dippers full and gave her a sip from the next before he polished it off. Threading his fingers through his hat-flattened hair, he cleared his throat. "I have planned the house again and again. No matter the arrangement, it doesn't work."

"It works if the beds are each against a wall. But you'll need to reverse them so Ma can still get in and out on her right side."

"But then she cannot sit by the window."

"She'll be a few feet away from it." Maggie shrugged. "The view's still the same."

He drank again. "I promised her the window, and she will freeze if her bed is against that wall. With us working, I knew you would not mind."

I do mind. You should have asked me rather than giving her the choice spot. "Her bed can be narrowed, can't it?"

"Nein. The frame—it is iron. The cabin is too narrow for the beds to go end-against-end." Wiping his brow with his bandana, he stared past her toward the house. "The harvest—perhaps the yield will be sufficient to let me add a room. For now, I plan to push our bed against the wall."

Months of only fifteen inches between them and Ma—and if the harvest wasn't great, mayhap years. Now that she saw the state of affairs and discovered they were deep in debt, expanding the house was only a dream. Todd kept track of every last cent to pay the mortgage.

Maggie tamped down a sick feeling. Complaining wouldn't solve the problem; hard work in the fields would. She'd get up earlier, go to bed later, work herself silly. What with the concessions he'd asked of her, he ought to grant her one tiny request as a sign of goodwill. "We'll make do, but I have to have a door on the outhouse!"

Todd shook his head and swung his arm to encompass the farm. "Around you, there are countless needs. Essentials, Wife. Not fanciful things."

"A proper door is not fanciful!"

"It is not done—a wife raising her voice. Ma, the house and meals, gardening, laundry—those are your concerns. The animals and fields—I see to those vital matters. With only two of us, the work is already too much."

Never once had she mentioned a repair without a man accomplishing it at once. It was the very reason she hadn't spoken a word about the roof back home, fearing Uncle Bo would run out, climb up, and kill himself. Even if Todd didn't see the most basic item as important, he could grant her this boon. Instead, he chided her for not being a good wife.

Raising her chin, she locked eyes with him. "I'll take care of it somehow."

"Better you rid my barn of the mess you brought." He dropped the dipper into the pail. "I need to help Toomel. We'll return for supper."

He left, and Maggie went to the barn. Todd wanted her things out of the barn? Then the only place to put them was the house. Aye, and he'd told her the house was her domain, so he'd accept whatever she chose to do.

Arms full, she headed back to the house. A small dust cloud in the distance grew larger. Soon, a dandified man rode up and doffed his hat. "Mrs. Valmer, I presume?" Simple hospitality combined with making sure her mother-in-law wouldn't misconstrue anything led Maggie to invite Mr. Walker in for a cup of coffee. "I understand you brought a very interesting chair from the Ozarks."

"My son will not take kindly to you trading." Ma glowered at Maggie.

"If, perchance, I were to represent my husband's interests and barter on his behalf," Maggie ignored Ma's gasp, "what would you be offering for such a rare piece?"

"I'd have to examine it for myself."

While he went out to the barn, Maggie took hold of Ma's hand. "Ma, you'd burn that chair if you could. If I can get us a door for the outhouse—" Ma's jaw dropped. "That's right. Just a blanket is hanging there."

Ma inhaled sharply. "If you take down that whirligig out my window, you may trade away my chair."

⟡

Setting a gunnysack down in front of the house, Maggie indulged in the fantasy of tossing it over her shoulder and walking clear back to Carver's Holler. When Ma had gotten into the bartering spirit today, Maggie thought they'd come to an understanding. But now Ma sniped at the inferior quality or ugliness of each of Maggie's beloved treasures.

"Lord, please keep whispering that thirteenth chapter of First Corinthians. 'Charity suffereth long, and is kind; . . . seeketh not her own, is not easily provoked . . . beareth all things . . . endureth all things.' "

As soon as she opened the door, Ma said, "Lord have mercy! Don't tell me you brought in more junk!"

"Treasures, Ma. I brought you something extra special to show my faith in how you'll recover." She lifted the cane from the gunnysack, thinking Ma would take heart.

"Don't weasel your junk in here by saying it's for me."

Maggie drew a deep breath, stepped inside, and turned to close the door. But her eyes caught sight of another visitor in the distance, driving a wagon—and this one wore a bonnet! Anticipation surged through Maggie as she rushed out to meet the wagon.

"Hi! I'm Linette Richardson." Short brown curls, dark brown eyes, and a willowy build made her look like a statue of Juno come to life. Her smile looked as warm as her voice sounded. "Our farm's over thataway."

"Linette, you don't know how delighted I am to meet you! I'm

Maggie Ro—Valmer." She laughed self-consciously as she accepted a big roasting pan. "Come on down and stay a spell."

"I was hoping you'd ask!" Linette scrambled down, then reached up for a basket. "We'll take supper on in and I'll pay my respects to your mother-in-law. Then we can get your chickens back in the barn. The hens are getting ready to set." Linette tugged at her apron. "I came to work. Having seen the boxes where Mr. Valmer wants those chickens to nest . . ." She slapped her hand over her mouth. "I'm sorry. I always wind up saying the wrong thing. You may as well know that right away. I didn't mean to speak badly of your husband. He's really a nice man. I would have married him in a heartbeat if he'd—Oh!" Linette whirled around and started back toward the buckboard.

"Don't you dare dash away! If speaking your mind is dreadfully wrong, then I'll be sitting on the sinners' bench beside you." Linette halted, and Maggie hurriedly closed the distance. "I've been surrounded by a surfeit of men with nary a woman for years. I'm so starved for a friend, I could weep for joy just meeting you. Saying my man's the buck any gal would have liked to marry up with . . . Why, I take that as the highest compliment."

"When you put it that way, it doesn't sound bad at all." Linette smiled.

"Then merciful heavens, stop scaring the liver out of me and promise you'll stay and share this supper. It smells delicious!"

"I'll stay—but to help out for a while."

Since their hands were full, Maggie bumped against her. "I'd have you stay even if you wanted me to quote Lincoln. That's how excited I am to have a friend without whiskers!"

Linette laughed in disbelief. She mentioned having several sisters; she couldn't fathom Carver's Holler's all-male population. Once in the house, Linette set down the basket and pitched in with a few things. She won Ma over in a trice by brushing her hair and pinning it up again.

"I'm so tired." Ma heaved a dramatic sigh.

Linette said she often helped the doctor, and it showed. She assisted with getting Ma back in bed for a nap. "We'd better go release the hens."

"I'm so thankful to you for keeping them in Todd's absence."

"It wasn't much. We have seven dozen, so a few more didn't make a difference." Stuffing fresh straw into the laying boxes along the wall in the barn, Linette warned, "Ornery things are pecky as the dickens."

Compared to Ma, anything's sweet-tempered. Maggie grimaced. *There goes my attitude again. Sorry, Lord. I'll try. Truly I will.* "I reckon that presages them to start a-layin'. The thought gladdens me. I never gave a thought to how much I use eggs, milk, and butter until I didn't have them. Preparing breakfast without those ingredients—"

"That won't be a problem." Linette unlatched the first of two large crates. The door barely opened, and a beaked head jutted out and hammered at her hand. "I brought butter and milk to tide you over until your husband gets a milk cow."

Necessary as she considered a milk cow, Maggie had a sinking suspicion Todd didn't. Clearly, this was a time for her to step up and be his helpmeet. Using her skills as a trader, she'd find out the value of a fresh cow hereabouts, who had an extra, and what they needed. But for now, the hens required her attention. Yanking her sleeves to cover her wrists as well as they could, Maggie grabbed for one.

It didn't take long to free the hens. The last one pecked at Maggie. "Try bein' mean like that again, and I'll introduce you to the inside of a pot!"

Linette laughed. "If Todd heard you threaten that hen, he'd likely tell you it was too bothersome just so he'd have a chicken dinner."

"The man could eat the hind end off a running deer, but he'd better leave these hens alone. I need to increase the brood so I'll have enough to cook for the harvest crew and for Sunday suppers all year. I figured close to five dozen, and I could sell the extra eggs."

"The coop would be the size of your house!" Linette's cheery smile turned into a mask of mortification. "I shouldn't . . . I didn't—"

"My uncle Bo would say the selfsame thing. Having someone who'll tease me and speak the unadorned truth makes me feel more like this is home."

Linette gaped like a landed fish. "You can't mean that!"

Maggie shrugged. "I'm sure other women's fancy manners make for pretty times, but I've been a lone woman. Solitude brings you down to the bare bones. More than anything I want a woman friend who loves Jesus and we can pass time together. It's plain to see you don't have a malicious bone in your body. If you want me to take offense, whomp me upside my head and tell me you're aiming to pay me insult. Until then, I reckon I'll stand on the trust of friendship."

Her new friend's shoulders relaxed as if a heavy yoke were lifted. "Don't expect me to insult the one person who ever took me just as I am. With everyone else, I have to be on my guard." She looked away, then dusted her hands. "I meant to say something sooner— you're wearing your Sunday best jewelry." Linette's hand grazed the base of her throat.

"Which cameo am I wearing?" Maggie unlatched it and smiled. "Paw-Paw carved it. Rose was my maiden name, and I love my roses so." She fastened it back on. "Come hither."

Linette sat in the whiskey barrel chair. "Piet told his brother about this—it's the good-luck gambling chair."

"I bartered it away today, and the man's supposed to return tomorrow to finish the trade. Folks with enough cash to gamble ought to be smart enough to double their money by folding the bill over and putting it in their pocket." She opened a long, narrow box and made a selection. "This day's had rough spots, but when I spied you, everything got better. After years of my pestering, God has granted the desire of my heart and sent a friend. Today will be a memory for me to treasure. I want you to have this to fasten the memory in your mind, as well. Here."

Linette gasped and shook her head.

"I insist. God creates every one of us as unique, and cameos mimic that. Carvers can't make identical ones, and that adds to their charm. A more charming gift God's never given than you, so it's a fitting remembrance."

Carefully, Linette handed back the pin. "Becoming your friend is unforgettable. A reminder isn't needed, and I can't accept this, Mrs. Valmer. It's too valuable."

"It's a gift." Maggie didn't reach to take it back. "And I'd like to be knowing why you reverted back to addressing me as Mrs. Valmer when we agreed to be friends. I'm calling you Linette."

Color filled her cheeks, and Linette's gaze dropped. "A married woman—especially a bride—"

"Is still in wont of friends." Maggie waggled her finger at Linette. "And I'm not a-gonna let you back out on me, seeing as you're the first woman friend I've had in nigh unto eight years now! Believe me, I spent far more time begging the Lord for a bosom friend than I did asking for a husband!"

"You didn't!" When Maggie nodded, Linette set down the cameo and her shoulders slumped. "No matter how hard I beg God for a husband, He's not listening."

Wish I had me a porch swing. Swaying helps comfort grown-ups just as much as rocking soothes a babe, and this gal's sore in need of succor. Maggie shoved aside plans for a swing. Their farm had far greater needs. "God's not to blame. A lame-brained oaf who isn't listening to our Father is at fault. Instead of pleading with God to hurry up, mayhap you ought to be thanking Him for taking the time to rub some of the rough edges off your man."

Linette reached up and touched the tips of her short curls. "And for my hair to grow. When I took a bad fever, Ma chopped off my hair to spare my life. Only what man would want a wife who could pass for his brother?"

Rearing back with an exaggerated start, Maggie paused. "I see. So you really don't like the cameo. She's ugly to you, but you didn't want to tell me so."

Snatching it up, Linette yelled, "I didn't lie. She's gorgeous!"

"Aye, as are you. The both of you thread a ribbon through a cap of curls." Maggie's fingers skipped over a few of Linette's curls. "I picked her out special on account of there being such a close likeness. It's time you start seeing yourself through the eyes of God and your Christian sisters. Me? I saw a gal who cared enough to bring over food for tired neighbors. Instead of turning up her nose at the mess, she pitched in all. She even went out of her way to tend my ornery fowl 'stead of shredding them into a chicken salad!"

Linette blurted out, "When you said 'ornery' I thought you were going to say—" Her voice skidded to silence.

Maggie rescued her. "Let's pin on your friendship cameo."

They went about doing a few more things. Suddenly Linette got a stricken look. "I've got to go home. I let time get away."

Maggie didn't mention that spying Todd and John in the distance appeared to trigger Linette's decision. "I'm more than grateful for your help. I'll see you Sunday at church."

"Yeah. Good. Great!" Linette bolted to her buckboard and raced off.

Maggie slipped inside, washed up, and set the table as the horses' hooves beat out the men's arrival.

"Linette's not staying for supper?" Ma sounded disappointed.

"Not this time. I asked her to, but she had to go. Wouldn't it have been nice for her to stay?"

The door opened as she spoke. Both men shouted, "Nein!" and "No!"

He'd done it now. He'd promised her woman friends, and she'd chosen the one he most hoped she'd just be neighborly with. But not his stubborn wife. She'd sung chapter and verse of Linette's strengths. Sly as can be, she waited until John Toomel lavishly praised her cooking to inform them that Linette made supper.

After eating, he and John strode to the barn. John smirked as he opened the door. "Linette's mama ought to hire your wife. She'll be able to barter that girl off as some man's bride. Never heard such a testimonial or so many selling points from someone at a supper table."

Todd grunted. His wife talked faster than a snake-oil charlatan trying to sell off a case of stolen bottles. "The box with block and tackles is here somewhere." Todd stood by the two stalls and felt his shoulders bunch up. In that jumble, who knew where anything was? For all the things Maggie now had in the house, he'd expected much of her mess to be cleared away.

"What's in those mammoth boxes toward the back?"

Todd shrugged. It wouldn't be right to say anything about his wife's flaws. Then again, it wasn't as if John couldn't see the problem surrounding them.

"Beans." John moved a big sack. "Reminds me I need to get to Clark's Mercantile soon. Without your supper—or should I say Linette's—I could have starved."

"Never!" Maggie's voice jolted them. She marched on up. "John Toomel, there's always a place at Valmer Farm's table for you. If you forget that, you'll be a very sorry man."

"That's right," Todd agreed, despite his vexation over his wife's interruption.

"But in the meantime, I'd be happy to share some of our goods so if the weather's bad, you can still have a hot meal at home." Maggie weaseled past them and opened a bag of pintos.

"Wife, where are the block and tackles?"

Silly woman knew exactly what to move to get to the box. "You'll see I brought fine merchandise, John. Back home, I was the region's trader. My man allowed me to bring along some of the finer goods."

Todd cast her a hot look. "John earned this by watching my farm."

"Absolutely."

Both men relaxed.

Maggie gave them a casual smile and wandered off to the far corner of her stash. Lifting a coiled length of hemp rope, she struggled past the obstacles and dropped it on the barn floor. "There. That still doesn't begin to repay all your hard work and dedication. My man and I are grateful for your kindness."

She was up to something. He knew it.

John held up one hand. "No. That's far too much."

"We think it's far too little—don't we, Husband?"

"Ja." There. That ought to put and end to this game.

Shaking his head and looking at the substantial collection, John ground out, "I don't feel right about it."

"See? Told you he was kind." Maggie threaded her hand through Todd's arm. "Man like him doesn't need folks to give him their thanks or remind him of his Christian duty. He's a gentleman through and through. You were right, Todd. We got ourselves grand neighbors."

"Thanks." John let out a deep breath.

"Don't mention it." Maggie let out a small sound of upset. "I was going to get you some viands. Tell you what—I'll have them ready for you next time you're over. Tomorrow night?"

She wasn't aiming to get anything, after all. Todd let the tension drain from him.

Face creased with an enormous smile, John nodded. "Tomorrow. Sure. Thanks."

Maggie grabbed a bar of soap Todd knew she didn't need and headed toward the barn's side door. Just as she exited, her words floated back to them, "Glad to have a fine Christian gentleman as a neighbor. Now I won't have to worry when my dear friend Linette needs someone to see she gets home if the time gets away from us."

John blustered for a moment, and then he threw back his head and belted out a laugh.

"You think it funny?" Todd gaped at him.

"Hilarious. That woman roped me into doing something, but you're tied to her for life. She'll have you in knots the whole time."

Todd lifted the rope and shoved it at him. "Don't be too sure. That rope could turn into a noose."

The next hour, Todd saw to things in the barn and considered what he ought to do about his bride. She'd outsmarted him and John, but for reason. They'd insulted her friend, and Maggie had already proven her staunch trait of being loyal. When he drew close to the house, he noticed the women sitting outside.

"Ma and I are enjoying a little night air." Maggie pressed a steaming cup of coffee into his hands. "Heaven's dazzling us with stars, like thousands of angels a-winking at us."

He gulped some coffee, then held the mug to Maggie's lips. "Beautiful—you and the thought."

Shyness replaced the spirited look in her eyes. She took a tiny sip. "Thankee."

Did she thank him for the coffee, or for the compliment? Slugging down the last of the drink, he wondered if he'd ever decipher what went on in her mind. But she'd keep him entertained. The corner of his mouth kicked up. And starting tonight, he'd keep her warm. Which undoubtedly accounted for that shy aura that suddenly surrounded her. He set the coffee mug next to the house and glided his rough hand down her oh-so-soft hand and held it. Together, they'd raise crops and rear children, then leave behind them a legacy of land and love. This was his land, his wife, his future. As God said at the end of each of day of creation, Todd declared, *"Es ist gut."*

"It is good." Her lips bowed upward in a smile—a wobbly one, but it counted. She cleared her throat and rasped, "What did you want to do?"

Raising his brows, Todd waited for her to direct the thought. Did she mean in the fields? Or how to spend the next half hour?

The second his brows rose, her eyes widened and she rushed out, "I mean, what did you have in mind?"

Todd lips twitched. She'd mistaken his reaction and dug herself straight into embarrassment.

"For the farm!" she blurted out before he could rescue her. Face aflame, she rubbed a shaking hand across her forehead and rushed, "I mean, what did you plan for us to do—" Groaning, she tried to jerk free.

Holding tight, he lifted her hand and pressed a kiss on the back of it. Jitters. She had bridal jitters, and he had desires. Even the most innocent phrases could be construed differently. With Ma sitting right there, he couldn't address the issue, so he acted as if everything she said held nothing other than the innocent, straightforward connotation. "First off, I'll get the fields in order. The winter wheat—it's heading up. This year is as dry as the last two, but my yield will be higher, praise God. The alfalfa—I hoped for it to grow better and restore the soil. Two neighbors will bring mares by this week so the stallions can stand stud. Next I must plant either sorghum or corn. Already, I should almost be done with that."

"Sorghum," Ma decided. "It tolerates drought best." She yawned.

Todd carried her to her bed and left so Maggie could tuck her in.

Soon Maggie stepped back outside. "I've got a notion. You have the far field and the section yonder that's ready for a crop. Sorghum's both drought resistant and grows in marginal soil. Seeing as we'll be working together, what if we plant both crops?"

A second field wouldn't take that much water and could bring in more money. Her suggestion tempted him. He resisted. "No. The garden will take that plot. To plant both would mean breaking sod for the garden. You're already too busy."

Gesturing to the right, she said softly, "If the vegetables and flowers grew there, Ma could come out and feel like she's part of things. I don't know a soul who doesn't perk up in the garden."

"We can put a few rows there, I suppose."

"While the horses are hitched, we may as well do it right." *We.* She'd done the same thing about the debt—immediately jumped in and committed herself to sharing the burden.

"So." He slid his arm around her waist and hoped she realized how much he appreciated her. If he could find the words, she'd probably think he was trying to talk her into bed. The sounds of the night filled the silence. Strands of hair fluttered across her cheek. Automatically, he reached over and used the back of his fingers to tuck them behind her ear. *"Weich."* He couldn't resist touching her cheek and smoothing back another wisp.

Her eyes widened.

"Du bist eine Schönheit."

Her lips parted and laughter spilled out of her. "Soft? You are such a beauty?"

He didn't think he'd actually spoken the thoughts aloud. She ought to be pleased, though. "Is it not good for you to know I feel this about you?"

She twisted away from him. "You said those exact things to Eve today."

Twelve

Her voice shook—but was it mirth of fear? Or anger? If he'd said those very things to the mare today, Maggie might well be furious.

"Are you afraid of me?"

Her rapid breaths answered him.

He took her hands in his. "There's no need. I'm your husband, and I feel much tenderness toward you." He jostled her hands. "I assure you, I have never said that to a horse."

A tremulous smile formed on her lips, but she wouldn't look him in the eyes. His bride's voice shook as much as her hands. "I suppose tenderness is . . ."

"A sweet beginning. Just as we will cultivate our land, we'll take care of our love. Soil and seed and water—you and me and the Living Water—the essentials are together already."

"You think like a farmer." She looked off to the side. "But you could be full of beans."

The earth beneath his boots grated as he shifted to a wider stance. "You would not have married me if you did not trust me." Slowly, he pulled her closer and wrapped her arms about his waist before he wound his arms about her and cradled her close.

She swallowed. "Uncle Bo told me a husband needs his wife."

Todd brushed his lips against her temple. *What she and I want is opposite. It is a wife's duty to submit.* Submit? The word hit him. Intimacy should be giving and sharing—not demanding or taking. A man was the head of the home, but his wife—she was the heart. There had to be a balance—a harmony between them he'd never considered before. *Ma and Dad always seemed to be of one mind. I don't even know my wife's mind.*

Maggie shivered, and a wave of protectiveness washed over him. How could desire and tenderness be at odds when they belonged together? *Perhaps it is my wants and her needs. A husband must be willing to make sacrifices for his wife.*

Sensible, practical Magpie. If he gave her a few minutes, she'd come around. Todd continued to nestle her, stroking his hand up and down her back in a steady, reassuring way. She'd plunged right in from the first moments to care for Ma and never stopped working since—other than when they shared a sled. The way she'd fumbled the conversation earlier left her unsettled. Giving her a chance to calm down ought to allow her to regain her poise and start feeling the stirrings of desire, too.

Clasping her hands together behind Todd's back, Maggie stayed as pliant as a marble pillar. She shivered again. That, and hearing her audible swallow tilted the balance.

"Margaret." He set her a scant few inches away and lifted her chin. Her lashes lowered so she didn't look him in the eyes. "To have you fear me, there would be no sweetness. Tonight. I will give you tonight to rest in my arms and in my tenderness. Tomorrow, you will trust me—then we will know one another and it will be good."

"Thankee!" The word lilted out of her, and she gave him a quick hug before dashing inside.

Scowling, Todd watched her flit away. He'd done the right thing, but did she have to act like she'd just been given a reprieve from a death sentence?

⟊

Todd's comb rested against her hairbrush on the washstand. Earlier Maggie had set down her brush to leave a tiny space between, but he'd finished combing his hair and now the pieces touched. Like them in bed. Both nights, she carefully inched away when he climbed in next to her. He'd swallow up the space in seconds—but he'd kept his word. The first night, he lay on his side, facing away from her. His warmth radiated to her and felt wondrous, but he'd kept his hands to himself. Last night, Todd wound his arms about her. Back in the holler, he'd earned her trust—but this was a deeper, unique kind of trust. Throughout the night, he'd cradled her as though she was his one and only treasure. Doing so gave her a glimpse of what the future could hold . . . and planted hope.

She'd made him a grand breakfast to show her appreciation for his sensitivity. As much as he ate, he'd liked it plenty.

And wait until this afternoon, when I give him some of this! She took a pan from the oven box she pilfered from her trade goods. Fragrant steam wafted from the loaf pan. "Whilst I tend to a few matters, Ma, you can borrow my hairbrush. I'll put up your hair after it's nice and smooth."

"It will take me too long."

Placing the hairbrush in Ma's lap, Maggie took a firm tone. "I'm willing to do all you need, but I won't have you feign helplessness. A family pulls together, each member doing their utmost. Half of your body might not obey your wishes, but that doesn't excuse you from doing all you can. Todd's counting on me to be out in the fields with him. I aim to be there, too, so I'm relying on you to pitch in as best you can. Valmer Farm needs to make up for lost time." A quick tug took the ribbon off the tail of Ma's nighttime plait.

Cheap and filling, beans were a good choice for supper. What, with one trade started, she wouldn't be surprised to have a caller or two. If no one joined them, she'd have leftovers. With beans set to soak for supper and a batch of soda bread started, Maggie finally turned back to Ma. "Tomorrow I'll mix up biscuits for you to roll out and cut with a cup. Aye, and put them in a pan. Todd will nigh unto burst his buttons when he sees what you've done."

Ma didn't respond, but she did rake her right fingers through her hair to unravel the plait. A halfhearted effort at brushing her hair ensued.

"We can ask Dr. Bestman-Van der Vort—"

"That woman—she was ashamed to take her husband's name. What woman clings to her past like that? Such a poor example. The Bible says the man is the head of the home."

"From the way she looks at her husband and speaks to and of him, I'm sure she's proud to be his wife." Did Ma always look for the dark side of things and judge? Steering the conversation, Maggie declared, "Todd's a fine man. A godly man. I count myself blessed and I'm sure you do, too, that he's the head of our home."

"It is good you feel that way." Todd's voice boomed from outside the window.

Maggie squealed and jumped.

He beckoned. "Come. We've much to do."

Hastily braiding Ma's hair, Maggie called out, "I'll be in the barn in a few minutes." A half-dozen pins slipped into place, and Ma's hair assumed its normal style. "I'll sit you by the table today. With a glass of water, the bell, and the Bible I've set out, you can fill your heart and summon me if you have need." She put a threaded needle in Ma's hand and propped the hoop-enclosed canvas in place.

"Put me back to bed."

"Nay. When Mr. Walker returns today, you'd be embarrassed to be caught lazing around." Maggie didn't give Ma a chance to argue. She positioned her at the table, then hurried to join her husband.

Adam and Eve dragged the plow back and forth, breaking the sod for the vegetable plot. Thick as it was, only the horses' combined strength made the task bearable. Riding Adam, Maggie echoed the orders Todd called as he manned the gang plow. Both blades bit into the earth, fighting against hundreds of years of stubborn grass roots tangled deep into the soil. Row after row yielded to their brute strength. "Haw!" she called, and the Belgians obeyed, veering slightly. Twenty feet more . . . fifteen . . . five . . . "Whoa!"

After turning the plow to go the opposite direction, Todd grinned. Exposed dark, rich soil gave a promise of good yield. "Hitched to the Belgians, this goes as easy as a spoon through stew. To prepare my other fields, my horses and John's took a whole day to accomplish this much."

"We'll have acres done in no time." Looking back at the field, Maggie slid off Adam. "Soon we'll have a bounty for our table. It's frosty in the morn. Unless you say otherwise, I'm thinking we might need to wait a bit before planting. I'll want to put in sweet corn, cabbage, potatoes, onions, and some melons."

"Watermelons are already putting out runners. It's too late. Gardening here is different because of the drought."

"So what's the normal rainfall?"

Todd let out a heavy sigh. "There is no such thing as normal with weather. There is an average, but each year varies. The driest year so far was last year, with ten and a half inches. The greatest known was forty-one. The *Farmers' Almanac* says this year will be as parched as last." Just like the earth they worked, lines plowed furrows across his brow. He said nothing about how the lack of water would impact the yield of all their crops.

"Kickin' a tin can won't open it." Maggie smiled at him. Her man needed her to prop him up. "Bellyaching about a lack of water or watermelons won't make a difference, either. We'll plant extra canta-loupe, and I can swap neighbors for watermelons and tomatoes."

"Tomorrow at church, ask Widow O'Toole or Hope Stauffer when to plant. Widow O'Toole's known for her garden, and Jakob, Hope's husband, has farmed here the longest. Their advice would be best."

"Uncle Bo encouraged me to seek counsel from others with more experience. The Flinn twins always knew the weather and planting times best." Just mentioning their names swamped Maggie with homesickness.

Squinting at something afar, Todd seemed preoccupied.

Heart heavy, she turned away. "Whilst you rest the beasts, I'll go check on Ma."

Drawing near the house, Maggie spied the end of a wagon. Hastening to make sure Ma was okay, she threw open the door and stopped cold. Ma sat at the table with two strangers. Nothing but crumbs and an empty loaf pan sat on the table. *The prune bread! She gave them the prune bread I baked specially for Todd!*

"Mr. Walker couldn't make it." Ma took a stitch—only the third—but it was a start. Even if she did it for show, it was prog-ress. "These gentlemen came for him, and they've already hung the door."

"Now that's good to hear. Thank you."

One belched loudly as the other rose. "Come on out to the wagon and we'll see to the rest, Mrs. Valmer."

Ma answered, "I'll take care of it here."

Breath freezing in her lungs, Maggie searched for the best way of handling this. "I'll be back in a jiffy, Ma."

Brows wrinkled, one man looked at the other. "Did Boss say which Mrs. Valmer—"

"I'm Mrs. Valmer," Maggie forced a smile. "Ma's surname is Crewel. Let's go on out to the wagon."

A minute later the man said, "Boss got too busy to get the wood last night. He sent this instead."

An odd item lay clear across the flatbed wagon. "What is it?"

The men exchanged a quick look. "It's practically a ready-made porch. Which side of the door d'ya want it on?"

Maggie ran her hand along the upraised edges. "This is going to cause trouble with Ma's wheelchair. I traded for lumber because it needs to be flat."

"Boss wanted to be fair. Said if you liked, he'd throw in this canvas. To make an awning. Just in case, he sent some rods. That must be some chair he's getting from you."

The fast-talking man's trying to saddle me with a skunk. "Bartering requires honor. Mr. Walker dealt for a special, one-of-a-kind item, and he's sending castoffs instead of prime goods. You already hung the door, but I'm a-gonna have to have you men take it back down."

"Aw, c'mon, lady."

The other leaned against the wagon. "Mr. Walker's not a man to be crossed, ma'am. And your man won't have to waste any time making a deck for the old cripple—"

"Now you've done it." Maggie stepped back and set her hands on her hips. "You just hightail it on out of here. I won't stand for anyone to be disrespectful. My man'll return the outhouse door."

The other got a stricken look on his face. "He didn't mean it the way it sounded!"

"Sure and certain enough, he did. You just go tell your boss the deal's off." She turned around and practically bounced off Todd's chest.

"You heard my wife." Todd wrapped his arm around her waist and stared at them.

As the men drove off, Maggie poked Todd in the chest. "You're stealthy as a mountain cat on the prowl. I nigh unto leapt out of my boots when I found you behind me."

"What are you doing dealing with Mr. Walker in the first place?" Todd set her away from him and kept hold of her upper arms.

His curiosity pleased her. Uncle Bo always wanted to know with whom she'd traded, how they met, and the details of the deal. "Piet told him about the good-luck gambling chair, and he sought it."

"Which tells you much about his character!"

"Aye, it warned he's a rogue with more money than scruples." Todd worried about her. Wasn't that sweet? She leaned a little closer. He smelled of fresh, rich earth and radiated a warmth that tempted her to give him a hug—but she wasn't that brazen. "Ma's too embarrassed to use the seat, and we have no space for it. Better to barter it than burn it. I can't abide waste."

"I will get what we need."

"I don't doubt that in the least. Best thing you got us was this farm full of rich soil. That will provide for us now and for generations to come." She bobbed her head. "Aye. And as your helpmeet, I'm supposed to work alongside you. I was just doing my part."

Lightning flashed from his eyes, and his voice went thunderously low. "Dealing with the saloon owner? Getting a pool table?"

"A table that's a pool? So we could have ourselves some ducks and geese?"

Yanking off his hat, Todd made an impatient sound. "Nein. It is a game. Sticks hit balls into holes. Men place bets and play it."

"Well, it's good I held my ground and sent them packing. They already hung a door on the outhouse—"

"I heard." A muscle in his cheek twitched. "There was nothing wrong with a blanket."

Jehoshaphat, he was prickly as a jar of toothpicks. "We'll go on ahead and make do with that blanket until God sends a door."

"God will not use a saloon owner to deliver what He wants."

"Most often, I'd agree with you." A quick kiss on the cheek never failed to sweeten her uncles' sour moods. Did she dare? *What's a-wrong with me? A minute ago, I wouldn't hug him and now I'm considering a kiss? Dour as he's getting, I've got to do something quick.* Maggie went up on tiptoe and gave Todd's cheek a quick peck. Pleased with herself, she got a little sassy. "But the story of Balaam comes to mind. God spoke through a donkey. Is a saloon owner then not a possibility?"

"Your words were as disappointing as your kiss." Todd yanked her close and kissed her silly. Her knees went weak, and when he drew back, he demanded, "You will work on both."

"Both what?"

A smug smile tilted his lips. "Your words and your kisses. You will work on them."

"That sure didn't seem like work to me just now." As soon as the words slipped out, Maggie smacked a hand over her mouth.

"Then you can put more effort in thinking about what you say."

The bell rang from inside the cabin. "It's time for Ma's nap. Could you go put her to bed whilst I . . . ." Maggie's face went pink as she nodded toward the outhouse.

"Sure."

She went around the house to the necessary and stopped in her tracks. "Oh no!"

Yanking out his sheath knife, Todd dashed out of the house and around to the back. Maggie stood stock-still, eyes huge. Rapidly scanning about her, he didn't see any snakes or critters, so what was she—

Shaking her head, she sighed. "Husband, no matter how much I work on what I say, I won't ever find the right words for that."

Following the direction in which she'd pointed, he stared at the outhouse. It now sported a fancy swinging saloon door. "Magpie!" His roar made her jump.

"Excuse me." She ran past him, through that swinging batwing door, and out of sight.

The stupid thing worked perfectly. Upset as he was at her for bartering as if he couldn't provide well enough, Todd didn't mean to frighten her. He could hear her muttering about wishes coming true, too. The roads her mind traveled were plotted with an eggbeater, not a ruler. He went back into the house.

"What's all the ruckus? Didn't we get my porch?"

"Porch." That's what his bride traded for? She got rid of that ridiculous chair and thought of something to make Ma happy. Instead of leaving her inside all the time, they'd be able to bring her out and have a special place for her. Lumber for a porch would cost a chunk. The outhouse door was undoubtedly a little extra Maggie dickered for—not her primary goal. At least Maggie didn't stand for the devious exchange. His bride tried to kill two birds with one stone: pampering Ma and getting rid of something in the barn. And wasn't that what he wanted?

"Well? Where's my porch? The outhouse door is up, and I've waited all morning for my porch."

"Mr. Walker tried to cheat us. Maggie wouldn't accept what he sent as a porch."

"Why not? Anything would be better than the dirt and pebbles out there."

"Then whatever I come up with to serve as a porch should please you." He put Ma back in her bed. "Putting in the garden comes first. You'll have to be patient."

"I'm thinking since we've already paused," Maggie said from the doorway, "we could grab sandwiches and take them back out with us. That'll allow us to work in an extra row."

"Excellent!"

Ma jerked on his sleeve. "Speaking of excellent, those men ate every last bite of your prune bread, Magpie."

Shoulders sagging, his bride sighed. "I made it for you, Todd."

"Spared this time," Ma said in a low tone.

From Maggie's bewildered expression, Todd knew she heard the unkind comment. His wife deserved to be praised. "Ja. We spared our treat for their sake. It was a good thing." The smile that started to flicker on Maggie's face melted. Todd quickly tacked on, "Texas is known for hospitality."

"Son, isn't Texas also known for tall tales?"

"And longhorns." Todd shot Ma a quelling look. She'd grown downright ornery. "Take a nap, and we'll tell you all about the garden at supper. Together, we are getting far more done than I dared hope. My Margaret is a hardworking woman."

They headed back to the garden and stopped at the windmill to fill a bucket. Maggie gave him a shy smile. "I'm glad you're pleased with my labor."

"I'm not."

Her gasp almost knocked her off her feet.

Grinning, he pulled her close. "I told you to work on your kisses, and you've not done a thing about that all day."

"All day? You only just gave me that order, and I'll remind you, Todd Valmer, I'm not a hussy!"

Trailing one finger down her cheek, crooking it beneath her chin, and lifting her face, he looked into her eyes. "I'm not interested in a hussy. I want a warm, loving wife." He dipped his head and waited until his lips were a mere breath away to murmur, "Get to work."

Fast as lightning, she wheeled around and made it a single step before he captured her. "What was that?"

Glee lit her face. "That, Husband, was *Love's Labour's Lost.*"

Feisty woman. He arched a brow. "Forget Shakespeare for a minute. I far prefer Milton's titles." He kissed her until she melted in his arms, then whispered in her ear, *"Paradise Regained."*

It took her a minute before she whispered in a husky tone, "What about *Paradise Lost*?"

"That was last night." Chuckling at her blush, he kept one arm around her waist and went back to the field.

When the horses rested later, Maggie checked Ma and started supper. Todd filled every bucket they owned and set them in the sun so they'd enjoy decent baths. Good thing, too. They came home dirty as peasants in a mud puddle. Though Maggie sponge bathed Ma and washed her hair, Ma fussed and grumbled that she hadn't had a decent bath.

Exasperated, Todd finally said, "Ma, you don't need a bath. You spent all day soaking in self-pity." She let out an outraged sound, and he glowered at her. "Don't be a dog in the manger."

"A dog—!"

Maggie stepped in. "Last evening, he spoke to me the same way he talks to the mares. Your farmer son's got critters on his mind."

"Be glad I know *Aesop's Fables*, Wife. Someday I will tell them to our children."

"Not if Ma thinks you called her a dog again." Maggie pointed to the corner. "I bet she could use that cane I fetched for her and—"

Ma actually laughed. Making a big show of it, Maggie handed her the cane. "Ma, you've gotta promise if Todd uses horse-talk on me again, you'll prod some sense into him."

A while later, Maggie's thick hair dried into a tumbling sheet of black satin Todd could scarcely keep his hands off of. Grabbing her shawl, he invited, "Ma's weary and needs to fall asleep. We'll go look at the stars."

"You do that." Ma went back to looking like she'd sucked on lemons. "It's a regular romantic symphony out there—that clattering windmill and a breeze stiff enough to teach a pig to fly."

Maggie waltzed to the door. "Hurry up, Todd! I can't tell you how many things I've been waiting for until pigs could fly!"

They weren't out for more than a minute when Maggie tilted her head to the side. "My woodicocks are like baby windmills, making some of that same whirring clatter. I like the sound our windmill makes."

"Good." He didn't tell her it had become such an integral part of the farm's sounds, he didn't hear it anymore. "If a pig flies by, what will you see?"

"Uncle Bo wearing a dress." Merriment filled her voice. "Aunt Maude swimming. Paw-Paw riding a high-wheeled bicycle . . ."

"I didn't know your aunt, but I'd glue wings onto a pig if it meant I could see the other sights." The conversation wended along, mostly thoughts and plans for the farm. Tonight wasn't fraught with the same awful tension as last night.

Maggie hugged herself. "The holler felt cozy, like I could hold it all close." A tinge of longing colored her voice. "Here, the land

and sky go on forever—like I could stretch out my arms and there will always be more."

Reaching to match her widespread arms, Todd threaded his fingers with hers. "Our life will be like that—full of possibilities."

"I believe you." Her eyes twinkled brighter than the stars. "Our years ahead are bound to be breathtaking. . . . What with such rich soil, sweet water, and that grand door on the outhouse!"

"That door's going back." He didn't bother to hide the amusement in his voice. "But I won't be surprised if someday that'll be embellished and become a family tall tale."

"You mentioned *Aesop's Fables*. Daddy told me stories every day. It was our special time together."

Arms sliding around her, Todd murmured, "When God blesses us with children, we will both tell them stories." He drew her close, lowered his head, and gave her a kiss.

She remained in his embrace as he rubbed his cheek against her temple and said, "For now, though, I am thankful God has given me you."

Staying outside, he gave her a chance to get into bed. When he went back in, Ma's snoring gave ample proof she'd fallen deep asleep.

Todd slipped beneath Maggie's newlywed quilt and played with the curls spilling across her pillow. This was the time. He'd reviewed the verses that went along with her quilt and now recited from Song of Solomon, " 'I am a rose of Sharon, the lily of the valley. . . .' "

Soon, in perfect harmony of spirit and timing, Maggie breathlessly added the woman's line, " 'His banner over me is love.' "

Perfect. The moment was perfect.

Then the curtain between the beds whisked back.

Thirteen

~~~~~~~~~~~~~~~~~

S on, I'd like a word with you."

   "Anything you have to say, Ma, you can say in front of my wife."

   "I tried to be delicate. You're making it impossible."

   He let out a derisive snort. Delicate? After last night? When she opened the divider with that stupid cane and whined that she felt like she was closed in her casket? She'd spoiled everything. Intentionally. Unforgivably. He'd bellowed last night, but plenty still remained to be said. He'd refrained from reading from Proverbs this morning. Of all the Proverbs, today's spoke of the things God abhorred—including those who devised mischief and sowed discord . . . and though that certainly fit, the second portion mentioned a man lusting after a beautiful woman. Though the verses were addressing the sin of adultery, he suspected Ma would twist the words and make things worse.

If that were possible.

Maggie avoided looking at him today. The one time their eyes met, she grew flustered and pivoted away. His bride hadn't said anything. Didn't need to. The way she'd lain still as a board beside him all night shouted volumes. Though his wife followed his edict and sat at the table for the meal, she'd barely nibbled the edge of a biscuit. She sprang from the table to get the coffeepot. Seeing as she always set the pot on the table, Todd surmised she'd left it on the stove as an excuse to get away. Pouring fluid made the only sound in the entire cabin.

"Ma, say what you must."

"You should sleep in the barn, son. Maggie can stay here with me." Hastily, she added, "Just for this month. It would be best."

The blue graniteware pot that had been in his wife's hand hit the dirt floor. Maggie backed away. "I'm not carrying another man's child."

Savage anger shot through him. Todd bolted to his feet. "You question my bride's virtue?!" One strong yank had Margaret flush beside him.

Ma reached out her right hand, a beseeching action, but too late to matter. "It is not what I believe. But others—they do not know. Should you conceive immediately and have the baby early, there will forever be suspicions and whispers."

"Suspicions and whispers? What kinds of friends do you think we have?" Maggie's hushed voice shook. "Todd's fine brothers in Christ minded the farm and livestock in his absence! One toted and unpacked your things whilst you ailed hundreds of miles away. Three dropped everything and helped when we arrived in the dead of night.

"And loving Christian sisters!" Passion and pain vibrated in her voice. "I've longed for them for years. My dear friend Linette kept the hens for us, brought supper, and pitched in to do chores alongside of me as if we'd been bosom friends all our lives."

Maggie drew in a deep breath and shook her head. "Such neighbors wouldn't tell tales and gossip. Love thinks well of others, and the people here have poured out that very kind of godly love and friendship. You worry what they'd think? Down deep in my heart, I know they'd consider us blessed."

Ma didn't look Maggie in the eye and stammered, "Those are only some of the neighbors."

He stood strong by his woman and was proud. She'd been shocked at Ma's obscene implication, yet she'd been a lioness about defending others. Now he'd end this vile intrusion into their marriage. "We live by what is right and good and pure—not by the worrying about what someone might think." Sliding his arm from Maggie's shoulder down to her waist to squeeze her tight, Todd growled. "Our private life is no one else's business—including you, Ma. Our marriage bed will not be defiled."

His sweet bride deserved far better, and he pulled Maggie out of the house to tell her so. Twice, he opened his mouth to speak; both times, words failed him. The emotions shimmering in her tear-filled eyes tore at him, so he wound his arms about her, pulling her into the shelter of his very being. Between her jagged breaths, Todd felt her heart thundering against him. Clasping his bride to himself, he tilted her face up to his and rained kisses down upon her. When his lips finally met hers, the kiss they shared quickly grew in intensity. She started to pull away, but he wouldn't let her. A woman ought to know her husband wanted her happiness. For that matter, she ought to know he wanted her. God's blessing on their union released him to freely share his caring and desire.

Maggie trembled in his arms. Soft as could be, she reached up and tenderly touched his face. Immediately, he gentled his hold and lightened their kiss. At the same time she shrank a few inches. Realizing she'd been standing on tiptoe to relish those moments sent a jolt of joy through him. He almost drew her back, but she turned her face away.

For a minute, he stared down at her kissed-rosy lips and deep blush. Beautiful. She was beautiful. And his. Nothing and no one was going to come between them. Abruptly, he rasped, "I must work," and strode off. If he'd stood there even a breath more, he'd give in to the temptation of throwing her over his shoulder and carrying her up to the hayloft.

Maggie watched her husband walk away, his usual loose, lithe stride traded for a smoldering, wrath-filled stomp. Instantaneous and complete as his anger came, she knew full well he'd been offended by his mother's words. Aye, and that was the one glimmer of positive she saw in the whole mess.

Lord, your Word says love takes no notice when someone does you wrong. I can't help noticing my mother-in-law's dead set against me and won't stop at any chance to criticize or cast aspersions. What am I to do?

But Todd stood up for her. Or had he? Reviewing the exchange in her memory, Maggie realized he'd challenged Ma, but not declared his own faith in her purity. He'd said it was nobody's business!

And there she stood—cheeks aflame and hair tumbling about her shoulders. When had it come down? Just the memory of his large hand sliding up her nape and fingers parting to cup her head left her wanting to tilt the direction he'd held her for that masterful kiss. *I'm standing out here in broad daylight, acting like a trollop.*

What must Todd think? The verse went through her mind again. Love thinks well of the other.

But Todd doesn't love me.

Plucking her comb from the dust at her feet, Maggie couldn't quite keep her hand from shaking. She rose, twisted her hair into an orderly arrangement, and wished she could discipline her heart and mind as efficiently. *I already surrendered my heart . . . and my husband doesn't even know.*

He disappeared into the barn, and she made up her mind. Whatever it took, she'd get him to love her. Even adore her. Determination swelled within her. He walked back into sight and Maggie promised herself, *I'm going to have wedded bliss if it kills me.*

Starting back to the house, her thoughts shifted from Todd to Ma. "Wedded bliss." She snorted. "It won't kill me. That ornery woman will get to me first."

Ma locked eyes with her the minute she stepped over the threshold. "You know I'm right. A little self-control would stand you in good stead."

Self-control? After that wild kiss just now? "Todd is right. It's none of your affair, Ma."

Nose in the air, Ma huffed. "Such disrespect!"

"Aye, I'll agree with you there. Your disrespect of a sacred, God-blessed union."

"You don't know what you're getting yourself into. Mark my words—"

Maggie cut off her interfering talk. "The words I listen to are my husband's. Aye, I stand strong by my man and his opinion. We deserve privacy."

"If my speaking prevents you from making the worst decision of your lives—"

"Carrying my husband's wee bairn would thrill me to no end."

"Children are a blessing and a responsibility." Staring at her, Ma intoned, "It's because I want the best for Todd that I spoke." Her omission was glaring.

"Your son became my husband. What is best for him, or for me, is one and the same thing. In Genesis and thrice in the New Testament, the Holy Bible says, 'For this cause shall a man leave his father and his mother; and cleave unto his wife, and they twain shall become one flesh.' " She sucked in a deep breath. "Marriage is a sacred bond. The parson calls it holy matrimony for just cause, and you're trespassing. What you did last night and what you've said today are the same as you crawling right betwixt us in our bed."

Ma spluttered, but she couldn't deny that stark truth.

Gathering the dishes from the table, Maggie reckoned she may as well lay out the truth once and for all. "You're kin. Having you live with us is both right and necessary. With respect and love, there's not a reason in the world why we can't have us a happy home. Your son is the head of the home now." She resisted the urge to add, *and I am the mistress.* "As Todd's wife, it is my place to respect and honor him—and to demand that anyone under this roof does, as well."

Sounding querulous and yet wounded, Helga sighed, "Even as the head of a home, men need advice."

"Be that as it may, if and when Todd sees a need, it's his place to choose the advisor." Maggie picked up another cup, then slid all the dishes into the sudsy bucket. If only life's problems would wash away as easily as the dishes!

～☙～

Todd added H. J. Baker's fertilizer to the newly plowed land. He'd bought it back when he had a tiny bit of money before the wolves got to the colts—everyone said it was the best, and it better be. He barely had enough to take care of the fields, let alone the garden.

Carefully, he calculated half for the vegetables and a quarter for each of the other new fields. Feeding his family came before all else. If the garden thrived, Maggie would grow, can, pickle, and preserve food year-round. Fresh tasted best, of course, but something she did when she put up her fruits and vegetables made them taste almost fresh-picked. By the time things came ripe, they would have eaten what she brought. She could use the same jars and spare that expense, too. That, in and of itself, provided a reason she shouldn't barter away any of his jelly. Yes, the garden deserved most of the fertilizer. They'd have food, and almost as important—he'd save money.

Todd didn't think in terms of dollars. Not even in terms of quarters and dimes, though that would be nice. Conserving pennies and nickels by making do or doing without kept his head above water. Though Maggie didn't understand that when she asked for the outhouse door, she knew now.

Diligently, he distributed the fertilizer. Shoveling manure atop it took the rest of the morning. After lunch, he'd use the spring harrow.

Waving a dishcloth in the air, Maggie summoned him at midday. Splashing off for meals wasn't good enough for her; if a man couldn't dust off what ailed his clothes, then he had to change. A white flour-sack shirt awaited him, along with a bucket of warm water, a bar of soap, and a flour-sack towel.

Mouthwatering aromas wafted from the house. Scrubbed Sunday-clean, he hastened to the table and fought drooling during grace. "Good food." He attacked Maggie's green beans first. Until their garden produced, the cans she brought along would be a rare treat. "Finding the shirt and washbowl outside—it was nice."

"You wash up good, plowboy." Maggie set down her glass. "If you didn't guess, I'm going to civilize you."

"Civilize him?" Ma's voice sounded shrill as a penny whistle.

"Aye," Maggie sighed. "I know you spent eighteen long years a-trying. Probably made fair headway, but two years on his own, and Todd didn't even own a pair of forks."

"Only needed one," he muttered. He didn't mind. The interplay proved his wife and Ma were still speaking.

"Ma's doing mighty good with her fork."

"It would be easier if the gravy had more substance." Ma whispered, "Next time, add a little more flour."

Once he cleaned his plate, Todd said the after-meal prayer, then rose. "Ma, I'll put you to bed for your nap."

Patting his chest with her good hand, Ma said, "The sun's beating through the window, and I'll never be able to fall asleep. Put me in the other bed so I'm behind the curtain."

"No." Maggie blurted out the word.

His wife had a right to speak her mind about her bed. Their bed. But Ma needed her sleep and the cabin was bright.

"Our side of the cabin is far smaller. Ma has a nice, big slice of our home—partly because she says she can't bear to be closed in." Maggie grabbed a blanket. "I'll tack this over the window right quick."

"Since it is daytime, if we pull the quilt halfway, it'll be dark enough for me and I won't feel pinned in." Ma's voice broke. "I won't mess your bed. I won't!"

Todd grimaced. Because he'd hollered at Ma last night, she'd stayed utterly silent—and embarrassed herself as a result. She'd been completely wrong in her actions, but he never wanted her to feel she couldn't ask for help. And that was all she was doing now. Simply asking for a little help so she could rest comfortably. "Okay, Ma. Just this once." As he carried Ma over those few steps, Maggie whisked away her Rose of Sharon, then yanked back the remaining bedcovers. Wordlessly, she folded her prized quilt with jerky moves and set it atop the table. He'd triggered her temper, but it seemed so petty. It was just once.

Lying on the bed, Ma cooed, "Oh my. What a nice bed. So comfortable. It's far more padded than mine. Softer, too. And I spend so much time in bed."

"I'll see to stuffing your mattress with fresh hay or corn shuckings." Maggie came over, bearing the chamber pot.

Todd stood back, then yanked the bedding off Ma's mattress. He'd wanted to do something simple and nice for Ma, but she was turning it into more work for everyone. "I'll be in the barn."

Rose of Sharon quilt over her arms, Maggie marched out to the barn. Bristling, she came in through the side door and headed toward the stalls holding all of her junk. A solid clunk let him know she'd put their newlywed quilt back in the dowry chest. Boy, he'd tweaked her temper. Maggie didn't bother to glance his way.

"Took me four years to gather the feathers and make that mattress. Your ma's nudged up against it, nigh unto crawled into it betwixt us last night, and now she's lying in it. You told her our marriage bed is private, but quick as lightning, she found her way in it—and she's angling to keep it, too."

"For crying out loud! It's just for a nap. And it's just this once." Maggie tossed him a heated look.

"It's what we will share in the bed that is private—not the bed itself. Take pride that she appreciates the fine bed you made."

"We have work to do." Eyes trained on the barn floor, she sidled past him and out toward the field. She was in a rare temper, but from the sound of the crazy insult she yelled to Adam, raging emotions didn't keep her from work. Good thing. She was more than a mite touchy, and if she indulged in tantrums each time he crossed her, nothing would ever get done.

By the time Todd made it to the vegetable garden, his bride had directed the Belgians a quarter of the length of the field. A fine sight they were—all three of them. No sluggard, she. The labor ought to do her some good—he always found putting himself to a hard task allowed him to work out thoughts and feelings.

The woman's emotions were the best and worst part of her. She cared so tenderly, but her sentimentality about objects tied her in knots. He'd have to work on that flaw.

She'd said something about her roses a couple of times now—wanting a "bit o' land" for "the flowering legacy" left to her. Women set store by those things. After last night's debacle and now him giving in to Ma, she felt put upon. Yielding a little room for her flowers would smooth her ruffled feathers. Yes. That would be good. Intending to tell her so, he signaled her to halt at the row's end. Instead, he thundered, "Where are your gloves?"

"They were too large, so I traded them for a box of laboratory beakers."

"That was a useless trade."

"Not at all. I use the beakers every year."

A disbelieving half laugh burst from him. "You bother to barter for something and keep it when you use it only once a year? No wonder my barn overflows with your possessions."

Her jaw hardened. "Once we put my roses to bed, that'll trim out a dozen crates. Yah! Thou fly-covered—"

"Whoa!" He'd actually meant the command for Magpie, but the horses halted, too. "A dozen—"

"Aye. The Flinn twins gave fair warning of that freakish storm, so we'd gone out and buried the bushes. My uncles crated some for me to bring so I'd keep my legacy intact. Five to the crate was all that fit."

"A dozen crates. Five apiece. Sixty! Sixty rosebushes?" He shook his head. "Wife, you haven't the time or water to indulge in such an outlandish notion. Plant one crate. Two, even. But that's the limit."

Blanched, she fisted her hands. They and her voice shook. "You don't mean it."

"I do."

"My legacy!"

"A woman's legacy is the children she bears, not the flowers she plants."

Shaking her head, she near scorched him with her anger. "How am I to teach my daughters to make the soap and perfume and lo—"

"A dozen bushes will be more than sufficient."

"That's scarce enough to cover our own needs, what with me slathering it on your ma."

He'd make her see his point, and by doing so would help rid his barn of useless nonsense. "A dozen bushes will be sufficient for now. That is as it should be."

She stared at him. Hard. A deep breath raised her shoulders, and she let it out very slowly. "It's been a bad couple of days, and a lot has happened. Todd Valmer, I'm giving you the benefit of the doubt here and letting you reconsider."

"I know my mind, Margaret. You cannot waste that much of my land for flowers or keep unnecessary goods cluttering up my house or barn. If they are not used several times in a year, they need to go."

She folded her arms around her ribs. "That's what you really think?"

He nodded once, emphatically. "Barns are for horses and tools."

Tears filled her eyes. "Your mother was right."

She left him standing in the field, then walked over the furrows they'd plowed together and into the barn. Tears clouded her vision, but she kept blinking them away. Once she was out of sight, she could fall apart—but not in front of him. He'd guess how she felt about him if she showed him any vulnerability, and she'd already been a big enough fool.

First things first. She brought a buckboard. Rightfully it and these other things were hers. A crate of her beloved roses, then a second . . . She was lifting the third when Todd came in.

"I'll help you." He took it from her and lifted it into the buckboard. Then he loaded the fourth. And the fifth. "The timing is good. Tomorrow at church, you can give these to your new friends."

Dozens of empty glass bottles tinkled inside the next box she lifted. "Nay."

He took that box and loaded it, as well. In fact, he quite happily helped her lift her flower press, the crates of glycerin, and all else that went with her legacy. When she lifted another box, he stopped her. "Nein. This one, you keep. See? Two. You keep the two. And now there is already much gone from my barn." He had the unmitigated gall to look pleased.

Maggie edged past him and shoved it up beside the others. As she lifted the last one, Todd stopped her. "What do you think you're doing?"

"Correcting a terrible mistake."

Fourteen

His eyes narrowed. "What do you mean?"

"You have your barn. You have your house. And your land and water, too." She stressed, *"Yours."*

"Ja. Margaret—"

"That's right. Call me Margaret. Margaret *Rose*. That's who I truly am. You didn't bring me here to be your helpmeet. You brought me here to be your help. I won't stand for it." The books she brought along weighed a ton. Hefting the box took all her strength. Voice strained, she rasped, "And as soon as I rid your barn of my things, I'll be gone."

He ripped the box from her and cast it aside. "What has gotten into you?"

"Belated good sense."

A disbelieving laugh cracked from him. "Nothing you've said

makes sense. After the way we kissed this morning, you believe I have you here as a servant?" His eyes shot fire.

"Facts speak for themselves."

"They do." His bellowed agreement almost bowled her over. "You get riled and think to run away? Nonsense. All of it."

"Nonsense," she choked back, "is what you spouted to bring me here. I'm going back home where they love and respect me."

"This is your home!" He roared the words.

He hadn't said he loved and respected her. That lack thrashed her heart. She shook her head. "Nay. Minutes ago, you declared this is your barn, your land, your house. Not ours. Yours. What I hold dear matters not a whit." A strangled laugh curled in her throat. "Your mother told me why you married me. She played the hostess to those men yesternoon and answered to 'Mrs. Valmer,' making sure I knew my place. But most of all, she kept us apart last night."

Palm on his forehead, he heaved a mighty sigh. "I'm sorry about that. I'm mad, too. It won't happen again."

"No, it won't." Bitter laughter saved her from bursting into tears. "I'm not stupid enough to be in that situation again."

"Wife!"

Turning away, she looked for what other small things might fit in the wagon. "I'm not your wife, and I'm not going to be." For all the tumult inside, she strove to treat it as a business deal that soured. "You gave your word that my treasures and legacy were welcome. It was the one condition I had, and you agreed. You just stood out there and reneged on it all. I gave you a chance to reconsider, and you stood firm. Well, I know my mind, too. And of this I'm sure: You just cancelled our whole arrangement because I'll never destroy my legacy, and I don't deal with men I can't trust."

"Don't question my honor, Wife." His harsh whisper cracked through the air like a lash.

"My honor was questioned this morning. And I've not done a thing to deserve such treatment. You, on the other hand, just backed out on our deal."

"I stood in your defense." He looked downright indignant.

It was good to know he was certain about her—but she still wasn't so sure of him.

The vein in his temple beat forcefully, and the muscle in his cheek twitched. Hands on his hips and standing like a colossus, he should have scared her, but she didn't. He'd never hurt her physically, but Maggie feared if she stayed, he'd tear her heart to shreds. Already it was ragged.

"Six. You filled six boxes with your treasures. I agreed to those and understood there would be clothing and cooking stuff. I agreed to *that much* and your legacy thing. I've kept my word. You took advantage."

She let out an incredulous laugh that was precariously close to tears. "I didn't agree to only six boxes. If you made an assumption, I'm not to blame." She promised herself she'd say no more, but the next words escaped without her intention. "You promised to try to love me."

"I am trying to, Magpie, but you are the most trying woman I know!"

"You can stop trying now." She couldn't take everything she'd brought to Texas, but she'd take the most meaningful. Her barrel of china came next. "Loving someone ought not be a miserable burden. I'll leave the bribe that hooked you. With time, Adam will become obedient."

Todd grabbed her before she lifted the barrel. "With time, you will be obedient, too."

"Don't liken me to a horse!"

He looked stunned that she'd screamed. "You vowed—"

221

"You don't hold to your vows, but you expect me to? Nay. That is no marriage at all. I'm putting an end to this now." Embarrassment scorched a path across her face—joining the searing burn his rejection left in her heart. She had to speak the truth quickly, before her mortification and tears overtook her. "We've not yet become one in God's eyes, so the marriage can be annulled."

"Nein! No." He wrapped his arms about her, clutching her as closely as he had that morning when they kissed. "You are my *wife*. A bed I have made in the loft. A love nest for us—"

Her hands came up between them, and she tried to push away. "Possession is not love, nor is it honor." Until now, she'd managed to speak with a measure of control, but that last line quavered and ended in a sob.

"Shhh." Swaying side to side, he kept hold of her. "Shhhh."

Ma's ugly words shredded her memory. "You wanted the horses—keep them. The tools, too. So your barn will hold everything you want."

"Only if you are inside it. I want you. It is you I am keeping." Each time he said *you*, he squeezed tighter.

"You put your mother in our bed, and you offer me a bed of hay?" Hands flat on his chest, she tried to push away. Beneath the fabric of his shirt, she felt his solid chest and rapid heartbeat. He looped one arm more snugly around her waist, then slowly ironed the other hand up her spine and cupped her head to his shoulder. Maggie tried to pull away, but he didn't yield in the least. She tried to stop crying, too—but failed at it, as well.

"I am lousy with words." Fumbling to speak, he sounded . . . irritated? Anxious? "Shhh, my Maggie. Shhh." He rested his cheek on her head, still swaying her. "I could handle only one fork and one skillet. Even then, I did badly with the skillet. I am finding it was much easier than handling a woman."

How could he say something so ridiculous and disarm her? Why was she even listening to him?

He made that hushing sound again before sliding into a deep, wordless, monotone hum. Oddly, it helped. Her feelings were just as raw, but he'd soothed her enough to calm her weeping. "Margaret. You are mine, thus all that is mine is yours. Do you not see this?"

"You're only saying so because if you don't make concessions, I'll go. But I don't want to be the wife of a man who b-b-barters his values." Her throat started to clog up with tears again.

"You are not." His swift, confident reply gave odd reassurance. His large chest lifted as he shrugged. "Well . . . except for one thing. I loathe prune bread."

A small watery laugh shivered out of Maggie. "Me too."

"We make a good team."

Snapping to her senses, she pulled away. She couldn't let her emotions cancel out common sense. *That's what got me here in the first place.* "The truth stands. You agreed to my treasures. Those things matter to me, else I'd have left them behind. And my roses!"

"So . . . some roses—they would help this be like home? When you spoke your uncle's name earlier, your voice ached."

Todd confused her, and she confused herself even more by looking up into his steady eyes. "That's only part of it."

"You have so many feelings. Women—especially you—are a mystery. The wrong pronoun upset you. To me, it is understood: Whatever is mine is yours. Those were your words on the train when I discovered the money you tucked in my pocket."

She'd said it back then, and he'd agreed. At least that much was true. Letting out a choppy sigh, Maggie allowed him take her hands. Then she decided better and took back one.

He rubbed his callused thumb on the back of her hand. "What little we have, we hold in common."

Maggie gave him a fierce look. "I'm not sharing my specials and sparkles if you're going to use it as an excuse to get rid of them."

One eyebrow rose. "You brought more than treasures."

The man was daft if he thought a businesswoman would leave behind all her stock! Especially since money was an issue, she needed her trade goods. But he had a point. She hadn't specified that as part of the bargain any more than he specified a few paltry boxes.

"And so we did not have the same vision of what you would bring." He had the nerve to wink. "The proof of a man lies in what he does. Here is proof of my honor, Wife—Adam and Eve each have a stall. You brought them, and you will stay here with them."

"Then I'm bringing my bed out here."

Amusement filled his voice and eyes. "You—and your bed— will stay in *our* home. And out here, for a while, you will have two stalls for your things."

For getting off to such a terrible start, this might yet turn into a worthwhile negotiation. "What about my roses?"

"Roses require much care. To have fewer here and to share them with your friends—this is wiser. Margaret, you have too much to do."

She shook her head emphatically. "Roses aren't work. My legacy is a joy."

He dragged her over to some hay bales and sat down. Maggie's world tilted as he swept her into his lap. Ignoring her gasp, he ordered, "Explain these roses."

"The roses must be kept and given only to my daughter. They've been passed down for generations. The roses, the recipes, the process for making everything is taught from mother to daughter. Or, in my case, from aunt to niece. It's a sacred trust."

"A trust, ja—but such things are not sacred."

She struggled to express it clearly. "It's a bequest of loving devotion. There are stories for every generation of my roses. Stories of a woman who lost her husband and all four children in one day to smallpox and was courageous enough to love again and have a daughter. Of one who was stone-deaf and could still sing hymns with perfect pitch. Of Moira Andrea, who counted the legacy so important she stood before an army and demanded they ride around the roses instead of through them—and the commander of that army came back and wed her.

"Generations from now a little girl will hear the stories as she tends the roses. The traits of courage and faith and fortitude take root early in life. As she grows, the virtues illustrated and wisdom borne of experience will guide her through thorny times, and she'll blossom.

"My daughter will be told of my mama marrying a man who came to Carver Holler just to hear her people's stories, and my aunt Maude who couldn't have a daughter yet took me on as her very own." Her voice shook. "I'll be able to pass on their legacy, their lessons of virtue and strength and love. I'll do it because I won't give up my roses. They're not just mine. They're for all those who follow."

He met her gaze and held it. Held her. "For this reason, I would have you plant a fraction now. That much . . . It is right and fitting."

She closed her eyes. He didn't understand. Couldn't.

"There is much to do. The water . . . It will barely be enough to nourish such a large vegetable garden. Yielding to emotion when we have so many other considerations and needs would jeopardize everything, Maggie. We will plant three crates—one each in honor of your mother, aunt, and father. I cannot promise more today."

Three. Only three. Then again, he'd already shown good faith by going up from two. She couldn't agree to just three, but he'd proven he'd listen and be somewhat flexible.

"Rosebushes put down roots. You must, as well. You will stay by my side. And so all points of honor are kept." He brushed his lips against her temple. "Someday, stories will be told of you marrying me and bringing the roses to Texas."

The promise of that shimmered for a brief second, and then he spoiled it. "Margaret, there is only one Mrs. Valmer."

Sadly, she shook her head. "You said the proof of a man is in what he does. You've shown your mother favor over me."

Todd had the nerve to look baffled.

Then Maggie thought of how her uncles were oblivious to subtleties. The times Ma sniped at her and he'd been silent—had Todd been unaware? She could mention him seating Ma in her place . . . but that problem was solved. Deciding to name the most egregious and apparent, Maggie looked him in the eye. "You gave her the choice of where her bed went."

He grimaced. "I didn't realize it would crowd us. Since she is sickly, the window seemed like a reasonable request."

"Reasonable?" She gave him a long, meaningful look. "As Mee-Maw said, 'When a man says something is *reasonable*, any sane woman ought to run, screaming, in the opposite direction.' "

"You are sane, but you are not running in the opposite direction." He was back to looking like a rascal. "So from now on, you will decide what will go where in the house."

"Does that include me saying your mother is not napping in our bed?"

His chest rumbled as he groaned. "I will never do that again." He heaved a mammoth sigh. "Magpies have special nests, beautiful. To share a nest of a feather bed or of humble hay—either would be beautiful because you are my Magpie."

Reaching up to move a rakish lock of hair from his forehead, she whispered, "Don't be expecting me to believe you the next time you say you're lousy with words. I guess I'm staying, after all. I really do love—" she caught herself—"my roses."

"Some farmer I am. I will be growing sorghum, wheat, corn, vegetables—"

"And roses!" She slipped off his lap.

"And children."

Her cheeks suddenly went hot. "We'd better get to work."

"Ja."

Relief flooded her. They could cease this intimate talk and get back to the field. "We've wasted enough time."

He gave her a sweet kiss. "But we will waste no more." Suddenly he lifted her and carried her toward the ladder.

"Todd!"

Climbing up to the loft with her over his shoulder, he let loose a rumble of deep laughter.

A few seconds later, she gasped. "Oh, Todd! You brought Rose of Sharon up here."

⟶⟨❧⟩⟵

From the few bits of hay in Maggie's hair and the way Todd's hand lingered at her waist, Helga knew she'd better hurry up with transforming the magpie into a woman worthy of her son. Once Magpie became a mother, she'd be too busy to learn the proper way of doing anything. *My body might fail me, but my mind is sharp. I can share my wisdom. Just as Titus exhorts in the Bible, I can edify her in the ways of being a godly housekeeper.*

Housekeeper. She meant housewife. But Helga couldn't help drawing the parallels. Her grandparents had been well-to-do. They and Arletta employed servants—and every last one was Irish. Just the sound of Maggie's lilting voice brought back memories of maids drawing baths, making beds, cooking and cleaning. When Maggie sat by her sickbed, changing the linen, tending her and feeding everyone, it seemed right. Temporarily being cared for by an Irish-woman actually comforted Helga.

But by marrying Todd, the girl reached far above her station. Arletta was the exception that proved the rule: When differing classes married, the better invariably sacrificed his standards and standing. Her own mother went from planning soirées to planting onions. Todd deserved far more than a horse-swapping hillbilly. Whipping her into a good farmwife—that was going to be quite a trick.

Unable to read any longer, Helga regretted her inability to snatch up God's Word and go to a passage that would make her point. No doubt, that technique wouldn't leave Maggie quite as touchy.

She's sensitive. And possessive. Already that girl pushed me away from my place at the table. What's to keep her from pushing me right out the door? Todd wouldn't let her . . . or would he? At first, he didn't have feelings for the girl. Only with each passing hour, he seemed to become more enamored.

What will I do if she decides I must leave? That's what Arletta had done. Her own daughter kicked her out. Helga couldn't return—they weren't even there. And even if they were, she couldn't travel alone. She couldn't do anything alone. And she didn't have a penny to her name.

Every second brought another terrifying thought. *Should that hillbilly girl stop taking care of me and tell Todd to make me leave, I have nowhere. No one.*

Helga needed to become indispensable. Important. Training Todd's bride about what foods to cook, tutoring her on housekeeping, explaining etiquette . . . The list went on and on. If she did all of those things, they'd rely on her wisdom and appreciate how she still had a place in the family. On the train, Todd invited her to teach his bride whatever she lacked. Ja. Helga would simply remind him she was following his wishes.

They left her alone in the house again—Todd out to the fields, but Maggie quickly returned with Helga's sheets she'd had to launder. "Next time, if you do not let the sheets entirely dry, they're easier to iron," she informed Maggie.

"I've got to get out there and stir the beans, and your ticking's aired, so I'll stuff it. The sheets'll just have to go without ironing this once." Draping the halfway-folded sheets over the footboard, her daughter-in-law didn't seem in the least bit ashamed of such shoddy housekeeping. It wasn't all that long before Maggie coaxed the freshly stuffed mattress through the door and dumped it on the bed. She started making the bed with the wrinkled sheets.

"Wait! Use the sheets that were on it earlier."

"No, ma'am, I won't. Both of these sets here are yours, clean and sunshine fresh. You didn't sleep in the other sheets, so I'll fold them and put them away. Their corners are embroidered to match my newlywed quilt, and I aim to keep them special."

So I am not special. A wagon rattled outside, kicking up a gigantic dust cloud. "Take off your apron. It is rude to wear one when company comes calling."

Opening the door, Magpie called out, "Mr. Walker, don't trouble yourself to climb down from that there wagon." She promptly closed the door and shot a grin at Helga. "Ma, he's going to be slicker 'n snot on a glass doorknob. But he tried cheating us, and if he still wants the chair, I'm a-gonna teach him a lesson."

Sure enough, someone knocked. Maggie let out a beleaguered sigh as she opened the door. But for pete's sake! She still had on her apron.

"Mr. Walker, I don't have time to waste with someone who lies to me. I told you not to come down off that wagon."

"Now, Mrs. Valmer . . ."

Magpie being called Mrs. Valmer was a pitiful truth. But there she stood, dickering in the open doorway.

"Let him come inside, Magpie."

Maggie half turned. "I'd be crazier than a rabid raccoon if I let a liar into my house. A home is for kith and kin. This feller here's neither." She pivoted back, heaved another sigh, pulled her apron over her head, and instead agreed to go out and look in his wagon.

From the window, Helga saw Todd striding to the front. Good. He needed to handle this.

"Todd," Magpie singsonged, "Mr. Walker's come back. If you go take the door off the outhouse, it'll save you a trip to town." What did she think she was doing? Todd's appearance should have sent her scurrying back inside. Not fifteen minutes later, she sashayed into the house carrying a kerosene lamp and set it in the middle of the table. Instead of a clear hurricane glass, blowsy cabbage roses covered this porcelain one, and a big white globe that bore matching roses topped it.

Here was a simple problem Helga could correct without much fuss. "Do not use that. It will burn up far too much fuel. And that is a parlor fixture. Diners cannot see through it. Simple and plain is best on the table."

"I love my lamp." Running a fingertip over the piece like a child about to be deprived of a favorite toy, she pouted, "Old Mee-Maw Jehosheba painted it for me herself. Nothing in the world beats a rose for beauty."

"Other than you." Todd stood in the open doorway. "You started as a Rose and are now the gorgeous Mrs. Valmer."

"Todd! You scared the daylights out of me!" Maggie laughed instead of thanking him for the compliment. Did she have any manners whatsoever?

He tilted her face to his and gave her a lingering kiss. "My rose by her new name still smells as sweet. Sweeter." Todd's grin proved that the woman had bewitched him. He lifted the lid on a pot and sniffed. "Did you settle with Mr. Walker?"

"Sure and enough, we came to an understanding. He was very motivated because there's to be a poker tournament tonight. With the train strike, the lumberyard isn't due for a shipment until sometime next week, but he reckoned I wouldn't take an IOU for Ma's porch, so he brought eight bags of gravel, eight of sand—"

"Sand will blow away, and it is too hard to push my chair through gravel! I know I told you anything was better than dirt, son, but—"

"Hold your horses." Magpie grinned. "And I got us ten bags of Portland cement. We can have a nice, smooth porch and do the space in here by the window and under the table!"

Todd's jaw hardened. Helga waited for him to tell Magpie how much work it was to mix and pour cement. Or that he could provide for them. He said nothing, so she did. "There's nothing wrong with a dirt floor. My son built a fine house."

"Yes, Todd, the house is expertly fitted and chinked." Maggie stroked his arm. "But you didn't anticipate a wheelchair. How could you? It leaves ruts, and when Ma begins to walk, those ruts will be dangerous."

He looked at the floor. "So."

"On the morrow, I'll do the last section of the vegetable garden so you're free—"

Ma snapped, "It is the man who assigns the work. A wife listens and obeys."

"Tomorrow . . ." Todd paused. "Tomorrow is Sunday."

"Glory be! I lost track of the days. We'll actually be going to a real church! When the one back home burned down, it seemed silly to build one for so few of us." She turned and gave Todd a smack on the back of his hand for trying to pilfer food. "We've got just about an hour until we eat—or at least, that's what I planned on since we know John's a-coming over."

John? "It is proper that you call him Mr. Toomel," Ma advised. "A married woman must be above reproach."

"My man's invited his best friend to join us at the table whenever he has a hankering. When someone's that familiar, why, they're practically family."

Fresh-mouthed. The girl had no respect whatsoever. "Remember, though. Your uncles—you called them by their surnames." There. That would help her understand.

"On account of me being of a younger generation. The aged deserve respect. Just like Linette—she calls you Mrs. Crewel, but she calls me Maggie. Were I to start calling John 'Mr. Toomel,' he might figure I'd gotten fed up with him. We can't have that—especially since I already started calling the Van der Vort brothers Piet and Karl. We all just got the handles set that first night."

Todd left without weighing in on the matter, probably reluctant to correct his bride in front of her. So Helga held her silence. Soon her brash daughter-in-law would discover that she'd been given sage advice.

At the supper table, Maggie mused, "The porch—pouring it isn't really work, is it? To my way of thinking, it's an act of love."

Mr. Toomel wiped his face. "The little lady's got a point. Toss in Sunday supper, and I'll come help."

To Helga's mortification, news of Maggie's bartering had attracted a pair of men. Bad enough, she'd haggled like a penny peddler in the Ozarks. Helga thought the trade to rid them of that gambling chair wasn't ideal, but she'd agreed out of necessity. Folks were gossiping already if these men came to examine Maggie's goods. Not only did Magpie wrangle deals with the men, she'd invited them to supper. Now with the temptation of Sunday supper, they didn't wait a heartbeat to volunteer to help with the porch. Ma couldn't see Todd's face. Maggie's ridiculous lamp blocked her view. Her daughter-in-law was enticing all four men to break one of the Ten Commandments.

The tallest cleared his throat. "With you gone for such a spell, seems to me, the ox is in the ditch. May as well do the inside, too."

"Are you calling me an ox?" Helga blurted out the question, then prayed he wouldn't answer. If she didn't weigh so much, the wheelchair wouldn't be causing ruts to form.

"Now, Ma, it's nothing more than an old saying." Maggie plopped more beans on the men's plates as she continued, "What we're discussing brings to mind when all those brawny men cut a hole in the roof and lowered their crippled friend to Jesus."

"This thought gives me peace." Todd pounded the table, and everything on it jumped. "Tomorrow it will be done!"

"Just like in the Bible, Ma." Maggie couldn't silence her chatter even after she got her way. "Only Todd's friends aren't taking the house apart, they're fixin' to make it better."

But I'm the cripple, and I'm not going to be healed.

❧

Dumping brown sugar on his oatmeal, Todd mused, "You wear that cameo more than the others."

Maggie's hand went to her throat, and her fingertips grazed it. "It's my favorite because of the story behind it."

"All your nonsense about stories." Ma Crewel made a face.

"See the woman here?" Maggie asked. "She's supposed to be Rachel, watering her sheep. In Bible lands, a well is out-of-doors and ringed by stones. Often, a large stone covers it to hold in the water. When Jacob came close to remove the stone for Rachel, it was love at first sight, and this cameo is to commemorate the event. But the carver didn't understand how his well differed from those in the Holy Land. That's why there's a cabin and a tree here. It's a well house. The man who created this worked according to his understanding, yet it was wrong."

"Why keep something made in stupidity?" Ma muttered under her breath.

Maggie gazed at Todd, willing him to understand. Did he? And if he did, would he stand up for her and preserve the special meaning of her cameo, or would it be ruined by an old woman's bitterness?

"The man was not simply carving a beautiful woman to appeal to a sense of worldly vanity, Ma. He was honoring God's union of marriage."

"He got it wrong." Ma shot a meaningful look at Maggie.

"Ah, but that's why it means so much to me." Tracing the shell's delicate relief with her fingertip, Maggie closed her eyes for a moment, then opened them. "Like that carver, I work to be pleasing to the Lord, and still I fall short. I make mistakes."

"But that's what grace is about." Beneath the table, Todd slid his hand atop hers and squeezed. "If we could live a blameless life, Christ's sacrifice wouldn't have been necessary. I, too, fall short."

If only she could take this feeling and bottle it up! She'd fill every container she owned and relish every last whiff that hovered in the air. Todd just confessed what most strong men would not—at least, not in front of his bride and mother—that he made mistakes. *If I were to name this scent . . . Bliss? Contentment? Unity?*

Ma heaved a stretched-to-the-limits sigh. "If the cameo is so special, you should keep it for Sunday best, like today. But you wear it other days, too."

"Because it serves as a reminder that God looks past my flaws and at the intent of my heart. He takes me just as I am. I want to be like that to other people. Whenever I wear this cameo, that sentiment sings in my soul."

Todd tightened his grip on her hand. "When we married you took me as I was."

The mention of their wedding touched her. "Aye, I did. Even though you'll forever be 'stuck in pants,' as Jerlund said." A smile slid across her face. "The shawl I wore is Clan Rose's ancient hunting plaid. I still have a man's full-length plaid. You'd look very handsome in it, too."

"Too?" Ma inhaled sharply. "Who else wore it?"

"I meant that my husband looks handsome in trousers, but he'd also cut a fine figure in a kilt. I traded for it as a gift, but God took Daddy ere I gave it to him."

"God could have taken me, but He did not show me that mercy. Everyone knows He has stricken me. You read about it yesterday in Proverbs. 'Therefore shall his calamity come suddenly; suddenly shall he be broken without remedy.' " Ma burst into tears. "That is me. I will be like this for the rest of my life!"

Maggie hopped up and wrapped her arms about her mother-in-law. "Nay, Ma. Don't think that way. Why, look how much better you are—your face doesn't droop as much, and you hardly drool at all. And you're feeding yourself."

"Ja." Todd nodded once with zeal. "And Maggie gave you the cane. She expects you to walk again. Thus we will prepare a smooth way for you today."

"We don't know that." Ma's shoulders shuddered with her sobs.

"We have faith." Maggie mopped some of the tears away and added, "But faith without works is dead. Now that you've recovered from the train ride, I'm going to start cracking the whip and make you put all your efforts into getting back to where you used to be."

"I cannot."

"Nonsense!" Maggie tapped the wheel on Ma's chair. "I'm too stubborn to let you sit around here forever."

Ma sniffled. "I cannot go back. Arletta is gone."

Does Ma want to live with Arletta? Maggie's mind whirled. *Is that why Ma's been so unhappy?*

"Sis cannot have you. You are ours." Todd set down the Bible. "No one's going anywhere but church."

⁓⁂⁓

They barely made it to church on time. Linette had saved the end of her pew for them, and Maggie grabbed her hand. "I'm downright giddy. I'm in a real church with a regular parson, betwixt my man and my new friend. Someone's going to have to shush me on account of me hollering praises to God Almighty long after the worship's done."

The woman in front of them turned around. "The Bible says to praise without ceasing."

"Mrs. Bradle, this is my wife, Maggie, and my mother, Mrs. Crewel. Mrs. Bradle is the parson's wife."

"It's lovely to meet you. I want to speak with you right after the service." Mrs. Bradle turned back around as her husband gave the invocation.

Maggie's heart glowed with delight at each part of the service. Hearing other sopranos and altos surprised her. She'd forgotten what it sounded like for the upper register to blend in harmony with the tenors and basses. Then the reverend plumbed truths from God's Word.

After the benediction, Mrs. Bradle spun around. "The reverend and I would love to have you all come to supper."

"Ma'am, your invite is truly generous, but I'd have a trio of hungry bachelors back on Valmer Farm upset with the both of us."

"Next week, then?"

"We'd be honored, wouldn't we?"

"Ja," Ma said as Todd nodded.

Two men in the pew behind them leaned forward. "You're feeding bachelors?"

"No, she isn't." Linette shooed them away.

A blond woman with a little girl on her hip replaced Mrs. Bradle. "This here's Emmy-Lou and I'm Hope Stauffer. Our farms are catty-wampus. Cowhands and farmers hereabout are like stray hounds. Once you feed 'em, they'll be showin' up, stepping on your door every evening, howling for food."

On the train, Todd warned her Hope invariably mangled sayings. He hadn't mentioned how endearing it was. Maggie leaned forward and gave Emmy-Lou and Hope a hug together. "They're not stepping on my door unless they've sung for their supper. You're welcome anytime—music notwithstanding."

"I tried to come, but I had too many feet in the fire. We'll make plenty of time in the days to come. I'll visit just to hear your voice. My mama had that same musical lip."

Todd's hand enveloped hers. "My Margaret's lilt is beautiful, isn't it?"

"Children's giggles are music to me." Ma reached out and gently stroked a little girl's cheek.

No one seemed in a hurry to leave the churchyard. It wasn't fitting to conduct business, so Maggie merely confirmed that she bartered when asked. That question came up several times as she met more people.

A couple of men helped get Ma and the wheelchair into the wagon, then Todd lifted Maggie onto the bench and unhobbled Axe and Wrench. "Carver's Holler boasted a population of fourteen. There's twice that many women here in Gooding!"

"I promised you woman friends." Todd climbed up next to her.

"Aye, that you did—and right quick." *But how long will I have to wait for your love?*

His gaze mesmerized her. "It may take some time, but I keep all my promises."

Fifteen

Sand, gravel, and Portland cement were all shoveled together, then mixed with water into a thick, heavy mess. "We can start smoothing it out," John said.

They'd emptied the house and started at the back. Grandy, a cowboy from a nearby ranch, had done masonry in the past. He'd pointed out two bags of cement had no sand or gravel with which to mix it. A dried creek bed provided both, and his calculations assured Todd they could pour both a floor in the house and a porch.

Todd looked at the rippled, wet muck at the back quarter of the cabin and glanced around the place. Floor, walls, and roof—those were his to worry about. The stuff on them and in between—that was woman territory. Well, except for what went in the pot. Maggie made the food, but he still needed to put meat on the table. Yesterday he'd snared a brace of hares Maggie fried up for their

Sunday supper. Every last piece was gone . . . and he'd done his part in making it disappear.

Knowing Ma needed rest, Maggie had hauled Ma's mattress to the barn. With Ma bedded down, Maggie kept herself busy. Walking around the work, she carried a bucket and gave the men dippers of cool water and wiped Todd's face with a damp cloth. As if his bride could sense the heaviness in his heart, she gave him a searching look more than once. "Hot, hard work," he explained.

"A grand result. I'm proud of you—of all of you—for this." She wiped his face again and went to refill the water bucket.

"That's some wife you caught." Grandy gripped the handles of the wheelbarrow.

Todd nodded. A man didn't boast about enjoying what others didn't have. The facts spoke for themselves—a good meal, freshly plowed fields, and a comely wife. In his absence, these men had all witnessed the decline of his farm. A few things still weren't quite up to Todd's standards, but the additional plowed field for sorghum ought to yield some profit. Ought to—but might not. The talk he'd heard at church weighed heavy on his heart.

After they finished the job, Maggie gave each man a paper-wrapped stack of cookies. The first few times he'd tasted Maggie's cooking, Todd acted just as crazed as these men. He and Maggie traded an amused look as they rode off.

They caught up on the essential Sunday chores, and he tested the edge of the porch. "Not ready."

"Reckoned it wouldn't be. I got Ma set up so she'll keep warm and snug in the barn tonight." In the waning light, he noticed the hectic color filling Maggie's cheeks.

"We will use the loft."

She bobbed her head in acknowledgment. "Back home, when

they set a foundation, it was customary for the owners to each make a mark."

"The last part over on the side's still able to take an imprint." Todd refused the pencil-thick twig she extended to him. "It is your custom—you make the first mark."

"Nay. As head of the home, it's your right and responsibility to lead."

Such a silly waste of time. He'd already been on his knees all day. The last thing he wanted to do was hunker down and mess up a glass-smooth finish. Only she stood there, eyes full of stars. He chose a spot and scribed, *Maggie and Todd Valmer March 15, 1893*. Once he started, the idea grew. His bride's soft, pleased gasp made him glad he'd done this. After scripting, *God bless our home,* he passed the twig to her. "Now it is your turn."

Beneath his writing, she drew a cross, a shamrock, a heart, and a rose. Between them she wrote *FAITH, HOPE, LOVE, CARE*. He thought she was done and cupped her shoulders to help her up. "One last thing." Leaning forward, she tapped and smoothed something and doctored it with the twig. Popping up onto her tiptoes, she whispered in a playful lilt, " 'Beware the Ides of March.' " Todd peered down in the failing light. She'd doctored the five, turning it into a three. He'd gotten their wedding date wrong.

⟊

Todd held Maggie close all night. If only he could stop time to the moments they'd marked the cement and he'd kissed the laughter off her lips but left it in her eyes. She'd been so happy. But for how much longer? Todd ran his hand down her luxurious hair. At some point earlier, he'd unwoven her nighttime plait, wanting it as wild and free as she was. Only from what he'd heard at church, they weren't free at all. Every hour of labor used to represent a greater yield; this week the price of grain plummeted to the point that it cost almost exactly as much to grow it as he'd earn. In the months between now and harvest, if the price dipped more, his production costs would be greater than the crop brought in. He'd poured that floor in a home he couldn't afford. Etching into the cement *God bless our home* had been a plea for the Lord to let this home remain theirs. But the bank had every right to sell the house—the farm—everything because he'd mired them in debt.

Sometime before dawn, Maggie woke. Pushing a lock of hair from his forehead, she murmured, "Your mind is troubled."

For an instant, he considered denying it. Though Maggie knew of the debt and that finances were real tight, he longed to shield her from the looming disaster. But his wife deserved the truth, and it should come from him. "It is."

She shivered.

"Here." Todd wrapped his arms about her as if he'd keep her world together and hold back any ugliness. But God would have to intervene, because their situation was far beyond what Todd—or the two of them—could handle. "Wheat. A few years ago, it sold for $2.24 a bushel. Last year, I got $1.09. It was enough to cover the mortgage note and met the expenses, but that was all."

Tilting her head back, she smiled. "You had unusual bills because of your horses—Hammer tangled with the barbed wire and the wolves preyed on Nuts and Bolts."

"Don't you think I took that into account? It is beyond that. At church yesterday I heard the price for wheat now is at seventy-eight cents. Seventy-eight stinking cents."

"But the yield this year will be higher—oft you've said so. What with the sorghum we've added, it should be more than enough. Especially since we'll need so little in the way of provender. The garden will yield plenty. The farm's self-sufficient when it comes to feed. Aye, then there are buyers for my rose goods."

She believed they'd be fine; short of a miracle, he knew they'd be lucky to hold on. More than half of the farmers who came west failed. He just never imagined he might be among them. "You deserve to know."

Snuggling back down, she murmured, "We'll be fine. I have faith in you and in God."

Todd let her fall asleep, then inched away and went out to work in the dark. He couldn't ask the Lord to bless his farm if he didn't put in his full share of work—and more. Maggie believed in both of them, and he refused to disappoint her.

❧

"You moved the furniture back inside!" Maggie's delight made Todd glad he'd gotten up early. Then she went up on tiptoe, gave him a quick hug, and whispered, "Next Monday's my turn."

"Next Monday?"

She beamed as she nodded. "I'll have to come up with something mighty special to match such a fine token."

"What are you jabbering about?" Ma voiced his question—and he was glad of it. His wife wasn't making a speck of sense.

Brow wrinkling, Maggie asked, "Germans don't do love tokens? On Mondays?"

"Never heard of it. Not with the Dutch or Spanish or English, either." Todd watched her expression go from amazed to saddened to resolute.

"Then it's Carver's Holler tradition, and we'll keep it. Our duty is to keep the heritage, so I'll explain. Sunday is God's day. Monday is for the man and wife. They take turns every other week, giving the other a little surprise. Todd beat me to giving the first token of love. Look how he got the house all ready for us so bright and early, and his instincts led him to do it. He kept the tradition going right from the very beginning. Next Monday, it's my turn."

Ma looked around and announced, "We need curtains. Purple, I think."

"A love token is a surprise. It can come at any time of the day on Monday, too. I'll have curtains up before then. I set aside some special cloth the same color as Todd's eyes."

"That'll do." Ma studied the window. "This place needs some color."

"Just like you said, Todd. I'll handle the inside things whilst you see to the beasts. Ma, when it comes to horsemen, Todd's got them all beat. I've never seen a man as talented as Todd. He charmed Eve straight away, and stubborn as Adam is, he still obeys Todd's 'whoa!' There wasn't a man in all Carver's Holler who could do the same."

All of Maggie's cheerfulness and compliments made him suspicious. Ma and Arletta both resorted to flattery to get their own way. Todd figured Maggie had to be up to something. "Halting a horse is nothing."

"Balderdash! It's the most important order to train horses to obey. They can't cause havoc if you stand 'em still."

"Magpie's right, Son."

Tension seeped from his shoulders. Clearly, Ma seemed to have turned a corner. She'd been pleasant about Maggie's choice of curtains and now agreed with her. Hopefully now life would go as smoothly as her wheelchair glided across the new floor.

After breakfast, he read Proverbs 8, then decided, "We'll finish the vegetable field. Did you ask Hope Stauffer about planting?"

"Hope told the beautiful woman with a little baby girl that this week would be the best time."

Ma enthused, "That was the prettiest baby."

"Sydney," Todd provided. "That was Big Tim Creighton's wife, Sydney. The baby's name is Rose. While we work, we'll set aside space for the flower bed."

"Oh! Thankee!"

"So much else wants doing. A rose bed is the last thing you need to waste time on." Ma fumbled with her napkin. "Today is laundry day."

"Monday?" Maggie's voice held puzzlement. "Friday is laundry and Saturday is ironing so everything's fresh and clean for the Lord's Day."

"No one does it that way." Ma quoted, "Mondays, laundry, Tuesday, ironing . . ."

He left the women and went out to the barn. First Todd mucked, then lifted the enormous hames to fit around Eve's neck. He'd rather wear the heavy thing himself than carry around the knowledge that all this hard work wouldn't be enough.

The day did not go as expected, though. Nothing got done about Maggie's roses, but it was her own fault. After church, she'd shamelessly confirmed that she bartered and brought things with her. They weren't treasures, as she'd claimed. They were trade goods, and she'd barter or sell anything for the right price. He'd seen it happen several times today. She kept leaving the planting to escort curious folks into his barn and wrangle deals. Good thing he'd hauled all of their belongings back into the house this morning; otherwise, she might have traded it off. By this time next week, she ought to have dealt her way through half of her junk.

Over rabbit pie that night, he asked for the Lord to send rain soon. All the hard work in the world and a miraculous jump in the price for grains wouldn't matter if the crops withered for want of water.

The next morning, Maggie said the blessing and thanked God for the dew on the ground. The woman was a cockeyed optimist if she believed it would make any difference. Todd didn't tell her so. Faith the size of a mustard seed—that's what the Bible said it took for a miracle. No use crushing the very innocence that might move this mountain.

But if she were innocent in that aspect, she certainly bore a pack of guilt when it came to her conduct. Folks continued to stop by, and whether they came to be sociable or to trade didn't matter to Maggie. She treated each visit like a business opportunity. When asked what they needed, folks answered—but Todd felt it was out of politeness, not because they wanted to confess money was tight and they couldn't much afford anything extra. Knowing the state of their own finances, Maggie hadn't asked him for a thing. But now she was dealing with neighbors, plainly saying what she wanted or needed and procuring things he ought to have supplied.

His wife might as well wear his pants.

When Jakob and Hope Stauffer came late in the afternoon, it didn't take long for Maggie to snoop into what they might want. At least she deferred to him when it came to arranging for Adam and the Stauffers' mare to share time in a paddock. Jakob traded his second milk cow for several tools. They would return the calf when it was ready to be fattened, but receive half of the meat. Jakob frowned. "This is not fair. We still will owe you."

"Twaddle! Tryin' to cook without milk or butter's been a mite wearing." Magpie flashed a smile. "I'll be in a much better mood, so mayhap Todd will owe you his sanity, too."

Gritting his teeth, Todd let out an obligatory chuckle. He'd failed to supply one of the most basic necessities—a milk cow. And his wife's bartering just got them one and put meat on the table. It was one thing for her to grow their food; another issue entirely when her haggling made them look like beggars.

"I'll go on home with them and bring back the bossy and her calf."

His wife frowned at him. "Todd Valmer, you're spoiling things."

Maggie twined her arm around Hope's. "We're asking the Stauffers to supper. Jakob can go home and round up his sister, Annie, and her husband, Phineas, and little Emmy-Lou whilst Hope and I visit over the stove."

"I do not think we need a bossy. My wife is giving orders enough to—"

"Pay no mind to him," Maggie interrupted, thoroughly embarrassed by what he'd said. Surely he couldn't have meant it the way it sounded.

Hope's laughter filled the air. "Just the other day, Jakob told me I'm off my feed! That's what we get for marrying up with farmers."

It wasn't long before everyone from Stauffer Farm arrived with the cow and calf in tow. Hope showed Maggie how to bake biscuits in a Dutch oven by an open fire. Maggie brewed coffee and made succotash out there, too. With that well underway, giggles filled the cabin as they cut up the meat, breaded, and fried it. Legs, thighs, and breasts formed a gigantic mountain on Maggie's largest platter. Excitement surged through her. She'd already planned a nice supper, and this would be their first time having another family as guests.

"Look here!" Todd brought in a leaf for the table. "We'll all be able to eat together."

"And why wouldn't we?" Maggie asked as she helped him slip it into place.

"The table would be too crowded."

Hope leaned into her and whispered, "German farmers—well, not just German, but especially them, when it's harvest or when it is crowded, the men eat first. Then the women come second."

The thought appalled Maggie. Back home, a man gave his seat to a lady. They'd never do anything so rude. She muttered, "The way they eat? It's a wonder and a marvel the women have strength enough to set the table, let alone cook!"

Emmy-Lou slid the flowers she brought into a canning jar, and Annie let Ma hold her baby boy so she could set the table. By leaving the door open and scooting the table over, Todd sat on a chair straddling the threshold and they all crunched together at the table. Heart overflowing, Maggie declared, "I'm afraid to close my eyes for prayer, because when I open them, everything and everyone will be gone!"

"Not everyone," Ma said, "but most of the food would be missing."

Ma? Ma had a sense of humor? Maggie tried not to gape. As soon as the prayer ended, a flurry of activity began.

Sitting on her mama's lap, Emmy-Lou sniffed appreciatively. "Do I get the wing?"

"Have a leg. Here you go." Hope served them and passed the platter.

Ma decided, "You can give me the wing."

"A leg will be easy to eat." Maggie stuck a fork in a juicy piece. "Here you are."

"I said I'd take a wing."

"The leg is handy, Ma." Todd reached over and steadied the platter.

Emmy-Lou got the giggles. "That's funny. Legs being handy."

Everyone set to eating, and Ma made short work of her piece. "This tastes like my recipe."

"Delicious," Jakob declared, helping himself to his third piece.

Busy holding her baby, Johnny, Annie leaned over and took a bite Phineas held out. "Mmm." The graveyard of bones on Phineas's plate declared he agreed.

Todd lost his sour look and actually winked at her! This was her first time truly entertaining, and Todd kept the conversation lively. He even fetched the coffeepot! Working together—they did that well, whether at work or play.

"It's yummy." Emmy-Lou's face lit up. "Who gets the gizzard?"

"There aren't any," Maggie nudged the jam toward her husband.

"Hope!" Phineas teased. "Did you sneak the gizzards?"

"Of course she didn't. The doctor told her to eat liver." Jakob's chest swelled. "For the baby."

Pink rushed to Hope's cheeks. "Well, you just let the chicken out of the bag!"

"It's not chicken. It's cat," Ma corrected.

Hope looked puzzled. "Ain't cat, neither. It's whistle pig. Didn't all y'all notice all the legs and no wings?"

"Are you feeling okay?" Maggie asked her new friend, giddy about the happy news of a baby. Ma started choking, and Maggie patted her on the back and kept talking to Hope. "You look chipper as a—"

"Whistle pig?" Todd dropped the picked-clean bone onto his plate to join the pile already there. His voice sounded a little strange. "*What* is whistle pig?"

"My daddy called 'em woodchucks." Maggie held a water glass to Ma's mouth.

"I mostly hear them called groundhog," Jakob added as he helped himself to another biscuit. "Good eating."

Not wanting Ma to feel left out of the praise, Maggie said, "Since it tastes like your recipe, Ma, we'll have to compare—"

Ma started moaning. "I don't feel so good. I need to lie down."

"Her tummy's full because she ate lots," Emmy-Lou said. "I do that sometimes, too."

Phineas snickered behind his napkin.

Todd repeated, "Groundhog."

"Not many people fix it up so juicy and tender." Hope wiped her little girl's fingers. "Your bride did quite a job of it."

"She sure did." Todd's agreement sounded less than sincere.

"Maggie," Annie handed the baby to Phineas. "I'll help you get Mrs. Crewel to bed. All of a sudden, she's looking poorly."

Understanding that Ma was frail, the guests took their leave quickly. Good thing, too. Ma got sick to her stomach. Maggie cleaned her up and tucked her in. Most men didn't handle sickness well, so she figured Todd hiked off to the barn for a while. Dishes washed and put back on the shelf, the table scrubbed, and a bit of rose lotion on her hands, Maggie stepped outside for some fresh air.

Her husband sat on the ground, leaning against the cabin. "The night we arrived in Carver's Holler, one of your uncles told me. But I didn't understand."

Stooping down, Maggie worried, "What? What's wrong?"

"He said you could fix anything and make it taste good."

Relief flooded her. She plopped down beside him. "You don't have to thank me, Todd."

"Thank you? Thank you?" he roared. "You fed our guests groundhog!"

She let out a big sigh. "From the way you gobbled it up, I reckoned it was one of your favorites. You don't have to worry that we'll run out. I already have a couple more soaking in brine." Snuggling up against him, she added, "Cooking with Hope was a lot of fun. We traded a few recipes."

⌒⟅⌒

Todd poked at the bowl the next day and gave Maggie a suspicious look. "Grits?"

"Aye. What with us having a cow now, there'll be butter tomorrow."

"*Hmmpf.*" It looked safe enough. Tasted okay, too—but so had the whistle pig. Maggie had fed them vermin. God bless Jakob and Phineas, they were true friends for not hurting his Maggie's feelings and spitting out what they'd had in their mouths.

Todd might have thought it was a joke, but Hope Stauffer didn't have a drop of guile or ability to put up a pretense. She'd cooked right alongside his wife, making it seem like everyone ate . . . it. He'd had nightmares about what Maggie would make next.

"Baked some prune bread, special just for Ma."

Normally, he'd laugh. Ma hated prune bread, too—but this was no time to mention that. Last night he hadn't had the words to explain the error of Maggie's ways. But he needed to set her straight.

Still looking peaked, Ma asked him to put her back to bed. She whispered, "We'll take turns asking. My new policy is 'Look before you leap and ask before you eat.' "

"What about, 'What you don't know can't hurt you'?"

"What you eat can," Ma fired back.

Maggie's shadow fell over the bed. "Is there a problem?"

Todd grimaced, but Ma hopped right in. "Your cooking. What possessed you to cook hedgehog?"

"I didn't. Hedgehogs don't live in America. Porkypines do, though. Haven't ever cooked one, but I hear it's mighty toothsome. Mayhap I can trade for some. Or even armadillo."

Immediately, Todd ruled out those dishes. "Armadillo shell is too troublesome and porcupine has nasty quills."

"Nothing's too good for my family." Maggie swished her hand in the air. "Don't trouble yourself over the work. One meat's about as easy to cook as the other."

"But," Ma coughed, "they are not as easy to eat."

"Ma," Maggie stroked her cheek. "Chopping it up for you is no bother. I'm proud of your good appetite."

"My appetite suddenly plunged."

"We've got a few days to perk you up. Remember—on Sunday we're a-going to eat at Parson and Mrs. Bradle's!"

"By Sunday afternoon I'll be ravenous." Ma glowered at Maggie. "Mrs. Bradle serves decent food. You shamed us all last night."

"Shamed!" His wife looked every bit as astonished and hurt as she sounded. "You said supper was good—just like your own recipe!"

"People don't eat rodents." Todd tried to keep his voice soothing, yet firm.

"Squirrel! Squirrel's fine eating and they're rodents, too. God provides a bounty—possum, beaver, frog legs . . . Waste not, want not."

"I don't want any of that," Ma stated baldly.

"Then why did you have a recipe? We thank God for our daily bread—"

Grabbing that lifeline, Todd declared, "Bread sounds great!"

Fierce as any badger she'd refuse to eat, Ma stood her ground. "I thought it was chicken."

"Then what's a-wrong? If you can't tell the difference, then there's no reason to fuss. Our neighbors knew what they were tucking away, and—"

"Good manners," Todd explained.

"Hogwash!" Maggie's confusion had slid into frustration—but

temper now fired that exclamation. "Hope said she and Annie just baked them up a tasty whistle-pig casserole."

"Low-class, white trash—"

"*Silence!*" He grabbed Maggie as she recoiled from Ma's ugly words. "Forgive Ma. She's still sickly and spoke too harshly."

Precisely, carefully, Maggie twisted her hand and released herself. Her voice shook. "About the food I cook? Or about how she'd attacked our neighbors' dignity? Or just about how she's demeaning me? Because I want to know exactly what harshness I'm to overlook.

"And you, Husband. You believe good manners led my sweet friend to cook alongside me and her family to eat with gusto when they could have just nibbled?" Aching hurt tainted her voice. "You've condemned me for having no manners—or bad ones."

"Don't put words in my mouth!"

"She doesn't have to. She already filled your mouth with—"

Todd bit out, "Ma! That's enough!"

"No, it wasn't. It was just right." Maggie gave him a brittle smile. Her skin was normally fair as could be, but it had gone stark white. Her eyes darkened to indigo, and tears sheened them. "A woman deserves to know where she stands. I've just been soundly put in my place."

"Your place is beside me, as my wife." He thought to reach for her hand, but she'd crossed her arms and was hugging herself. The best thing he could think of was to move and stand by her and slide his arm about her shoulders. "This is simply a misunderstanding. Our ways of living are different. You are a barterer. You know it is possible to come to an agreement."

"That's where you're wrong. I don't barter when there's no respect." Leaning away from him, she oh so carefully unlaced Ma's boots and removed them. Then she rolled up a towel and tucked it beside Ma's hip and thigh so her weak leg wouldn't rotate out and make her ache. Maggie pulled up a quilt, set the bell within Ma's reach, and wordlessly slid the breakfast dishes into the washtub.

"Yesterday was Proverbs nine. 'She has killed her beasts and mingled her wine, she hath also furnished her table.' And that's what I did." She left the cabin and shut the door very quietly behind herself.

"She cannot pick and choose verses. The same chapter says " 'A foolish woman is clamorous: she is simple and knows nothing.' Ach! What a disgrace that girl is!"

Looking at his mother, Todd's heart sank even further—if that were possible. "Margaret is knowledgeable and she followed the Word. *She* was not clamorous. The disgrace is not on her. My wife deserves respect, not insults. This will not happen again."

"I'm not eating hedgehog again, either!"

"Groundhog, Ma. And if my wife fixes it, we will eat it," There. That settled the issue—or at least a very small part of it. He still had to deal with Margaret.

"You'll still read the Bible to me." Ma sounded tearful. "Just as your father did. Ja? That will not change, too, will it?"

For a second, he paused. When upset, Maggie seemed to like a little time alone. He owed her that, and there was no better place to go for guidance than the Bible. He lifted the black leather book. " 'Hatred stirreth up strifes; but love covereth all sins.' " He paused for that verse to sink in, then continued. The last verse hit hard. " 'The lips of the righteous know what is acceptable; but the mouth of the wicked speaketh forwardness.' "

"See! It is our duty to tell her what is acceptable." Ma snuggled down.

"Acceptable by whose measure? Everyone else liked it. You speak of shame—but the shame was our ingratitude and your contempt. Asking her to forgive you because you are still weak—it was wrong of me. Your body is afflicted, but your mind is sharp. Ja, and your tongue is sharper still."

Ma snorted. "Sharp tongue? She bosses me and prods and nags. The way you twist a pretzel—that is what she does to me. This way and that."

Livid, Todd grabbed her footboard. "All for your welfare. She cares for you, and you complain. You embarrassed yourself and me, calling her a vile name and complaining. There will be no hatred or stirring up strife." He paused before speaking slowly and precisely. "It will not happen again."

Todd strode outside, determined to set matters straight. Maggie wasn't in the garden. He walked into the barn. Something dropped down on him, and everything went dark.

Sixteen

Maggie froze at the deep bellow. She hadn't known Todd was below. Peeping over the edge of the loft, she spied Todd's arms windmilling as he fought his way free of the quilts she'd dropped. He tilted his head back and spotted her. He looked hostile as a bull in midcharge.

"I'd apologize, but I don't have any manners." The second the words left her mouth, she jerked back out of sight. It would be wrong to laugh. But she did, and she made no attempt to muffle her reaction. Either she'd laugh or she'd weep, and Todd Valmer wasn't going to see her cry. Nay, he'd not. She'd kept her tears from falling while in the house, and that counted as a miracle. Only now she'd had a few moments to think matters through, and anger replaced the hurt. Resilience. Uncle Bo taught her well.

"It tasted good, Margaret." Todd's deep voice carried to her. "The groundhog. I'll eat it again, and so will Ma."

Todd expected her to come down the ladder. Maggie could hear him waiting beside it. But he'd miscalculated. Arms stuck out to balance herself, she walked almost all the way across a beam. As the space narrowed, she sat and straddled the beam, scoot-hopped another couple of yards, and bit her lip.

"Margaret, come on down." The coaxing tone of his voice brought back memories she quelled at once.

Adam shuffled below. From the way he snuffled, he smelled her, and that gave her a burst of confidence. Maggie held the beam and slid her leg over, then barely kept from losing her grip as her body swung with the force of a wild pendulum. Pointing her toes to add a few more inches' reach, she searched in vain for Adam's form beneath her. Though not afraid of heights, Maggie didn't want to look down. She kept craning her neck, trying to see the base of the loft's ladder.

Shuffling sounds below restored her confidence. Even if she had to drop a yard or so, Adam's back could bear the brunt of her fall. Dismay washed over her when she dipped her head, for Adam moved. *The minute I depend on him, he strands me.* "Komst," she whispered to the horse.

He looked up at her and shook his mane. At that moment, Maggie spied it—the rope about his neck. It was tied to a post that kept him just far enough away from her.

Dangling from the side of a beam, her only choice was to inch sideways and land in a pile of hay. Whatever it took, she'd do it to get out of this barn and be alone.

Todd was talking, but she couldn't make out exactly what he said. That didn't much matter since he'd already said plenty enough.

She was entirely focused on slowly moving along the beam. But, oh, how her arms ached.

"Bullheaded pain in the neck!" Todd's voice sounded near. "Wife, are you going to hang around there all day, or are you going to see sense?"

"One of the two of us sees things clear as can be, and it's not you!" An enraged sound curled in her chest when Maggie spied him again. Todd sat astride Adam—bareback, no less—and the traitorous stallion followed every little nudge and nuance Todd gave until they were right below her.

"We're waiting for you."

Maggie refused to give in and drop into that oaf's arms. "Go away." Drawing up her knees, she punctuated her rejection. Only her hands couldn't take it much longer.

An impatient growl sounded a mere breath before a firm yank ripped half the hem out of her skirt. "Wife!" A second jerk made her fingers lose purchase, and she landed in Todd's arms. "Are you trying to kill yourself?"

"No." She shoved a lock of hair out of her face. "I was trying to kill you. I had it all figured out and was going to poison your dinner today. Groundhog was on the menu, but now I'll have to come up with another plot."

Todd threw back his head, and his deep rumbles of laughter almost knocked her from his lap. "And just to think I came in here and told you we'd eat it. I've spoiled your plan." Fast as lightning, his expression changed. Cupping her cheek, he said, "It's not the only thing that's spoiled around here."

She knocked his hand away and tried to slide free. "I'm not spoiled."

Gripping her apron bow to hold her in place, he growled. "I

never said you were. Stop looking for reasons to be offended. Are you always this touchy?"

"No." She retreated into sarcasm to hide her hurt. "Low-class, white trash hillbillies develop thick hides from totin' rifles and eatin' skunk. Let me tell you, farmer man, skunk roast with collard greens and corn pone is the best Christmas Eve supper you'll ever have."

"Collard greens are sweetest in winter. Everyone likes corn pone." To her irritation, he tried to snuggle her close. "But no one eats skunk."

Giving him a scathing look, she pushed one arm away and said, "I have. Twice!" She jabbed her elbow between his ribs and slid free.

Quick as a whip, Todd was on his feet behind her. He grabbed her hand so they both stroked Adam together . . . whether she wanted to or not. "Adam deserves reassurance and praise."

"Then go ahead and give it to him. You've won *his* obedience and devotion."

"Margaret, Margaret." His whisper rumbled against her temple. "You are a better woman than that. Come." He lifted the rope tied across Adam's stall and ducked beneath it. With his arm around her waist, she found herself dragged over to a barrel. "Sit here. We need to talk."

"To my reckoning, there's been more than enough talk."

"What happened. It was wrong—"

"You already told me that. I've never seen anyone kick up such a ruckus over anything this piddly. Then again, there are other things I'd never seen before—like folks saying two prayers over the same meal. Or a woman bein' dead set on what day another does the laundry. Sure and certain as I live and breathe, no one's ever eaten my food only to turn and revile it."

She couldn't sit still any longer. Hopping to her feet, hands fisted, she nearly got a crick in her neck, looking up at the man she'd pledged to love. If only it were just a crick in her neck and not in her heart, too. "Up till then, what all got said hurt, but sometimes problems gotta get aired. Aye, that's the way it is, and I accept that."

"So." He managed a lopsided smile and reached for her hands. "I knew you would see it thus. It was a misunderstanding."

"There's a misunderstanding, all right." She wouldn't let him touch her. "Uncle Bo told me that love means seeing someone through God's eyes—not trying to mold them to suit our wants."

"That is very wise."

"And I've been incredibly foolish because I've confused respect and acceptance. When you proposed, you claimed to respect me. As it turns out, you respect my ability to work, but unless I learn your ways and fix your foods and change into your idea of what a wife is, I'm not acceptable. You're ashamed of me. Well, the joke is on you, because you're stuck with me as your wife." She turned away. They didn't have a milking stool yet, but her dress was ruined anyway. Maggie snatched up a pail, dashed over to the cow, and squatted down. But the steady *shhhh-shhh-shhhh* of milk streaming into the bucket and the repetitive action failed to calm her. Even that simple pleasure was gone.

Todd crowded by her, down on one knee as if he were proposing all over again. Only he gently tugged her back and seated her on his thigh. "If the result of a joke is having you as my wife, then I'll be a very happy man."

"No, you won't. You're going to eat groundhog every day for the rest of your sorry life."

"I hope you know a lot of ways to cook it." He heaved a sigh. "Enough of the nonsense. These problems must be solved. Mountain ways are different than German ways. The issues themselves are small."

"Groundhogs aren't all that small. I—"

His fingers pressed against her mouth for just an instant. "I'll gladly eat it again. Surprises sometimes are shocking. And the differences come as a surprise, thus we were shocked. Just as you were about Monday laundry. But our home will be richer for having more knowledge and ways. In the first months, things are bound to come up. We will pray before and after we eat the groundhog, and our family will be happy."

"Ma's never happy."

"I have spoken to her." His voice took on a harsh edge. "As I said, what happened was wrong."

Ohhh. He wasn't saying it was my fault.

"That was one issue, but there is another. I am proud to have you as my wife. I told you, there is no other woman I ever considered to be the mother of my children. But we talk differently. It makes for misunderstandings. For me to say the Stauffers had good manners, you took that to mean I consider you rude. It is not so. I think highly of you. To say that I am grateful or that you are beautiful . . . these things are facts—yet I give them no voice. It makes them no less true.

"The week in the holler, I heard more praise given from one person to another than in all my life, combined. Among you, the words were of encouragement. In my culture it is assumed that all will do their best, and to praise is to make them haughty."

His voice rang with sincerity, and his words held true. But it saddened her to think there had been such a lack of everyday, ordinary appreciation. It sweetened life.

"Two ways of life. They have caused a misunderstanding in how we see the situation, not in how we see one another. My nature is to talk of the weather and crops and animals. Consider this a measure of my regard for you: Twice, now, we have had long, important conversations. And they were not about weather and crops."

She couldn't give in. Not yet. "It was about animals. Ground-hogs."

"See? Even trying, I fell short."

"I am far different from your horses—you cannot speak soft words and stroke my back a few moments and win my trust." He said to withhold a truth was the same as lying. In the holler, she'd have let the conversation end now. But this wasn't the holler, and the time for stark truths ticked with the same measure as her aching heartbeat. Maggie struggled to find the words and failed, so she blurted out, "I don't like you right now. Not one bit. You'd best know that my heart, mind, and soul aren't always in accord. My soul tells me to forgive, but my heart aches, and my mind will always remember."

"For you to forgive is all I ask. It's enough."

"Enough for you. You are absolved, and yet I—" Scooting off his leg and kneeling in the hay, she leaned into the cow. Tears poured down and robbed her of the ability to say anything more.

He remained so close, Maggie knew when he breathed. After a long stretch, when she finished the milking, he set aside the milk pail and helped her up. *I'm an idiot. Why did I take his hand?* She tried to separate, but he didn't turn loose.

"Margaret, I'm sorry." He used his free hand to wipe her cheeks. "My heart aches to see you thus. I will always remember this day, too. Guilt does that—not just that what I did was wrong, but even more, that you are the one who will bear the wounds."

⤙⤚

He and Ma sat down to sauerkraut and ham for supper. Maggie fried up the groundhog, but the only pieces on the table were on her plate. It smelled great. Savory steam wended up from it. Todd knew exactly how it would taste, too. After he prayed, he asked, "Where's mine?"

"Your supper is fine," Ma said.

"It is fine. But that is excellent. Margaret, you fried up more than two measly pieces."

She scooped up a bit of leftover succotash. "You only use Margaret when you're mad or want something. Which is it this time? Or is it both?"

"He's not mad at you anymore." Ma set down her fork. "Maggie, could I trouble you for a little honey, please?" As soon as Maggie's back was turned, Ma whispered hotly, "Don't be stupid. Eat what she put in front of you."

"Too bad we didn't follow that advice yesterday." Suddenly, an idea struck. Todd cut into his ham. "This is good ham, Margaret."

She let out a small, disdainful huff.

As Maggie returned from the shelf where she kept the honey, Todd made a show of lifting half of his ham and putting it on her plate. Fast as lightning, he grabbed one of the fried pieces from her plate. She smacked his hand. He had trouble trying to look innocent and hurt. The look on her face was priceless.

"What's mine is yours and what's yours is mine, Wife."

Maggie made a show of sitting down and picking up the ham. Dropping it on his plate, she said, "You got it wrong."

"I did not!"

"Sure and certain, you did." Calm as could be, she speared the other half and plopped it on her plate. "*That* half was by sauerkraut. You took the bigger piece off my plate. A fair trade is for me to get the better half of the ham."

"You did."

A funny sound bubbled out of Ma. "He's right. Sauerkraut is—"

Holding up a hand, Maggie silenced her. "Excuse me, Ma, but Todd and I are having our first fight, and I aim to win it."

"First?" Had he heard her right?

She arched a brow. "First. It's a new beginning. But I'm taking a stand here and now: Keep your sauerkraut to yourself."

Borrowing the word he'd seen her use at the end of her bargains, he felt joy clear down to his toes. "Deal!"

A new beginning. They'd cleared the air, and he'd made sure to straighten out Ma's attitude.

❧

Over the next few days, Maggie's smile wobbled a little now and then, but now that Ma decided to be her better self, things would be far better. To top it all off, he could now drive Adam and Eve.

At breakfast Saturday, Maggie mentioned, "I brought some of Mee-Maw Jehosheba's tomato seeds with me, and I promised to share with Hope and Annie. Remind me to take them tomorrow."

"There are better reasons to go to church." Ma scooped up a bite.

"Yes, ma'am. Like the beautiful music and the prayers and listening to Parson Bradle read the Word of God and expound upon it. I'd saddle up a jackrabbit and ride it to get to church—even if we hadn't gotten an invite to Sunday supper."

Unexpectedly, Hope's giggle came through the open door. "I'd sit alongside the road to watch!"

"You wouldn't just watch. You'd cheer for me." Maggie embraced her friend, who had come to switch her Dominiques for other hens that laid white eggs instead of brown. "How are you feeling? Have you been drinking enough milk? If you're craving something, I'll get it for you."

Maggie's heart and arms stretched wide open to gather and hold her woman friends. They all took a shine to her, too. Linette stopped by every morning on her way to work and again on the way home. Leena Patterson dropped by on Thursday, wanting a particular feed sack so she could sew something. Maggie hadn't yet located one, but Todd felt positive she'd come up with one—maybe even two.

With the farm hanging by a thread, he couldn't ignore that some of her bartering was advantageous. But in truth, he needed those stalls. Adam and Eve deserved more space, and before long, the colts would need stalls of their own. A barn was for animals—not an array of oddities and essentials. Certainly not for providing a woman with space to conduct a business of her own—especially when she obtained the necessities her husband ought to provide. Running horses or bartering—the barn was large enough for only one enterprise.

"Todd?" Maggie gave him a quizzical look.

"Huh?"

"I asked if you're still hungry. Normally, you're hotfooting your way to the barn."

He took one last swig of coffee. "Never ask if I'm still hungry. I have a hollow leg."

Her features dimmed. "Paw-Paw jokes about that."

Intentionally misunderstanding her, he nodded. "Paw-Paw did tease me about it. He asked if my head was hollow, too." Heading toward the door, he told Ma, "*Donnerwetter*. Stay inside."

"Thunder weather? It's going to rain?" Maggie rushed back to the door. She frowned. "It's too far away."

"Wouldn't matter. It's a dry storm. Clouds are wrong." Todd set to his chores, wishing he'd been wrong. Nothing would make him happier than a good soaking rain.

☙❧

After church the next day, the men milled about and discussed the weather. Underlying it all was an ominous threat. Ranchers and farmers alike worried that they'd lose everything. Todd watched the bank manager hasten home. He attended worship, but he didn't want to mix business with church. Too many of the congregation owed money and couldn't meet their obligations.

"I don't envy his position," Pastor Bradle said at lunch. "He can't loan to men who desperately need funds because they're so close to the edge and the risk is too great. One minute of gratitude when he first makes the loan, then men resent him for years to come. I'm afraid it's going to get worse."

Maggie set down her fork. "We'll be sure to invite him out to supper."

"At that rate, you'll be inviting a handful of other people, too," Big Tim Creighton said. He, Sydney, and baby Rose were also the Bradles's guests. "Places like Clark's Mercantile have extended credit and all sorts of grace periods. They own the feed and lumber and are having to turn away requests."

"Well, I have a request." Sydney shifted the baby to her other arm. "Tim said the carriage feels wrong. I'm afraid to ride home in it until the Van der Vorts check it. Could you give us a lift as far as your place?"

"If, perchance, we hopped off at our place and let you drive our buckboard on over to your ranch, could Ma hold the baby? I'll tie my plaid to form a pocket that'll keep Rosie safe and warm against Ma." Maggie waggled her brows. "And I'll have you know 'tis the proper clan for your daughter: Clan Rose!"

Tim and Sydney exchanged an uncertain look. Todd didn't want them put on the spot. He cleared his throat. "That plaid is mighty soft, too."

Not long thereafter Maggie and Sydney sat on either side of Ma's chair in the back of the buckboard. Pocketed in the Rose plaid, baby

Rose slept the whole way home. Ma curled her right arm around her and beamed.

While the women chatted, Todd took off his hat and wiped his brow. "Hotter than ever out here."

"Drier, too." Big Tim grimaced. "My catch basin is bone-dry and my pond is down to half of what it ought to be. I went through this once before, and we had beef dying on the hoof."

Never Forsaken had a better water supply than any of the other ranches or farms. His admission underscored the desperation they all faced. Tim added, "Checkered Past is drilling for the third time, and still they haven't tapped into water."

"My water is still clear. Several others have to strain their drinking water."

Watching crops and livestock fail was one thing; with hard work, they could be replaced. Losing a clean supply of drinking water risked loved ones. The men exchanged bleak looks as Todd pulled up to his place.

"We cannot be home yet," Ma complained. "I want to hold the baby longer. Take us for a Sunday ride."

Tim teased Ma and helped get her into the cabin. Walking back to join Maggie and Sydney, Todd overheard his wife. "I'm thanking you from the bottom of my heart. I'd never suggest anything that would put little Rosie in danger. Your kindness earned the first smile I've ever seen on Ma."

Tim held his daughter and pulled his wife closer with his other arm. "You don't know what worry is until you have a family."

"You got what you asked for. Don't complain now." Sydney gave him a feisty grin.

"No man knows what he's asking for when he proposes. Does he, Todd?"

"Absolutely not."

A look of mock outrage on her face, Sydney declared, "You knew more or less what you were getting, Tim Creighton."

"More *and* less." Tim's voice softened. "Less than I thought I knew; far, far more than I imagined."

As they rode off, Maggie wore a winsome expression. "Daddy loved Mama like that."

The undertone in her voice tugged at him. Todd refused to feign what he didn't feel. Then again, he'd said love would grow—even promised her uncle that he'd court her. *I've done well at that so far—I made a bed in the loft for us, didn't I? And I got up early and took care of the furniture.*

Maggie avoided looking at him when he remained silent. Wrapping her arms around herself, she rasped, "I'd better get my apron back on."

"Your uncle warned me you grew up on fairy tales." Todd let out a frustrated growl. Though he hadn't meant to fling hurtful words at her back, she'd turned around at the same time he spoke.

In that momentary pause, Maggie lifted her head and squared her shoulders. "Aye, it's true." The lilt in her voice disappeared. That was bad enough, but she blinked rapidly.

Reaching out, he captured her shoulder. "Margaret—" He sounded too gruff. "Maggie . . ." He ought to say something more now to reassure her—but what? Suddenly, it came to him. "We are doing well. Remember? On the train, I said life was good with God in my heart, crops in the field, and you in my arms."

"God is in your heart, and there are crops in the field and a vegetable garden ready to plant." She drew a deep breath.

There, she understood. He relaxed.

Until he realized she had focused on his hand. On her shoulder.

Thick-hearted man! her heart cried out, but Maggie couldn't afford to allow him to see how deeply his indifference wounded her. Likewise, she refused to pretend everything was right . . . let alone good.

"I'm not in your arms; you hold me at arm's length—and not just this moment. You keep your heart and mind every bit as far from me."

His hand tightened on her infinitesimally, then he dropped his arm.

"And I'll be changing my mind, as is a woman's right." Gathering her nerve, she looked him in the eye. "I didn't grow up on fairy tales. I grew up with them. Surrounded by them, aware every moment my parents were together or Uncle Bo and Aunt Maude kept me under their roof that love might well have been pouring straight out of the windows and door, yet there was still so much it spurted out the chimney top, too." The torrent of the emotion and the flood of memories robbed her of her breath.

"Our marriage is ours." His words vibrated with restraint. "Yours and mine. And God's. What others did or had was their marriage. I spoke of fairy tales, not of family. Someday, our marriage can be as strong as any—but it cannot be built on a foundation that is chipped away with comparisons."

She turned away again. "I need to change out of my Sunday best." As she walked to the house, she avoided looking at the words they'd put in the cement.

Like it or not, he had a strong point. It wasn't right for her to compare him to other husbands. She was to love him just as he was, not the way she hoped he'd be. Sure, she'd like some changes, but she did love the lummox.

Tomorrow was Monday—her turn to give him a token of love. *Aye, and that's just what I need to do. Keep reminding him that love grew despite rocky soil. Todd needs me to teach him how. Aunt Maude had to wait two years until Uncle Bo finally showed her how precious she was. I don't want to wait that long.* Still, she'd do things that spoke to a man's heart, and he'd make gestures back. Soon he'd realize they weren't empty gestures on his part. She had to keep hope.

After a light supper, Todd sat at the table, reading a farm journal aloud. "There are some recipes here."

"For anything good?" Ma's comment set Maggie's teeth on edge. "It's been weeks since we've had *kase knoephla*. You always liked my kase knoephla. And yeast bread. Remember my loaves, how you couldn't wait for them to cool?"

"Your bread was always tasty, Ma." He named off several of the recipes, his voice rich with enthusiasm.

Soda bread, biscuits, corn bread—those were what she made. With no means of refrigeration, she couldn't keep a cake of yeast. Most of the foods he mentioned, she'd never heard of, let alone made. And Ma kept egging him on, reminding him of how much he liked the food she used to prepare. The third time Ma mentioned bread, Maggie said, "I'll see about trading for some yeast."

"Sehr *gut!*" Todd flashed a smile at her. "And then Ma can teach you to cook."

⌒☙⌒

At last! At last she had a job. She'd prove her worth. Helga could scarcely sleep that night. Lying in bed, she made menus and determined she'd teach Magpie how to cook like a good farmwife.

And baking! They'd have so much fun. Raisin cream pie. Shoofly pie. Pumpkin custard. Cinnamon rolls. And she'd demonstrate using a knife to carve wheat stalks on the piecrust, like a farmer's wife should—not a design of berries or cherries like Maggie did. Then, too, Maggie always cut a cross on the top of a loaf of that

271

heavy soda bread prior to baking it. Odd. The girl was odd as a three-eyed trout.

Why, it would be almost as if Helga was doing all the work herself. Todd's wife would be her hands.

All day long, Helga tried to teach Maggie everything she could work in—a quick way to tighten the broom since it was dropping straws, how to tell when the farmer's cheese was starting to curdle, and how to make *pfeffernuesse*.

Some things, Maggie acted glad to learn. Others, she dug in her heels. Helga did her best to ease past those rough patches, pointing out that farmer's cheese, butter, and all the dairy products would be different because they had a fine milch cow—not a stinky goat.

At midday, Maggie folded her arms across her chest. "Today's my turn to give my husband a love token, and I plan to surprise Todd with a special dessert."

In the interest of getting along, Helga didn't say the cookies they'd made were enough. That night Todd ate the kase knoephla with gusto, proving it had been a successful day. Then Maggie put aside the plates and produced a cake she'd carefully covered with a water bucket so it would be a surprise. "It's my turn. I made you a love token."

"After you do the dishes, we will eat the cake." Todd pushed aside his coffee cup. His eyes twinkled. "Not often do I say this, but I am full!"

Smile fading, Maggie said, "Fine."

While Maggie did the dishes, Todd read from the *Gazette*. The drought was expected to worsen, the railroad strike persisted, and the news from Chicago World's Fair cited decadent waste of luxuries like California fruit while elsewhere people were struggling to make ends meet because of the stock market's plunge. Eventually, he folded the paper and set it down.

Maggie picked up a knife and turned toward the table. Helga muttered, "After that grim news, I don't want cake."

"Me neither. I'm still stuffed."

Maggie almost dropped the knife.

"I shocked my wife." The boyish smile Helga thought Todd lost when his father died lit his face.

"Are you sure?" Maggie sounded incredulous. "Not even a little piece?"

"Nein. Tomorrow I will. But have some yourself."

"No."

Todd gave her an exasperated look. "You wanted some. Go ahead."

"I wouldn't touch that cake if it were the last scrap of food on earth." She picked up the platter.

His voice tinted with laughter, Todd said, "You just said you wouldn't touch it—"

"You didn't even look at it! It was your love token!" She wheeled around and opened the door.

"Margaret! What are you doing?" Todd shot to his feet.

"Slopping the hogs. They'll appreciate getting a love token. You couldn't care less."

He grabbed her arm, and she jerked away. The cake slid off the platter and landed just outside the door. "What has gotten into you?"

"Certainly none of the cake." She stared down at it with tears in her eyes.

"The top layer is still good." His voice guarded, he suggested, "Lift it back onto the plate."

Shoving the platter into his hands, Maggie shook her head. "Go ahead." Helga gasped, but Maggie barely drew a breath. "You need to practice carrying something over the threshold."

Seventeen

Todd watched her run out into the night.

"Let her go, Son. She needs to collect herself."

He had no notion of how to handle a woman—let alone a weeping wife. Proud as Maggie was, she probably didn't want him to see her crying. Squatting down, he tried to figure out what had gone so wrong. Something elaborate swirled and dipped on the cake. Once he forked his fingers between the layers, plopped the top back on the platter, and put it on the table, the lamp illuminated the design: their monogram.

He might manage to clean up the porch and his hands, but he doubted he'd ever remedy the mess he'd made. He'd do his best, though. He went in search of her.

The smallest circle of light gave away her whereabouts. He ought to have known: She went to her treasures. Strewn around her on the barn floor in a kaleidoscope of color lay a trove of whimsy and wealth. Several small dolls dressed in a rainbow of colors, a host of carved angels, a lace collar. She had to know he was there, but she hadn't turned around.

"Maggie."

"Hmm?" She scooped up all the angels and dropped them back into the box.

He couldn't think of a thing to say.

Her hands shook, yet she swiftly rolled the dolls into a scrap of an old quilt and laid them back to rest with a lacy covering. "I'll be there in a while." She still had something, but he couldn't see what.

"Together, we will walk back, and I will carry you—"

"Don't." She looked over her shoulder at him. "You were right from the start—to not give me a taste of what won't be. Pretending is for children."

"The Bible commands me—"

"That's between you and God."

"—to love you."

As she stood, several bits fluttered to the ground. "From the start you told me there is more than one kind of love."

"Time is needed. But for now, it is not good for the sun to go down on your anger."

"It didn't." Something in her strained denial rang true. In a softer voice she added, "It went down on my hurt."

It's your love token. If he'd given her a gift and she set it off to the side without a thank-you or kind word or just a smile . . . he'd be upset. Not that they were madly in love, but warm affection had flowered between them. He'd rejected her and her cherished tradition all at once.

"Tonight I will sleep out here." Todd didn't give her a choice. He threaded her hand through his arm—the same way he had back by her barn so she wouldn't slip on the ice. He'd even taught Jerlund the proper way to escort her. *Jerlund wouldn't have blundered the way I have.*

Part of the way across the yard, she released him. "This is far enough."

"Nein. We are only halfway."

"Halfway can be good enough." As if to convince herself, she stood straighter and said with resolve, "Aye. Halfway can be good enough."

He didn't relent. He walked her to the door. Once she went inside, he trudged out to the barn. Curiosity led him back to all her stuff. Setting the lamp on the very box into which she'd delved, he looked at the scraps of paper littering the ground. The letters were printed in classic German typeset, and there seemed to be a hand-tinted illustration. It didn't take him long to piece together enough scraps to know what she'd done. She'd torn out the last page of a book. One that said, *They lived happily ever after.*

❧

Maggie flew out of the house. *Lord, you couldn't reassure me of your love any better way than this!* "Linette!"

"Mercy and I baked up a storm yesterday, just so I could have a day to spend with you. Can you put up with me?"

"Aye, but the true question is, are you thinkin' you'll survive the encounter?"

Linette helped her pamper Ma by giving her a proper soak in the tub. Ma had an early luncheon, let them exercise her, then fell into an exhausted nap.

As they started hemming the other half of the curtain, planning to meet in the middle, two loud blows sounded from outside. Linette jumped. Maggie cast an anxious look at Ma, but Ma still snored. They smothered giggles as they dashed out to see the source of the noise.

Long, loose strides carried Todd away, and a flurry of clatters made Maggie wheel around. "My woodicocks!"

"Your what?" Linette looked up and made a face. "I'm going to have to teach you to talk Texan. Those are whirligigs." She sighed. "Oh, to have a husband. Just look at how he spoils you."

"Uh-huh. And I never know what he'll spoil next."

They took the curtain outside to work on. Linette's thread tangled. "Oh, Maggie, my life's knotted up just like this. I'm never going to live down the stupid things I did in the past. Katherine and Marcella—since they're younger, folks held me to blame. Well, not so much the women. But the men. I've thought about moving away—"

"Don't you dare." Maggie tugged gently on one of Linette's curls. "If you worry about your beautiful hair being short now, just you wait until I shave it off. Don't try me, because I'll do it if you start packing."

"Then I'm doomed to spinsterhood—just like everyone predicted."

"Nonsense. A plan. That's what we need."

Tears filled Linette's eyes. "You're the only one who thinks a man might want me. Even my own parents talk about me staying with them forever. I could wear a dress spangled with five-dollar gold eagles, but men would run away the minute I show up."

"If a man wants you for what you own or what you're wearing, you don't want him. I know in my heart there's a feller who'll want you for all the right reasons. Men are like little boys—they want most what they can't have." Maggie almost leapt up. "That's it! From now on, you're what they can't have. You're going to be unattainable."

"I am? How?"

Maggie winked. "By turning the tables. Instead of you working to catch them, they're going to have to notice you."

"They notice me and run."

"Whatever you do, Linette, don't think about a sleek, whitetail doe." She paused. "Now what are you thinking about?"

"The doe."

"Aye. Men are hunters at heart, a-chasing after a doe. In the end, it's nigh unto the same amount of meat as the steer in his pasture, and the addled man's worked harder. But you've heard men boast and brag about the doe they caught. You're sleek and have big brown eyes—just like a doe. You're going to be man-wary like one. They'll spot you, but you're going to flit right past and ignore that they exist. It won't take long ere they'll take it as a challenge."

"I'm not going to be good at this." A hopeless sigh filled the silence. "There's not a man in three counties who would bother."

"I already set up a practice for you. Whene'er you stay late, John Toomel's bound to escort you home." Linette's lips formed his name—she looked hopeful and horrified all at once. *I thought so. She's sweet on him.*

Nothing wrong with giving love a nudge. "Once someone spies him passing time with you, it's going to be deer season in Gooding. So starting tonight, you gotta stay late. He's too proud to come to supper every night, but he'll be here for certain."

Delighted with their plan and the finished curtains, they went in to check Ma, made lunch, and took it back outside. Maggie waved to Todd to let him know it was time to eat.

"Linette, you are here to help plant the roses, ja?" Todd asked the question before taking a bite of his sandwich.

"I love roses!"

"Gut. Sehr gut." He took another bite and nodded as if he'd solved

a great philosophical riddle. "Later this week we'll plant vegetables. Today, you plant roses."

Maggie couldn't hide her amazement. "Where?"

"Roses belong closer to a house. They will come first, then the corn, and finally the sorghum." Todd shoved the last bite in his mouth and strode off.

They finished eating and went out to the garden. Gently patting the earth, then drawing a circle in it around the first rosebush, Maggie whispered, "Welcome to your new home."

"You haven't said what color they are."

"Vivid pink. You've never seen such a color, and you never will again. They're my treasured legacy for my daughters and granddaughters and great-granddaughters. It's essential I make them thrive."

"Okay, so show me what to do, and we'll get this done before that grouchy mother-in-law of yours beckons you. You haven't said anything, but I can't ignore the truth. Todd's mama would test the patience of a saint."

Resisting the urge to agree, Maggie leaned forward and stabbed into the earth. "Here's how I do it. Dig a hole . . . this deep. This is my desiccated, ground-up kelp, and here's bone meal. Molasses, too."

"I knew it! I just knew it! I helped old Mrs. Whittsley plant roses last year, and she had me pour her secret formula in the hole and a few drops at the base. I said it smelled like molasses cookies, and she told me I'd be one sick and sorry girl if I tasted from her bottle."

"And well you might. The molasses for cooking has the sulfur removed; agricultural molasses doesn't. I made that mistake. Once."

"Look. Todd is bringing out another crate. I thought you said he'd decided on three."

Maggie's breath caught. Four! That meant a total of twenty bushes. Since her roses bloomed throughout the year, that would produce enough not only to meet their needs, but for her to make a few gifts. When Todd set the box in the dirt a few paces away, she smiled up at him. "Thank you."

Linette waited until he left. "I saw the cake. Don't you dare think he gave you more roses to make up for whatever he did. He's not that kind of man."

Pretending not to hear her, Maggie planted another rosebush.

Todd brought out two more crates!

"He's so romantic, Maggie. I'd die to have a bucktoothed, bow-legged pauper give me a smile, and Todd's showering you with the thing he knows you hold so dear."

Still, they came—crate after crate. At first, Maggie wasn't sure. But Linette opened her eyes. Todd knew how much she treasured her roses. This couldn't be a mere apology—it was far more! *He might not love me . . . yet. But he's trying. Things can still work out. I need to be patient and persistent.*

Finally, Todd brought out the very last one. Maggie's heart was so full, she almost wept.

Wiping his neck with his red bandana, he came closer to survey the dozen bushes they'd already planted. "It's practical to have the roses between the corn and the house. It keeps vermin from the house."

"Aye, 'tis practical." *Though not nearly as sweet. I was foolish to let my hopes run wild.*

Knotting the bandana around his neck, he added, "With the rose garden close, Ma can sit outside and talk with you."

Maggie fought the urge to help him tie the bandana much, much tighter.

"Better, too, for me to yield land outside the barn than to leave boxes in the barn."

Maggie stared at him in disbelief. She'd actually started to believe that he wasn't just sorry, but even developing deep feelings for her. But he wasn't penitent in the least. And certainly not passionate. No amount of patience or persistence would soften his hard heart.

Maggie made a snap decision. She wasn't going to win him; he had to win her.

⌁

"Not again." Smacking his hat against his thigh, Todd growled, "Margaret."

He'd had ulterior motives in having her plant all of the roses: It would clear out a dozen crates, Maggie would get involved with her beloved legacy, and she'd be busy enough that she'd stop all of her haggling. Friends remarked on the deals they'd made with her. Even Daniel Clark said something—undoubtedly because he'd noticed a dent in his business at both the mercantile and the lumber and feed. Todd growled her name again.

Maggie's head popped up over a wheelbarrow. "Uh-oh. What did I do this time?"

"Someone's coming. Whoever it is, make it quick. Time away from the fields is wasted."

Men came to the farm, and Magpie talked with anyone. She had no idea of her appeal. Cowboys and farmhands didn't want to have to wait until Sunday to catch sight of a pretty woman. As long as men came to his land, Todd would have to bird-dog his wife—for her safety and to scare the men off instead of feeding them.

Shading her eyes, she looked down the road. "It's one of the boys from Checkered Past. Those five whiskered boys stay clumped together like marbles in a bag. They're about as sharp as marbles but not nearly as useful." Maggie shook her head. "I'm guessing at his age you had work to do, not notes to carry for Mama. Are any of them worth a hoot when they get a job?"

"Fencing. They're good at fencing."

Maggie quirked a brow. "Useful fencing, or waving-skinny-swords fencing?"

In spite of his irritation, Todd cracked a smile. "Useful. Two can rope." They went into the barn.

Dragging his feet in the dust, the young man mumbled, "Mrs. Valmer, ma'am? I got a note." He patted his shirt pocket, then crammed his hands in his pants pockets. "Here."

Maggie took the note, opened a ledger, and frowned. "Can't do this. Go back and tell your mama that it's got to be a full half of a steer."

Todd felt anger surge, but he kept silent until the kid left. "When it comes to providing meat—"

Maggie penciled something on a tablet. "Meat. Go ahead. I'm listening. The Van der Vorts and the Pattersons are supposed to get this meat. The Van der Vorts could eat the whole thing in two meals, but then the Pattersons' boys wouldn't muck the livery." She looked up and asked, "The trader's fee is a few cuts of beef, depending on what they are. What do you fancy?"

"What does Checkered Past get?"

"Their choice of two Van der Vort IOUs: Either they shoe eight horses, or they'll take one of the boys and apprentice him for a month—which was why I was asking if they can do anything useful." Tilting her head to the side, she asked, "How does a roast sound?"

"That barter did not get rid of anything. Emptying the barn of all your things—that is the goal. There is too much to do here. No more, Margaret. Clear out everything."

Slapping her ledger shut, she said, "You have another think a-comin' if you believe I'll do so."

"A wife does not speak thus."

"Neither does a husband," she shot back. "Just look about you. Go on ahead. What do you see?" She didn't give him a chance to answer. "My things—and I'm not talking sparkles and specials—I'm talking your basic, start-up-a-home stuff. All of it except for the washstand are stuck out in the barn. Not in the house. In the barn! That's Ma's table and chairs in there. Her dresser, too. Mayhap if I had some of my things in the house, then you wouldn't be bumping into them out here."

He compressed his lips.

"I can't move the furniture by myself, and you're too busy. I reckoned we could blend things in and store the rest here until we have a wee bit of elbow room."

Standing with his arms folded across his chest, he met her hot look. "The pots in the house are sufficient."

"Not when harvest rolls around and I'm cooking for a couple dozen men."

She had a point. He cast a look in the stall. There was more now than when she first arrived. Given free rein, she'd take over the whole barn. "Most of this, you could get rid of. We would not miss it."

"You might not. I sure would. I'd delight in setting my rose china on the table."

"You have your rose garden. It is fair Ma has her plates."

Maggie's jaw tightened and her eyes sparked. "Those plates were given to her by a husband who knew the importance of a woman having the dishes she dreamed of. A man who loved his wife and paid his last cent to be sure she got them."

"So you hold against me that I have not bought you new china."

" 'Tisn't the truth, and well you know it." Her voice shook.

"Do I? I've given you nothing but debt. You chase all over, bartering because I haven't given you what you want or need."

Bang! She thumped her ledger on the table. Upending an envelope, she sent slips of paper flittering in the air. "Have a look. Just have a look! There's not a soul in the whole town who hasn't needed to barter. And I said *need.* Did you think less of Piet and Karl because that is how they get their meat? Or of the Pattersons? There's not enough money, but plenty of necessities. One neighbor helping another."

One by one, he flipped or turned the papers. "A cord of wood. Butchering. Credit for Clark's Mercantile?"

"Daniel Clark suggested it. He's getting coal for his home and store. He wanted some of my lotion and soap, so we have a little store credit, ourselves. I didn't tell him how much Mrs. Ludquist sent us for the soap and lotion she wanted. He's been so good to everyone, I wanted him to take it for free—but he wouldn't."

Shaking his head, Todd continued to look at the things people had to offer. In her ledger, she listed what everyone needed.

"We're a team—yoked together and pulling a mighty weight called debt. Every chance we have, we're dropping it—by putting in the sorghum, planting a huge garden, and by snaring meat and dozens of other ways. What kind of wife would I be, to go against my very nature and not do something that will ease things? Bartering is natural as breathing for me." She paused a second and added in a wry tone, "But when it comes to farm stuff, I've got a sore, sad case of hay fever."

Pride and need warred inside him.

"I'd rather see you handling lots of the deals. . . . I don't know enough about farm tools to fill a thimble. And I don't know if I should accept some offers. One lady says she'll sew a fine church shirt for a man. I'm not sure any of the men would take that deal."

"Widow O'Toole and Linette can both sew well. A married man has a wife to do the sewing, but a bachelor won't touch that trade."

"See?" She reached out and rested her hand on his arm. "I didn't even mention names. So why don't we work together?"

He pondered the idea.

Maggie squeezed his arm. "For our future."

"Did you say we'll get a roast?"

⤙❦⤚

Two chairs sat out on the porch that very evening. Maggie's dowry chest now served as a bench on the far side of the table. Ma looked at the china Maggie drew from the barrel. "Oh." It was so . . . ordinary. All it had were little sprays of roses on it.

"You're speechless. I was, too, the first time I saw it." With a grand flourish, Maggie put a cup and saucer on the table. "So now that you've seen it, we need to decide whose china is for everyday, and whose is for extra-special occasions."

Helga thought for a minute. "Yours are plain and mine are fancy. Someday, my granddaughter will want to use my china, so we'll save the best for best. No putting it in that barrel, though! It's getting stored safe and snug in your dowry chest." She poked at Maggie. "I expect German food on my plates for the holidays."

Maggie looked at Todd and laughed. "Your ma sets a mean bargain."

"All the trading and swapping I'm seeing, it's fair I do some, too."

"You are going to see plenty more, Ma. Maggie and I are going to work on it at the table every couple of nights. Maggie, the rear axle on the buckboard is cracked. That's the first thing we have to arrange. You already traded the axles you brought. But what about a wagon jack?"

"Jakob owns it now. He gave two water barrels to Widow O'Toole, and she promised me she'd come help do the canning. I don't doubt he'd be willing to let you borrow it, but I'll send along some of my lotion. You can tell him it's because Hope and Annie have fragranced my life with their sweet friendship."

Todd grunted. Helga liked how he did that because he sounded just like his father.

"As for the axle, Mr. White has a spare. No doubt he'd part with it for half a day of Adam and Eve's labor—but he'd dicker over it for the other half of the day. Millie Clark has her heart set on a jet intaglio for her sister. I have one she particularly likes. Millie could extend store credit to Piet Van der Vort, and I'm sure he has an axle."

Helga croaked, "Todd, you can't mean to go begging."

"Cooperating, Ma; not begging. Maggie and I—we've kept it from you, but things are more than tight. We're hanging on by a thread."

Helga stabbed the needle in her work. "I've got the perfect trade. Simplest thing you could do." Cocking her head so she could see them both, Helga said, "Write Arletta. Tell her to send money, or you'll send me back."

"We will not!" Maggie threw down the dishcloth as she yelled. "I'm not selling you!"

For all the times she felt like a burden, Helga drank in the vehement reaction. But they needed the money. "You're not selling me. She got rid of me before. The girl won't take me back—especially like this."

"She'd better be beautiful, because sure and for certain, that girl doesn't have brains or a heart."

Todd folded his arms across his chest. "Sis looks just like Ma. Same brown hair and eyes."

Heart twisting, Helga whispered, "No one looks like me. Not like this."

"No one looks like anyone else. It's like my cameos. Sometimes, though, it's not what's carved on the outside. On the most beautiful, it's the light that shines through it." Tender as could be, Maggie pushed in one of Helga's hairpins. "Think on that, Ma."

"The intaglio cameo—that would be the best choice for the axle." Todd studied Maggie's face. "But I know you love your cameos."

"I have my favorites. I'm a barterer. Getting rid of things is my job, and just you watch me do it." Maggie turned to her. "And you are not a thing, so don't you dare think that applies to you."

Maggie went out to get her ledger from the barn.

"She's fond of you, Ma."

"She did it for you, not for me."

"Then make her change her mind and be glad she did it for all of us."

✦

Weeks passed, and Maggie fell into a routine. Each Sunday, she'd relish not only worship, but an afternoon of friendship. Heart and soul—Sundays filled her up.

All her friends held to the cockeyed notion that Monday was washday, so Tuesdays Maggie ironed. Other than that, she worked in baking and cleaning.

In many ways, it was like life back in the holler. Everyday chores were the same. But here, the bartering was much, much brisker. And she was working in the fields. With the weather growing hotter, they'd rise up early of a morn and do chores before the worst of the day. Every drop of water had to sink in—and Maggie learned the tricks of "dry gardening."

But she missed the cool mountain breeze and the mist. And the impish twinkle in Uncle Bo's eyes. Paw-Paw's wise counsel. The sound of Jerlund planting both feet on each step. But most of all, Maggie longed for the contentment she'd once taken for granted.

Men back home spoke their hearts freely and did so in a musical, run-together way. Cowboys and farmers—especially the German ones, guarded their hearts and hoarded their words.

The blue curtains looked . . . fair. Strung on twine, they dipped a bit in the middle. So she drove a few pegs above the window and swagged her beloved Rose plaid across.

"The blues match." Coming from Ma, Maggie took it as a compliment.

"Like from our wedding." Approval warmed Todd's voice.

Black lines separated the jeweled green and blue squares—making it handsome, yet reminiscent of a stained-glass window. She'd always had a plaid across her mantel. Depending on her mood, she'd choose one of the three belonging to Clan Rose, but the ancient hunting one had been Daddy's favorite. The change made this feel more like home . . . but it also made her feel much, much farther away from Carver's Hollow.

Maggie anticipated the weekly letter she received from Uncle Bo and read it over and over. In his letters, Uncle Bo told of the happenings. Often her uncles sent notes, too. And bless her dear uncle, he had Jerlund write his name on envelopes and sent them with stamps affixed. She never breathed a word about how their farm was at risk; no one in the holler ever asked about finances. But Maggie suspected Uncle Bo knew. About every other letter, he'd include money and receipts for some of Maggie's trade goods he'd sold. Every penny of it went in the jar that held their savings.

Two magnificent double eagles sat in the bottom of the jar—ten whole, blessed dollars from Mrs. Ludquist. She'd requested Maggie send a bottle of perfume and some soap to her home in Boston—a rush order, because she wanted to take it with her on her travels. Maggie couldn't help seeing the irony of it: Mrs. Ludquist wanted the roses as she left home; all Maggie wanted was to grow roses at home!

Saturday morning Maggie wrapped her own plaid around Ma's shoulders. "I aim to go pamper my roses. They're struggling. Come on outside."

"You're bossy."

Maggie dropped Ma's embroidery in her lap. "I'm honored you noticed."

Maggie fretted over her beloved roses, and Ma's stitches improved each week. Todd stopped by to admire both.

Linette sashayed up. "I hope you don't mind, but John Toomel is meeting me here so I can measure him for a shirt."

"We don't mind at all."

Todd waited until Linette was out of earshot. His hot whisper sounded appalled. "We don't mind? You said we were helping our friends and neighbors with this bartering. Don't even consider trying to play matchmaker between your friend and my neighbor."

"What's mine is yours." She frowned at a leaf. "I'm just helping along two folks who are our friends."

"I'm saddling up and warning my friend about yours. He can't possibly know what he got himself into."

A moment later, while Ma stayed in the shade, Linette yanked Maggie into the house. "I can't believe John really asked for this trade."

"Aye, and you're going to be proper as a stiff-rumped professor. No fluttering or small talk. And I'll chaperon. Afterward, we'll cook a roast. The other one was so delicious, Todd's been wrangling all sorts of deals to bring in another."

Plopping down on the edge of Ma's bed, Linette gave her a woebegone look. "You're smart and beautiful and talented. You even had Belgians. Todd is blind to what a bargain he got. If that didn't get you love, then I'm sunk."

It was the first time Linette implied Todd didn't love her. Maggie turned away. "Love can't be bought. And I'll have you remember you are a sleek doe—a very talented and smart one that can sew and bake. In a few months, I might change my mind. Could be, love isn't bought, but a man can make a first payment on it with a shirt."

She poured lotion into Linette's hands. "When you measure his collar and cuffs, you want your hands nice and soft."

"This smells heavenly. Do you make other fragrances?"

"The rose is my specialty, but I can mix other things. What would you like?"

"I don't know. Can you ask John what his favorite flower is?"

"I'll do it today."

Linette rubbed her hands a little more, then inhaled. "You ought to sell this. People would buy it!"

Maggie looked out the open door. "No one has that kind of money. Wheat and corn prices dropped again. We're all praying to make ends meet. Luxuries, like fine perfume, soap, and lotion . . . Only the very rich are indulging."

Until now, Maggie hadn't let herself imagine what would happen if they lost the farm. They could start over again. *Todd did it once, and he'd get us through anything. . . . But if we leave Gooding, I wouldn't be with my dear friends anymore.*

John arrived. "Hello, Miss Richardson. I'm looking forward to getting a new shirt for church."

"Did you have any preferences?" Linette pitched her voice just right. "Some gentlemen are having shirts with the collar and cuffs attached instead of removable. And would you like the sleeves standard length, or longer so you can uhhh . . ." Linette didn't want to say "garter."

"Band it," he supplied. "What do you recommend?"

"Removable collars and cuffs make it easy to freshen a shirt and make it last longer."

Cutting butter into flour to make a pie dough, Maggie said, "It never ceases to amaze me how we are all so different. Like those preferences for a shirt. What makes one person happy displeases another. Todd is very easy to please. But he has taken a special liking to my peach jam and dried-peach pie."

"Now if you'll pardon me, Mr. Toomel . . ." Linette measured the length of his sleeve, trying to act casual.

"What about you, Mr. Toomel? What kind of pie is your favorite?"

"Maggie, I have yet to eat a thing here that isn't great. But the thing I recall enjoying the most is that apple pie Miss Richardson made."

"Mmm-hmm!" Dusting the table with more flour so she could roll out the dough, Maggie said, "Linette, you have a way with spicing things just right."

"Thank you. Oh my. Twenty-nine across the shoulders!" Scribbling down the measurement, she said, "Daddy likes his shirttails extra long so they stay tucked in better when he rides."

"If you could do that and work in a little give around the arm, I'd appreciate it."

"John!" Todd shouted from outside. "John, I need to talk with you for a second."

Irked, Maggie pushed the rolling pin so hard it spun around and around when she lifted it. She wasn't going to let Todd ruin

Linette's chance for happiness. Determined to get the information from John she'd promised, she had to keep him there. "What about the collar?"

John had to lean down for Linette to measure his neck. His eyeglasses reflected Linette, proving he was staring at her. She measured him with trembling fingers.

Maggie took pity. "I'm still learning Todd's favorites. Like the dog he'd like to get, or flower. I've seen your dogs. Do you have a favorite flower?"

"John . . ." Todd called again from outside.

John jerked upright, away from Linette. "I . . . um . . . flower? I didn't know there was anything other than Best." With Todd bellowing for him, he left.

Linette wilted into a chair. "Best?"

Maggie stared down at the table in utter disbelief. There, in a white powdery cloud, sat a bag emblazoned *BEST*.

Holding up the flour sack, she sighed. "Linette, they're hopeless."

Eighteen

The small oven box limited how many cookies she could bake at a time. Since Todd and Ma adored pfeffernuesse, Maggie took most of the morning to make a batch. She developed a rhythm—heating the iron while she spooned the next pan of cookies to bake, ironing while the cookies baked, and repeating the cycle. By the end of the morning, she'd finished her ironing and had a big tin full of cookies.

Ma set aside her crewel work and swiped another cookie. "Todd's fit to be tied over you playing Cupid. That whole shirt-measuring scheme from yesterday rubbed him the wrong way."

"Something special is blossoming between Linette and John." *If only Todd looked at me the way John gazes at her . . .* "I wish my roses were coming along as nicely." *I wish my own marriage was going as well. Our romance is as dry and barren as the rose garden.*

"You're wasting your time—on the matchmaking and on the flowers."

Maggie needed to go tend the roses—because they needed the attention and because she didn't want to hear Ma's grousing. Wrapping cookies in a tea towel, she said, "Todd loves pfeffernuesse hot from the oven." She brushed a kiss on Ma's cheek and headed out to surprise her husband. It felt good to be outside . . . until she looked around.

"No!" The word tore from her chest as she raced to her rose bed. Falling to her knees, she scooped away everything at the first rose's base. Desperately, she crawled down the row. Thorns raked her flesh, but she had no time to put on gloves. It was probably too late already.

Todd pulled her to her feet. "Maggie?"

"My roses! They're burnt. It's killing them." She jerked away and fell to her knees again. "Help me."

Shoveling off the mixture of manure and fertilizer, Todd moved with blinding speed. "They weren't growing. I tried to help."

They worked furiously, but it was too late. Maggie looked at the yellowed and brittle stems and leaves—damaged. More than damaged. This would kill her beloved roses.

"It was yesterday's love token. I traded for fertilizer."

Maggie gave him a tragic look. "They won't make it. They're dead or burning."

⌘

The sizzle of fried eggs was the only sound at breakfast the next morning. Todd's five filled the skillet. Soon as they were done, she slid them onto his plate. She and Ma ate two apiece—the second round. The idea of eating turned Maggie's stomach, but she'd force herself. Wasn't she the one who always told her uncles back home that an empty stomach stayed sick and one with a little something in it calmed down? But it wasn't her body ailing—it was her aching heart.

Now without the refuge of her roses, she'd plunge back into ceaseless hours of Ma's advice. Learning a new recipe or how to account for the dishes you took to someone else's house at harvest rapidly trapped her into listening about any and every opinion Ma held. Only Ma didn't have opinions; she believed she had the truth.

"Charity . . . beareth all things, believeth all things, hopeth all things." No matter how much she chanted that verse, Maggie didn't think she could bear much more of this, and she didn't believe more than half of what Ma said. If only God would send Linette or Hope—or anyone—to come rescue her.

Outside the woodicocks clattered and the windmill whirred. Everything else about her remained the same—but she'd lost her legacy and sacrificed that bequest for her daughters and granddaughters. Future generations would hear the stories, but they'd mean so much less. The hours and days of two or three generations working together, talking about what it meant to love, to sacrifice, to face the worst with courage . . . Gathering petals, smelling the fragrance, and helping press out the essential oil . . . the fragrance brought back hundreds of memories. The tenderness of a mother dabbing the tiniest dot of perfume on her little girl's wrist . . . lost. All of that lost.

Maggie's chest ached—some from crying, but mostly from the crushing feeling each heartbeat made.

"Go water the vegetable garden." Ma sounded as if she'd been dosed with a vile-tasting curative. "The important matters in life— those are what you must work on."

Anguish welled up. "My roses are—were—important!"

"Sewing warm quilts is important. Putting up food is vital.

Helping my son in the fields is essential. These are the things that count most."

"I've sewn curtains to warm the cabin. I'm tending a large vegetable garden to have food to preserve, and there's not another woman in all of Texas who helped her man with every row of sod he broke."

"Basic things a wife ought to do. No one's going to lavish praises on you like those hillbilly geezers. Children crave praise; wives do the work with a willing heart and know labor is its own reward."

The eggs she fried earlier hadn't sizzled half as hot as the thoughts in Maggie's head. Careful to put a cup of water in Ma's reach, she finally said, "Chores are waiting. Before I go, though, I've something important to tell you: Mama taught me, 'If you don't have something nice to say, don't say anything at all.' Aunt Maude taught me the importance of respecting others. And the importance of gratitude. They were fine, God-fearing women who passed on those common courtesies and eleven generations' worth of wisdom that is twined with my special roses.

"Our beds are warm with my quilts and meals are ready on time. But those quilts will be threadbare in a generation, and a meal is eaten and gone. Twelve generations from now, whatever I salvage of my roses will have multiplied. Those roses and the lessons that belong with them will still survive. Families will be sweeter, lives touched, hearts softened by the legacy. And someday, the women whose faith blossomed, who lived and learned those lessons, will reap one last sweet reward by meeting at the Savior's feet.

"But in the meantime, the fine gentlemen you're calling 'hillbilly geezers' are my family. You will speak well of them, or you won't speak at all of them."

Ma looked a little thunderstruck.

"As I said, I've got chores waiting." Maggie stepped outside.

Scanning the farm, Maggie couldn't find Todd. A few nights ago, John mentioned he could use some help. Of all days, her husband could have been here today when she'd see if a single one of her rosebushes survived. Deep in her heart, she hoped a few might have escaped the chemical burns. The minute she noticed what her husband had done, she'd cleared away as much of the mess as possible—but after a whole night and most of a day, the newly transplanted roses took a lethal dose. Row by row, she saw the truth. This place had ruined them. *Just like it's ruining me.*

Against all logic or sanity, she still watered each one before she watered the vegetables. The full buckets weren't as heavy as her heart.

Todd rode up, dismounted, and walked over to her. Eyes and voice somber, he held out a gunnysack. "For you."

He couldn't find pink, so he'd settled for something kind of orange. That lone rosebush didn't lie amongst the graveyard of Maggie's dead plants. She planted it with the vegetables. Nothing could replace what she'd lost, but he'd wanted her to have something similar. Brokenhearted, she cried as she opened the gunnysack and the whole time she planted the bush. But each time she passed by, she'd caressed the leaves.

Roses—they did odd things to a woman. Ever since he'd given her that entire rose garden, Margaret had changed. She no longer skipped over to him with a greeting on her lips and a hug. Instead, she had rarely left the stove. At the supper table, the Magpie had been less talkative with him—even though she'd liven up and be the belle of the ball if anyone came by. They'd plotted out barters and prayed together—and in those times, she had seemed almost herself—but the rest of the time, she'd taken on an odd reserve.

A wife ought to treat her husband differently. Ja, she should. And she did—but in the wrong way. She had stopped seeking him out. He had to go to her. But she was fairly easy to find since every spare moment had been spent among her flowers. She'd smiled plenty—but it qualified more as a mysterious one, like on her cameos.

Now that he had killed her precious legacy, though, Todd wondered if she'd ever smile again. But wanting to do something, he gave her that one silly rosebush. She'd given him a hug.

Nailing shingles to a twister would be simple compared to understanding his wife.

Maggie.

Her uncle—all of her "uncles"—were right. She was a magpie of a woman. She couldn't be around people without chattering or trading. Those days on the train, she'd been bubbly. The first week on the farm, she'd done her best to settle in and help Ma adjust. Singing and chattering all the time, she made a point of staying cheerful for Ma. Goodness only knew how hard that was.

Now each morning Maggie walked along the rows of ruined roses. Every so often, she'd bend down and inspect one, but whenever she did, her shoulders slumped as she straightened up.

"Baffles me why Maggie tends those dead thorns." John's voice pulled him from his thoughts.

Todd let out a heavy gust of a breath. "It's a family legacy. The women use them to pass down stories that teach their daughters, and they make rose lotions and soaps from the petals."

"Those women must have been saints to inspire devotion and instill the patience Maggie shows your mother."

"Ja. Ma was a bad patient, yet my Maggie graciously cared for her." He shot John a wry grin. "I couldn't do it. I'd sort rattlesnakes before I'd take on Ma as a patient. But she has gotten better."

Hunkering down, John gave him an odd look, then plucked a weed. "Is Linette coming this afternoon?"

"I never know. Sorry I can't warn you since Maggie roped you into—"

"I don't mind." John rose. "Miss Richardson is an interesting young woman."

"So Maggie says. Be careful, though, that she doesn't mistake your friendship for—"

"Courting? That's exactly what I want. Confound it, now that I'm noticing things about her, she couldn't care less about keeping company with me."

Maggie and Linette had lively conversations at the supper table—about everything from their friends' new babies to Chicago World's Fair. The friendship between them had grown strong. They were two women so thirsty for a friend that everything else paled in comparison. Once an awkward, man-hungry gossip, Linette had changed. John's comment knocked Todd into taking a fresh look across the supper table.

"Your cantaloupe is so juicy! Ours didn't do well this year." Linette ate another bite. "Everyone has tomatoes, but something must have been wrong with the okra seeds. Nobody's got much to harvest or trade."

"It might not be the seeds. It can be something else," Ma opined. "Some things won't grow here. Like roses."

"Roses most certainly do grow here!" Linette nearly shouted.

Turning the color of a wisp of smoke, Maggie said, "They do. Old Mrs. Whittsley has lovely bushes. They're already budding. And—"

"I meant here. On our farm." Ma directed her comment to Maggie. "Rose was your maiden name, and you can't stop talking about your past and how wonderful everything was back home. I'll bet the barn is filled to the rafters of trinkets those old men gave you."

"Halt!" Todd boomed.

Ma kept right on. "God destroyed those roses to teach you a lesson."

In cold fury, he bit out, "It is my fault, not God's. I burned them. Apologize to my wife. Now."

Ma didn't make a sound.

Maggie stared at her. "God isn't a despoiler of beauty; He's the Creator and Author. Things that go wrong . . ." Her voice trembled. "They aren't to be dumped at God's feet and the blame heaped upon Him. The rain falls on the just and on the unjust."

"By your logic, Mrs. Crewel," John said, "when one farmer's crop thrives and another's fields fail, it's a spiritual punishment. You're condemning every farmer, because we all have good and bad years. Especially this year—we are all suffering."

Ma argued with great feeling. "You made my point. You are suffering. So am I. God struck down my first husband and then my second. Now He's stricken me."

"All are staggering losses," Linette said, "but you just proved what Maggie said. Good things happen to terrible people just as bad happens to the good."

John leaned forward. "Ma'am, if you can't accept that theology, then you're saying God won't extend grace to you."

Todd let them speak. A man controlled his temper, and he could scarcely hold his in. Let them handle the theology now. He had to address the other issue. He'd not let anyone revile or wound his wife.

"I'm older. Wiser. Much I have seen. God is the God of wrath as surely as He is a God of love. He's every bit as much the God of Revelation as He is of Genesis."

"Husband," Maggie said in a strained voice, "where do you stand?"

Between a wife who will praise God no matter the circumstance, and a mother who—like Job's friend—felt cursing God and dying was the only option. "We are responsible for many of the problems in our lives—through sloth or greed, lying or lust. There are consequences to sin. But in sending His Son, God proved His mercy is far greater than His wrath. He forgives and forgets our sins when we confess them. Children of God are still rained upon, but we have the umbrella of His grace."

"Amen!" John stood and started gathering dishes.

Maggie hopped up. "I'll get that!"

"It won't hurt me to do the dishes. I'd gladly wash and dry every last one of them for a meal you and Miss Richardson cook."

Maggie's lids lowered. "Someone else once said that to me." Forcing a smile, she added, "Only Linette wasn't cooking with me at the time."

I'm the one who told her that. In the holler, the men always did the dishes. Here, I haven't once. Not a single time. Maggie does them three times a day. And much of the time, they weren't the ones she dreamed of, but Ma's.

"The two of you don't have much leisure time all to yourselves." Linette made a shooing motion. "Go take a walk. We'll do the dishes."

"Thank you!" Though his towering rage would defy the coldest of nights, Todd grabbed Maggie's plaid and yanked her outside before wrapping her up. "We're going to the barn."

She dipped her head and shook it. "Nay, Todd. I'm not—"

"When are you finally going to learn to trust me?" He tugged on her arm.

Digging in her heels, she jerked back. "Trust is earned."

He did the expedient thing. It had worked once before. Tilting her over his shoulders, he crossed the yard and entered the barn.

Nineteen

Blood rushed to Maggie's head, making her dizzy. "Put me down!" She pinched his back. "I said, put me down!" It still didn't work, so she fought just as dirty. Strong as an ox and twice as stubborn, her husband had one weakness. He was ticklish. Seizing his sides, she tickled and shouted, "Put me down!" The minute he obliged, she stepped away.

Todd gave her an icy look. "How am I to learn of you, to love you, when you refuse to trust me?"

Thoroughly incensed, she shot back, "I came to Texas. How much more trust is there?"

"There is the trust that you can come to me with anything— everything. Such trust demands complete truth." Arms akimbo, he demanded, "Have you withheld truth from me?"

How do I answer that? I don't want him to know I love him.

Cupping her jaw, he stared into her eyes. "Your silence is answer enough." He let out a cross between a moan and a growl. "Every night I shut our door and know the land surrounding us has taken all we have to give—and it may not be enough. All of my strength and knowledge and vigor are aimed at providing what you need." He patted the mare who stuck her head over the stall gate for affection.

If only I could do that—to reach out, confident of our love. Sorrows swamped her. "If you're asking if I trust you . . . Yes." The colts came to her, and she babied them. "So much so, I will gladly follow you to start again wherever you take us."

"That is a large trust. I pray it's not one you have to exercise, but knowing you feel thus—it is good. Should I become blind, would you stay with me and lead me where I needed to go?"

She stopped playing with the ponies and gave him an outraged look. "You don't need to ask that! Of course I would."

"I am blind to see what you need. My own friend knows better. He spoke, and there was such longing in your eyes and voice—"

Maggie stepped toe-to-toe and jabbed her finger in his chest. "Have you lost all good sense? Me? Long for John Toomel? Have you so little faith in my loyalty to you and to my dearest friend?" As her voice rose, the horses all shuffled and let out nervous sounds.

Todd looked thunderstruck. Then he had the nerve to laugh. "You misunderstand."

"You want me to trust you when you make my hair stand on end and laugh afterwards?" She turned her back on him and paid attention to Nuts and Bolts.

"To trust someone, it means you can depend upon them for large and small things. Why, Maggie? Why didn't you ask me to wash dishes?"

Maggie made an impatient sound. "You washed dishes in Carver's Holler. Why pretend now that you were 'blind' to the need?"

Grazing a set of blinders on a hook, Todd said, "I borrowed John's eyeglasses for an instant, and then I saw things clearly." Then he pushed away the gelding who had edged up to him. "Ma is another thing. Does she treat you the same alone as when I am there?"

Maggie kept her distance from Hammer's stall. Considering his temperament, it was a marvel Todd hadn't sent him to the glue pot. "Overall, nothing I do is right. It's not good enough. The bread I bake, the color of a dress—she plans to change me."

She sighed. "Loving someone means taking them just as they are. God did the job right the first time. Nobody else needs to come by and redesign His work. His work isn't ever done, so we can change—and I will. But that's betwixt me and God . . . and sometimes you. But I don't see a time coming soon when Ma takes a mind to be happy that you married me. She can't find a loving thing to say, and you . . . you can't find love at all."

For an instant, Maggie felt free. She'd told the truth. Then she felt dreadful. "Only thing that came of me giving you the truth is that now we're both miserable."

"This is not so, Magpie. My eyes are open. I will help you with dishes just as you help me in the fields. Together, we will talk to Ma. You come first in my home. We said we would not ask Arletta to take Ma back, but that depends on Ma. I would sooner send Ma to my sister than have my wife mistreated in our home."

Maggie gave him a sad look. "I love her, you know. I see so much good down deep inside her heart. Some days you'll have to help me look for it, though."

"I'll put a request in the bartering book." He winked. "For a magnifying glass. Or a microscope."

Sliding the back of his fingers down her cheek, he shook his head. "I set my greatest burdens before you, and you have been my helpmeet. Instead of leaning on me, you stand alone. The time has come for you to trust me to be your helpmeet, too."

Her flower press sat in a stall. Boxes of bottles and jars surrounded it. Ma was wrong. Maggie didn't have any doodads or junk anymore. She'd traded away all of her "specials and sparkles" without a complaint. The only things she insisted upon keeping belonged to her legacy. "I'm grieved about the roses, Magpie. When you trusted me with what they meant, seeing you plant them gave me joy. I know how precious they were to you."

Grief mushroomed, but also sorrow. "You said it was better to get the roses out of the barn than have them stay in here."

Todd nodded. He looked pleased with himself. Maggie thought about what he'd said. *Dear heavenly Father—I resented his words when they were meant to be good.* "Oh, Husband! We're newlyweds. We're supposed to make mistakes and figure out better ways of getting along. But we're supposed to do it together. I apologize. I'll try to trust you more."

"Men—especially this stubborn German farmer—don't like to admit they'd done poorly. But I have."

Distress clouded her eyes. "No! I've never seen anyone work so long and hard. Don't say that!"

They stood by the barn door. He gestured outward but looked at her. "The fields around us have taken my time, my consideration, my labor—"

"And I'm so proud of you."

"I'm not." Her sweet support only made him feel more like a failure. "The most important field I have is our marriage. You are the crop. I was lazy. I cut off weeds instead of pulling them out, yet even the heartiest crop can be choked out. I have prayed for rain, but I have carried too few buckets to the field. I complain of the drought on the farm, but the worst drought has been in our marriage. In every way, I will do better to tend to you as that which is most dear to me."

"I reckon we've got a deal. Second one we've made." Her pitiful attempt at a smile hit him like a punch.

He pulled her into his arms. "This is our first deal, Maggie. Getting married was never a deal. We held hands and took a leap of faith."

Her head tilted to the side. "There's a fine thought. I'll ponder that."

Todd knew there was no better time than now for him to speak his heart. "I've made a decision, Maggie. With the additional crops, I doubt that we can meet our debts. I cannot run horses and start a farm at the same time. It was a footloose bachelor's dream. Hammer and Wrench, Nuts and Bolts—we don't need them. Not with my gelding and the Belgians."

"You love your horses!"

"They pale in comparison to my family."

Tears filled her eyes. "We didn't pray about it together. Can't we do that?"

"God provided the horses and preserved them through their injuries for such a time as this." Her distress tugged at him. Weeks ago, the decision would have bothered him, but tonight, he'd come to the decision without difficulty. "Don't be sad, Margaret. About your roses, yes, but not about the horses. Most of all, let's think of this as a time when we saw hope for our future. In all ways."

He pulled out her ivory comb. Using his fingers, he untwisted her hair. She shivered—but he knew it wasn't from cold. "I like your hair down. It's your crowning glory."

She cleared her throat and pulled away from his touch. He'd seen her eyes dilate and the unconscious way she leaned into his hand as he stroked her soft hair. The distance she tried to put between them wouldn't last long if he considered his actions, courted her far more aggressively, and sought God's way of falling head-over-heels in love with her.

"I don't want you to sell the horses. I want you to have your dream. The Bible says, 'Where there is no vision, the people perish.' You saw my hope for the roses and tried to make it possible. I want you to have the horses and start that business. Once the harvest is in, then we'll see how God provided. Until then, don't sell them."

It was something that could wait. He nodded. "I need to speak with Ma, and she will give you her apology at breakfast. You need to take butter to town. Once she is dressed, go have a little time of your own and do as you like. I'll keep close to the house to mind her."

"Thank you."

His arms closed about her. It felt good, but she pushed away. One quick tug, and he had her against him. "You are my woman. Don't do that."

"You're wrong. I was your bride. And the preacher pronounced us man and wife. But *woman*—that's what God called Eve when she was created as Adam's perfect mate. It's what Daddy and Uncle Bo called their wives. You're my man, but I'm not your woman. Not until you love me."

He inhaled sharply and tilted her face upward. "You love me."

It wasn't a question, so she gave no reply. Lowering her eyes so he couldn't look into them, she tried to hide her heart with silence.

"You do. Why have you not told me?"

Her shoulders rose and dropped slowly, but with a choppiness that denoted her fighting not to cry. "I did tell you."

Without question, he would have remembered that moment, which left only two possibilities. "Was I sleeping? To sneak such a declaration in when the other is sleeping—that is without courage.

Or is it when you sing that song in Gaelic? So I could not under-stand? I expected more of you, Wife."

Her head came up, and she muttered, "You're relentless as a nagging toothache."

Silent, he waited.

Gathering herself, she said, "I made my declaration, and it took more courage than I had on my own, so I was sure to wear the hatpin Daddy carved for me."

"That was fitting."

"Aye, but still I didn't have sufficient, so I put on two little things that belonged to my mama."

He still didn't understand. It was no wonder he didn't love her yet. He couldn't understand her to save his soul. "What?"

"Her veil and plaid." His arms clenched about her. "Aye, Hus-band. We took a leap of faith on our wedding day, but I was wearing my heart on my sleeve."

Again, he inhaled deeply. The breath came out slowly. Oh, so slowly. Tucking her head back down, he held her with every scrap of tenderness he could summon.

Honor demanded he not say what she longed to hear—but the temptation pulled at him. Three little words, and he'd warm her heart and soothe away some of the ache of these last weeks. Now that his eyes were open, he could see all the ways she'd given him her love.

His fingers played through her hair. "I'm humbled by your love. Were I to proclaim more than what is true on my part, it would cheapen the value of what you give me. When I love you, it will be with my whole heart and soul and being." He kissed her crown. "Someday, my dear, sweet wife, I will tell you I love you, too. You are perfect for me as Eve was for Adam. I will do whatever it takes to be the man you deserve. God brought us together—surely He will work in my heart to let love flourish. Give me your trust a little longer. I promise, you will be my woman."

⌒🙟⌒

The next morning, Helga felt a shift in the home. Linette had put her to bed last night, and no one said anything today about last night. Todd rolled her to the table. Before taking his place, he seated Magpie and gave her shoulders a little squeeze.

Once he finished praying, Helga rasped, "I need to speak."

"Ja, you do." Todd stared at her. "You owe my wife an apology."

"About last night . . . the things I said, I stand by. But I should not have said them in front of others. Magpie, I should have said them to you when we were by ourselves."

Maggie set down her fork. "Nay, Ma. If you're afraid to have others hear what you say, then you oughtn't say it."

"At the beginning, I was harsh. I admit this—"

"So you knowingly hurt my wife." His eyes and voice were both cold and hard as sleet. "Changes will be made."

"B-but we have been doing better." Helga turned to Maggie. "What about all the fun we shared, baking cookies?"

"The cookies were fun—but I'm a grown woman and don't need someone to boss me around."

"I'm trying to help you. Give you instruction."

"Ma'am, on occasion you've told me some fine tricks and short-cuts around the house, and I'm glad of it. But instruct means to equip or train. To put something together. It doesn't mean tearing someone down by finding fault or pushing them to change on account of them being different. I don't need to change what I cook or how I wear my hair."

"But you do! If people accept you, they will help you more."

"Ma'am, if I gotta be someone else to garner their help, I'd rather do it on my own." Maggie rose and scraped her eggs into the swill bucket.

"Go on ahead," Todd rumbled. "I'll take care of this."

Maggie wrapped her plaid around herself. "We have a lot to do. As soon as I get to town, I'll check with the doctor or Widow O'Toole."

Todd looked his wife in the eye and nodded. "So." He went out to help her into the wagon, then came back, and looked at Helga.

"Still you did not apologize. I do not deserve Maggie. She is far too good for me. All her loving care, and yet you hurt her." He shook his head. "Things must change." He turned away and rolled up his sleeves.

To Helga's utter astonishment, Todd put the breakfast dishes in the aluminum tub. Big, strong hands washing china. She'd never seen such a sight.

That was proof. Everything had changed. Everything but her.

After finishing the dishes, Todd wheeled her to the window and went out to work. Regret and worry tangled inside her as she looked through the window. A few hours later, a horrified cry tore through her at what she saw.

Twenty

As the Belgians halted in front of the house, Maggie beamed. "Todd! I brought home a little Sunshine. Isn't it wonderful?"

"That stove is bigger than the one you had in the holler."

"From the awe in your voice, I can tell how pleased you are." She couldn't resist. "And it's the exact same style, but one size down."

"It won't fit, Maggie. Even if we enlarge the cabin, it will have to stay in the barn."

"Then you'll be comfortably warm when you sleep out there . . . alone." In comparison to the house, it was gigantic—and she knew it. "I can't send it back. My uncles sent it as a wedding gift. We'll have to find a way to make this work." Standing on the edge of the buckboard, she waited for him to help her down. His hands went about her waist. She jumped and flung her arms around his neck.

"You don't have to pretend, Todd. I can see how grateful you are to have it."

He held her tight and growled in her ear, "You test me, Wife?"

"If, perchance, I did, could you not still appreciate the result?" She tilted her head to the side. "I'm holding you to your word. You told me to do as I wished."

"I didn't say I'd like it."

She wiggled free. "Think of how our farm will benefit! Once you look at it that way, you'll share my delight." Thunder rolled across his features, and she laughed. "Things could be worse. Jerlund is urging Uncle Bo to send Ma that chandelier."

The muscle in his cheek twitched. "The stove stays. But that abomination stays back in the hills!"

"Well, well. I just might make a trader out of you yet."

He gave the stove a disgruntled look. "That's not going in my barn."

"I could turn the sod wall into a summer kitchen. If you put it there, I promise I'll never use it to bake prune bread."

"Deal!"

Maggie went inside. She took care of Ma's needs, but Ma balked at doing exercises.

Exasperated, Maggie demanded, "What do you expect me to tell Jerlund in my next letter? This sad state of affairs is going to disappoint him."

"I'll do better." Ma caught Maggie's hand. "Not just about my exercises."

"I'm counting on it."

Steering Ma through the door, Maggie promised herself she'd water all the vegetables before she checked her roses.

"You're going to do it." Ma burst into tears. "You're going to make me stay with her." Ma was beside herself. Sobbing, she babbled an incomprehensible stream of words.

Maggie grabbed a pair of dish towels and a glass of water. "A hanky would be a waste of time. Here, now. Take a sip." It took a fair bit of work to calm Ma—though that term seemed generous. "What's upset you?"

"You went to town, and you got that . . . that *thing*. That stove. It says it all."

"I've yet to hear a stove talk, Ma." Maggie teased softly, tenderly wiping the sagging side of Ma's face. "It's a gift from my family. Think of the delicious meals that'll come from it."

Ma shook her head. "I will be gone. Why would I want to think about that?"

"And where, I'm asking, are you supposing you'd be?"

"Living with Eunice O'Toole. You went to town and met with the doctor and her. And then you brought back that oven so there won't be any room for me."

Dropping the dish towel and spilling the water, Maggie yelled, "What kind of silly notion was that? Am I the only one in this house whose heart and mind work right? You're not going anywhere!"

Temporarily stunned, Ma simply blinked.

"Your son won't risk his heart, and you think I haven't a heart a-tall. You think I'd shove you out the door so a block of iron could take your place? Nay! True and to be certain, you've been a handful and sometimes a heartache. But you're *our* handful—and you can quit being a heartache if you set your mind to it.

"Paw-Paw said you could foster happiness and add to our joy— or sow hurt and discord. It's a choice you make each day, each hour, and with each thought. You're our kin, and we take care of our own. I'd have it no other way. But kin doesn't make war on one another.

No folks ought to—but certainly not people under the same roof. The time's come for harmony, and you have to do your part.

"You're stuck with me, Helga Crewel. Your son wed me, and I've pledged my heart to him. I left everyone I love behind and came west because I was convinced it was God's will. Day by day I've come to love my man more. He's too blind to see. You're just as blind if you think I'd boil up a pot of hatred and serve it to you until you had to leave. At eight, I lost my mama. Arletta's half the world away. I'm missing a ma and you're missing a daughter. God could knit us together if you'd stop tying a bunch of knots.

"Blessing or curse—you decide what you want to be. We've all made mistakes. We're bound to again. But if you think I'd strand you with anyone, then take your pick of who it'll be and get yourself out of that chair and walk to 'em. Because the only house I'll ever push you in is right behind you."

⟨❦⟩

"What is this?" Maggie sat down to the breakfast table.

"Piece of paper," Ma muttered.

Todd's smile stretched from one side of the cabin to the other. "It's Monday. My turn for the love token."

"Hmm." The paper envelope rustled as she unfolded it. " 'IOU a lifetime of roses.' " She looked at him. "How touching."

"I mean it. I telegraphed Uncle Bo, and he's sending more of your legacy. They arrive tomorrow night."

She squealed his name, and he swept her up. Later, Maggie tucked her IOU into her dresser drawer. It meant far more than a dozen roses. It meant Todd loved her—even if he was too blind to know it yet himself.

Over the next weeks, her hope grew along with the roses. Almost half the injured ones recovered, and the new ones flourished. Though he wouldn't touch the roses whatsoever, Todd wandered by as she tended them and even plucked weeds as they'd discuss something minor. With water as precious as could be, he'd haul out bathwater for the garden and dishwater for the pigs—but each day, he left two buckets of fresh water by her rose garden.

After putting Ma to bed, he'd take Maggie for moonlight walks in the rose garden, too. What could be more romantic than that? He'd promised a lifetime of roses—and was sharing it day in and day out. Some evenings they traded memories of their pasts, others Maggie shared the tales that accompanied the roses.

"They've put down roots, Wife, and so have you," he told her one night.

"Then plan on keeping the farm, plowboy."

"Only if God wills and the price of wheat holds." Letting out a soul-deep sigh, Todd said, "The balance is so close, one small tilt of His hand will make the determination."

Maggie gave him a steady look. "Faith. I have faith in Him and in you."

⌇

Wheat rippled in the wind. Sun scorched down on Todd, and tomorrow would do the same. He walked the field, reached out, and ran a head of the grain through his palm. Wheat and chaff. Useful and useless—just like all the labor they'd exerted to raise this crop. According to his calculations, when they finished harvesting, they'd make enough to cover the mortgage. By sheer grit and God's grace they'd keep their land. But that was it. Wheat had dropped to fifty-five cents. Pathetically, shamefully lower than it had been in years and years.

A man ought to enjoy the fruits of his labor. But their daily bread was about all his labor yielded. He wanted more for Maggie and Ma. Especially Maggie. She'd worked alongside him, been the helpmeet he'd prayed for. Todd stopped. Surrounded by a sea of rippling gold, he was a pauper—but also a very rich man. Because he and Maggie would reap a crop of togetherness for years to come because of the time they'd spent out working together.

Lord, she's the answer to my prayers, but I am not the answer to hers. I haven't been the provider she deserves. I wanted to make enough just to add on a little room.

Loud rustling sounded nearby. He strode toward the noise. "Maggie!"

"It's my turn for the love token. Simple as it is, I'm hoping it'll hit the spot. How's about a sip o' sweet tea? I wish it were cooler, but it'll still help your parched throat."

He accepted the glass but tipped it to her lips first. "That sip was no more than a bird would take." He tilted it again.

"I'm a magpie. And don't you be forgetting it!" Flashing a smile, she stepped back just enough to avoid the glass.

A few long, steady gulps and he drained every drop. Rolling the glass against his forehead, he cooled off. "Ahhh. How did I live without you, Magpie?"

"None too good." She laughed. "Not from the taste of the meal the one time you cooked!"

He looped his arms around her, pulled her close, and took a breath. "I've been looking at figures. Yours, I like. The ones for the farm, I don't. Because of the extra crops and bartering, we'll barely make the mortgage when the harvest is in."

"I'll thank you for the compliment, but I'll beg to disagree with your disappointment. We're holding on to our land. Someday our sons and daughters will play among these wheat stalks, and later help harvest them. That's good by me. We'll have lean years and good ones, so I reckon landing in the middle our very first year together is a success."

"Being penniless is not a success. I will sell the horses to provide for the seed and staples next year. We can make it through that way. It's not much, but it's the best I can do."

Wheat rustled all around them. She closed her eyes. "That's music, Todd. I told you music is important to my people, and you gave me a wheat symphony, a whole season of listening to the soft brush of stalks. I learnt the pride of eating my daily bread, appreciating everything that went into the flour I dumped into my bowl." Her eyes opened. "Things like that can't be bought with cash money. And they can't be bought with a broken dream. We're keeping the horses. Furthermore, you're mistaken if you think my love for you would change depending on the bank account. I didn't marry you for money."

"Good thing."

She stepped closer. "I didn't marry you for your land."

"You didn't?"

"Nay." A coy smile tilted her lips as her skirts brushed his pant legs. "I didn't marry you for your good looks nor for your strong back, neither."

"Hmmm."

"You know I married you on faith. With love."

"I'm sure glad you did."

Her hands slid up his chest to rest on his shoulders. "But I really married you . . ." An impish spark lit her features. "For Ma and apple pie!"

Encircling her waist, Todd lifted her high into the air and listened to her laugh. She might like the symphony of wheat stalks, but her laughter was the most beautiful music in the world. Slowly, he brought her back down and claimed a kiss.

Later that evening, Todd took Maggie's hand in his and walked through her rose garden. In the very middle of it, he stopped. "There is something I want you to have. It does not come alone, though."

"We have a crop to bring in, wonderful horses, and my roses are in bloom. My mother-in-law can find a nice streak every so often . . . I love my husband. What else do you think I want or need?"

He reached into his shirt pocket and withdrew a ring. "The one thing that's been missing from the start. A ring is a symbol of love. It has no beginning and no end. I believed there would be a beginning of my love for you, but I cannot look back and say for certain when that moment was. With your fire and your fierce love, you have captured my heart. This was my grandmother's ring. I want you to wear it as a reminder—not just that you are my wife, but that I have come to love you."

Tears of joy shimmered in her eyes.

"I prayed for a wife, and God used the worst of circumstances to bring about the most unexpected and best in my life. Serendipity is when happiness sneaks in unplanned. Serendipity I call it, when God brought us together. Karl knows silversmithing. Inside this wedding band, I had him inscribe *serendipity*. In our years together, we will look to see the touches of God's love and grace in the unexpected places."

He slid the band on her finger and kissed her.

"Come here, *Woman*."

She gasped as he lifted her into his arms, but that made it all the sweeter. Todd carried his love over the threshold, and everything in their world settled into place.

Twenty-One

Maggie's world turned upside down. "Here? They want to start here with the harvest? That's not the order you told me it's supposed to be in. Why isn't it at the Stauffers'?"

"Annie's sick. After the influenza the area suffered last harvest, no one wants to spread a sickness. Mr. White's got summer complaint, so that makes it smartest to start here." Todd hadn't bothered to dismount. "You have two days, Maggie. You'll have everything ready."

Ma sat in the shade of the sod wall, fanning herself. "There's a fine line between faith in a mate and foolishness."

Hands on her hips, Maggie demanded, "You'd best tell me this is some kind of Texas tall tale or jest."

"I am serious as a heart attack, Margaret." He flashed her a bolstering smile. "All you need to do is have the food ready."

Pushing her hair back from her forehead, she watched him ride off on Axe and shouted, "That line Ma just mentioned? You've crossed it!"

Three hours later, she arched and rubbed her low back. "I bet there's a special place in heaven for farmers' wives who don't strangle their men at harvest."

Laughter surrounded her. Linette and her mama, and Sydney Creighton and Velma from Never Forsaken Ranch showed up as soon as they heard the news. Sydney tacked on, "It's right next to cattlemen's wives who don't shoot their men during roundup!"

Every last pot, pan, kettle, and crock Maggie brought from Carver's Holler now formed an arsenal next to the sod wall. Ma held Sydney's baby and snapped out orders to anyone in earshot. Velma kept adding to a list of who would bring different dishes and what Maggie needed to do. Since Valmer Farm didn't have a springhouse, Linette's mama took home all the coleslaw, cucumber salad, and potato salad they'd made.

Pulling her nine hundredth loaf of bread out of the Sunshine oven, Maggie shot Linette a glance. "Don't know why I bother with the oven—it's so blessed hot out here!"

Velma fluttered the front of her bodice. "Days like this, I know just how a dumpling feels when it's dropped into the soup. Sydney, I'm taking you and the baby home. Can't risk little Rosie getting summer complaint."

"Donnerwetter."

Maggie wheeled around. "Todd! You surprised me. What's a-wrong?"

"Donnerwetter. Thunder weather," John translated from beside him. He kicked the dry ground in disgust. "All this humidity, and not a drop of rain."

The men helped Sydney and Velma into their buckboard, though

Ma didn't want to give up the baby yet. "It is only right that I hold her while you put bread into some sacks and have Velma store them for us at the ranch. We have nowhere to put it."

John gave Linette a stern look. "You're staying here for supper."

"Am I?"

"Yep." He nodded.

"Well, since the place is turned upside down, there's only a seat for one guest. It's awful nice of you to let me take it." Linette kept a straight face.

"You're not." John sauntered over to his horse and mounted up. "I'm taking it. You're sitting on my lap."

"John Toomel, I'm not that kind of woman!"

Taking a moment to adjust his eyeglasses, John seemed in deep thought. "You're right, Miss Richardson. But since you're familiar enough with me to use my first name, I suppose I'll just sit on your lap."

Maggie murmured in a conspiratorial tone to Sydney, "I haven't had woman friends. Is there something I'm supposed to say right about now?"

"If you know what's good for you, Magpie, you'll let me take care of this." Todd declared, "You'll each have your own seat. Maggie is sitting in my lap."

Both men left. Linette slid a flour sack filled with rolls into the buckboard and added another of bread loaves. Sydney got her daughter back, and they left. Plopping down on a bench, Linette wailed, "I'm doomed. I've eaten half the bread we baked today. If I ever sat on his lap, I'd break John's legs."

Maggie quickly handed her a handful of crumbs. "A man with a broken leg would be easy to catch."

Ma pointed at a flash of lightning in the distance. "Two . . .

three . . . four . . ." The air rumbled with thunder. "Four miles away. That is God laughing at us. Dry lightning."

Another flash of lightning struck, so Maggie started pushing Ma's chair toward the house. "We'd best get inside." Halfway there, Maggie whooped as more thunder rolled. It covered the sound of the approaching wagon until it was nearly upon them.

"Fire!" Velma yelled, fighting to keep control of the horses. "C'mon!"

Linette and Maggie looked at an ugly bit of smoke in the distance. Without exchanging a word, they scooped up Ma and heaved her into the wagon. Sydney clutched her baby and reached down. Linette grabbed hold and jumped.

"Maggie!" Linette screamed as the wagon careened away.

"Maggie!" The sight of smoke way over on the other side of the Whites' farm made Todd's guts clench. Fire. On the prairie, fire was every farmer's worst nightmare. Nearly impossible to contain, sparks jumped from one field to the next, one farm to the next, leaving entire communities as nothing but ashes. In no time at all, his farm would burn—but not until he sent Maggie and Ma to safety. Todd wheeled around and ran from the field to the sod wall.

Every pound of his foot, every beat of his heart drummed with desperation. As he rounded the wall, the buckboard clattered off. Ma was in the back, but what about Maggie? A breath later, he saw her on the other side of where the wagon had been. Instead of just standing there, she lifted her skirts up to her knees and sprinted toward the barn.

"Maggie!" Todd rushed alongside her. He swept her along, away from the fire. Nothing else mattered. Only his wife. He begged God with every shred of his being to save her. His stride was longer, but it had never taken so long to reach the barn. She'd never outrun a prairie fire, but a horse would carry her to safety.

"Ride Wrench! *Go!*"

Maggie had her fists fill of skirts, and she turned toward Wrench's stall at once.

Assured Maggie would get away, he released Eve. Nuts and Bolts ran out, letting him know Maggie had to be mounting Wrench as he'd ordered. Adam didn't need a crazy command. He bolted, too. Hammer ran through—but how had he gotten out? Todd bellowed, "Woman! *Raus!* Get out! GO!"

She had simple rope halters on Axe and Wrench. Todd threw her atop Wrench. "I love you!" He slapped the mare.

A well-trained gelding, Axe stayed just long enough for Todd to vault on. They followed Maggie, but only a short way. Turning for an instant, Todd saw the Whites' fields going up in flames. Desperate after two dry years and poor crops, White had grown some of everything this year. And against all common sense and consideration, White worked his land right up to the fence. The extra-wide ring Todd plowed around his own fields to act as a fire-break wouldn't be enough. One spark in the wind was all it would take, and there were millions. Spots of fire already began in areas of White's cornfield—it and his wheat were all that stood between his and Todd's place. In the distance, the church bells clanged wildly. Their sound would serve only as a warning. Men couldn't put out a blaze of this magnitude.

My place next. Ours—Maggie's and mine . . . Every hope, every dream . . . But Wrench carried Maggie away. She was safe. So was Ma. That was all that mattered.

Todd found he couldn't turn away from the sight.

The fire moved fast. The sticky, heavy air of the day changed to almost blistering waves of heat. Smoke didn't just rise—it sent a dingy cloud in every direction. Each second, the flames grew in intensity and scope, consuming more of the corn. White's horses ran past in a blind panic. Todd prayed he'd gotten his wife and kids out.

The roaring wind would send countless sparks in a firefly-like plague. Valmer Farm was bound for utter destruction, even with the wide firebreak rings about their fields. It wouldn't stop there, either. Fire would take John's crops, as well. Then the next farm and the next, all with ripe crops that provided abundant, dry tinder and a landscape where wind would wreak havoc.

Todd said another prayer as he set into motion. There was no choice. He ripped off his shirt.

Speeding toward Maggie's new stove by the sod wall, he scanned for something—anything that would work. One of the boards he used as a ramp to get Ma's chair into the wagon—it would do. Todd grabbed it. Every heartbeat seemed an eternity as he opened the stove and wrapped his shirt around the end of the board. Knotting the sleeves to tighten it felt unbelievably difficult. He thrust the shirt end of the board inside where the fire was down to mere embers. How could time be so slow here, when in the distance the flames destroyed months of work in mere seconds? One bucket of water—he poured it over himself and his gelding, then a second. His bandana got soaked. Yanking it around, he covered his lower face. Scalding heat and smoke made it hard to breathe.

He'd never controlled a horse around fire. Everything in its nature—and his own—demanded flight. Todd gripped the rope with his right hand as his shirt caught flame in the oven. Firmly holding the board, he waited for a split second while Axe sensed his lead to veer to the right, then dug his heels in and shouted. His gelding tore off, carrying him on a mission of total destruction.

Lord God Almighty, keep Maggie safe, and help me!

Here, where Maggie brought him water so often, he touched

down the makeshift torch and dragged it. All the way down the field, he set his own crops afire. Where Maggie spoke of the symphony of wheat, the wheat now caught and crackled with a sickening sound. Just a little farther . . . to the spot where he and John met for the first time. It was fitting. He'd give up everything he owned for his family and friends.

That was it. He shoved the remains of his torch into the stalks as behind him fire started licking at his barn.

Charred nothingness filled what had been an ocean of gold. Todd stamped out some glowing embers where his barn once stood. Tiny wisps of smoke spiraled into nothingness. From a distance, he could see Eve. It was a rare horse that would willingly go through ground still heated by a fire, but Eve would do anything for Maggie.

Raven hair tumbling down her back and looking like she wrestled a few dozen cougars, Margaret kept her shoulders back, her spine straight, and rode like a queen. She was the most unkempt woman he'd ever seen. And the most beautiful. Todd met her close to where the Sunshine stove still sat. Coated in ash, it would clean up and be perfect. At least she'd have that. And their cabin. Sliding off Eve and running to his arms, she chanted, "I love you. I love you. Praise Jesus." She clung to Todd.

He smoothed hair back from her forehead. "I love you, too. We have each other. We do."

"Yes. You're okay. You're really okay. Todd, we have each other. That's all that matters."

"But I have to tell you." He inhaled deeply, his parched throat and aching lungs letting him know he'd survived only by God's grace. "Margaret," he rasped, "I did this."

"I know. John and I saw." She wrapped her arms around his waist. "I'm so proud of you."

"Only the house is left. Everything, even the barn—"

"You set it afire. 'Greater love hath no man than this, that a man lay down his life for his friends.' You risked your life and laid down our livelihood. My thoughts weren't of what was to be lost—but of you." Tear tracks ran down the ashy dust on her face. "My treasures are laid up in heaven, but my heart—" She pressed her hand to the left side of his chest and patted. "My heart is here. As long as I have you, I don't care."

She knew he'd done it—and in her love, she looked past their struggles and saw only triumph. Everything they fought to achieve— he'd laid waste to it all. Todd did what he had to—and when she quoted the Scripture, he knew she understood. They were of one accord. The fire took away things—but it couldn't touch them.

Jakob Stauffer and John walked up.

Todd extended his hand. They shook, but no words needed to be said. It was finished. But it had stopped on his land because of the backfire he created. His sacrifice meant the others would keep their lives, their homes, their livelihood.

"Ma's fine. She's with Velma, and they'll take care of her for as long as you need." Linette slid off Wrench. Disturbed by the scent and heat, Wrench danced a little. John grabbed her halter.

Big Tim had ridden alongside her. He thrust a canteen at Todd.

Todd gave Maggie the first sip, then took a swig himself. Finally, he rasped, "Your story, Margaret. This is a story for generations to come."

His words drew everyone's attention to her legacy. "God used the rose bed as a firebreak," Linette said in awe.

"And the sod wall," John said. "It funneled the wind."

Linette grabbed Maggie. "You didn't quit. You replanted, and it saved your home."

"I replanted because Todd made me want to." A wealth of emotions swam in Maggie's eyes.

"You're not going to give up and leave, are you?" Though Linette asked, Todd knew she'd voiced what everyone wondered.

Studying the horizon, he waited a moment. "It is harvest. I'll help. Perhaps join a team and follow the harvest north. Whatever it comes to, we'll trust in God. He never fails."

⁕

The next morning, Todd watched as Maggie made grits. For the first time in his life, he had no chores to do. Grateful the Lord spared their home, they'd wanted to spend the night there in spite of the smoky smell. Knowing Ma was in loving hands, they'd given in to exhaustion and slept hard.

The landscape out the window was a stark study of opposites— ugly black directly against John's golden stalks. But that couldn't begin to hold Todd's attention. They'd gone through utter devastation, yet his wife hummed softly at the stove. He'd lost everything, yet he'd lost nothing. He had his beloved wife.

Wiping ash from a bowl, Maggie smiled. "Did you notice? Last evening John stood there with his arms about Linette."

"That didn't surprise me at all. I couldn't believe she finally let him. She's been elusive as a doe."

They shared their very first breakfast alone. Todd picked up the Bible. "Proverbs thirteen." He reached the seventh verse. " 'There is that maketh himself rich, yet hath nothing: there is that maketh himself poor, yet hath great riches.' That is me. I have nothing and am rich. I don't know what's to become of us, though."

Maggie didn't answer. She leaned into him, and they shared the silence.

It wasn't long before a buggy drove up. Parson and Mrs. Bradle alighted. Others dropped by, too. No one came empty-handed. They came to help. Sweeping the entire interior and the exterior lessened the ever-present smell of smoke. Men shoveled ash off the porch and others cleared around Maggie's roses. Buckets of water, loaves of bread . . . the most ordinary things were blessed gifts. That was the way Gooding lived—to share in the sorrows as well as the joys.

Several friends and neighbors stood on the porch as the banker's buggy arrived. He got out, looked long and hard at the blackened remains, and shook his head.

Tucking Maggie against his side, Todd waited.

After collecting a slim stack of papers from the buggy, the banker approached. "I see you had a problem."

"My wife and I know that in life, there are inconveniences at times. This was nothing permanent."

"He's right, you know," Jakob agreed.

John stepped shoulder to shoulder with Todd. "We're all in the same circumstance. One . . . inconvenience, and the consequences could be permanent." He swept his arm in an arc. "And long ranging."

"That's why I made this trip." Squinting at the distance and scanning neighboring farms, the banker mused, "Mortgages are heavy responsibilities. Legal responsibilities. A bank can't afford to have debtors default." He drew out a sheet of paper. "It might be an inconvenience for a bank if so many farms had a problem at the same time. In recognition of that fact, I'd like to suggest a one-year deferment on your loan."

"Praise God!" Todd lifted Maggie and swung her around and around.

Epilogue

SIX MONTHS LATER

"M aggie?" Linette called out, giving a quick hug when she emerged. "I put my Wishes Come True recipe on your table, but I need to get home. I'm borrowing your boxty bread recipe because tomorrow is John's birthday, and he loves it. I thought I'd surprise him with a picnic lunch."

Maggie smiled. "Are you sure you don't want to stay for coffee?" She motioned to the big Sunshine stove. While Todd had been away earning what he could as a harvest hand, her uncles had surprised her by showing up with "the other part" of their wedding gift: They built a "kitchen" to hold the stove. It looked so much like the one back home, they kept working—until the house matched her foursquare in the holler.

"Another time . . ." Linette motioned toward the porch and whispered, "Ma's really grouchy today."

Maggie gave her an odd look. "I thought this was one of her better days."

"Heaven help you!"

A big new barn presided over their farmland. Dan Clark had sold them the lumber at cost, and the bank added the sum to their existing loan. People from far and wide arrived as soon as harvest ended, and they'd raised the barn. Others sent love offerings—hay, fertilizer, seed, oats, chicken, and food . . . And God provided for every need. Todd and John even used a few miscut boards to make a chicken coop.

The fire's ash enriched their soil, and even with the drought plaguing them, God provided sufficient water for the fields, the garden, and Maggie's beloved roses. Halfway into carrying another set of twins, Wrench slurped water from the tank in her paddock. Eve was in foal, too—but it was early enough that she didn't have to be separated from other mares. She was fully capable of working, but Todd babied her.

Yet the most beautiful thing Maggie saw was her dear friend, Linette, as she rushed home.

And the most handsome was Todd. He wandered inside and started inspecting the shelves. Maggie knew what he was up to, but she couldn't resist letting him get away with his shameless ploy. "Hmm. This jar's almost empty." He grabbed the jelly and unlatched the spring wire lid. "Peach."

"Suppose you might do me the favor of getting rid of that wee dab?" He grabbed a spoon while she continued, "It's just taking up room on the shelf, you know."

"I'd do anything for you, Magpie."

"Mrs. Ludquist sent a letter. She's back in Boston. I think she'll probably stay put for a little while because her daughter is getting married. She's buying soap and lotion and perfume as favors for the houseguests and bridesmaids."

"Good," he replied in his usual understated style.

"She found pretty little bottles she wants me to use, so I won't have that expense."

"Uh-huh."

"Todd?" He gave her a guilty smile. "If you stop spooning the jelly from the jar to your mouth, you might want to see the bank draft that came with her order."

Stubborn as usual, Todd scraped the last glob of peach preserves from the jar as he took a look at the paper on the table. "Well, well. Wishes Come True."

She snatched it from him. "The other one."

The spoon clattered to the floor. "That's—"

"Half of what she offered." Maggie slipped her hand in his. That simple touch never ceased to make her heart beat a little faster, but now her heart raced. "The other half will be paid upon delivery."

He set down the jelly jar. For the first time since she'd known him, he didn't scowl at the bottom of the empty jar. The amount on the check was, to the dollar, their annual mortgage. "Half?" he repeated in a strangled tone.

"Now, Mr. Valmer!" Maggie struck her serious bargaining pose. "Fine perfumes are exceptionally pricey. The market is very exclusive, but since the Panic, few people are buying. I didn't think it wise to ask for more."

"My wife's roses are legendary. Any bottle filled with their essence is priceless."

"Peace of mind that we can pay the mortgage this next year is priceless. And just one other thing: Mrs. Ludquist says I'm to give a special name to the scent."

He lifted her hand and ran his thumb over her wedding ring.

"Serendipity. There's nothing more fitting. It's how you met Mrs. Ludquist on the train, but even more so, it is how we met."

"That's perfect!"

"And so are you, my love." He gathered her close for a kiss.